DEFIANT LOVE

She saw the anger enter and narrow his eyes, and felt safe. In his anger she felt no threat. It was his gentleness she feared, for it touched a vulnerability within her she could neither admit nor reveal.

"But now you tell me, woman of the Ordovices, who is the true target of your spite?" He grabbed her, his fingers biting into the flesh of her upper arms like talons. "Is it the handful of men who violated you or the *one* man who let you be? Or the men who have since forced upon you a shame of which you are undeserving?"

His hold relaxed slightly, but his tone remained stern. "Look at me. *I* am none of those men, Rhyca. I have sought to prove it to you with more than words, and now I also say it: I will not harm you—or let you be harmed."

"You are the fool, Roman." She twisted from his touch. She could not—would not—take his pity! "You speak of my courage . . . Well, I tell you now, it is hatred for your kind that sustains it—hatred that burns within me like a flame."

"No flame can burn without fuel."

There was no warning, no betrayal of his intent in the bronze features. Before she knew what was happening, his mouth came down upon hers with a force that crushed her lips between his. He sought from her a response, an answer to a question only her soul perceived. And perceive it, it did.

Taylor—made Romance From Zebra Books

WHISPERED KISSES (3830, $4.99/$5.99)
Beautiful Texas heiress Laura Leigh Webster never imagined that her biggest worry on her African safari would be the handsome Jace Elliot, her tour guide. Laura's guardian, Lord Chadwick Hamilton, warns her of Jace's dangerous past; she simply cannot resist the lure of his strong arms and the passion of his *Whispered Kisses.*

KISS OF THE NIGHT WIND (3831, $4.99/$5.99)
Carrie Sue Strover thought she was leaving trouble behind her when she deserted her brother's outlaw gang to live her life as schoolmarm Carolyn Starns. On her journey, her stagecoach was attacked and she was rescued by handsome T.J. Rogue. T.J. plots to have Carrie lead him to her brother's cohorts who murdered his family. T.J., however, soon succumbs to the beautiful runaway's charms and loving caresses.

FORTUNE'S FLAMES (3825, $4.99/$5.99)
Impatient to begin her journey back home to New Orleans, beautiful Maren James was furious when Captain Hawk delayed the voyage by searching for stowaways. Impatience gave way to uncontrollable desire once the handsome captain searched *her* cabin. He was looking for illegal passengers; what he found was wild passion with a woman he knew was unlike all those he had known before!

PASSIONS WILD AND FREE (3828, $4.99/$5.99)
After seeing her family and home destroyed by the cruel and hateful Epson gang, Randee Hollis swore revenge. She knew she found the perfect man to help her—gunslinger Marsh Logan. Not only strong and brave, Marsh had the ebony hair and light blue eyes to make Randee forget her hate and seek the love and passion that only he could give her.

JUDITH HILL

HEARTS ENSLAVED

ZEBRA BOOKS
KENSINGTON PUBLISHING CORP.

ZEBRA BOOKS are published by

Kensington Publishing Corp.
475 Park Avenue South
New York, NY 10016

First Printing: January, 1994

Printed in the United States of America

To my husband,
for his love and unceasing faith and support,
and my sons: Matthew, Jason and Daniel

and in memory of my father,
Anthony Tanana
I know it was from him that I acquired
my enthusiasm for history.
I wish he could have seen this book completed.

Prologue

She lay beneath him, still cloaked in comforting darkness, yet trembling in knowledge and anticipation. Rumbling his intent, he descended. She rose up to meet him, opening in acceptance. His touch was cold, his breath heavy, and she shuddered as he entered her. A sudden light erupted at the moment of their joining. Again he thrust, and again, each time sending forth the bolts of lightning to strip away the protecting night. As she must, the goddess of the soil suffered the mastery. And with a great terrifying roar of thunder the god of the sky achieved his climax. The fruit of their union was immediate; the life-giving rain fell upon their people.

But there were others among their people, strangers who knew nothing of their ways and beliefs, invaders from across the sea who would make use of this mating to destroy life. . . .

To these dark-skinned horsemen the storm was only that—a storm of the kind that was so common at the winter end of spring upon this damp and drizzly isle. Cursing the discomfort it caused them and their mounts, they nevertheless blessed the cover it provided. In the darkness their approach of the unguarded village went undetected, the hoofbeats of their horses muted by the pelting rain that ceased just as they readied their charge. As one, their voices rose in a cry of blood lust, and they attacked,

But what ensued was not a battle, rather a massacre. It could not be otherwise: ninety-six soldiers—three *turmae* of cavalry—pitted against a score of farmers. In only moments the native tribesmen fell under spear and sword and arrow. With one appetite satisfied, the victors readied themselves to assuage another.

They fired the huts for light, yet were as unmindful of the mud and cold as rutting beasts. Some of the women fought. Others fell upon their husbands' swords rather than suffer the violation that would precede their deaths. Still others with infants in arms and children clinging to skirts sought the refuge of the forest.

Those invaders who relished the added challenge gave chase. Afoot and on horseback, their way lighted by smoking torches lit from the burning roofs, they crashed through the underbrush to seek out their prey.

Of all who ran, none escaped, and only one survived.

She was called Rhyca, but the three men who pursued her into a small clearing had no interest in her name. Dismounting, they were of no mind to rush their sport and instead cuffed her to and fro among them. Laughing and jeering, they pulled at her garments and tore them, reveling in each bit of flesh revealed until she stood naked in their midst. Tall and proud as were the women of this island, she was a fine prize. With her labored breathing her firm breasts rose and fell in a most inviting manner. A flood of golden hair the color of ripe wheat fell to her knees.

Ever she would remember what came next, though the memory was to be one comprised only of pieces: the acrid smell of the torches and the damp of the rain, the reflection of orange flames in the men's bronze armor and the sound of her own screams as she struggled in one's grasp, then another's, until they threw her to the ground, each to take his turn at her.

After the first searing pain she ceased to struggle, and when the weight of the grunting man atop her was replaced with a second, she felt nothing but the hatred that would give her the strength to endure what they did and live—never to draw another breath that did not curse their name and kind: *Romans*.

One

Legionary Fortress of Deva
Permanent Base of Legio II Adiutrix
Roman Britain, A.D. 78

In disciplined ranks they stood, awaiting his command. Upon their burnished armor the summer sun shone bright and fierce. He knew the sweat was trickling down their backs, as it was his. And while he was not helmed as they, he knew all too well the feel of a heavy iron helmet heated by the sun.

Unconsciously he raked his fingers through his hair, jet black like all of his bloodline, and shorn close to his head per army regulation: more difficult for an enemy to grab in battle, in order to slit the throat of a wounded man or to behead a dead one.

Once more he let his hooded gaze sweep down the line of a dozen men. Oyster-raw, this newest lot of recruits, more boys than men. He'd wager that better than half did not yet sport face hair beneath the cheek guards of their helmets. But then, had he when he joined up?

Sixteen years, half of his life, Galen Mauricius had spent in service to the legions of Rome. In the shadow of their Eagle standards he had grown to manhood and risen through the ranks to become an officer, a cohort centurion. In all, four hundred and eighty men now stood under his command. And whether they lived or died in battle depended largely upon the level of training and discipline he was willing to enforce—and the loathing he was willing to instill.

The recruits were growing restless, he noted with an inner smile, though the emotion was not revealed upon his face. Long since had he learned that manner of control. Purposely, he allowed another moment to pass, then beckoned the first man out of ranks to face the stake. Designed to fit the height of a man and inspired by the methods used to train gladiators, the post did service as a target for those trainees still too inexperienced to face off against a living opponent.

"Remember, thrust. Do not swing your sword. A slashing blow can be seen coming." Narrowing his eyes against the flash of the sun's rays reflecting off the youth's plated armor, he awaited the response to his instruction.

Lunging forward, the recruit delivered a stabbing blow with his practice wooden sword, sharp enough, but too high.

"Lower. Go for the belly—always the belly. Elsewise you will find your blade stuck in the breastbone or rib cage."

Though his words were quiet and his tone matter-of-fact, the chilling message underlying his low command was unmistakable: kill or be killed.

Clearly shaken, the recruit lunged again at the stake,

this time delivering a well-aimed thrust, yet dropping his shield in the process.

The laughter of his comrades was silenced immediately with a single look from their commander. Striding forward Galen grimly took up a practice shield. With the easy deftness engendered only by long experience, he hefted the heavy wicker framework into position. "All right, recruit. Pick it up and face me." Aware of the dozen pair of eyes upon him, he waited impassively as the youth retrieved his shield.

In another quadrant of the amphitheater a grizzled veteran paused in his own weaponry practice with the *pilum* to watch. A survivor of twenty-five years of campaigning, Rufus Sita knew well what was to come, for he knew well the bronze-skinned Moor facing off against the blond recruit.

The Fourth Cohort's new commander, though just arrived at Deva, was no stranger to Rufus, who had served under him ten years earlier in Palestine. Controlled and unapproachable even then as a junior officer, Galen Mauricius was a disciplinarian and taskmaster of the highest order. Another might wait to teach this lesson—or might not teach it at all—but not Mauricius. He cared too much about the men in his command, a trait that would earn him few friends among the officer corps here. At Deva the discipline of the centuriate was slack and morale of their men low, with too many, centurion and common soldier alike, having been assigned here—to the Empire's farthest frontier—as a sentence of punishment.

Certainly it had been so for Rufus, who had received his transfer as a result of insubordination, if it could be called that. In spite of the outcome, his feelings about the incident had not changed. No use did he have for an officer who accepted bribes in exchange for assignment to easier fatigues. He had told his commander at Novaesium as much, and promptly found himself on the next ship bound for Britain. That had been a year ago. . . .

With a stoic shrug he walked forward to retrieve his practice javelins, all the while keeping his attention surreptitiously upon Mauricius and the blond recruit. The boy didn't stand a chance. Mauricius stood better than a head taller. Equally impressive in build, the implacable Moor also possessed the power, speed and lithesome grace of his race.

". . . correct fighting position . . . left shoulder into the shield and sword held level, ready to thrust . . ." As Mauricius spoke, he gestured with the staff of twisted vine wood clutched in his right hand. A badge of his rank, the staff also handily served as an instrument of instruction.

Rufus watched. There was nothing in either Mauricius's stance or expression to betray his intent. There would not be. The man was too good—and hardened, shaped by the brutal training that taught its survivors to give no quarter and ask for none.

And then it happened.

Though he expected it, Rufus was still startled to see the swiftness with which the vine wood rose and arced downward. The youth saw it, too. But training not yet honed into instinct was little better than no training at all. Despite the shouted command to raise his shield and take the blow, his response was late and unsure. As the staff came crashing down upon his shield, he stumbled backward. His left arm appeared

14

to drain of strength. His shield lowered. At that moment, with cold calculation, his opponent struck a second time—a sharp, thrusting, vicious blow to the youth's belly. The recruit instantly doubled over and dropped to his knees, clutching his midsection as he labored to breathe.

Maricius's face was like a bronze mask. If he felt anything, it was not betrayed by so much as a muscle twitch. "On your feet, recruit. Over the next several days this aching in your guts shall serve to remind you of a shield's purpose. Lower it in battle and you die."

Rufus watched the youth stumble to his feet. As he struggled to rise, an undisguised loathing appeared in his eyes for the dark man before him. Rufus smiled. And so it commenced—the process whereby a soldier was made. The burning humiliation and hatred would forge courage. For as steel was strengthened with each tempering, so was a man.

Rufus continued to watch as each recruit was summoned forward to take his turn. Indeed, the example made of the first had not been lost upon his comrades. Not so much as an inch did a single shield lower, and every blow delivered to the stake was true.

Galen Mauricius was not so easily satisfied. Though the sweat now ran in rivulets from beneath their helmets, he ordered his men through the exercise again and again, all the while assiduously watching for the slightest deviation of aim or shield position.

Finally, when he knew they could not lift their arms to wield another blow, he gave the command to stand down and disarm. Shields and swords thudded instantly to the ground. "An enemy will not care if your arm is weary. Beginning tomorrow—" he spoke slowly, weighing his words for effect and pinning each man in turn with the same warning stare—"neither will I. Today, however, I am in a generous mood. You are dismissed."

Like smoke before the wind, the line broke, and the recruits scattered for the amphitheater's exit passageways. No doubt headed for the legionary bathhouse, Galen thought. He followed the progress of several, noting in satisfaction that save the dust and sweat they appeared none the worse for the afternoon's training. Were that he could say the same! He transferred the vine wood staff into his left hand and flexed the muscles of his right arm. The impact of his blow upon the recruit's shield had aggravated an old wound.

Resigned to the pain he knew would burn in his shoulder for days, he fixed his attention instead upon a handful of seasoned men paired in mock combat in the arena's center. Only one did he recognize as belonging to the Fourth Cohort, a broad-faced fellow with large protruding ears who went by the name Facilis. Though known to be something of a buffoon in the barracks, in his handling of the *gladius* the Northern Italian was anything but a fool. His opponent had just cause to thank the gods this swordplay was but a training exercise and Facilis's blade therefore leather-tipped.

"Your staff falls heavy these days, Mauricius."

Galen raised a brow at the sound of a familiar voice and slowly turned. There were few men at Deva whose criticism he would suffer, but the huge bald-headed Thracian was one. "Not as heavy as an enemy sword," he answered, allowing himself a half smile of amuse-

16

ment as he regarded the bearlike man before him. "And lest you seek still another transfer for insubordination, Sita, you would do well to add 'Centurion' to my name."

Rufus Sita laughed and tugged at the leather chin ties of his helmet—at the moment caught in his steel gray beard. "And to what new dunghole could I be assigned, *Centurion* Mauricius? Take my word, there's no worse on this island. The question is . . . why are *you* here? Last I heard, the emperor himself had ordered you transferred to the Fourteenth *Gemina*. Something about 'a need for trusted officers to consolidate the loyalty of the Rhineland legions in the Upper Province.' "

Pointedly, Galen avoided the older man's gaze. "And now Vespasian has ordered me here. That is all you need to know, Sita."

The massive shoulders rolled with a shrug. "Just as well. I don't want to know. It'll happen soon enough. The Eagles will fly."

"And the reason for your certainty?" All traces of Galen's earlier amusement vanished.

But if Sita had marked the change in tone, he did not show it. He pulled off his helmet and ran a huge paw over the top of his head before replying. "I'm talking about the new governor's arrival. Rumor has it, Agricola intends to take up where Frontinus left off with the mountain tribes."

Galen relaxed. "Would that the man himself traveled as swiftly as gossip and rumor! I would not count on a new call to action very soon. Agricola's reputation may precede him to his new posting, but he is no Caesar. Besides which, he crosses the sea with the

17

summer campaign season better than half-spent. We will not march again until we come out of winter quarters in the spring—if then. In the meantime Agricola will surely pass his first year in the routine affairs of a governor. Indeed, he will sit bored and inattentive as reports on civil matters are presented and amuse himself with pageantry and ceremonial visits. Once he has investigated such pressing matters as the state of revenues, the progress of road building, crop prospects, and labor requisitions, then—and only then—will he tour the legionary posts."

Sita lifted a shaggy brow. "The years have taught you rhetoric, Centurion."

"Not rhetoric, Sita, cynicism—the cynicism of a man too long acquainted with the political machinations behind army command."

The bald head nodded in agreement. "Politics should be left to the politicians, and the army to soldiers. You're right enough in that. I hope you're just as right about Agricola. I'm five months from retirement. I wouldn't mind spending it out of combat gear. But . . . I think you're wrong. Frontinus may have cowed the Silures to the south, but there's been new talk filtering out of the mountains about an alliance between the northern federations—the Ordovices." Sita looked to the west.

Galen knew his focus was not upon Deva's twenty-foot red sandstone walls looming behind the amphitheater, but upon what lay farther: the menacing hills and beyond, the mysterious mountains of the last tribe unsubjugated to Roman rule. Warlike and hostile, they presented a need for control—as pressing as the Empire's need to control the mineral resources in their

18

territory. Wild and ragged, a land of rivers and peaks, it was not a region that would be easily conquered—not by traditional methods. . . .

Sita continued. "Dug in they are and gearing up. Last spring there was a cavalry massacre of one of their villages—a farewell gesture by Frontinus. Strangely, it's yet to be avenged. My guess is that the bastards have purposely waited. They know a new governor is arriving. When they strike—and they will—it'll be for revenge *and* to test Agricola. Summer, winter or spring, Centurion, when that happens . . . we'll march."

Not if Agricola's plan were successful first. Galen forced a nonchalant shrug. "Then we will march."

Rufus Sita stared at the lean, sun-bronzed face of his former—and current—commander. Ten years could change a man, true enough. But something did not feel right. . . .

"Return to barracks, Sita." Mauricius's voice cut off the thought. "The Fourth has pulled forage patrol tomorrow. You are going, along with Facilis, the Spaniard Drausus and six of the recruits. I'll lead it."

Rufus was helpless to keep his surprise contained. "That's only ten men," he murmured.

"Do you offer to dispute your orders, soldier?"

The cool tone of Mauricius's voice clearly threatened against further comment. Rufus shook his head.

At the mute reply Mauricius turned on his heel and strode toward the arena's center, where Facilis and the others were still engaged in their weapons practice.

Pack your kit, Facilis, Rufus thought, letting his attention then return to Mauricius's odd behavior. A cohort centurion did not lead patrols—forage, scouting or otherwise. There were five junior officers under Mauricius, and to the best of Rufus's knowledge only one was excused from active duty—in the infirmary barracks with an infected leg ulcer. Any one of the remaining four could be sent instead. And then there was the size and makeup of this particular patrol: ten men, with most not yet blooded by battle—the Moor had taken leave of his senses! There was no telling what could await them a day's march into the mountains, burdened by mules besides. It was not unheard of for native war bands to lie in ambush for forage parties. Sometimes they took prisoners, but more often not. Mithras god! Was Mauricius trying to get them all killed—or worse?

"He surely is a bastard, that one."

Rufus's head jerked up. The unfamiliar voice belonged to the blond recruit. Helmet in hand, he stood with two of his comrades, regarding Rufus with a sardonic grin and nodding toward Mauricius's departing back.

"And you make that judgment based on what, recruit?"

The youth took a startled step backward. The grin slid off his sweat-streaked face.

"I asked you a question, boy. By what right do you judge him? Your years of service to the Eagles, or the *phalerae* upon your chest?" Rufus looked pointedly to the youth's armor, begrimed with dirt and sweat, and bare of the medallions and decorations he wore himself, proud badges of honor won in battle.

"I . . . I overheard the . . . the way he talked to you just now. I merely thought you'd— "

"You thought I'd agree with you—a little mutual

commiseration among the lower ranks? You got a lot to learn, boy: like watching your tongue—and your rear. Mauricius was right to knock you on it. Caught you a fine blow, didn't he?"

At the blatant, mocking reference to his earlier lesson, the youth colored in embarrassment. Rufus, however, was not finished.

"Before you talk ill of a man, you best know of what you speak." He glared at the trio. "Twenty-five years I've given the Eagles. I've known a thousand officers, maybe more, and there's never been one I'd rather have at my back. Despite what happened today, he's not overly heavy with the vine wood like some, nor does he ask more from his men than he's willing to give himself. During the Judaean rebellion in Palestine I served under him. Twenty to one we were outnumbered. But we held their charge and pushed them back. When the battle was won, Mauricius's shield was brought to the legate. The same man who is the Emperor of Rome now, but then he was the legion's commander."

Rufus paused to allow the full meaning of his words to be felt. "Vespasian counted the holes in it himself. There were over a hundred. Right then and there, for services to himself and the Empire, Vespasian transferred Mauricius from junior centurion of the Seventh Cohort to senior of the Sixth. That's a jump in eleven grades, boys—if you've not been in the legions long enough yet to know the ranking system. And normally they're made one step at a time. A man with the ability to rise like that through the ranks is rare indeed—and him being all of twenty-two years of age at the time."

Rufus smiled wryly. "One thing more. That day

21

they counted the holes in his shield, they counted something else as well. The fatalities in his command—they were half those of any other century afield that day. So you go right ahead and hate him. But fear him, too. And you learn what he's got to teach. Come the day when you see battle, you stick to him like a bare-assed babe to its mama—and you just might live to tell the story to some loud-mouthed recruit that don't know enough to recognize the best of the best when he's looking at it." With a final snort of derision, Rufus turned away.

Left speechless as they watched his departure, the recruits quickly recovered. Laughing and jostling one another, they feigned an indifference to the verbal onslaught just inflicted.

"Pay the graybeard no mind, Gaius," one of them consoled the blond youth whose imprudent remark had incited the scathing rebuke. "You know how they are. Ready for pension and settlement in a *colonia*. Talking about past glories revives their former manhood."

"Valerius is right, Gaius," the second spoke. "Why, I'd wager a month's pay every time the old bear tells that story the number of holes in the shield increases tenfold! 'The best of the best' . . . bah!" he then scoffed, throwing his arm around his comrade's shoulders. "He's not a god—that black-eyed Moor—underneath he's still a man. Cut him, and he'll bleed just like the rest of us. Mark my words . . . one day he'll be brought to *his* knees!"

The blond youth scowled and gingerly rubbed his belly in remembrance of the painful and humiliating

22

blow. "I hope you're right, Sextus. And by the gods, I hope I'm there to see it!"

They communicated with hand signals, knowing how in the still air even a whisper could carry. For three nights they had lain in hiding, watching from their mountain aerie as their enemy, like so many ants, scrambled about on the valley floor below. Despite the fate of their brothers to the south, they were still unconquered themselves, and so their arrogance remained. At this sight of Roman might before them, they were wholly unimpressed, just as they were with the patrols that left each morning through the massive gates only to return at sunset. Thus far their quarry had not ventured beyond the foothills. With such caution, could cowardice be far behind? Why, then, the need for their orders? But theirs had not been a vow to question, rather a blood oath to obey. Hence the war band waited in growing impatience, listening to the morning and evening calls of the trumpets that rose with the smoke of the cooking fires above the fortress's high walls.

Slowly they wended their way up the steep, rocky terrain. The road they followed upon leaving the fortress had long since given way to a native track, bordered on the south by a swiftly rushing stream and on the north by thick forest.

From his position as rear guard Rufus Sita looked up the line of men fighting their way over the stones and rocks in their path. With each mile they covered

23

his uneasiness grew, and the prickling sensation on the back of his neck intensified. There were unseen eyes upon them. He would wager his entire pension on it. At least the pair of pack mules were each being led by a recruit, leaving Facilis and Drausus at the column's head with free hands to draw their swords— as were he and Mauricius at its rear. Not that in the event of ambush four swords would be worth a camp whore's promise of faithfulness!

Typhon! Why were they heading ever deeper into the mountains? Already they were beyond the point that would allow them a safe return to the fortress by sundown. They would have to make camp. What was Mauricius doing—or thinking? Theirs was a forage patrol. Where were the fields, orchards and villages from which they would appropriate the foodstuffs and supplies they sought, the provisions to be laid in both for winter and to supplement the garrison's daily rations of grain?

He turned his head to look at the dark, stalwart man beside him, and from out of the corner of his eye he saw something in the trees move. He whipped his head around. There, behind that fallen log—a shadow!

"Ambush!" Facilis's voice called out the warning, even as Rufus slung into place the shield hanging from his shoulder—barely in time to intercept the spear that thudded into it. Another spear sang past his left ear. He hurled his javelin into the thick underbrush suddenly alive with men leaping from the cover of the forest.

Caught off guard and off balance, the soldiers fought for footing on the rock-strewn incline as they attempted to close ranks and draw arms. The mules bolted, crashing through the already weak line of defense. More precious reaction time was lost. The enemies' advantage increased. The element of surprise was a valuable one, as was their greater number.

Better than two to one, Rufus guessed. They were trapped, caught between the charging tribesmen and the rushing stream. It was only a matter of how many they could kill before they were themselves cut down.

Instinctively, his thoughts melded with his body's response. To block the blow of a long sword that came flashing, seemingly out of nowhere, he raised his shield. Then, with the first strike staved, he lunged forward, closing the distance between his attacker and himself. A grim smile twisted his mouth. Now the advantage was his. Unlike the tribesman's slashing sword, which could not be effectively wielded in close combat, his shorter *gladius* was specifically designed for this deadly close-in assault. He thrust, and the wild-eyed Briton caught the blade with the rounded edge of his oval shield, deflecting the blow into his thigh. His scream of agony filled the air. From behind him Rufus heard Mauricius shout to the recruits to form a defensive circle and overlap their shields.

Lost in the shock of shields and the clang of swords, the command went unheard, and hence, unheeded.

Even as he had given the order, Galen had known his breath was wasted, his voice drowned out by the war cries of the enemy. Helpless to prevent it, he saw the first of his men die—a spear lodged in his throat. His shield still hung from its strap on his shoulder.

Acceptable losses . . . necessary sacrifice . . . unavoidable. With a cry of rage Galen denied the truth of the words resounding in his mind—Agricola's truth,

25

not his! He slammed his shield into the face of a Briton on his left, and then, aware only of a blur of color from another's multihued tunic, he parried a blow that would have taken his head. Feinting with his sword, he took a step back, lunged and thrust.

His blow went in true, just under the Briton's shield, and Galen felt the familiar sensation of blade sinking into soft flesh. He heard a groan, felt the sticky warmth of blood on his hand and pulled back his arm. A shower of red dotted his armor. *Acceptable losses:* the terms agreed upon by both parties.

As the man fell, Galen caught sight of the battle raging on the mountain slope. Seasoned and trained, Facilis and Drausus had closed ranks and were fighting side by side. Holding their own against a pair of Britons, they were drawing back, attempting to reach Mauricius and Sita. But of the three remaining recruits, two had already panicked. Tossing their shields to the ground, they were making a frantic and futile bid toward the river. Only the blond recruit had held his position—and was drawn off in a frantic fight with a burly tribesman twice his size.

With a fervent hope the boy had remembered the lesson taught the afternoon before, and would keep his shield raised long enough for Galen to reach him, the centurion hacked his way toward him, reaching the youth's side just as he succumbed and collapsed beneath an unrelenting rain of sword blows. Putting himself between the tribesman and the prone youth, Galen took the intended death blow. Pain exploded in his right shoulder. But his armor had served its purpose. Instead of slashing into flesh, the Briton's cutting blade bent sidewise upon contact with the iron plates of the *lorica*.

Watching his eyes, Galen saw the warrior's surprise and confusion. The stunned tribesman fell back. Lacking time to dig the sword's point into the ground to straighten the bowed blade with his foot, he tossed the now useless weapon aside and drew his dagger.

Galen braced himself. Strangely, the anticipated lunge did not follow. For some inexplicable reason the nature of the battle—its very mood—had suddenly changed. With no command given, either by voice or trumpet bray, the tribesmen still pulled back as if purposely to allow the Romans to regroup into a defensive formation in their midst.

Surrounded and trapped, the soldiers looked to Galen.

"By your command, Centurion." The veteran Sita spoke for all of them. "Give the order, and we'll take a good number of them with us before we fall."

Galen looked out into the faces of the enemy. The one he sought he would know instinctively—their leader. His eyes found a massive warrior whose long golden hair had been made more so with an application of lime. Thickened and stiffened by the treatment, the mane was drawn back from the Briton's forehead, with a resultant appearance resembling that of a Satyr—a custom Galen knew from his time in the Upper Province among the *Celtae* of the Rhineland, who were not so distantly removed from these tribes of Britain. And indeed the comparison to the woodland demon was accurate enough.

The man's blue eyes were bright with blood lust; the grimace that resembled a smile beneath his long mustache, sadistic. Around his neck he wore a collar of three strands of twisted gold. The *torc* was the symbol of a free-born male, but the choice of metal and quality of workmanship were clear indications of wealth and position. Not only was he a member of the exalted warrior class, this man had ties to a royal bloodline.

As Galen recognized him, so did he Galen. "Surrender, Roman, and live," he demanded in the harsh tones that functioned among the *Celtae* as language. "Fight, and you will all die." With a half turn of his leonine head he gave a signal that brought two of his men to stand on either side. Each held in his grasp one of the recruits that had attempted escape toward the river.

The chieftain nodded, and the soldier on his left was shoved forward by his captor. Quaking with fear, the recruit seemed not to notice immediately that the detaining hold upon him had been removed. Then, before he might have reacted, the Briton leader stepped behind him and laid the edge of his sword along the right side of the captive's neck.

In wide-eyed terror the youth looked at Galen. Even though the boy was tall enough to meet or exceed legionary height requirements, the top of his head came only to the warrior's shoulder. Thus Galen's view of the man's face was unobstructed.

Galen's gaze shifted from the recruit and met and held the Briton's. Pitted against one another in individual combat, theirs would be a formidable matching, a contest of comparable strength and skill. . . . But this was not the time.

28

As if having heard Galen's thoughts, the Briton smiled. "Your swords, Roman—or his head."

A long moment of hesitation passed in silence. Galen tossed his sword to the ground. A rumble of disbelief and protest issued from Drausus and Sita. Either they had also understood the Briton's demand or had guessed at it.

"Do it," Galen commanded quietly.

One by one they complied, their swords clanging atop his.

"Now the shields and helmets."

Again the men waited until Galen had first thrown down his armor.

The Briton's grin now spread into a complacent, triumphant smile. "You—" with the tip of his sword he pointed to Galen—"on your knees."

Never breaking his stare, Galen went down, first on one knee, then both. His features betrayed no emotion, not the fury seething within him or the strain of controlling it.

Suddenly the smile vanished from the Briton's face. A look came into his eyes, and Galen knew. He knew before the warrior laughed and before he swung his sword back for the wide, slashing stroke.

"Sextus."

Galen alone did not hear the horrified whisper of the blond recruit invoking his comrade's name. Nor did he watch, as did the others, the severed head that rolled for several feet before coming to a stop against a rock. Teeth clenched against the outcry of rage he would not release, he denied the Briton his triumph— and cursed the inner voice that drowned out all else: *acceptable losses.*

Two

"There! Look, Rhyca!" Dafydd clawed at her arm to gain her attention, then pointed excitedly toward the hill fort's western gate. "They're coming!"

Try as she might, Rhyca could not stop herself from heeding the child's urging. Drawn as if by a lodestone, her gaze followed the direction indicated by his small hand which had pulled itself from her protective clasp. Though the heads and shoulders of others in the growing crowd blocked her view, in the mere knowledge of their nearness her heartbeat quickened. The fearful images faded by time returned.

She should not have come. She should have ignored the order. But one did not refuse a command from Cerrix the King, soon to be Great King of all the Hammer Fighters, the Ordovices—if the talk of the council were to be believed. Yet why? Why had he decreed her presence?

She let her gaze sweep across the throng of men, women and children. Farmers from outside the hill fort's ramparts and craftsmen from within stood with the warriors of Cerrix's household and their servants.

She was sure the hilltop settlement's population of several hundred was swelled to twice that number—an occurrence that happened only when those who lived outside the walls fled to the hill fort for protection. But this day it was not war or threat of attack that had generated the influx. Nor was the mood of those in attendance one of fear. Indeed, it was the news of live captives that had caused the gathering of the crowd and its excitement. The return of Mouric and his war band had been anticipated since last nightfall. To all save Rhyca, the spectacle was cause for merrymaking.

A tugging at her gown forced her thoughts to the immediacy of the moment. She must keep Dafydd close, safe. She reached out to set her hand upon his shoulder, to draw him near. Too easily could he stumble and fall beneath the crush of the curious. Then, too, in the feel of his small body next to hers there was a strange comfort, a sense of strength regained.

But he broke free of her grasp to join the other children, limping after them with the jerking gait that proclaimed his deformity.

She tried to follow, pushing past those who blocked her way. Angry curses erupted in her wake until their speakers saw it was she. Then they merely looked away in uncomfortable silence—especially the women, who found it most difficult of all to look at her.

She lifted her chin in defiant pride. Yes, in the beginning she had wished she had not survived. But she had—and for that she would not feel guilt or don a mantle of shame for an act not of her choosing.

Suddenly a great clamor burst from the crowd.

Mouric had come into view. To shouts of his name, cries of welcome and praise, the warrior passed through the gate. In one fist he brandished a severed head, in the other his sword, flashing in the sunlight. Immediately behind him there followed a score of swaggering men.

Numb and deaf to the roaring din around her, Rhyca stared into the procession of strutting victors to the guarded prize in their midst.

There were six of them, shackled at the neck and joined by a single chain threaded through the slave collars. Their own spears had been used as staves to pinion their bound arms behind them. Their faces were concealed, hidden beneath cloaks which had been tied tightly over their heads.

Prodded by those warriors who walked alongside, they stumbled forward. Someone in the crowd threw a rock, another a clod of dirt. More rocks followed. Others hurled only insults or laughed, cheering as several dogs snapped and bit at their legs. Blinded by the cloaks, they could neither fend off the dogs nor dodge the missiles. To a man, however, they uttered no curse or outcry of pain.

Rhyca watched, unmoved. The compassion she would have felt for an animal so helpless and tormented did not exist within her for these beasts. *Romans.* Like the most bitter bile the name rose in her throat as she continued to stare at them. That she could not see their faces mattered not. She had seen others of their kind, had seen how evil and cruelty could assume human form.

The line of captives and warriors had advanced farther now into the settlement, and the crowd parted, allowing them to pass through. Mouric took no haste in leading his band, first passing the round huts of the bronzesmiths and then the horse enclosure, his aim a platform in the center of the village. Eager for the best view of what was about to occur, the mob converged around the raised framework of wood. The warriors pushed their captives through the spectators, and Mouric stepped onto the platform, mounting his bloody trophy upon one of the support poles.

Rhyca tried to draw back. As if trying to swim against the current of a river, she found herself instead swept up in the movement of the crowd, helpless to do anything but allow herself to be jostled forward to the very edge of the wooden structure.

In eyeing his amassing audience, Mouric's gaze fell upon her. "Come you, sister-in-law, in hope of seeing Roman blood spilled? Say the word, wife of my slain brother, and I will take the head of your choosing." In support of his vainglorious boast he flourished his sword toward the line of captives now being forced by their guards to climb the platform.

Still covered by the cloaks, the bound soldiers could not see to gain balance or footing. Brutally they were shoved and pushed onto the framework, and then into standing positions facing the crowd.

Rhyca quickly turned her eyes from the cruel sight. She was angered and confused by a sudden feeling of pity for the prisoners, a feeling she did not expect—or want—to feel.

"Choose, Rhyca." The tone of censure in Mouric's impatient prompting was unmistakable. And there was no denying the malevolence in his heated stare. She burned beneath it. He had judged her, found her guilty,

33

and had condemned her to suffer his contempt. Yet for the benefit of the onlookers, because a warrior must ever honor the ties of family, he would now put forth this show of avenging kinsman.

The crowd, seeing in her hesitation a delay to their own entertainment, began to vent their annoyance with loud jeering.

Then, as swiftly as it had commenced, the heckling ceased. Rhyca guessed the reason. So did Mouric. His handsome face darkened instantly, and he turned to watch the approach of the one man whose current position in the tribe eclipsed his own.

Cerrix mounted the platform, and the crowd quieted completely. Well known was the discord between their king and Mouric. Whereas Mouric advocated all-out war with the Romans, Cerrix had seen a lesson to be learned in the fate of the Silures to the south. He believed that the Ordovices at all cost must avoid the pitched battles which would favor the invaders' greater strength. Hence by his command there had been no retaliatory attack for last spring's massacre. As long as he was king, the path followed by his people would be one not of warfare for blood lust's sake, but one directed toward survival. Thus far the council had seen fit to support his leadership, thereby thwarting Mouric's bid for the kingship—a bid supported by maternal blood ties equally as strong as Cerrix's paternal claim.

It was this rivalry between the men, as well as their present and tenuous truce, that now brought the mob to near utter silence. For the moment even the Romans standing behind them upon the platform had been forgotten. All eyes were fixed upon the two warriors, equal in strength and stature, faced off in silent and controlled animosity.

It was Cerrix who spoke first. "Sheath your sword, Mouric. Well it has served our people, but now the time for bloodletting has passed. Killing these men will serve no purpose. To their great legions the loss of six is as inconsequential as the taking of so many buckets of water from a river."

"You have grown soft, Cerrix—and old," Mouric retorted grimly, setting his blade into the sheath at his side. "Despite the smoothness of your skin, you are as an aged man—no longer with enough blood in your veins for courage and honor."

The crowd gasped, many shocked by the boldness of the insult.

"Courage and honor? That is what you call it, Mouric? Your desire for personal glory at all cost?"

"Not personal glory. I fight for the glory of our people. But you—you, Cerrix, have lost all claim to honor. To let an enemy live is unworthy of a warrior, much less a king."

Rhyca drew back in alarm from the combatants. Taught as youths to fight with words as well as weapons, these men were indeed as much at battle as if they wielded steel.

Now others, mostly hot-headed young warriors loyal to Mouric, rallied to agree. Shouted opinions and disparagements from supporters of both men began to flow freely.

Cerrix ignored the rising tide of voices. "But I *am* king. And for so long as I hold the kingship, you will obey my command."

"So once again you allow the murder of our clansmen—my brother among them—and the rape of our innocent women—" he looked to Rhyca, the reproach in his eyes belying his words of indignation—"to go unavenged? What of our laws? Even within the tribe the taking of a life must be repaid."

"Either by private revenge or compensation. *That* is the law, Mouric." The soft-spoken voice of Myrddin the Druid immediately brought both men to deferential stances. The priest alone held the power to interpret the law and to pass judgment, for he alone held the power of divination.

Stepping from the crowd, the white-robed figure raised an arm for the silence that had already descended with his mere approach. He paused to lay a hand upon Rhyca's shoulder, and she tensed. But beneath the jutting brow the deep blue eyes were filled with kindness and understanding.

Could he know? she wondered. Could he somehow by virtue of his mysterious powers know the secret she harbored?

With a reassuring—or was it answering—nod of his dark head, Myrddin turned to climb the rude steps. With an almost fatherly gaze toward the two men, he seemed to regard them as one would quarreling children, though both were of a like age to himself. He directed his words to them, yet gave his voice such strength as to carry it to the crowd.

"Each of you speaks words of truth. Cerrix, you rightly recognize the futility of vengeful slaughter of our enemies. And, Mouric, you recognize their evil and know the penalty for their crime under our law. By tradition the taking of a life *is* punished by the giving of a life. This is done, however, to appease the gods' desire for balance—not vengeance. But while balance must be served, so, too, should justice. You, Mouric . . . you would slay your prisoners in the name of exacting justice for your dead brother and for his widow. But I ask you . . . in that *she* is very much alive, would not justice be better served in another manner?"

Rhyca felt a shudder go through her. Though Myrddin spoke in riddles, she had the gnawing sense that she was about to learn the reason for Cerrix's summons. Desperately her eyes sought his face for some hint. Undeniably standing in confident silence since the priest's appearance, Cerrix seemed wholly unsurprised by his words—as if he had previous knowledge of them.

Abruptly Myrddin lowered his voice. Rhyca could still hear him, but knew that to the crowd his speech was now lost. "To kill one or all of the captives will neither undo the wrong done to her nor bring back your brother, Mouric. Nor was their taking for that purpose—but another, already agreed upon by the council. The death of these men will not serve 'the plan.' "

"A plan doomed to failure," Mouric growled.

"So you have said from the beginning. But it still shall be attempted." Cerrix at last broke his silence with a finality to his quiet proclamation that quelled Mouric's protests.

Rhyca looked in confusion from his face to the Druid's, then Mouric's. Clearly this "plan" was known to them all.

Cerrix continued. "Give over your prisoners,

Mouric, to the slave block—as you agreed to do. Or is your word without worth?"

Mouric ignored the goad and looked to Myrddin. "You cannot convince me that this is the right course. However . . ." He then shifted his gaze to Cerrix and smiled. "I will follow your command—for as long as you hold it," he added softly.

Myrddin nodded in satisfaction and turned to face the crowd, raising his arms high above his head, as if through his body a message from the heavens might carry to earth. "To serve the gods' need for balance, I decree in their name that these captives shall *not* be put to death."

Despite the Druid's exalted place in the tribe, angry shouts of protest and disbelief immediately burst from the crowd. Myrddin glared the mob into silence and continued. "This is not to say their lives are not forfeit. From this time forth they are no longer free men, but slaves who shall perform the labor that would have been performed by those no longer of this world. Among you are several who have sent sons and fathers, brothers or husbands to the Otherworld. You shall be given one of these slaves in their stead."

Rhyca felt as if she could no longer breathe. Denial of what she had heard and frantic hope that she was wrong in what she now suspected were like twin hands at her throat, fighting to tear off a fist of fear closed around it. Even as she saw Myrddin beckon to her, she could not believe it.

"In the name of Belenus—no!" she gasped, evoking the name of the god from the dark depths of the subterranean that embodied the clear light of reason. Surely the madness of this could be seen! How could she accept this judgment and take a *Roman* as slave? That very name sickened her. She could not look upon his face or suffer his presence without reliving the horror of what had been done to her.

In a desperate plea for help she looked to Mouric. "Please," she whispered, knowing her entreaty to be futile even as she spoke it, for her kinsman only stared past her, refusing to meet her eyes.

Myrddin turned to the warriors guarding the captives. "Remove the cloaks and unchain them. Let us look upon the faces of our enemy."

The mob's fervor, dampened only moments earlier by the priest's pronouncement, was now rekindled. With invigorated enthusiasm the spectators clamored for Mouric. As the war band's leader, it should be he who revealed the first prisoner's face.

Clearly reveling in his regained sway over the crowd, Mouric feigned a reluctance he knew would fuel their fevered excitement. He waited. And still they cried out his name more loudly, until at last he strode toward the first captive. He flung back his head and, turning slowly, let his triumphant gaze settle upon Cerrix.

As plainly as if he had shouted it, Rhyca heard again the challenge so recently issued: *For as long as you hold it*. Then, a smirk still firmly fixed upon his features, he wheeled on the line of captives, tearing off the cloak that shrouded the first.

As loath as she was to watch, Rhyca stared. This man was the embodiment of everything she remembered of those who had come into the village that night. Small, but lean and wiry of build, he possessed the dark hair and olive skin that bespoke the people from the great and distant Middle Sea. His face was contorted with hatred for his captors.

Mouric moved on to the second man. As he whipped off this one's cloak, laughter rang out from the crowd. Numbly Rhyca realized the cause—the man's ears. Large, and sticking out from either side of his head, along with a shock of bright red hair and a sprinkling of spots across his face, they gave him an appearance far from ferocious. Then, too, absent from his face was the flagrant hatred of the first man. In fact, this one stared out into the crowd with an almost imbecilic expression that invited not malice, but amusement.

Finding disfavor with the mob's changed mood, Mouric strove to recall its hostility. "You, Laeg! Find your humor in beholding the ilk of those that slew your father? And you, Gwydyr! Does your mirth show a forgetfulness of the stump that hangs in the stead of your arm—that your woman must wield the scythe and harvest your fields? Make no such laughter, but rather a bid, a bid on a Roman slave! Bend his back to the plow and the whip. And you, Neirin, as well. Wealthy are you in cattle, but to what good now that the son to whom you would have passed on that wealth has gone to the Otherworld, dispatched by Roman steel."

Like oil thrown on a smoldering fire, Mouric's words inflamed the crowd anew. Shouting in agreement, they clamored with revived rancor for him to proceed. His aim achieved, Mouric threw off the cloaking of his third prisoner. Like his companions, the soldier was bareheaded, his helmet with its distinctive cheek plates and neck guard having been removed.

Helpless to do otherwise, Rhyca studied this man as she had the others—though this one, she realized with a start, was more boy than man. Pallid beneath his tanned face, he stood frozen in place, his eyes empty and unseeing. Suddenly the pity she had felt earlier threatened again. Sure that the cause was merely the boy's youth, she turned her eyes to the next prisoner as he suffered Mouric's unveiling.

With this man there was no danger of sympathetic feelings. He was a great bearlike man, fearful in appearance, yet of an age past prime. Curiously, although the lower half of his face—indeed his entire body—was covered by a thick matting of hair, dark upon his arms and legs, and steel gray in his beard, the top of his head was utterly bare, shiny like the bottom of a polished bowl. Pointedly he diverted his gaze from Mouric's contemptuous one and stood steadfast. He was a man who had lived his life by the sword. Be it now his fate to die by the same, he would accept it.

Not so with the captive revealed beside him. Another boy. This one was as fair in skin and hair coloring as her own people. He was terrified, yet valiantly tried to control that terror. He could not have seen more than eighteen summers. His show of courage pricked at her more deeply. That she should feel such compassion defiled reason. What was wrong with her?

She willed herself to look away—and instead found her gaze locked upon the uncovering of the last man, who wore an officer's cloak of scarlet. But it was more than that brilliance of color contrasting against the others' mud-brown garments that drew her attention inextricably to its wearer.

He was tall, this Roman, as tall as any man of her tribe, with wide-set shoulders and a hard, well-muscled body clearly evident beneath his armor. His hair, blacker than a raven's wing, was shorn close to his head in a fashion that allowed neither distraction from nor softening of the harsh lines of his face—taut planes beneath high cheekbones, a straight brow and square-cut jaw.

Chiseled features, handsome, yet honed and hardened by time and deed, she thought, stiffening in sudden wariness as his dark eyes swept the gathered crowd. There was not the slightest element of fear in his proud face or steely gaze. His clean-shaven jaw was locked in arrogant defiance. Indeed, something akin to a smile curled his lips—as though he held an utter disregard for his present circumstance, viewing it with detached amusement.

She was not alone in her thoughts. An uneasy murmuring drifted through the crowd. Even bound, with his neck shackled in a slave collar, he inspired intimidation. This was a dangerous man, a formidable foe, an enemy not to be underestimated.

Apparently viewing their focus of attention upon the Roman as a diminishment of the acclamation due himself, Mouric's irritation with his audience's reaction was obvious. He hastened to draw focus from the captive by commanding his men to remove the chain threaded through each prisoner's neck shackle.

One by one their arms were next unbound. Then, in a final degradation, the soldiers were publicly stripped of their armor: first, the empty dagger belts with their aprons of iron-edged leather straps hanging from the belts; next, the curved, overlapping plates of shoulder armor; and last, the leather tunics upon which small segments of iron plating were laced. With the final piece removed—a leather scarf—the captives now stood clothed solely in brown-colored tunics that reached mid-thigh and leather sandals cross-thonged to the knee.

It was not Rhyca's imagination that each man, before stoically enduring this ritualistic humiliation, had looked first to his commander. From him they clearly took their lead, following his example. The arrogant Roman betrayed no trace of discomfort. If anything, the removal of the armor served to reveal within the man an additional pride and power that had lain dormant until now beneath the iron plates.

Mouric was not pleased. He glared at his prisoner, who met the mute fury with undaunted silence. Unblinking, each held the other's gaze.

Rhyca could almost feel the hostility between captor and captive. It went beyond that of men made enemies merely by respective allegiances to nations at war. The enmity between these men was personal. She had no way of knowing its cause. But to see that Mouric would act upon it, she needed only to continue to watch.

She saw a smile cross his face an instant before he turned upon the blond captive beside the tall Roman. Cruelly he drove his fist into the youth's now unprotected belly, dropping him to his knees.

The Roman's reaction was immediate. Eyes blazing, he thrust himself at Mouric with a speed one would have thought impossible for his size. He heaved a massive shoulder into the warrior's chest, sending him stumbling backward. As Mouric struggled to right himself, the Roman stood defiant, awaiting Mouric's advance. "To attack another of my men, you will first have to kill me," he growled.

Rhyca started. He had spoken in their tongue. The sound of it, along with the cold conviction and authority of his voice, sent waves of grudging respect through the crowd. In truth, Mouric had attacked an unarmed man, a prisoner who posed no threat. That this man, his leader, would now challenge the boy's assailant to combat was a selfless act worthy of a warrior of great honor and courage.

"Cease this!"

Striding to the center of the platform, Myrddin placed himself between the combatants, effectively halting any further action. "Stand down, Mouric," he commanded quietly.

Already incensed at having been caught off guard by the Roman's attack, Mouric eyed the priest furiously. His hand twitched for his sword before reason rallied. The Druid's interference had cheated him of the opportunity to regain face. But he had no choice but to obey. "There will come another time, Roman," he hissed, drawing back.

The Roman's response was no more than a barely discernible nod of his head. Not merely accepted, the challenge was welcomed.

Standing at the edge of the platform, watching the interchange between Mouric and his captive, Cerrix smiled in secret satisfaction. Striving to move his prisoner to violence, Mouric had sought to sabotage the plan ere it commenced. Yet he had failed. As Cerrix had recognized Mouric's actions for what they were, so had the Roman, refusing to be caught in the trap.

Again, Cerrix smiled. Rome's governor had chosen well his envoy. The centurion was not only trustworthy, but sensible, a man not of hot temper but cool control. Even in his fury—justly roused by Mouric's unprovoked attack upon his man—he had demonstrated that deadly hold of emotions that marked a man of discipline. After his initial response he had not charged ahead, but had waited for Mouric's advance. While that tactic might have put him at greater risk by losing him the advantage of first strike, the strategy had gained him a greater edge—the respect of the onlookers. *Yes, Agricola had chosen well.*

With that thought Cerrix turned his attention to Myrddin, who now addressed the crowd. Calm and commanding, the priest's voice carried to those even at the farthest fringes of the throng, holding them captive to his message.

"By sword reckoning a man has the right to exact justice himself. A woman, however, must depend upon the justice meted by our laws. For this reason the first slave shall be given to her who, while having suffered grievous loss at the hands of the invaders, can exact no justice for herself. Come forward . . . Rhyca . . . and choose."

Rhyca felt the hundreds of eyes instantly upon her and swiftly directed her own at the ground with a mixture of fear and shame. She had known from Myrddin's first words that this was to be his intent. And while she had no willingness to accept his "gift," she was as helpless to decline it or disobey his command as Mouric had been moments before.

With her eyes thus averted she did not see the satisfied leer Mouric directed at the Romans' leader. Nor did she note Cerrix's thoughtful observation of it.

"Choose, Rhyca."

Myrddin's voice compelled her to act. She raised her gaze. Without looking again upon the line of captives she knew which must be her choice. She clutched tighter the mantle about her with her left hand and began to raise her right, to point to the blond youth who had suffered Mouric's brutalization.

"Give her the tall one."

"No!" Rhyca cried, whipping her head around to look at the man stepping forward from the platform's edge. The fear gripping her was neither fully formed nor rational. And still she knew. More so than the others, the dark and arrogant Roman was a threat to her, posing a peril she could not identify, yet instinctively recognized. Cerrix must relent and recant his proposal. He must!

"I . . . I would prefer the boy," she insisted with as much firmness as she dared display.

Cerrix smiled, and she wilted in the sudden knowledge that his recommendation had not been counsel, but a kingly command, now to be repeated. "Take the tall one."

Without giving her time or opportunity to reply, he then shifted his attention to Mouric. There was no mistaking the confusion—and suspicion—evident in his rival's face. "Can there be a greater insult rendered a warrior and leader of men than to be forced to accept absolute domination by a woman?" In accompaniment to his question Cerrix offered a casual shrug. "I should think the sting of this humiliation would appeal

46

to you, Mouric. Still, he *is* your prisoner. Prefer you to spare him the indignity of being enslaved to your brother's widow?"

Rhyca waited for Mouric's answer, holding her breath in a silent and furtive prayer. That he hesitated was cause for hope. Defeating that same hope, however, were the sudden cries and shouts of the crowd she heard over the sound of her own pounding heartbeat. The onlookers might have respected the Roman for his honor and courage, but so, too, did they fear the selfsame.

"Give him to the woman!" they clamored, their voice and desire as one.

Galen turned his hooded gaze from the men upon the platform. That the war band's leader, the warrior he now knew to be called Mouric, would heed the mob's will, he had no doubt. Too dearly did the braggart covet their favor and support. Rather than watch as Mouric made his decision, he looked out into the crowd, his eyes seeking the woman the Druid had addressed, the woman called Rhyca.

He knew he had found her the instant his gaze collided with a pair of ice blue eyes, intent with loathing. She stared at him with such bitterness he felt it drive like a knife into his belly. For the briefest moment he experienced a sensation so utterly foreign to his nature that at first he did not recognize it. Then he realized that the shield of indifference he put between himself and others had been pierced, but with a much more devastating effect than the stripping of his *lorica* moments earlier. Bereft of his emotional armor he found himself inexplicably vulnerable to her hatred, which seemed without reason—until he thought back to all he had overheard. Instinctively he knew that this woman was the widow of Mouric's brother, the brother for whose death he craved vengeance.

Galen looked at the woman. Now he understood. At the hands of men like himself—men of Rome's legions—she had suffered the loss of her husband. Could there be small wonder she looked upon him with such hatred?

Suddenly, from the thick of the crowd the figure of a small boy emerged to cleave his way to her side. Galen flinched. The wife widowed, and the child orphaned. But there was yet more he was to learn of her. For as she lifted an arm to draw her son into her embrace, she let go of the mantle that had been clutched closed at her throat. The garment's folds fell open to reveal her tunic-clad form.

The woman was with child.

Three

"Rhyca?"

Rhyca shook off feelings of hatred and loathing . . . and of fear. At Dafydd's awe-filled whisper, she looked from the platform down to the small boy wriggling in her embrace. A sad smile touched her lips. She knew why he had come back to her side. He was bright and inquisitive, insatiable in his need to understand the world about him. The events of a moment ago had surely filled his head with questions—which she must now answer. "Yes?"

"Why did Myrddin and Cerrix give the dark soldier to you? You don't want him . . . do you?"

The straightforwardness of his questions, the innocence of his confusion, tugged at her. "No, Dafydd. I do not want him. But Cerrix and Myrddin are being—" she groped for the right words to explain to the child what she herself did not fully accept—"helpful. They know I cannot work my fields alone."

"But you are not alone! I can help you." His bright blue eyes sparkled—then dimmed in painful understanding. He brushed a shock of straight, straw-colored hair from his forehead with the weariness of an old man. "It's because of my foot, isn't it?"

The tightness of his voice, the tears that threatened to rise, tortured her. "No, Dafydd, no." She set her hands upon his bony shoulders and knelt down so that her eyes were level with his. Pointedly she avoided looking at the misshapen foot on his left leg. "The work to be done is a man's work. Not a woman's or a boy's. Your foot has nothing to do with it. The oxen are too strong, the plow too heavy . . . for us both. That is why Myrddin and Cerrix have given me the soldier—to do the work."

"Because you no longer have a husband?"

She flinched at the brutal truth hidden beneath the simple explanation. "Yes."

"Will he live with you, then?"

"No!" Without meaning to, she snapped her response—and promptly regretted her harshness as the boy recoiled in fright. "Forgive me, Dafydd. I . . . I am not displeased with you."

"I know. You don't want the Roman," he stated matter-of-factly, seeing with his child's eyes what the men in command upon the platform had not. "The Romans hurt you and killed Keir. You hate them, don't you?"

"Yes, Dafydd."

The blond head nodded in satisfaction. "Mouric hates them, too, because Keir was his brother."

She thought to explain that Mouric's hatred had little to do with love for his brother. In truth, there had been no love or compassion of any sort between them. Yet she did not. "It does not matter. All of the soldiers will be kept here, under guard in the hill fort. Warriors will bring them to the fields, then bring them back at day's end. We shall not have to see much of them. Now . . . I must go home, where it is rather lonely without anyone to talk to. Will you come stay with me for a while?"

His head swiveled to look about the crowd.

Rhyca knew he searched for his mother. She knew, too, the woman would not care even if her son absented himself a fortnight from her hut. Widowed, then rewedded to a warrior who regarded the crippled boy as no more than a loathsome burden and responsibility, Luned had no time for Dafydd. She gave her full attention, and love, to the two healthy children she had since borne her second husband.

Rhyca straightened her back and stood. Her growing girth made the kneeling position an awkward and uncomfortable one. "Find your mother," she coaxed gently, "and tell her I have asked if you might stay until the new moon."

She was immediately rewarded with a delighted smile. As the boy limped away to seek out his mother, she reluctantly turned her gaze back to the platform. With a twinge of irritation she noted that Cerrix was now gone. Surely it was coincidence he had appeared at the proceedings—and remained as an observer— only long enough to make his selection of her slave.

Her slave. The words forced her thoughts again to the tall Roman. In relief she saw that he was being taken from the platform—no doubt to the guarded pen she had mentioned to Dafydd. She had been right about that much. But could she be equally accurate in the other assurances she had made to the boy? Could she control the loathing and distaste she felt at the mere knowledge of the Roman's presence in her life?

She had told Dafydd she needed his labor; now she must force herself to believe it.

Galen watched the woman rise. With her face turned from him, he saw only the fair hair, plaited in a single braid and shining in the sun like the palest gold. Tall and slender, her condition not yet advanced enough to impede her body's grace, she was very different from the standard of beauty of his world. . . .

Before he could think further, he was seized by a pair of warriors who unceremoniously shoved him toward the platform's steps.

Silent, their eyes darting furtively toward him as if they anticipated an escape attempt, they led him from the wooden structure and away from the crowd. Several of the onlookers cast cautious glances at him as he moved past them. For the most part, however, the attention of the mob remained upon the Druid.

Galen heard his voice continuing to issue the "gift" of a Roman slave to those he deemed in need, and knew by the priest's accompanying description which of the captives he designated: The small, dark one was Drausus, the Spaniard; the red-haired one Facilis; Sita was called the "bear"; and then the two recruits, Valerius and Gaius, were both identified by the word "youth," one "mute" and the other "blond."

The Druid had nearly completed the distribution of slaves when Galen reached his guards' destination. The round hut before him, alone in the hill fort's center and larger by three times than any of the fortress's other thatch-roofed structures, could belong only to one man.

His silent nod of satisfaction was followed immediately by a rough shove through the hut's open doorway.

Instinctively his eyes searched the dwelling's dim interior. His body tensed in anticipation, and then relaxed in the knowledge he was alone. Galen rubbed his right shoulder. At last he allowed himself to acknowledge the fiery pain that had burned in the joint since the training field exercises, and which had increased in intensity since his capture. The blow he had taken in that battle had almost been his undoing. Yet to none—his men nor their captors—had he betrayed his agony. Only now, in private, did he permit himself that luxury—and weakness.

"I was told I would know you, Centurion."

Galen started and jerked toward the direction of the voice.

Its owner remained hidden in the hut's dark recesses, but his words continued. "In that the trader was right. Let us hope for the sakes of both our peoples that he shall be proven right in other matters as well."

Galen recognized the speaker. Now he would confront the man face-to-face.

As if in response to these thoughts, the shadows gave up their occupant. "I am Cerrix. You are called Galen Mauricius, yes?"

Galen nodded in acknowledgement.

"So . . . again the trader's information proves accurate. A knowledgeable man, that Painted One. Of course, it is his business to know, moving as he has all these years between the tribes and now among the fortresses of your legions as well."

53

Knowing already of the trader, a Pict from the north, who had acted as go-between for Agricola and the Ordovician king in the negotiations of their scheme for peace, Galen concentrated instead upon the warrior before him. Having inherited the kingship a year earlier upon the death of his father, Cerrix was king of only one of the many federations of the tribe known as the Hammer Fighters—the Ordovices. However, his bearing and appearance clearly reinforced the image of a powerful ruler.

Like all of his tribe, the king was tall and well built, with a mane of pale yellow hair. Unlike the warriors of the war band, however, Cerrix wore his hair untreated by the lime and chalk. Two long, thin braids hung loose on either side of his face. The remainder of his hair he wore thonged at the nape. About his forearms he wore a pair of massive bronze armlets, embellished with red enamel. The gold that proclaimed his exalted rank was around his neck—a heavy *torc* with sculpted boars' heads meeting in the center. Like the others of his kind, he, too, displayed a pride of appearance that bordered on vanity. His knee-length linen tunic of small red and green squares worn over tight, close-fitting *bracae* was elaborately fringed and belted at his waist with a girdle of gold links.

Galen returned his attention to the man's face. The jutting chin and blue-green eyes, void of the hostility of Mouric and his followers, revealed an inner strength and wisdom, a confidence of self. Beneath the long, luxurious mustache there might have even been the hint of a smile.

Intuitively Galen knew that the Ordovician king, although his enemy, was nonetheless trustworthy. He bowed his head in respect, not of the title but of the man.

Cerrix noted and understood the gesture. He smiled. As the Roman had examined him, so had he studied the captive upon the platform and thus had already learned something of him. The decorated discs on the leather harness of the centurion's chest armor Cerrix knew to be awarded only for bravery in battle. Certainly, that valor would be put to ample test in the coming months.

"Sit, Centurion." Breaking the silence between them, Cerrix motioned the man down, then took his seat across from him. In surprise he saw that the Roman lithely assumed the cross-legged position of his own people. "You have spent time among our kind," he stated quietly.

"Among those similar in custom," Galen amended, lapsing easily into the Celtic tongue. He accepted an offered cup of wine, resin-thickened and diluted with water.

"That explains your knowledge of our language as well." Cerrix nodded. "I am thus far impressed, Centurion. If your governor displays equal wisdom in his handling of this island as in his choice of emissary, there may indeed be peace between our peoples."

"The time for peace has come," Galen agreed, bringing the cup to his lips to drink.

"Yes." The blond head nodded in agreement. "Since my grandsire's day we have taken refuge in our mountains, swamps and forests, ever hoping to wear out the invaders, believing from the days of your Julius that soon you would all merely sail back to your home-land."

Galen permitted himself a smile. "We do not re-treat."

"This I know, Centurion. As I know, too, that war begets only war. Yet we do defy Rome's subjugation. Here in these mountains freedom has found refuge. We are quite safe hidden in this remote stronghold."

"Hiding is no guarantee of safety, Cerrix the King. Frontinus's army mastered all of the territories of the southern tribes. And under a new governor, it is only a matter of time before Rome turns her eye northward. Once the legions move against you in earnest, we will have no difficulty in subduing your 'remote strong-holds.' This I think you also know already, else I would not be here."

Cerrix tugged at his mustache, refusing to confirm the allegation. "No other can hold the Ordovices as one people, save I," he continued at last, pointedly turning the direction of their conversation. "Yet the wolves are waiting for me to falter."

"Mouric," Galen interjected.

Cerrix smiled. With this Roman there would be no games of words, only straightforwardness. He re-spected that. "Especially Mouric. Were he king, he would pursue war's path for blood lust's sake. Mouric hungers for personal glory, whether in victory or in defeat."

"The path you have chosen has been a wise one," Galen assented. "But it is not one that will lead to peace. You cannot achieve peace without some form of surrender. Always it has been the way of the Eagles to devastate the countryside in order to force the people to stand and fight. Once committed to war, their fate is sealed. In open battle the imperial legions are supreme."

For the first time Cerrix revealed anger. "And so, Roman, are you one of those who is blindly convinced of the invincibility of Rome?" His accusation, though softly spoken, was bitter. "And is your governor of a like mind-set?"

"No." Galen marked the man's change of mood with caution. "Neither Agricola nor I believe we shall prevail merely because we are Roman. Rome is not invincible."

"In this we agree." Cerrix relaxed slightly. "Do not mistake my desire for peace as weakness. The time for diplomacy comes to all men. But if this plan fails, I shall not hesitate to wage war upon your 'Eagles.' Know, too, I will not favor haphazard raiding or pitched battles. These would be disastrous. Mine will be strategic attacks, warfare designed to cut off supplies and reinforcements."

Galen smiled tightly. That Cerrix was confident enough to divulge his strategy in the event of war had to do with the terms agreed upon by the Ordovician king and Agricola. Both leaders wanted peace, Cerrix in order to unite all of the federations of his tribe with himself as their Great King, and Agricola to avoid costly and recurring campaigns. To this end both men had agreed to a time of mutual watching and testing—hence the "plan."

For six months Agricola intended to study Cerrix through the eyes of his emissary, Galen Mauricius, to judge whether the tribal leader truly had the power to unite the Ordovices under a bough of peace. For his part, Cerrix would learn whether Rome could be trusted by observing Agricola's handling of his new governorship. Should Agricola fail, Cerrix fully intended to kill Rome's envoy. Galen could guess this much and knew that his skill and training would then be tested, as well as the faith placed in him by both Agricola and Vespasian. Rome's emperor himself had chosen Galen for this assignment. The gamble was great—but the rewards greater. If Galen could escape, he would have learned enough of the Ordovician force of arms, their terrain, and their secret mountain passages to secure annihilation of the tribes for Agricola and his legions.

"Regrets, Centurion?" Cerrix's soft laughter was filled with confidence.

Now it was Galen's turn to refuse an answer, redirecting the conversation. "Tell me of Mouric."

Cerrix betrayed no surprise. That the Roman would have recognized the greatest threat to the plan's success was not unexpected—especially after what Cerrix had witnessed between the two men upon the platform. "Through the bloodlines of his mother, his claim to the kingship is no less strong than mine. But weaker is his support from the Council of Elders. They denied his challenge. While none disputed his courage or prowess as a warrior, many disputed his ability to rule justly and with wisdom." Cerrix allowed himself a wry smile. "Their decision was not one he accepted well."

"He knows of the plan?"

"Yes. And he supports it only because he is convinced of its failure, and because he must submit to the wishes of the council which has voted in favor of it for the present. Like the rest of the council he has been sworn to secrecy and cannot share this plan even with his fellow warriors. The memory of the massacred village is too fresh in the minds of our people to speak openly of peace. Indeed, Mouric hopes the defeat of this scheme will bring an end to my kingship and initiate the beginning of his own. He is dangerous."

A curious expression entered the Roman's eyes. Cerrix could not read it. Still he knew, as he had known while watching them earlier, something had passed between the two warriors that had made them mortal enemies. "Avoid him, Centurion."

"That may not be possible, Cerrix the King." Careful to mask his emotions, Galen considered what he had learned. What he had believed from the beginning had been proven out by this conversation. Although the attack upon the forage patrol had been part of the arrangement, Mouric's needless slaughter of the recruit had been of his own volition. No such orders had come from his king. Cerrix had honored the terms. Both he and Agricola had recognized that for the capture of the forage patrol from Deva to appear unstaged, a way to bring Galen to Cerrix without raising suspicions, there must be the risk of loss of life for each side. Still, they had agreed to "acceptable losses." For that reason Galen had carefully chosen the men to accompany him. Deliberately the patrol had been comprised mostly of raw recruits, who would either panic or put up little resistance in the face of a better trained enemy. And yet, Galen needed to be sure. . . .

"What happened on the platform—Mouric's unprovoked attack upon my man—I want your word such will not occur again."

Cerrix nodded at once. "You have my word. Mouric will not risk my retribution. Your men will be safe—as long as they do not try to escape. Myrddin supports the plan. His choices as to those who received a slave were well thought out. Your men shall be treated well."

"And *your* choice, Cerrix the King?" Carefully Galen treaded the strange emotional ground. "Why the woman?"

"My reasons are personal. Suffice it to say I saw in you the best man—given her past."

"Which is?" For a reason he could not fathom, Galen needed to know all he could of her.

"As you no doubt determined, her husband— Mouric's brother—was killed by men of your kind. Their village was overrun and burned. The only survivor, she was left for dead. Any more that you need to know, you shall learn from her."

"Fair enough." Galen squared his shoulders and looked at Cerrix. Since manhood he had offered few men friendliness and even fewer friendship. He had been separated by age from the other senior officers— and from the common soldiers by the unbridgeable gulf of rank, for a centurion who grew too close to his men lost effectiveness. Ironically, with this man before him—a man destined by fate to be his enemy— he felt a bond. Under other circumstances he knew they would have been friends.

Cerrix rose to his feet. "Well, Centurion . . . it begins. I believe you a man worthy of the trust Agricola and I have placed in you. I will have you taken to your men now. While what you say to them is your decision, the plan itself must remain secret. There is much at risk here—the fate of both our peoples." Extending his right arm, his sword arm, he smiled. "May the gods watch over you, Galen Mauricius."

Galen clasped the man's forearm. "And also you, Lord Cerrix."

His men knew enough to remain silent, greeting his return with quick glances cast from beneath lowered lids. *Give an enemy nothing he might use against you.* It was an old soldier's creed—but one whose truth had been borne out by time and adversity's test. Not until they were alone would they break their silence.

If the guards at his back found the reticence of the captives unwonted, they did not show it. Without entering the circular enclosure themselves, they shoved their prisoner forward through a narrow opening in the stockade's walls. Well over two meters in height, the top of the split logs driven into the ground would have prevented even a very tall man from seeing over them.

The gate was pushed shut behind him; a rattle of chain followed. Up over the wall and through the apertures between the logs men's voices drifted. Galen knew they belonged to the guards, who would now no doubt be posted continuously. He turned his attention to the men inside the compound.

They had been left unbound. As with himself, only their iron neck shackles remained—the slave collars which would proclaim their status to all who beheld them. A slight, shadowy form ranged along the inner perimeter of the pen. Like a wild animal Drausus paced, acquainting himself with the confines of his cage. Facilis sat calmly on an upended bucket, tracing patterns in the dirt with the hob-nailed sole of his sandal. The two recruits squatted near him, their eyes now fixed upon their commander. Leaning against the wall to Galen's right, as if testing its strength, was Sita. The bald Thracian spoke first.

"I was beginning to think when next I saw your face, Centurion, it would be mounted along with the rest of your head on a pole."

The irreverent reference to the fate of the recruit, Sextus, drew sharp intakes of breath from his friends.

Galen ignored the youths' reaction, as well as Sita's comment, and cast a glance at Drausus. Of the five, the Spaniard might prove the greatest problem. "I was summoned for an audience with their king. We were discussing your future, Sita," he growled, still maintaining his attention upon Drausus rather than the man at whom his levity was directed.

His sarcasm elicited laughter from the large man. "Heartened I am, Centurion, to know I still have one."

"Future?" Drausus wheeled to face them. "What future?" He spat and continued. "Sacrifice to one of their gods? Or emasculation—with our organs being offered to their goddess of fertility?"

"Like our swords and shields in the river," the youth beside the blond recruit murmured, his eyes hazy, drifting to the memory of the war band's votive offering of the Roman's weapons to the water goddess in thanksgiving for their victory. Clearly his mind remained still upon their capture and the horror of his friend's beheading. Galen doubted he had even understood the import of Drausus's tirade.

The blond recruit had, however, and his eyes widened in fresh terror. "Emasculation?" he whispered.

"It's all right, Gaius." Facilis reached out to pat his shoulder in comfort.

"No!" The youth jerked away from the touch. "Drausus is right! I've heard of their blood-stained altars. They sacrifice more than animals!"

Galen's brow lifted in grim amusement. It served his purpose to let them speculate as to their fate a while longer. Their safety depended upon acceptance of their slave status. If they feared barbaric reprisals, so much the better.

Drausus continued, having found a willing listener for his gruesome scenario. "No altars, boy. Their ways are not so civilized. They weave colossal wickerwork figures and fill the limbs with living men. These they set afire—with the victims screaming in a sea of flames!"

This time even Facilis reacted. The spots on his cheeks seemed to darken and stand out more prominently as all color left his face. "I do not fear death—only this form of it," he whispered, looking for confirmation to Sita, the seasoned veteran they all knew had served among the barbarians on the Rhineland frontier.

"Burnt offerings are made only in times of crisis . . . ," the older man answered. Though his voice was calm, his eyes, fixed upon Galen, were turbulent with unanswered questions. Since his commander's entrance into the enclosure, he had been watching him in a probing, insistent manner. Now, seeing that Galen had become aware of his staring, he turned toward the blond recruit "plague, famine and the like."

"What about a foreign army in their territories . . . ?" Not assuaged but heightened, the youth's fears caused his voice to crack. "Or a massacre upon one of their villages?"

"Enough!" Galen barked. He was suddenly haunted by a pair of blue eyes filled with hatred. "I have their king's word of honor. No harm will come to us as long as we do not attempt escape."

"And you believe him?" Astounded, Sita transferred his attention from the recruit back to Galen.

"Yes." Galen's tone brooked no argument. "We are here until spring, and we will do nothing to endanger our survival."

"Slaves." Drausus spat in disgust.

From the corner of his eye Galen watched Sita. He had seen how the Thracian's bald head had snapped up at his mention of spring. The flicker of suspicion that had been burning in the old soldier's eyes now sparked.

"As slaves," Galen repeated, "if that is what it takes to survive. Think as soldiers . . . all of you." He let his gaze sweep across and encompass each of his men before redirecting his full attention to Drausus. "Coming here, we crossed rivers by fords the Ordovices know well. Those same rivers would have delayed a legion without similar knowledge. The route we followed, the passage through the mountains, think you a scouting patrol would have found it? If our eyes and ears are kept open, there is much we can learn . . ."

"But why wait until spring, Centurion? Why such a length of time? Surely two or three months would be long enough to give us the knowledge you seek?" Drausus queried.

"The longer we are here, the more we shall learn. Then, too, escape in the winter months will be more difficult, and whatever information we learn could prove useless. This hill fort could be deserted by the time the legions are ready to leave winter quarters. The new governor will not be prepared to march sooner. Auxiliary units are scattered all over the province. Once Agricola arrives, he will watch where danger threatens, launching no new campaigns until spring."

"It does not make sense," Drausus still protested. "Talk was that Agricola was especially selected by the Emperor to put an end to the hill tribes' resistance. Why would he not continue what Frontinus started?"

"The Emperor's favorite former consul?" Galen scoffed. "Think you Rome would be so quick to risk his life? Agricola received this posting *because* of his ties to Vespasian, *and* because he knows the island, having been stationed four years ago at Virconium as legate of the Twentieth."

Rufus Sita listened in silence. The thoughts and suspicions that had swirled about in his mind like dried leaves upon a stout breeze began to find direction.

Mauricius continued. The Moor's words were now weighted with the finality of command. "Our duty is to Rome and to the Eagles. If we must be slaves to honor our vows of service, we will be slaves." He looked from man to man, clearly daring any to dispute his orders. "Frontinus left this island ruthlessly scathed. The Ordovices' need for vengeance has been left unsated. We will give them no cause to quench their thirst with our blood."

As four of the five men nodded in acquiescence to

the command, one man inclined his head, not in response to the order issued, but to his own thoughts. Mauricius had led them deliberately into ambush and capture. Of that Rufus Sita was now convinced. The question was why. *Why?*

Four

The distance between them did not matter, nor the presence of better than twenty men scattered in the fields that bordered her own. Even stripped, he was completely recognizable. She marveled at the stark contrast of the bronze skin against the bleached whiteness of his linen undervest and loincloth. No, there could be no mistaking him, his size, his bearing. Scythe in hand, he was still a soldier—his foe the rows of harvest-ready grain before him.

Her grain, she reminded herself in a futile attempt to quell the resentment she still felt in acknowledging her new possession. After all, she conceded reluctantly, whatever labor her slave performed was labor spared her. Certainly it would have taken her an entire day to do what he had accomplished just since sunrise. In his wake nearly half of the field now lay felled. To a steady rhythm the tasseled stalks succumbed beneath the cutting sweep of his curved blade like enemies to a sword.

"Do you see him, Rhyca? Why, he does not even look tired—and he's cut most of the field!"

The childish awe and innocent remark of the boy walking beside her fueled her fury. "Demons do not tire, Dafydd." She pulled her gaze from the field and looked straight ahead toward the river lying at the path's end. In response to her anger her fingers tightened their grasp on the hemp handles of the buckets she carried. The left bucket knocked against Dafydd's knee and swung back sharply against her knee. She winced. "Besides, he's not done *most* of the field—but only half. And he still must sheave and stack what he has cut. By day's end—demon or no—his accursed back will burn with fatigue."

The thought of the Roman's pain served to ease her anger somewhat. She slowed her pace to match Dafydd's uneven gait more closely.

The boy glanced back over his shoulder. "He's very tall, isn't he?"

"Mmmm."

Her gruntlike response seemed to encourage rather than discourage him. Clearly he was fascinated by the man. "I've never seen anyone of his coloring before. He looks like a carving of golden oak. And his hair is so black—like a raven. I wonder—"

"Dafydd, please!" Rhyca regretted her outburst the moment she had made it, but could not undo it. Although the boy dipped his head immediately, she still caught a glimpse of his lower lip caught between his small teeth.

"I'm s-s-sorry, Rhyca."

His stuttering reply, so different from his light-hearted chatter of only a moment ago, made her wince again. He was only a child, with a child's natural curiosity. Why had she not bitten back her brusque reproof? Surely she could better control her emotions. *Curse him!* It was the Roman's fault. His very presence even thirty meters from her had set her nerves on edge.

She glared at the object of her spite. A second oath resounded in her mind. Laying down their scythes and sickles, the freemen had ceased their labors, while the warriors guarding the Romans had already begun herding their charges toward the river. Even slaves must be given rest and water.

"It's all right, Dafydd," she murmured more for her own benefit than the child's. The margin of the river was broad all along the edge of the fields, allowing easy access at any point. There was nothing to make her believe the Romans would be brought to the same stretch of sandy bank from which she drew water. Nothing except the gods' perverse desire to test her—for no sooner had she knelt down and submerged the first bucket than she heard their approach, the soft tread of footsteps upon the hard-packed earth and the faint rattle of their slave collars.

"Rhyca?"

"Ignore them, Dafydd," she whispered. With both hands she pulled the filled bucket from the river, dragged it across the bank, and set it to the side.

Silently the child handed her the second bucket and leaned close to speak in her ear. "He's watching us."

"Ignore him," she hissed, slapping the bucket against the surface of the water and raising a splash that wetted the front of her tunic. Again she cursed, this time aloud.

Galen felt a smile tug at the corners of his mouth. The boy beside the woman must have seen it, for a

69

shy, hesitant one formed on the young features. Galen nodded. But the overture was too bold. The boy hid his face against the woman's shoulder, thereby leaving his observer free to study them both.

He had watched the woman and her son walking toward the river and noted the boy's peculiar gait. Now he was close enough to discern its cause. The foot on his left leg was deformed, misshapen and turned downward, with the sole exposed inwardly so that only the toes touched the ground.

Knowing the intolerance of the *Celtae* for such imperfection, Galen felt innate pity for both child and mother. Theirs was a society that revered strength of body and personal beauty. That the boy's defect of birth had thus made them outcasts was obvious. Not a single Ordovician now at the river's edge—farmer, freeman laborer, or warrior guard—had offered so much as an acknowledgement of their presence, much less a greeting or offer of assistance. In fact, the men of her tribe pointedly ignored them. As did she them, he noted in wry afterthought, continuing to study her.

There was a singular strength about her, a determination that such censure could not weaken. In the square set of her slender shoulders and outward thrust of her chin, her pride was evident. He found himself hoping she would turn her head that he might see her full-face but knew she would not.

He moved toward her, paying no heed to the young warrior who had stood watch over his every movement since their dawn departure from the hill fort. Galen knew the youth was too inexperienced to act on his own initiative without direct orders. Rather than risk a confrontation, he would merely follow his prisoner at a cautious distance.

"Rhyca, he's coming toward us!"

Dafydd's strangled gasp and simultaneous clutch at her elbow startled her enough that she lost her grip on the last bucket. She had to plunge her arm into the water to retrieve it, then struggle to lift it out. Intent on her task, she kept her head lowered. Suddenly she felt a shadow fall over her. Instinctively she knew whose it was. She refused to raise her gaze. Never again would she look up at a Roman, any Roman—but especially not this one.

"You are called Rhyca?"

The strange lilting accent he gave to her language, even her very name, combined with the fact he had dared approach her, much less speak to her, filled her with outrage. She scraped the filled bucket across the sand, set it next to the others, then slowly stood. She glared at him, her eyes steady under his dark and penetrating stare. "A *slave* does not speak unless spoken to."

She expected a reaction of some sort, perhaps his face to pale or color at the affront. But there was nothing. No trace of any emotion at all. He simply brought his hand up to his forehead and raked his fingers through the cropped hair. And with that unfeigned action his heretofore formidable image acquired a trace of vulnerability. She turned away, unwilling to see in him anything that was human.

She reached for the handle of one of the buckets. A large brown hand closed over hers. Irrational terror took hold, and she recoiled from the touch as if his

71

flesh were flame. "Do not. Do *not* touch me, Roman!" she hissed.

Her outburst brought his guard running forward. Spear in hand and at the ready, the warrior looked first to her, then to his prisoner, seeking from either an explanation or course of action.

"I intended no offense . . . and no harm." Never taking his eyes from her, the Roman made his explanation. "I meant only to assist—as a slave. I would not see her whom I serve labor while I stand idle."

Despite his servile words, carefully chosen no doubt to pacify the guard, she heard mockery in his tone. She chafed beneath his blatant arrogance. "I can carry water," she spat in furious response.

"As can I." And with that he took a bucket in each hand.

Rhyca stood for an instant at a complete and utter loss. She had no desire to stand toe-to-toe with the Roman cur and argue further. From the corner of her eye she could see Dafydd waiting and watching. He had taken up the last bucket and was struggling with a two-fisted grasp of the hemp handle to keep from spilling its contents. If she did not help him, surely most of the water would be sloshed out before they were on the path. "Then, carry it, Roman."

She reached out and took hold of half of the handle that the child gratefully relinquished. "Come, Dafydd."

Galen watched the change that occurred in her the moment she looked to her son. The gray-blue gaze that had been brittle when leveled at him, softened. The venom in her tone vanished. With her free hand she lifted her gown slightly to ensure a better footing up the incline of the riverbank.

He purposely waited until they reached the path, then started to follow. At once he heard the guard's presence behind him and ignored it. His concentration was on the woman walking several paces ahead. He realized in annoyance that he had still not seen her face clearly. Each of the times he had faced her, his gaze had been locked with hers, forcing his full focus to remain upon the hate-filled stare she reserved solely for him. It was a deliberate tactic to maintain distance and thwart closer contact. He knew—because he often used it himself. In spite of her efforts to the contrary, he had learned something of her. Nodding in secret satisfaction, he continued to scrutinize the feminine form before him.

Her clothing, a sleeved knee-length tunic of deep blue over a long saffron gown, was plainer than that worn by the other women of the hill fort. Along with their men, they favored the striking, variegated patterns made of squares of every shade and color. Absent, too, was the glint of the gold, bronze and bright enamel which was worn in almost garish profusion about the arms and necks of both the men and women of the settlement.

Neither did this woman rely upon feminine enhancement by artifice. Her fingernails, short and work-worn, were unreddened by elderberry juice, nor did she use that same dye to darken her cheeks and lips, as so many did. He could not be sure, but he was confident her brows had not been dyed black either, as was the practice of the wives and daughters of the tribe's warriors and craftsmen. Was her sorrow so great that she did not bother to make herself up? Or did she simply not care to attract another man?

His thoughts ended with the pathway. With a soldier's eye he took careful reconnaissance of the village, a feat he had been unable to accomplish in the predawn obscurity. The small rectangular fields that had bordered either side of the narrow track from the river to the village here had given way to smaller clearings, grazing plots, and patches of dense forest, all scattered among several dozen dwellings. The circular huts with conical thatched roofs varied in size, from five to fifteen meters in diameter, he estimated. Each stood within an enclosure demarcated by a palisade of interwoven cane which encircled the dwellings, creating a compound with a single entrance facing the worn path.

He noted that each could serve as a miniature fortress, but communications or movement of defending warriors between them would be difficult. Once in position Rome's well-organized legions could easily surround and overwhelm any Ordovicians attempting such a defense. And the cane breastwork surrounding the individual huts could quickly be fired by torches while the legionaries merely waited for the barbarians to emerge or perish in the flames as they spread to the thatched roofs.

The woman headed toward one of the compounds. Suddenly his calculations of a moment ago seemed not so much sound military strategy as inhuman, unspeakable cruelty. Who, indeed, was the barbarian?

Somewhat removed and smaller than the others, her enclosure was bordered on two sides by woods. In fact, the thick underbrush had begun to encroach upon the farm. The palisade was in need of repair in places, nonexistent in others where the land had already been retaken by the forest. More than anything else this neglect and disrepair bespoke the absence of a man.

That thought brought Galen to others. Whose farm was this? She was reputedly the sole survivor of the massacre that had claimed her husband's life, and yet he was certain the village attacked by Frontinus's cavalry was several days' march from Cerrix's hill fort. How had she come to be here, and in possession of land? He knew that by Celtic law a woman might inherit property only if there were no male heirs. Was her ownership of this farm therefore a result of her father's death, with no son to whom his properties would otherwise have gone?

As with all of the questions he had about her, these, too, would have to wait for answers. She had just entered the enclosure.

As she had since leaving the river, Rhyca fought to ignore the searing gaze she felt upon her back. But the effort was futile. The trickle of sweat running the length of her spine had nothing to do with the late morning heat. If only Dafydd could have walked faster, the scrutiny of the Roman cur would at least have been less prolonged, though surely no less infuriating!

Immediate guilt over her uncharitable thought arose. She looked down at the boy beside her and smiled.

"Inside?" he asked.

The water was for cooking. But as she nodded at Dafydd, she realized the implication. Unless she said otherwise, the Roman in his insufferable arrogance would surely follow her right into the hut. She was torn between avoiding speech with him at all cost and the need to keep her home undefiled by his presence.

Suddenly Dafydd stumbled on the wide wooden sill of the doorway. The decision was no longer hers to make. The Roman reached out, catching the child in the crook of his strong brown arm and preventing his backward fall. She grabbed for the bucket, and before she knew it, he was inside the small passage area between the hut's inner and outer doors.

Her body tensed instantly. He was not actually inside the living space yet, but certainly within her walls—and that was enough! "Just leave the water," she gritted between teeth clenched in anger.

Acting as if he had not heard her, he looked beyond her into the hut's interior. Then, without a word, he walked right past her, straight to the hearth in the room's center. And as she looked on in silent fury, he emptied the buckets, one by one, into a large earthenware vessel located there for that very purpose. That he had known what to do was somehow an intimate violation of her private life, and she glared at him even more fiercely. "If you are so willing to carry water, you can return to the river and do it again, about a dozen times."

"The vessel is full," he answered, his dark brow lifting.

"For the garden, Roman," she spat, turning away from the sight of him, dismissing him.

"I have a name."

She paid him no heed.

"Galen."

She wheeled on him. She wanted to know nothing of him, not even his name.

76

He bowed mockingly. "A dozen times you said, *domina?*"

Only with effort did she stand still, ignoring the foreign term with which he had addressed her, but certain it was an added insult. "You can hear me perfectly well."

He acknowledged her accusation with a slight nod. "Might I make a request of you, *domina?* That is a great amount of water. Might I borrow the boy . . . to help?"

It was impossible for Rhyca not to see how Dafydd's face brightened instantly, before he turned to her.

Curse him! He had known all along what the child's reaction would be—had known what it would mean for the crippled boy to believe his help was needed and wanted. Not even to spite the Roman could she steal that light of excitement from the shining blue eyes now beseeching hers for approval. "Go with him, Dafydd. See that he knows what to water . . . and does it well."

As the boy's head bobbed in understanding, he looked to the tall, dark man and offered a diffident smile. "My name is Dafydd."

Rhyca turned away, but still heard the Roman's response.

"I am called Galen."

"I know." Dafydd giggled. "But her name is Rhyca . . . not *domina.* Why do you call her that?"

Rhyca listened, curious in spite of herself to discover just how vulgar his insult had been.

"It is a word in my language which means the mistress of a household. It is a term *not* of disrespect, but one that merely implies ownership. And since I have been given to her to serve her, she is my owner, my mistress."

Rhyca bristled. She knew the latter part of his explanation had been specifically for her benefit. And she knew, too, despite his words to the child, it was unlikely the proudful Roman considered himself either given or owned!

Rhyca knew each time they returned from the river. At regular intervals the two voices—the man's and the boy's—drifted inside the hut through the open doors. From where she knelt by the hearth she could make out none of the words exchanged. She heard only the laughter—Dafydd's laughter. So rarely had she heard it, that at first she did not recognize the high-pitched sounds that floated into the dimly lighted space like sunshine.

She reached for another handful of grain from the basket beside the hearth. She threw the kernels into the hand mill set before her, disregarding that which jumped from the stone bowl to scatter about the hut's clay floor. She sat back on her heels and took up the grinding stone. Like the meal in the bowl already ground, this last handful was soon reduced under her vengeful force to flour—flour much finer than need be for daily bread.

Noting the sudden silence from outside, she quickly added water and formed the loaves on the flat stones beside the mill. These she carried outside to set to bake in the yard's dome-shaped clay oven, whose fire she had thankfully built before setting out for the river.

She would seize every opportunity to avoid even sight of the Roman.

As she walked back toward the hut, her gaze fell toward the small garden plot off to one side. The furrows beneath its ripening rows of peas, lentils and beans were wet with pools of standing water beneath the vines. On impulse she skirted the garden and headed for the opposite side of the enclosure, to the small covered structure which housed her single milk cow and the pair of oxen each farm kept for plowing and pulling the two-wheeled carts and sledges used for harvest.

She knew before she looked, yet did so anyway. The long wooden trough was filled. Her slave was thorough, and becoming far too familiar with that which was hers, judging by what she saw, and now suddenly heard as well. The snap of breaking cane was unmistakable. She knew instantly the willful cur was pulling down the palisade behind her hut!

By the time she reached the shady, cool retreat formed by the overgrowth of the forest, the seething fury that had fueled her steps was in full flame. "What are you doing?" she demanded, hands on hips, ignoring Dafydd's startled gaze.

Standing at the Roman's side, the boy was diligently tossing pieces of broken sticks toward a pile at their backs.

Lifting up a large section of one cross timber, her slave paused to favor her with a bemused smile. "Labor. Or does it appear otherwise, *domina?*"

"I can see *what* you are doing!" she snapped.

"Then, why do you ask?" He tossed the timber

down upon a second pile—one that looked to contain salvageable pieces.

"Very well, Roman . . . if I must speak to you as if to a thick wit . . . *why* are you tearing down that barrier?"

He looked at her as if she were the thick-witted one. "Because it is needed," he answered calmly.

"I gave you no such command . . ." She noted how the dark brow lifted—but not in his usual mocking manner. Deliberately she drove the barb deeper. *"Slave."*

The hard line of his jaw seemed to become more hard, as if he might be clenching his teeth. In anger? Elated at the thought, she plunged scornfully ahead, turning her gaze from side to side. "Where is your guard, slave, your keeper?"

A muscle twitched in the lean face.

Suddenly, Dafydd's giggle pierced the tense silence. "He got tired, Rhyca. He said he wasn't about to trek back and forth to the river, and if Cerrix trusted Galen's word of honor not to escape, it was good enough for him; and if Mouric wanted him watched, Mouric could do the watching!"

The child's second giggle went unheard by Rhyca. Nor did she stop to realize how uncharacteristic was Dafydd's comical mimicry of the young warrior, given his normal sad and taciturn demeanor. Instead, she was absorbed in a flurry of thoughts: Cerrix trusted the Roman not to attempt escape? Despite knowing how she felt about him and his kind—and with good cause—he would grant this bronze-skinned demon unguarded freedom of movement? Why? What could her king know of this man that should make the way in

80

which he was treated so different from any other prisoner of war or captive?

Before she could speak, the Roman did. At some unconscious level she noted that his composure—and mocking arrogance—had returned.

"I assure you, *domina,* I am trustworthy *and* competent. The ancillary skills essential to the soldier's art are not so very different from those of a field-worker. In addition, I can quarry and cut stone, fell and shape timber . . . upon occasion I have also done the labor of carpenter, lead molder—"

"Do the labor of farmer," she hissed, cutting off this boastful recital of his skills. Despite the coloration of his flesh and hair, he was underneath no different from the men of her own kind—even in his diminished status. Be they Roman or Ordovician, they were blustering braggarts all! "Return to the fields," she concluded, her tone scathing, "for I want not your presence anywhere save there."

She turned on her heel. His voice stopped her.

"I see little point, *domina.*"

She spun around. Her heart leaped with hope. If she could go to Cerrix and tell him this Roman could not be ordered about by a woman, at the very least his insolence would earn him the lash—and how she would relish seeing those proud shoulders bared to a whip's bite! And there was a chance Cerrix might recant his decision. She would be free of him!

"Do you refuse to obey my command, slave?" She narrowed her eyes to conceal her eagerness.

"I do—when the command is ill-judged." His dark gaze held hers steady for a moment, then lifted toward the sky. "There will be rain tonight. It is better to leave the remainder of the field uncut. Later I will return to sheave and stack what has already been felled. Right now, *domina,* you need a new storage pit dug to store this harvest once the grain has dried and been winnowed."

Rhyca tore her gaze from the Roman's and glared at Dafydd in silent accusation. That morning as they had walked to the river, she had spoken those very words. Once dried and the grain removed by beating, the harvest would be stored in pots in granaries to be milled for later use. The seed for next season's planting, however, would be buried in a deep hole, then covered with a wooden lid and sealed with clay. But her present storage pit—its basketwork lining having rotted over the years—was ready to be abandoned and a new one dug. Only Dafydd could have told him of her need.

"Do not blame the boy," the Roman interceded. "I asked him where the harvest would be stored."

Rhyca knew he lied. That he donned the mantle of protector, inviting her to target him with the anger she might have unleashed against the boy, incensed her still further. But why did he choose this role? It was as if between them he had willfully drawn a clear line of battle, with Dafydd in the middle. But she would not engage in this game. She would not give him the satisfaction. "Then, dig it."

She took only a single step before his voice stopped her once again.

"With what?"

She stormed to the hut, ignoring his footsteps close behind. Before he could follow her inside a second time, she entered and exited quickly. In her right hand she carried her father's iron spade set into an oaken handle worn smooth from years of use. In her left was a pick made from the antler of the red deer he had slain the previous fall.

Wordlessly she threw the tools at the Roman's feet, then turned and stalked toward a site several meters from the hut. He would not force her to speech on the pretense of needing instruction or answers to inane questions for which he already knew the answers. That particular tactic of his she had learned.

She stomped the ground with her foot. "Here. The depth of half a man's height, the width of his arm's length."

Confident she had at last outwitted him, she turned toward the oven. Whether baked or not, she would retrieve the bread. Not one step would she venture outside again as long as he was in clear view of her door.

Usually it was a comforting sound, rhythmic and lulling—the clacking of her loom. This day it was not. Above the clicking of the bone bobbins of the shuttles and the soft scratch of the horn hand comb closing up the weft threads, another sound could be heard. Steady and rhythmic in their own way, the scraping and thudding of the Roman's tools intruded upon the loom's song—and her solace. Even without sight of him, she could not ignore him—or force him from her thoughts any more than she could now force him from her life. Cerrix had seen to that. Why?

Was this Roman who had been pressed upon her a punishment for having refused to enter into his house-

83

hold, the plight of kinless widows—to be one of the half dozen women who served the king's wife? In the name of the goddess! She was entitled to this land—her father's legacy—*and* to the independence its ownership granted! Never again would she fall under any man's dominion or suffer his mastery. That lesson had been driven into her with every thrust she had endured that night. With every slobbering grunt her violators had uttered, she had repeated a silent vow: No man—ever.

A bead of sweat trickled from the base of her throat to slide between her breasts. It was hot inside the hut, the air bereft of any breeze entering through the open doorway. Normally she was never inside during the heat of midday. That she suffered was because of him, because she would avoid the Roman.

Her stubborn pride rose. No man would dictate her actions by means of his mere presence. And no slave would make of her a prisoner, unwilling to venture outside for fear of contact!

As she went to the doorway, the sound of the pick biting into the earth grew stronger. She blinked at the sudden assault of bright sunlight and instinctively turned her head aside. Her gaze fell upon the site where the Roman worked.

She saw immediately that he had stripped off the white linen undervest and was now clothed only in the loincloth. His back was to her, and for the first time she was able to look upon him without enduring his stare in return. She noted that the deep brown of his skin, that which Dafydd had likened to golden oak, was not merely a result of the sun's coloring, but a legacy of his bloodline. The loincloth covered little.

Every bit of his exposed body—the tops of his muscled thighs, the buttocks, the broad back—all were of the same bronze color.

Clearly unaware of her, he swung the antler pick up, back over his head, and then down into the hole at his feet. With the downward swing the muscles of his arms and back rippled beneath the taut skin glistening with sweat. As in a wild animal, there was a beauty and grace in his body's power and strength.

She turned her eyes away, furious at her thoughts. She was no giddy maiden like those of the hill fort who whispered among themselves of the eye-pleasing form of a particular young warrior.

"Rhyca!" Dafydd's excited cry halted the stumbling, retreating step she made to return inside. "Come look at our hole!"

No, an inner voice shouted. And still she found herself crossing the sill and walking toward the boy limping hurriedly toward her, his hand outstretched to take her own.

Dafydd half led, half pulled her toward where the Roman labored. At their approach he stopped. Bronze muscles gleaming with sweat, legs slightly astride, the pick resting on the ground at his feet and its handle propped against him, he watched her. He never broke his stare—even as he wiped his brow with his forearm.

Dafydd released her hand. "It's almost dug. See!" He pointed to the gaping hole in the earth.

"Yes, I see, Dafydd." But she did not even glance at the pit. Her gaze remained upon the Roman. Lean, virile, his chest and arms crossed with scars and marred with calluses from armor, he was the essence of a soldier, a man who had fought for the Empire of

Rome and for his place in it. What she had known at first sight of him, she now acknowledged to herself. His blood was not Roman. His people, too, had been at some time conquered by the very legions he had served. But it changed nothing. She had no sympathy for this man. Whether by blood allegiance or no, he was her enemy. The loathing she felt surged within her to fill her eyes.

He saw it, she knew. His dark gaze narrowed.

And yet when Dafydd, having noted the Roman's pause, dutifully pressed a gourd dipped from a nearby water bucket into his hand, he smiled down at the boy and winked.

Rhyca refused to see the change wrought in the hard features, and watched instead the path of the water he poured over the back of his neck and chest. Straight down the center line of his breast, bypassing the raised scars, the rivulets of water trickled down until they were absorbed by the linen at his waist.

He accepted a second gourd. This he drank. He handed the bowl back to Dafydd and took up the pick. The arrogance that had settled across his face at the sight of her, yet which had disappeared when he had regarded the boy, returned.

"Domina." Inclining his head in a mocking nod, he resumed his labor with a pointed indifference to her presence.

For some reason she remained where she stood, watching him. The pick began its upward swing, and suddenly she thought she saw him wince. She backed up, moving slightly more toward the left, taking up a vantage point that would allow her to see his face more clearly. Again he swung the pick. She felt an instant sense of satisfaction as she saw the same flicker of pain betrayed.

He tossed the pick aside and took up the spade. Jumping down into the hole, he threw out the loose dirt at the pit's bottom. Then, pitching the shovel out first, he pulled himself out. She noted instantly how in doing so he favored the right arm, bearing his weight on the left.

He looked straight at her, then bent down and picked up the discarded undervest. Deliberately he waited to speak, first wiping his face. "I believe it meets your specifications of depth and width, *domina*."

Rhyca felt her lips thin into a smile, the mirror image of his own mocking smirk. "No."

"No?" The black brow arched sharply.

"You heard me, Roman. Dig it deeper." She was sure he must know she lied. She did not care. "*Much* deeper."

She had fully anticipated a reaction of anger from him, or at least protest. She was disappointed—for he simply shrugged, tossed down the vest and picked up the pick. She waited for the first swing, watching for a sign of the pain she now knew he felt in his right shoulder.

For a second time she was disappointed. In the proud features she saw nothing but amusement.

Five

With the gathering clouds the afternoon's heat abated. Galen lifted his gaze to the sun cloaked by a gray sky that promised rain. His belly rumbled. He had not eaten for three days, not since departing Deva.

Pointedly the Ordovician war band had not fed their captives; a man weakened by hunger was less inclined to waste his strength fighting his bonds. Then, too, in the event of escape, he was a prey more easily hunted down and recaptured. The reason for the forced fast lasting yet another day was purely disciplinary—to teach a sobering lesson: The Romans were now dependent upon their captors for survival.

Feeling Dafydd's eyes upon him, Galen set aside his thoughts and looked down at the boy. The child had tailed diligently at his heels all day, but now his small shoulders drooped with fatigue. He was probably hungry as well. "You should go and eat," Galen prompted. The gentle tone came with an ease he had not expected. "I have nearly finished here."

Too weary to protest or even voice compliance, Dafydd nodded, moving toward the doorway. Then he stopped and asked with concern, "What about you? Are you not hungry?"

Galen smiled wryly. "I expect that when the need is seen, I will be fed. Now go." He watched the boy limp toward the hut, then tensed slightly, turning as he heard another's approach into the compound.

"Back to the fields, Roman," his guard from that morning ordered with a tight-lipped smirk.

Galen knew the retrieval came more likely than not from the young warrior's desire to alleviate boredom. With the restlessness and impatience of youth, he was no doubt chafing under the monotony of his post, his mind on the hunt he had been forced to forego or the weaponry practice this guard assignment had precluded.

Galen acknowledged the command with a curt nod that implied only that he had heard it. He returned his attention to the child now at the hut's door.

"Will you come tomorrow?" The small voice carried across the compound to him.

"Yes." Despite the distance, he clearly saw the smile that appeared on Dafydd's face as he ducked inside the open doorway. Galen stood for a moment, ignoring the guard, and lost in his thoughts of the woman inside those wattle and daub walls.

She held a strange fascination for him. Although he was aware of the dim luster of beauty that seemed repressed by the sad, weary brow and ice blue eyes, he did not look upon her with lust. She was a woman with child. Certainly were his masculine needs to be aroused, the cause would be one of the far more comely women of the hill fort who had lingered last eve about the captives' enclosure, wantonly eyeing guard and prisoner alike.

He was equally confident that what she stirred within him was not pity. She displayed a pride and strength of endurance that defied sympathy. Yes, he was sure . . . his interest in her was no more than curiosity; what intrigued him was simply the challenge to break through her malice.

So he had used the boy deliberately, seeing in the woman's love for her child a weakness in her strength, the one softness in an otherwise hornlike mien. Only—Dafydd was not her son. That startling revelation had come while they were at the river. And though the boy had giggled at Galen's false assumption, there had also been a wistful quality in his reply: "I sometimes wish she was my mother, because then she wouldn't be alone. Or me."

Galen had considered learning more about her through the child—for whom, though not of her own flesh, she nevertheless held a clear affection. Yet he had not. The mystery that she presented and the confusion she had wakened within him were more personal. He would have the answers to his questions come from her. To that end he was content to wait.

"Let's go, Roman." His guard gestured impatiently with his spear, his eyes darting toward the hut, then back to his prisoner. He sneered as his gaze took in the dirty, sweat-streaked man, his contempt clear. Such labor was beneath a warrior. He looked down at the freshly dug pit and the mound of earth beside it. "You've made twice the work for yourself, Roman. Tomorrow you'll be shoveling what came out of that hole into the old." He pointed to a round wooden lid set in the ground several paces away from the new pit.

Indeed, the holes were close enough that Galen could simply have deposited the dirt removed from one into the other with little effort. He wondered if she had deliberately neglected that added instruction.

Masking his features to cover the annoyance he felt, he donned the discarded undervest, then picked up the abandoned tools and strode toward the hut. He noticed the door was now closed. He leaned the spade and antler pick against the wall beside the door's heavy support post. At his feet, lying on the hard-packed ground, was a flat, torn-in-half round of bread. For him. The fact that it lay not upon the wooden sill but in the dirt told him who had placed it there. He smiled as he reached for the bread and tucked it beneath his vest. It was a gesture, poor perhaps—and no doubt grudgingly made—but a gesture nonetheless.

The gray sky continued to darken. By the time the Roman slaves were led by their guards from the fields back toward the hill fort, the clouds hung low and ominous. A menacing rumble of far-off thunder and an occasional strike of lightning in the west bore witness to the ever-approaching storm.

Galen lifted his head and narrowed his gaze against the sting of the rising wind. With a practiced eye he appraised the tall timbered walls of the hill fort looming ahead. Cerrix had chosen its site well. Clinging to the upper shoulder of a rocky mountain, the fortress commanded the only approach to the narrow mouth of the shallow, sloping valley running the length of the mountain slope, thus protecting the lush pasture-lands and fields nestled therein. Guarded on the other flanks by a ring of steep hills and forest, the Ordovician stronghold possessed unmistakable strategic advantages for defense.

The thickly wooded and hilly terrain made approach by infantry, who would be unable to march in formation, very difficult—and virtually impossible for cavalry. An enemy would be forced to make a frontal assault up the steep, slate slope that led to the fort's wide gateway. There an attacking force would be confronted with a series of three immense earthen ramparts that completely surrounded the fortress, each of these in turn separated by wide and deep ditches.

Yes, to take the hill fort would be difficult. But if Agricola's plan of peace failed, and the need for war were decreed, the Ordovices' stronghold *would* fall. As had other forts and cities, nations, and kingdoms throughout the Empire, so, too, would Cerrix's mountain fastness succumb to Rome's mighty legions.

That realization neither elated nor saddened the cohort centurion and imperial emissary, now made slave. Above all, Galen Mauricius was an officer of the Eagles. His was a stoicism born of years of service. He had marched too many miles, dug too many camps and seen too many men die in the service to the stern, demanding eternal legions of Rome to be swayed from his course by any emotional attachment to these people to whose defeat he could contribute. Honor sworn to carry out the orders given to him by his superiors, his duty lay in the subjugation—by whatever means necessary—of all who would resist Roman rule.

And yet . . . why did he again find thoughts of the

woman, Rhyca, creeping into his mind? Why had the blatant loathing he had seen in her eyes upon their first meeting continued to haunt him—as did the continual knife-edged bitterness in her voice that seemed to compel him to decipher her, as a new language might challenge his decoding?

At that moment a shouted greeting from a pair of warriors posted just inside the fortress's gate to those escorting the Romans seized and diverted Galen's attention. He cast a thoughtful glance about. Though only sundown, the sky had grown as dark as late twilight, with the hill fort as still as the dead of night. Save the two men standing watch, the settlement was deserted, the impending storm having sent the inhabitants to their huts. The large, open central area that had yesterday teemed with people and activity upon the war band's return was empty. The only sounds to be heard were the nervous whinnies of horses and the insistent rustle of the wind against the thatched roofs.

As blowing dirt and debris pelted the men, they bowed their heads and shielded their eyes with their forearms. Galen heard the huge Thracian, Sita, mutter a curse. Without prompting by their guards the Romans entered the penned enclosure, grateful for the shelter it provided. To a man they wearily wrapped themselves in their woolen cloaks before hunkering down against the stockade's lee side.

Drausus was the first to speak. Leaning forward, the wiry Spaniard stared at Galen. Anger and frustration burned in his eyes. "This is what we are to endure, Centurion? To be starved and worked as beasts, slaves to these barbarians!"

"To be sure, it's no fate for a soldier," Facilis agreed

with a weary sigh. "I should have gone for that bastard, Mouric, and cut him down when I had the chance."

"Typhon take them all!" The blond recruit, Gaius, his courage no doubt bolstered by the older men's complaints, hastened to add his own voice.

Galen ignored the three. He knew the yoke of slavery was not easily donned, and these men had justifiable need to release their pent-up emotions. He removed the bread from beneath his vest and handed it to Facilis, who sat upon his right. "Divide it among yourselves," he commanded quietly, noting at once how Drausus's eyes widened at the sight of the bread.

Galen turned his head, pointedly seeking out the one man who had remained conspicuously silent. "Sita, you have not offered *your* opinion."

The bald man shrugged. "I am a soldier, Centurion." He glanced at Drausus beside him. "I have no opinion—only orders."

Chagrined at the implied reproach, Drausus lowered his head.

The look that then passed between Sita and his commanding officer needed no words. At least for the time being, Galen had the large man's support. With a slight, barely discernible nod, Galen acknowledged both the Thracian's promise and his own gratitude. The influence Sita possessed over his comrades would be imperative until the men grew to accept their slave status. But they would grow to accept it—for such was the way of things.

Only Drausus would continue to chafe beneath slavery's yoke. Still, his training and discipline might serve to keep his emotions in check. If not, and if he acted upon them—to the point that he posed a threat to the plan—it would be Galen who would have to either subdue the threat—or eliminate it. He looked to Drausus.

Somehow the man seemed able to sense the danger of further defying his commander. He offered a grim smile. "I will obey my orders, Centurion. I will take whatever these bastards give. But know this . . . for every swing of pick, scythe and spade they force from me, they will receive a thrust of my sword in return. When we leave this place in the spring, I intend to request transfer to the legion that will march against this hill fort. It will be one campaign I shall enjoy."

Galen detected an unexpected and sudden tightening of his guts he had not experienced earlier when thinking himself of the hill fort's inevitable fall. What was it about Drausus's personal promise of bloodthirsty revenge that now caused him to feel something approaching regret?

Feeling Sita's questioning eyes upon him, he forced the thought aside. "Enough talk," he commanded thickly. He wrapped his cloak more tightly about him, realizing suddenly that it had begun to rain.

His voice a fearful roar of need, the god of the sky summoned his lover forth. He was impatient and weary of waiting. It was time. He ached for the fulfillment of their mating and hungered for the power of their union. Their people were turning from them, looking toward the strangers. Like disobedient children they must be scolded, reminded of the might and the glory of their mother and father, shown the order of what was and always would be.

The goddess of the earth heard his call and felt his want. While his strength and rule were the forces of destruction, as the giver of life, her powers were wisdom and prophecy. But she knew that in all life there was also death—even for the gods. When the belief that sustained them died so too would they. But for a while yet they would live, and she surrendered herself to life's most glorious affirmation. She embraced her lover, opening to him. At the moment of his utter possession of her, as he defied their fate with a deep, prolonged cry of triumph, she accepted it.

Quietly her tears fell on the receptive earth.

Rhyca stared unseeing at the glowing fire pit. She drew no comfort from either its heat or light. Her body was exhausted, yet her mind refused to rest—crowded with thoughts that raged within her with the intensity of the storm without.

She hated the rain. But mostly she hated the crashing thunder and the flashes of lightning. Always the noise and light evoked the same memories. But not this time! This time she refused to allow the familiar and terrifying images to return.

She turned her head toward the small form an arm's length from where she lay. Curled in his bed of furs, Dafydd slept peacefully. If he dreamed, they were good dreams, dreams which had carried over into slumber the contentment of a small boy who had at last felt worthy. He had been like a bird flitting about the hut that evening, chatting incessantly. The smile, the easy laughter, the lightheartedness—all had been instilled in the child by the Roman. With no more effort than a few kindly words and a bit of solicitous attention, *he* had done it, this *Galen*. So often had she heard his name from Dafydd that she had thought she might scream with the very sound of it!

And yet . . . in thinking now of the tall Roman her blood suddenly warmed, as if the loathing she bore him and his kind somehow comforted her in a manner the fire could not. Indeed, his face came to her clearly . . . the sharply chiseled features, the determined mouth with its mocking half smile, the steely eyes. . . . Even in his slave status he was the embodiment of Roman arrogance! But why should it be he whose image came so easily to thought, his the features so indelibly etched into her mind?

By all rights, it should be another who haunted her. But after the passing of only five moons she could no longer draw forth a real memory of the man to whom she had been wife. She could scarcely remember his face or the sound of his voice. In the name of the goddess! Ten years he had been her husband, having wedded her when she had come into womanhood with her fourteenth summer. But now, as with his death, she felt not a sense of overwhelming grief but one merely of loneliness—and betrayal.

Keir had failed to protect her as he had failed in so much else. Born into the noble class, he had nevertheless disclaimed it and its way of life. After completing his fosterage he had declined to take up the arms of a warrior, choosing instead to wield a ploughshare. Like a common freeman laborer he tilled the

97

land belonging to his father's clan, content with his decision.

But in a society where war was venerated and deemed the only suitable choice for a man of noble birth, that decision was unacceptable. The ridicule that initially greeted his choice did not die with the passage of time. A dozen or more years passed, and he remained an object of disgrace to his family and disgust to the tribe's warriors. Some even claimed that the childhood illness that had nearly taken his life had instead taken away his manhood. She had heard the talk and the cruel jokes whispered behind his back, yet what could she—still a child really—truly have known of such things?

Her father had eagerly accepted the marriage contract. With her mother having died three springs earlier, he had felt burdened by his daughter. Cheated of a son, he'd seen at last his chance for a male heir. Tainted though it might be by cowardice, the blood that would flow through his grandson's veins would still be of a royal line.

And Rhyca, too, had seen some appeal in this marriage, even though Keir had been nearly twice her age. Unlike the swaggering, reckless young men who had lustfully eyed the lowly daughter of a farmer, he had possessed a gentle nature. When they'd been together, walking beside the river or alone in a secluded glade, he had been content with her mere companionship, never forcing himself upon her.

The reason for this restraint soon became apparent. The vicious talk was true. Upon the wedding night the consummation of their marriage was reduced to a fumbling, futile effort between a child who feared the act and a man who could not complete it. Keir could not function as a husband, could not even reach complete arousal. Though he had entered her and breached her maidenhead, he had been unable to spill his seed within her. Each time was the same, and over the next several years he gradually lost even that ability. So there was to be no grandson, no child. After a time they no longer touched as man and woman. Her life with him became no different from what she had known under her father's roof. She had merely traded the care of one man and his control over her for another's.

But the farm and the land were different. The land she worked with Keir was hers; the life she built would be her future. But even this security was soon to be taken from her. Three years after their marriage Mouric returned, having completed his own fosterage of several years within his mother's clan as was the custom. And though he came back at last a warrior in his own right, the taunts that had followed him his entire life—that he might be no different than his cowardly kin—remained. Forced to defend his honor, his very manhood, he felt he could not escape disgrace other than by publicly renouncing his brother. Mouric would suffer dishonor no longer, and Keir would not fight for the right to remain.

And so she and Keir had left, driven out by a man of Keir's own flesh. In a village several day's journey from the hill fort, they had made a new life. There they'd been safe from Mouric, but not from the threat of a far greater enemy. . . .

Suddenly a crash of thunder seemed to shake the hut to its very foundations. Almost in response the child within her stirred. Rhyca laid her hands upon her belly. Of late she had been able to feel the tiny being move, and the undeniable truth of the life growing inside her womb had filled her with doubt and fear.

Had she been wrong not to rid herself of it? There were ways . . . herbs known to the Druids that could poison what she bore. Yet she had not gone to Myrddin. Why? Was it because of the longing that had come upon her years earlier—the longing for children she could never bear to Keir? Did she somehow look upon the ripening seed within her as the fulfillment of an oft-repeated prayer to the goddess that she be with child? Yes, the seed was from one of her ravishers, but was it not her womb that gave it life? Was not the child, therefore, mostly hers?

Or had she made her decision to spite Mouric? His had been the war band to find her abandoned in the forest, left by her violators for dead. She had seen the contempt in his eyes.

As with all he said and did, his vow to take vengeance upon the murderers of his brother and to care for his widow had been no more than a braggart's show. With no place else to take her, he had been forced to bring her back to the hill fort, where she had returned to her father's house and keep. Immediately she became a public spectacle for pity and whispered speculation, and once again Mouric suffered the sting of ridicule, his name dishonored this time not by his brother's shame but the widow's.

All hope he might have held that with the passage of time the talk would die was abandoned once her belly began to swell. Whereas others merely questioned the babe's siring, Mouric had ascertained the indisputable truth. Knowing of his brother's impotence, he entertained no doubts that it was out of the rape that she bred a child.

Furious, he had come to her, demanding she rid herself of it. He did not intend to be humiliated further by her birthing of a Roman bastard—a black-haired babe whose sire would be known to all who laid eye upon it. She had refused. And by law he held no control over her as long as her father lived. Though ailing, her father was then very much alive, and when he died during the dark of the next moon, it was too late. Myrddin's herbs would have poisoned her as well.

Again the tiny being within her stirred, and the agonizing fears returned. She had prayed to the goddess that the life within her take nothing from he who had seeded her. Had she made the wrong decision? When it was born would she be able to look upon it should its hair be dark and its skin olive? Would she not feel the loathing she had long nurtured against its faceless father? The child could hold no blame for the circumstance of its conception—but knowing and doing were separate actions. *Could* she love this baby? Or would she be like Luned, who had no love in her heart for the son she had borne. Was her black-haired baby destined to know the same rejection and ridicule as the blond-haired boy asleep beside her?

The hands upon her belly clenched into fists. What had she done? Awash in a sea of confusion and despair, her fears crested like waves. She was afraid and alone. She had no one.

There was a flash of lightning, and suddenly the memories she had kept at bay broke free. Her weakened defenses gave way to a flood of images and sounds from the past . . . the roar of the rain that had first hidden the horses' approach, the raging crash of thunder, the lightning that aided her escape into the forest and then betrayed her refuge. . . . Most vividly of all she remembered their laughter and their grunting as they had lain atop her. But she had won a small victory. She had willed her body numb, and no sound did she make. Her hatred was her armor. They could not pierce it, and she would let nothing in—or out. She would not let herself feel what they did to her. She did not feel at all.

But this night her armor failed. She did feel. This time the enemy, the invader, was not without her shield but within. From the corner of her eye, closed and focused upon the past, a single tear fell.

"Doubts?"

Turning from the warmth of the fire, the white-robed figure moved toward the tall blond man standing in the open doorway staring at the weather raging beyond the hut's comfort.

Then Cerrix turned away from the dying storm. The large heavy drops that had fallen earlier, spattering upward when they hit the ground, had ceased. Now a fine drizzle fell. With the wind's lessening intensity, the mist would creep in. "Not doubts, Myrddin," he answered quietly, wrapping his great cloak tighter against the damp chill. "Concerns."

He looked beyond the priest into the interior of the huge hut made cheerful with burning lamps and colorful wall coverings of cloth. To the right, seated before a roaring fire, were a half dozen of his retainers gambling with carved-horn dice. To the left of a screen made of wattle partitions which divided the space into two rooms sat his wife with several of her attending women about her, guarded from the warriors' sight but not the raucous sounds of their sport. At her breast she nursed their daughter, Namor. On the floor before her, bare and rolling on the furs with a litter of half-grown pups, were his sons, Traian, four years of age, and Brychan, barely two. "The fate of my people—my family—lies with this plan. If this path is not the right one, there is much at risk, Myrddin—much that can be lost."

The Druid bowed his head in understanding. "Do you believe you can trust this Roman, this officer of their Eagles?"

Cerrix nodded. "He is a man I would have called friend if things had fallen differently. Yes, I can trust him. It is others whose word I doubt, and their actions I fear." Slowly he let his eyes travel around the hut again, lingering briefly upon his wife and children. He tilted his head toward the open doorway. "Walk with me, old friend."

Without waiting for reply, Cerrix stepped out into the night. The smoke gray color of his cloak blended so well with the rising mist that Myrddin almost had need to reach out to locate him by touch.

"Whose actions do you fear, Cerrix the King?" he asked, falling into step beside the silent man. "Mouric's?"

"He is one," came the disembodied reply. "But more than Mouric's actions I fear my own."

Myrddin allowed no surprise to surface in his voice.

"Why do you say this? You seek to lead our people into peace."

"So that we may spend the rest of our days with Rome's heel upon our necks? All my life I have been taught to face danger, even if my only weapons are strength and courage. For a warrior to perish is preferable to retreating. Yet nature has ordained that a man should love his children and protect his woman and kin above all else. How do I protect them by waging a war against an enemy I cannot defeat?"

"I think you have already found the answer to that question yourself, Cerrix," Myrddin replied gently. "Only through peace can you protect them."

"But at what price does this 'peace' come? We have not yet been forced to feel that yoke, yet I know what submission to these conquerors shall entail—their taking of hostages to guarantee obedience, garrisoned forts within our mountains, taxation, our land stripped of its harvest to fill their granaries . . ." His voice died for a moment, then resumed with a new fervor. "Part of me says that we cannot hope for mercy. We must take courage before it is too late and strive for what we hold most dear: honor rather than life. We must not surrender but fight instead to preserve our freedom!"

Myrddin stopped and touched the arm of the man beside him. "Listen to me, Cerrix. As a boy you were quick to fight, yet with maturity I saw that rashness become tempered with reason. You have learned what many men never do. Force is not always the wisest choice. Do not recant out of fear." He spoke with clear affection, but with a firmness that bespoke his position as priest and lawgiver. "Fight, and you shall truly doom your people, as the fate of the other tribes has taught us. Rebellion begets only reprisal. The tribes to the east all sought to resist, and all have fallen: the Iceni, the Belgae, the Coritani. Deva, from whence your Roman has come, stands in what once was Cornovian territory. This enemy cannot be defeated. Fight, and like so many leaves they shall sweep us into the wind. Our only hope *is* this plan."

Cerrix stood in silence for a moment. When he again spoke, however, the strength of conviction and of self had returned to his voice. "Why do you support it so, Myrddin? This plan for peace with the invaders. You above all men have just cause to hate and fear the Romans. Without mercy they have hunted down the Druids, putting many to death for leading the resistance to their armies. Why do you deliberately choose death?"

"Because I do not fear death, Cerrix. If it is to be my fate to join my brothers in the Otherworld, I welcome it, for there we join the gods. Death is the center of a long life, not the end. Now . . . enough of this. Whom do you mistrust besides Mouric?"

"Others of his kind. I fear this plan shall not be given time to succeed *or* fail. News goes through the hills like the wind. There is talk. Despite my argument against it, my pleas for patience, there are those who intend to test the temper of this new governor. I do not know when, but there will be an attack upon one of the Romans' cavalry fortresses."

Myrddin muttered a curse. "Does your Roman know of this?"

"No. Nor shall he be told. He must not be given cause to see us still as his enemy. Part of this plan's success depends upon his forming ties to us—ties that if strong enough might serve to weaken his loyalty to Rome."

Myrddin shook his head. "In this I think you are wrong. This man is not one to falter. He was chosen with care by men who were so convinced of his loyalty that they were willing to risk the control of Britain."

"He is still a man," Cerrix rejoined pointedly.

Myrddin looked up sharply in sudden understanding.

Six

With every sound and strange noise, she started. The anticipation was worse with the waiting. Still, she knew he would come. He had told Dafydd as much. Then, too, as her slave, where else would the Roman be brought if not to her? That he was not yet arrived was no doubt because of the heavy fog to which she had wakened.

Enshrouding the entire valley at daybreak, the gray mist had clung to the mountainsides, rising around the vale, leaving even the highest peaks hazy in the damp morning air. Until the vapor was burned off by the sun, travel down the steep shale pathway from the hill fort to the village would be hazardous and a foolish risk that the slaves' warrior guards would not take. Too easy would it be for a man to slip away unnoticed, swallowed up in only a few paces by the shrouding of shifting mists.

Rhyca stared at the cauldron of water that hung over the hearth fire, suspended by hooks and chains from the rafters. During the storm she had used up most of the wood Dafydd had brought in before it began to rain. There had been but a bit of dry brush and twigs left to build the small fire which scarcely gave off enough heat to warm the hut, much less bring the water to boil. If Dafydd did not return soon with more wood, they would be eating raw porridge.

Concerned with the boy's long absence, she looked toward the hut's inner door, carelessly left open with his departure. The heavy outer door several feet beyond stood firmly latched. Through the cracks between its oaken planks there was still no sunlight visible. She reached for a striped woolen mantle of amber and brown hanging on a peg driven into one of the wall posts. Taking care to close the inner door behind her, she stepped across the threshold into the short passage designed to provide draft protection between the doors. If the first door was closed before the other opened, there was less risk of a sudden inward rush of air blowing sparks from the hut's central hearth upward to set the thatched roof afire.

Just as she released the iron latch, she heard voices, men's voices, but unrecognizable and faint with distance. She pushed the door open and stepped outside. At the end of the yard by the entrance to the enclosure, there were two men, their forms shadowy in the lingering mist, their features obscured. Still, she had no difficulty in recognizing the one on the left. His scarlet cloak was like fire against the gray fog. He seemed to be engaged in argument with his guard. She was about to venture closer when the shorter figure, wrapped in a multihued mantle of subtler tones, abruptly pointed toward the fields, then walked away.

Curious, yet confused and uneasy with the Roman's obvious victory, she was at a loss. She was considering calling the guard back when Dafydd suddenly appeared on the path before her. His arms were laden with a precarious pile of sticks and branches broken off by the storm. She looked at the burden he so proudly bore and knew that what was not wet from the rain would be too green to burn without smoking abominably. But before she could think of a gentle way to redirect his efforts, the boy spotted her.

Inclining his mist-dampened head toward the red-cloaked figure now approaching them both, he spoke. "Galen wants an ax, Rhyca. There's a big rotted tree that fell in the night's storm. Not very far. There."

He turned, gesturing with his elbow toward the woods off to his right. The action upset the pile of sticks in his arms, and as the branches on top threatened to tumble from his grasp, she reached out to take several from him. In her haste to come to Dafydd's aid, the Roman was upon her before she could react.

"Domina." He inclined his head in greeting. "The boy tells me you are in need of firewood."

She bristled slightly at his continued use of the foreign form of address, as well as his habit of never asking but merely doing. Yesterday she had not told him to repair the palisade, and now she did not ask for firewood. That she needed it was irrelevant. Her suspicions of him and her loathing of all he represented seemed not to allow her a rational response.

But where objectivity was lacking, weariness served. She had slept very little, kept awake by the storm and the resurgence of memories it evoked. She was now simply too tired to engage in a battle of wills—if indeed there were one being waged between them. That admission, however, was made on a level

109

deep below conscious thought. Consciously she was aware only of his presence an arm's length from her.

Without speaking, she stared at him, her focus fixed for some reason upon his cloak. The length and copiousness of the garment were akin to that which would have belonged to a man of her kind who held the noble title and social rank of king. But even without the mantle—and despite the slave collar partially concealed now beneath the neck of his tunic—his bearing would have still been one of omnipotent strength and command. It was innate, his sureness of self, his control. Nothing anyone could do would touch him if he did not want it to. Not pain or fear or doubt.

She bit the inside of her lower lip and looked away. In spite of the hatred she bore him, she recognized and esteemed his strength—even envied him for it.

"Domina."

His voice—and that accursed foreign word—served to shatter her reverie. She blinked and shook her head to clear her mind of disturbing thoughts. Was it possible that the Roman seed within her exacted some power upon her, warping her reason? Else she must surely be going mad to see anything admirable in this man who was her sworn enemy!

Wordlessly she turned on her heel, went to the hut and returned with an ax in hand. She tossed it to the ground, then spun away, calling for Dafydd.

Inside, she numbly threw the sticks she still carried in one hand upon the dying flames and removed her mantle. But the wood was wet. Instead of catching fire, it smoldered and smoked, threatening to smother the glowing embers. Outside she heard the sound of the ax. The rotten tree was not far from the hut.

"Dafydd, please shut the door," she scolded, hearing the boy's entrance. Ignoring him, she knelt before the hearth. Eyes stinging from the billowing smoke, she tried to get close enough to blow the embers to life, tossing on a bit of dry brush in hope of creating at least enough fire and heat to dry the rain-wet bark.

She heard the doors close, and almost at once, with the lack of draught, the smoke rose upward toward the charred vent in the roof. Beside the hearth, gathered up and scooped into a basket, there were some dried grain stalks left from the milling the day before. These she also threw onto the rising flames, breathing a sigh of relief as they quickly caught fire, at last lighting the wood.

She sat back on her heels and wiped the tears from her cheeks. Silently Dafydd crept up beside her. "I'm s-s-sorry, Rhyca," he stammered.

Rhyca knew the child could not know for what he apologized. It had been she who had nearly let the fire die; she who had thrown on the wet wood. But the sight of her tears had frightened him, and he now sought to comfort her. She shook her head and reached out to touch him reassuringly. From the corner of her eye she saw the pile of sticks he had dropped between the hearth and the door. She pointed. "Let's look through that and see if we cannot find something that will burn."

A semblance of order had been restored, the wood stacked beside the hearth, and the water at last in a rolling boil, when a knock sounded at the door. Rhyca looked up from the cauldron. Her hand, poised above the pot to pour a bowl of meal, stilled.

"It's Galen," declared Dafydd excitedly from where

111

he sat toying with two sticks he had been attempting to fashion into a sword with a length of cord. He lumbered to his feet, the toy forgotten.

Rhyca pursed her lips and grudgingly watched as the boy limped quickly to the door, opening it and then the outer one to the Roman's entrance. Immediately the fire sparked, and the gray rope of smoke that had passively wound upward to the roof vent began to unravel and swirl about the room. "The door, Dafydd!" she snapped, her annoyance less at the surging smoke than with the bronzed man upon her threshold.

He took a single step forward to allow Dafydd to duck behind him and pull the outer door closed. Then he stood there, his eyes on nothing in particular. Yet she knew he noticed everything—and if he was awaiting an invitation, he would wait an eternity! With a resounding "plop" she dumped the meal into the cauldron, glaring at him . . . forcing him to ask permission to enter.

Intent on issuing her silent challenge, she forgot about the long-handled wooden spoon she held in her left hand . . . a spoon resting in the cauldron of boiling water and meal that now bubbled upward. . . .

She cried out in sudden pain as the mixture boiled over, splashing hot, runny gruel over her hand and between her fingers. She dropped the spoon and grabbed her wrist.

He was at her side in an instant. He reached past her, seized her arm and plunged her hand into a bucket of water sitting to the left of the hearth. The cool water stopped the gruel from continuing to cook on her flesh. But she was beyond reason to realize that.

"You are hurting me!" she cried, trying to pull her arm loose from the iron clasp that only tightened with her indignant struggle to free herself from his grasp. Horrified, she realized he was leaning over her, the muscled chest pressing against her back, his hard length allowing her no escape.

"Be still!" Galen clamped his left hand down on her shoulder, forcing her to obey his command. Pressing yet closer against her, he used his weight to keep her bent forward at the waist, forcing her hand to remain in the bucket. At his touch he felt the shudder he expected go through her. She ceased to fight and slowly turned her head to look back up over her shoulder at him. Her eyes were lifeless, filled with bitter hatred. Her gaze sought and found his.

"I do not want your aid. From the likes of you, *Roman . . .*," she hissed, making of it not a name, but a vile curse, "I do not want—or need—*anything!*"

Immediately he released his hold, standing upright. "You need to keep your hand in the water until the pain ceases," he retorted flatly. "And you need drier wood." Stepping aside, he waved his hand at the skein of smoke and steam that rose from the hearth. "I will be outside."

At last her loathing gave way to rage. "Where you belong—and shall remain," she screamed at his departing back, "with the other beasts of burden!"

Without seeing him, Galen brushed past the small boy in his path and slammed the hut's inner door behind him. Upon his entrance he had noticed the tools set against the wall inside the small passage between the two doors. Now, despite the darkness that filled the space, he easily located the spade. His fist closed about the handle as if it were a sword hilt, and he swore a silent oath.

His confusion at his own inexplicable reaction to her hatred, his need to break through it, the anger and frustration he felt in his inability to do so, all had found an added ally—another demon now to torment him. When his body had been pressed against hers in the effort to keep her still, his blood had stirred in response to the contact. As much as he would deny it, he could not. He had felt a man's awareness of this woman—a woman who despised him and all for which he stood, a woman whose belly swelled with the child of a husband slain by such as him!

He kicked the outer door open and hefted the spade to his shoulder. He had not been with a woman since his arrival in Britain. His energies and concentration had been centered upon Agricola's plan. He'd had neither the time nor inclination to purchase the favors of one of the numerous women residing outside Deva's gate for that express purpose. And while many a camp whore and noble Roman lady alike had lain beneath him, the pleasures of their soft, pale flesh had never meant any more than the simple gratification of a need as basic to life as food and drink. To sate that need he had also taken the spoils of war due a soldier—the right to a vanquished foe's womenfolk—but never had he allowed his urges to override his control. And now would be no different. The arousal he had felt with this woman would not happen again, nor would he permit guilt over her circumstance to prey upon his mind any longer!

He looked out into the compound, his gaze settling on the mound of dirt shoveled from the storage pit yesterday and now compacted from last night's rain. He thought briefly of his shoulder, then stoically shrugged. He had dug miles of trenches with the old wound. What was one small mound of dirt? Besides, the pain would give him something to concentrate on—something other than this woman he would drive from his thoughts. When he was finished chopping and stacking the firewood, he would fill in the old pit.

"Rhyca . . . why . . . ?"

From across the room Dafydd's hushed whisper, filled with confusion and distress, sounded. The sight of his face, skewed with emotion, tore at her. What the child had witnessed should not have occurred in his presence.

"He was only trying to help . . . why? Why . . . ?" The boy's voice faded, yet the look upon his face said what he did not need to. In his eyes she was wrong.

"Dafydd, there are things you do not understand." Helplessly she struggled to find the words. She looked at the small form that would not come closer even at her silent beckoning. "You are too young to know—"

"I know Galen was not hurting you. I know he was trying to help because you burned your hand."

"Please, Dafydd . . . try to—"

"No." He pressed his lips tightly together as if attempting to stop himself from crying. "I'm . . . I'm going to go outside and help Galen."

Rhyca could only watch him leave. The child had made his choice, and the door closing behind him echoed in the emptiness of her heart. Suddenly she was cognizant of the pain in her left hand. Pulling it from

115

the bucket of water, she stared at it. The skin was red but unbroken, nor were there blisters raised on the flesh. His swift reaction had done that, had spared her worse injury. Dafydd had been right. What was wrong with her that a mere child should possess clear vision while hers was made murky with hatred? Slowly she submerged her hand again in the water to ease the residual stinging left by the burn.

With hatred. The words resounded within her mind, and at last reason awakened. She could not view either the Roman's words or his deeds without distortion. Her hatred was too deep and that armor too strong. For her to endure his presence any longer would drive her mad. He was not relegated to the fields as she had believed he would be. And now she knew she could not ignore him—he would not let her ignore him. Always it would be as these two days had been, his dark eyes watching her with a steadiness and cold curiosity that made her hate him all the more. Cerrix would have to listen! He must see that he had commanded the impossible. If she must have a slave, let it be another, but not this one!

With her mind set upon a course, a sense of calm washed over her. She thought about what she must do as she wrapped her hand in a poultice of pain-dulling herbs and a strip of clean linen. Even when she opened the door and heard the sound of his ax, the serenity borne of her decision did not waver. Knowing she would soon be rid of his presence would enable her to confront him.

She stepped outside and shivered in the cold sunlight. The air was still, carrying the ring of his ax to her ears, telling her where he was. She followed the sound toward the woods, to where Dafydd had gestured that the fallen tree lay.

As she had known he would be, Dafydd was with him, stacking the logs he split. She saw the dark head rise up and knew he heard her. He turned to Dafydd, and whatever he said sent the boy scurrying into the forest. Rhyca was sure the child had not even been aware of her approach.

She came up from behind him and stepped around to face him. "I would speak to you."

He ignored her, bringing the ax down to split a log set upon a stump. Clean and powerful, the blow neatly halved the wood. One piece fell to the ground; the other remained standing on end upon the stump. He leaned forward, grabbed it and tossed it aside, setting another log immediately in its place. "Galen," he stated suddenly. "My name is Galen. If you want to speak to me, address me as such."

The ax fell.

She drew a deep breath. "Galen. I intend to speak to Cerrix. I cannot have you here."

He set another log in place. "I am not leaving."

The words were quietly uttered, but their force was unmistakable.

At first she was so undone by the response, she could conjure no retort. And then she recovered. "The choice is not yours, *Roman!* You will go where told and do whatever task given."

Leaning the ax handle against the stump, he slowly straightened and stepped toward her. The expression upon the bronze face was unreadable. "Those are orders for a slave." And as his black eyes bored into her, she heard his unspoken words more clearly than had he uttered them aloud: *I am no slave.*

A shiver of awareness rippled through her. What she had earlier admired in him, she suddenly feared. And her fear goaded her to fury. "Roman dog!" She raised her arm.

With the instincts of a trained warrior he had sensed the blow that would have otherwise met his cheek and now blocked it, seizing her wrist in the same fluid movement. Maintaining his hold, he pulled her a single step closer.

Though trembling, she still lifted her chin defiantly. "Let me go, or I will scream."

He acted as if he had not heard her threat—or did not fear it. "You are filled with hatred, woman of the Ordovices. And until now I have allowed you to release it. But no longer. No longer will I endure the lash of your tongue, for the cause of your hatred is not of my doing. Nor am I a threat to you. For my own reasons I have given my word to remain in this place, hence the chains that bind me are self-imposed—as is my obedience. Make no mistake, it is not obedience to *you,* but my *own* choice that has caused my compliance. If I obey, it is because I choose to do so."

His voice was a low growl, and a dangerous fire burned in his eyes. Strangely, however, her fear of him abated. His hold, though firm, did not cause her pain. Somehow she knew his show of force was no more. Though he could break her like a twig, he did not intend to harm her.

"You are alone," he continued, his voice suddenly softening, "with just cause to distrust and hate a man of my kind. But for now I am not your enemy. Abandon this battle you would wage between us, and allow me to prove the truth of my avowal. I know it is difficult . . . what I ask. I know—"

"You know nothing," she whispered hoarsely. His words, his attempt at a truce—indeed, his sudden gentleness—were together far more disturbing than had been his anger and strength. She did not know how to respond to either except to flee from what she could not understand. "You know nothing of me!" She pulled her arm free and ran blindly back toward her hut.

But once inside, knotted anger with herself and womanly weakness uncurled within her. What had she accomplished with her flight? She should have stood steadfast and faced him. To what purpose, though? There were but two paths before her. She could attempt this truce or she could go to Cerrix and beg for his reconsideration. And if he refused? He might well do so, given the peculiar esteem he seemed to hold for this Roman. Was theirs a leaders' pact of honor between them? Was that the cause for the freedom allowed this slave?

Amid the storm of confusion that raged within her there was a single certainty: Unless and until she had attempted what the Roman proposed, she could not go to Cerrix. He would only ask her why she had rejected so willing and cooperative a slave. Therefore, for the present at least, she must go about her daily tasks in as normal a routine as possible. Even now she could hear the soulful cries of the cow proclaiming her swollen udder and her need to be milked.

Reluctantly Rhyca left the hut and headed for the

oxen's stall. As she crossed the yard, she was acutely aware of the Roman's location. He had finished splitting the logs cut from the fallen tree, and he and Dafydd now stacked the firewood beneath a covered area against the hut's outside wall. His position accorded him clear view of the entire compound, and just as she had felt his eyes upon her the instant she had stepped outside, she continued to feel his surveillance as she began her chores.

The knowledge that he watched her was unnerving, and her hands trembled in the performance of the simple task she had done countless times. The cow seemed to sense her nervousness as well and responded in kind. The usually docile beast refused to stand still and kicked over the bucket not once but twice. Irritation and frustration joined the emotions already teeming.

Rhyca's mood was not improved nor her uneasiness assuaged when the Roman, having completed the stockpiling of wood, turned his attentions to the palisade's repair. The section he chose to work upon was close to the stall. She fed the oxen quickly. Thankfully, the rain had replenished the animals' water trough. Hence, she was spared from either having to fetch the water from the river herself or making her need known to him. Nor was she of a mind to ask Dafydd to lead the cow to pasture as he usually did. She would do it. And rather than have to walk past the Roman to take the milk inside, and then walk back again, she set the bucket in the shade. She had just prodded the cow forward when Dafydd approached.

"I'll take her, Rhyca." His offer was accompanied

120

by a hesitant smile and a darting look back over his shoulder—a look met by the Roman's nod of approval.

"Thank you, Dafydd." She forced a smile, trying to quell the annoyance she felt in knowing the boy's gesture had been prompted by her slave. "We'll eat when you return."

"Can I eat outside . . . with Galen?"

The question caught her off guard. She had not intended to feed the Roman, but could think of no way now not to—not without diminishing herself yet further in the boy's eyes. She nodded and reached for the bucket of milk.

The acrid odor that greeted her the instant she stepped back inside the hut was unmistakable; in her absence the porridge had overcooked and scorched. She kicked the door open to ventilate the room, all the while cursing the cause of the burn on her hand and the pot of ruined porridge.

"Feed him?" she cried aloud, slamming earthenware pots and wooden bowls about as she searched for the last bit of honey she had, knowing beneath its sweetness she could perhaps hide the burned taste. "It should be a handful of yew berries I stir in his bowl! Poison the cur . . . it would be one way to be rid of him!"

Despite her vengeful mutterings and the temptation to spoon into his bowl the burnt scrapings from the bottom of the cauldron, she refrained from doing so. She dipped two gourds into the bucket of milk and stood in the doorway to await Dafydd's return from the pasture. Unable to prevent it, her gaze went to where the Roman continued to labor.

Using the blunt end of the ax, he drove a loose post

more deeply into the rain-softened ground. The strength of the blows seemed effortless, and there was no sign of the pain he had yesterday betrayed. He set down the ax and pulled at the top of the post. Apparently satisfied with the firmness of its setting, he turned and looked straight at her. "If you hold the crosspiece, I can lash it into place."

Two thoughts assailed her instantly: Though his back had been toward her, he had been aware of her watching him. And did he ever ask? As with his proposed truce, he merely stated what he would do.

She drew a deep breath and walked toward him. The crosspiece that needed to be reattached was still lashed at one end to a support post, the other end resting upon the ground. At her approach he lifted the length of split timber, showing her how to hold it steady by resting it upon her shoulder. He took a step to the side and carefully transferred the weight onto her left shoulder.

"Too heavy?"

She shook her head.

"All right, then. Hold it against the post. Use your hand . . . here." He took her right hand in his and pressed its palm to the post. "Balance yourself. If it becomes too heavy . . ."

She did not hear the remainder of what he said. Staring at the large hand over hers, she wondered why she felt no revulsion at his touch.

He removed his hand and set about the task of winding a leather thong above, below, and around the timber and post, lashing the two pieces together.

He had just finished as Dafydd entered the enclosure. Wordlessly she stepped away and walked to the hut. She heard the boy greet him, and when she exited a moment later with the bowls of porridge, both were outside the door, the Roman leaning the ax and spade against the wall. She handed Dafydd the bowls, then went back inside for the gourds of milk.

The Roman was waiting for her when she stepped out. "You did not give me the opportunity to thank you for your help."

She avoided his eyes and extended the gourd. "There is no wine or mead," she found herself explaining.

"I am grateful for what is offered," he answered graciously, as if knowing how difficult those few civil words had been for her to speak. And then he continued. "The sun's rays will have dried the fields enough for the sledge. After I have eaten I will finish the pit, then harness up the oxen and begin to bring in the grain. If you do not need Dafydd here, I will take him along."

She nodded, at some level aware that he had done no more than state his intentions. Once again, no permission was asked—or given.

She lost count of how many times Dafydd and the Roman made the trek to the fields, returning with the sledge laden with the stalks felled the day before. By late afternoon the boy was exhausted. The Roman ordered him to rest and made the final trip alone. The sun had nearly set, descending in the western sky like a ball of molten fire, when Rhyca heard the now familiar tread of the oxen and the jangle of the iron rings on the yoke. She had only just returned as well.

Dafydd had fallen asleep, and loath to wake him, she had fetched the cow from the pasture herself.

From the doorway of the hut she watched their entrance into the compound. The Roman walked alongside the oxen, prodding the beasts with a length of stalk he flicked over their backs. He was not alone, however. With him was a warrior guard, but not the guard from that morning or yesterday. This one Rhyca knew well from the hill fort. Too well. He was called Balor, and was one of Mouric's warriors. Much feared for his vicious nature, his reputation for cruelty was well earned.

The bucket she had come to retrieve was forgotten. The milking could wait. Something was amiss. She could see it in the set of the Roman's shoulders. Once before she had seen that same posture of tension and carefully reined control—just before he had charged Mouric upon the platform.

She continued to watch both guard and prisoner.

As the Roman unharnessed the oxen, without provocation Balor suddenly drove the butt end of his spear into the Roman's side.

"Get on with it! I'll not be wasting the last of daylight on the likes of you. Unlike you, *I* have a hot meal and a warm body ready and waiting."

Rhyca walked cautiously toward the stall, taking care to remain just outside Balor's line of vision. While she could not see his face, she heard his words clearly.

"What think you of that, slave? To know there is nothing awaiting you for the rest of your days but the cold ground and scraps unfit for my hunting dogs? You know what I shall do? I shall think of you, slave.

Tonight. When my belly is full of food and wine, and I have a woman beneath me. Each time I bury myself in that hot, wet sheath, I shall think of you." He grabbed himself grotesquely between the legs and thrust his hips forward, laughing. "Perhaps you will hear her screams of pleasure."

Rhyca saw the Roman's eyes narrow, yet knew he would not permit himself a reaction to the warrior's taunts. Balor seemed to know as much, too. Determined, however, to elicit a reaction to his goadings, he thrust his spear a second time, this time with more force.

It may have been her dislike of him, or the distaste and disgust she felt at his loathsome gestures and references, but for whatever reason, she stepped forward. "Are you prepared, Balor, to explain your actions to Cerrix should it come about that my slave is unable to perform his labors due to broken ribs—or worse?"

Balor glared at her. Still, he seemed to have realized the weight of her threat. He looked back to the Roman. "Be quick about it!" he spat. Then, eyeing them both suspiciously, he turned and stalked through the gate without glancing back.

The Roman looked at her, arching a dark brow. "I did not need your assistance."

She exhaled an angry, indignant breath. "Injured, you are of no use to me."

"Fear not, *domina*," he stated flatly, "for I have suffered worse from better men."

"As, too, have I," she retorted, staring pointedly at him, "but from *lesser* men."

Galen watched her wheel back toward the hut. What had she meant—from "lesser men"? He was convinced from her look and the venom in her tone, she had meant men of his kind. But what suffering? Was there more to what had happened in that village than the loss of her husband and the orphaning of her unborn child?

A possibility he did not want to consider seemed the only logical one. He was a soldier. He knew what happened to the women left alive after an attack, and death was a far more merciful fate.

More disturbed by the thought than he wanted—or expected—to be, he turned his attentions back to the oxen only to look up several moments later at the sound of approaching footsteps.

Ignoring his questioning gaze, she stopped short a dozen paces from him and hurled what looked to be a bundle of clothing at his feet.

"You stink," she declared. "I may be forced to suffer your presence, but I'll not endure your stench. See that you bathe before next I lay eyes upon you, Roman, and put those on that I may wash what you are wearing. It's filthy."

Galen nodded. But she had already turned to head back to the hut. He stood for a very long time and stared at the door she had shut resoundingly behind her. This woman eluded understanding like a fox a snare . . . but then . . . he never had been very fond of trapping prey. He preferred to hunt it down.

Seven

His eye took in the changes almost at once. There was a marked sense of restored order about the small farmstead: a neatly stacked supply of firewood a few paces from the hut's door, newly repaired sections of palisade, harvested grain drying on racks in the yard, and the freshly dug pit of course. . . .

Cerrix smiled: the infamous pit. More than once he had heard the story of its digging, how she had insisted her slave dig it twice the usual depth, while neglecting to mention the necessity of refilling the old pit with the dirt removed from the new one, thus making twice the work for him. And yet when the warrior Balor would have mistreated him, she had stepped in. A curious contradiction, this kinswoman of Mouric's. But then, it was in that very paradox of her masculine strength of will and her fervent woman's soul that Cerrix had seen fertile ground for the seeds he would sow. That those seeds were planted he had no doubt. Balor's report confirmed it. Despite her loathing of the Roman, she had been unable to allow his maltreatment. Now all Cerrix could do was wait for the passage of time. Whether life would spring forth from those seeds would depend upon fate and the will of the gods.

He entered the enclosure, summoning the two men at his back to follow. Balanced upon their shoulders they carried between them a pole from which hung the wild boar Cerrix had hunted that morning—a gift to the widow and also his excuse to see firsthand what progress had been made. After all, he had reasoned, by law it was his kingly duty to act as father to his tribe, serving the needs of family for those who had none. The fresh meat would be welcomed.

Rhyca heard the dogs barking and went to the doorway in alarm. Hunting dogs were a luxury belonging only to the tribe's warriors. Suddenly alive in her mind was the vision of the pack of beasts that had snapped at the Roman captives as they had entered the hill fort. Ignoring for the moment the men entering her enclosure, she sought out her slave. Before she could locate him, however, a harsh command was issued to the animals. The trio of great gray hounds that had been coursing back and forth across the yard, their noses in the dirt, immediately sat back on their haunches, tongues lolling, as their master affectionately cursed them.

At her appearance in the doorway Cerrix lifted the heavy boar spear in his hand as greeting, bowing his head respectfully. "Forgive the unannounced nature of this visit. I have brought you the efforts of my morning's hunt in the hope you will regard me more kindly for the disruption I have brought to your life." He turned and gestured his men forward.

Rhyca gave his weapons bearers and their burden

no more than a cursory glance. As king, Cerrix did not have either to explain his actions or bribe her. Besides, if the "disruption" he spoke of was his pressing of the Roman upon her, it would take more than a fortnight's supply of meat to buy her forgiveness. This visit was because of the incident with Balor.

He seemed able to read her thoughts, for his eyes crinkled in amusement as he held her mute stare. "It is customary to express a word or two of thanksgiving when a gift is presented," he stated, his tone light.

"Of course." She dipped her head. "Thanks given, Cerrix."

"Now . . . about this incident of several days ago . . ."

As her head snapped up, he turned toward his waiting men. "There is a rack not yet in use erected near those upon which the harvest dries. Hang the boar that she may later dress it." At their obedient withdrawal he then returned his attention to her. "I have spoken with Balor. His actions were unwarranted. They will not be repeated. However, when Mouric returns and learns of your defense of the Roman he may be less understanding than I. As your kinsman he does not accept your autonomy, preferring to place you among the women of my household. I can understand his position; were you widow of my brother, I might feel the same."

Rhyca heard nothing of Cerrix's words save that Mouric was gone. Now she knew why it was not her brother-in-law who stood before her. "He is gone?" she asked in confirmation.

"Yes. He leads a scouting party to determine if the soldiers of the fortress have dispatched searchers for their absent men. Though no trail was left for them to follow, I would be sure they do not stumble into our mountains unwittingly."

"Would the loss of so few matter to them that they would send more to find those lost?"

Cerrix smiled. "Probably not. But it provides Mouric diversion." He cast a sudden and curious glance about. "Where is your Roman?"

"In the fields." At his nod of approval, she risked the voicing of the question that had gnawed at her from that first day at the riverbank. "Why is it that he enjoys such freedom of movement? He is not kept under guard save to be brought to and from the hill fort. I should think an enemy to be less trusted."

Cerrix's smile faded. Clearly her inquiry displeased him. She was, after all, merely a woman, possessing not the right to question the orders of any man, much less her king. "Has he given cause that you fear harm from him?"

"No."

"Or reason which would lead you to believe he would abuse the freedom he has been granted?"

"No."

"Are you in any way displeased at the labor he has performed?"

Again her answer was no.

"Then, I see no cause for your concern."

"But he is—"

"He is what, Rhyca?" His impatient tone cut sharply through her.

"A Roman," she finished weakly, realizing how feeble her protest was and knowing instantly that had she gone to him when she had considered it, her request

130

to have the Roman removed would have been denied—just as he now denied even her simple expression of unease.

Cerrix brushed a hand across his mustache to hide
from the woman his returned smile. Were there the
slightest complaint, she would have freely voiced it.
The planting appeared to be sure indeed. "Let us go
to your field. I have heard for days now that this Roman possesses the strength of an ox. I would see him
labor. Then, too, perhaps I might view something that
would cause me to rethink my decision."

He knew the hope—albeit false—which he had purposely instilled, that he might recant, would command
her accompaniment more than a direct order. Without
waiting for her he crossed the yard to where his men
struggled with the boar, their task made no less difficult by the dogs milling about their feet in anticipation of the scraps that would normally be tossed to
them once the prey was gutted and skinned.

Cerrix handed over his spear to one of them with
the instruction to both that they could return to the
hill fort once the boar was hung. A shrill whistle
brought the hounds reluctantly to heel. The woman
awaited him at the palisade's opening. The silence with
which she had acknowledged his intent was not broken
until they were well down the path that ran between
the fields.

"There." She pointed to the left of the path.

Viewed from the hill fort, the small, square fields
in their various stages of cultivation and harvest had
often looked to Cerrix to be as a cloak donned by the
goddess of the earth, a cloak in pattern and color not
unlike those worn by her people. But from here, the

fields looked to run together, not individual plots of land, rather a continual expanse. What the woman called hers was no more than a cleared area thirty meters or more from the path, in the center of which a solitary figure guided a pair of oxen pulling a plough. The bronze color of his naked torso identified him easily as the one Cerrix sought.

But despite the fact that he had come to view this Roman, Cerrix found his gaze drawn instead to the sight of another, one who stood in a field that bordered the woman's. With sickle in hand, the slave faced not the crop to be harvested, but an encircling trio of men—Ordovician warriors who each leveled a spear at the small, dark man, daring him with sharp stabbing motions to strike.

Cerrix quickly cast a glance back toward the woman's slave. He had to be able to hear the warriors' jeering, and yet, except to dart an occasional interested eye in the direction of the four, he did not appear concerned at his man's peril. Cerrix found this action strange, given the tall Roman's protective nature toward his men days earlier upon the platform. He returned his attention to his own men. If the Roman was not going to interfere, neither would he.

The taunting continued, the warriors edging ever closer. The slave raised the sickle.

Suddenly a command rang out. "Stand down, Drausus!"

The small, wiry man hesitated; then in slow compliance to the order he threw down the weapon in his hands. Their sport ended, the warriors still gave a half-hearted jab or two in the hope of stirring up the slave's temper anew. One spat in disgust, yet they all backed away.

"I don't understand."

The softly spoken comment of the woman beside him echoed Cerrix's own thoughts. Before he could respond, however, his attention was captured by the Roman. Pulling the oxen to a stop, he left the beasts and headed toward his man. Their confrontation was too distant to afford a hearing of their words. That they were heated, though, was clear. The smaller man threw back his head in defiant response, and in the next moment he was on the ground, felled by a blow delivered to his belly.

Cerrix had heard tell of the unflagging level of discipline instilled in and demanded of Rome's legions. Obedience to orders and adherence to the chain of command were absolute. Mutiny within their ranks was punished by a practice the Romans called *decimatio*. One in ten men, drawn by lot, was put to death—stoned in front of the remainder—while a lingering death of crucifixion awaited those deemed directly responsible for the dissent.

What he had just seen transpire between these men pricked at his curiosity so that he could bear it no longer. He left the path, stepping over the field's boundary, a bank of soil formed at the field's lower end by time and constant ploughing. At the field's upper end there was a hollow formed by the same factors and serving the same demarcation function. It was there, after pushing his way through the waist-high stalks, that he met up with the Roman who was, the Ordovician realized in surprise, curiously clad in *bracae*.

"Lord Cerrix." The dark head bowed in greeting.

Cerrix noted instantly that whatever emotion had led him to strike his man was now so well controlled as to be indiscernible. The bronze features betrayed nothing save minor surprise at the presence of the man before him.

"Centurion." Cerrix inclined his head toward the man in the next field, rising now only to his knees. "You would perhaps favor me with an explanation?"

The broad, bare shoulders rose in an unconcerned shrug. "It is a matter of little import. A lapse in judgment upon his part that shall not be repeated."

"You will tell me no more?" Cerrix pressed him for an answer.

"Your warriors have been trained to fight with words, Lord Cerrix, casting insults like spears. Mine must learn to raise as shield a deaf ear."

"Perhaps you expect too much of them, to suffer degradation and impugnation of honor in silence?"

"No more than I demand of myself. Words do not draw blood—only heat it. And heated blood makes a man lose sight of his better judgment." Abruptly the hard lines of the masklike face softened with a smile. "Once that occurs, he is sure to react foolishly . . . and *then* blood is shed—his blood."

In contrast to the man's outward control and complacent calm, Cerrix suddenly detected a restiveness about him. It was well disguised, but still there, deep within the dark eyes that had moved from Cerrix's face to stare off at something—or someone—behind the Ordovician. Upon the path perhaps?

Cerrix turned his head slightly, his gaze following the Roman's and confirming his suspicion. The source of the centurion's distraction and focus of his attention were one in the same. At last the seemingly impervious invincibility thus far exhibited by Agricola's envoy suffered compromise. But it was not the words or actions of a man that accomplished this feat, rather the silent presence of a mere woman. That she was as equally intent upon him was obvious despite the distance that separated them. Like a thread stretched taut between them, each's stare at the other was perceived and returned.

Cerrix concealed an instant smile of satisfaction. In the Roman's handling of the incident with his man, there was positive proof he would not hesitate or waver in regard to his duty. His utter loyalty was to the plan, and he would crush down any who threatened it—even his own. And in regard to the woman, Rhyca, and Cerrix's private plan. . . . Indeed, with all he had learned and seen this day, the future Great King could not have been more pleased.

Not so, however, with another who had also witnessed the confrontation. In a field adjacent to the one in which his commander now stood addressing the Ordovician chieftain, a burly man paused in his labors. He rested the blade of his scythe on the ground and its handle against his furred chest. Shaded beneath a meaty palm, his gaze darted from the two men engaged in conversation to the kneeling figure of the Spaniard. For the moment, Drausus had been cowed. He would think twice before he again challenged the bronze-skinned Moor. But by siding with the enemy against one of his own, Mauricius may have lost more than he had gained.

Rufus Sita shook his head. Of late his commander's

actions seemed to defy all rules of command. First the ambush. Now this. . . .

Suddenly the veteran's gaze locked with that of the man rising awkwardly to his feet. Between them no words needed to pass. Theirs was the silent language of comrades in arms, and in Drausus's face, beneath the visage of unrelenting defiance, Rufus saw his own doubts revealed and his fears confirmed. With his actions of a moment ago Mauricius had set foot upon a dangerous path.

Before she saw him Rhyca felt the malevolence of his stare. Still, she was not surprised with the sight of him. The women from the hill fort at the river that morning had talked of the scouting party's return last eve—not that Rhyca had taken part in the weekly ritual of gossip exchanged while pounding wash upon the flat stones along the bank. She simply would have had to have been deaf not to overhear what was shouted down a twenty-meter length of the river's edge.

She shifted the basket of heavy, wet wash to a more comfortable position on her hip, unwittingly away from the front of her where its bulk had served to hide her belly.

The man waiting at the entrance to her enclosure stepped forward. His eyes went instantly to her waist. "It thrives," he remarked coldly, his inference clear: She should have ridded herself of it when she had had the opportunity.

"Did you expect otherwise?" she retorted, her tone flat.

"Not expected, but hoped. I had hoped that the goddess would see fit to spare you the shame of birthing the bastard."

"The shame you would spare is not mine," she countered, burning beneath his malevolent glare. "Why are you here, Mouric? Surely it is not to inquire about my health—or the child's."

At the sound of the word "child" he worked his mouth as if he intended to spit. Then, apparently thinking better of it, he swallowed. "I come about your slave."

Had she no personal experience with rumor and gossip, or been unacquainted with Balor, she might have been surprised at the speed at which word of the warrior's encounter with the Roman had reached Mouric's ear. She had knowledge of both, however, and so she was not. He had only returned last eve after an absence of better than seven days, and though the sun was not yet risen to the sky's center, Mouric was here to confront her.

"What of him?" she asked in a colorless voice she hoped reflected apathy and disinterest. She pushed past him into the yard and headed toward her hut. Though she knew he would follow, she still wanted it pointedly known that his was a visit neither welcomed nor desired.

"I have heard he does not accept his status."

She kept her gaze straight ahead. "You have heard wrong."

"Have I?" His hand on her arm halted her in midstep.

She winced as he tightened his hold, repeating his accusation.

"Have I, sister-in-law? What is there between you and this Roman?"

Furiously she pulled her arm free. "How dare you!" she hissed. "Do you forget the choice was not mine? For Cerrix's whim he was thrust upon me—regardless of my outrage, his presence is to be endured."

"And yet it would appear you have readily enough accepted your 'outrage' *and* his presence—to the point that you dare confront one of my warriors to protect him! Balor told me what occurred."

"Then, he should have also told you my words. Heed them now, Mouric . . . what I told him, I say to you. I care not what happens to that Roman cur. But if I must be forced to have him, I will have him healthy. Like any other beast of burden, he is of no use to me if he cannot labor. However . . . ," she paused and raised her eyes to meet his, "if as my kinsman you would like to go to Cerrix and demand he rescind his order, by all means proceed. Nothing would please me more than to be rid of him!"

She saw the anger rise in Mouric's narrow stare and knew instantly its cause. While he disapproved the kingly command, he possessed neither the sway to demand its recanting nor the power to defy it. That she now challenged him to do so was a blatant reminder to him of his failing.

"I thought as much." She turned away from him and stalked toward the hut. From the corner of her eye she noticed the Roman. He had stopped in his labors, the ax in his hand seemingly forgotten as he stood upright. The log he split to form a new cross timber for the palisade lay ignored at his feet. His entire focus was upon Mouric. Despite the distance between herself and the Roman, and the even more considerable area that separated the men themselves, she could feel the animosity he directed at his enemy. It was evident in his stance and in the set of his shoulders. He was like a wolf, poised to strike yet holding back, holding back to watch and to study. . . .

She darted a glance to Mouric. He was equally aware of the Roman. His teeth bared in a snarl. Still, Rhyca knew that unless one made an overt move toward the other, each would merely continue to assess his foe in the savage, instinctive manner of all dominant males, whether two-legged or four.

Their contest of mute scrutiny and unvoiced challenge ended as the Roman broke his stare, the action more a bored dismissal of his adversary than a concession of defeat. He resumed his attack upon the cross timber, cleaving the edges of the log straight, with steady, calculated strokes of the ax.

Rhyca exhaled the breath she had unconsciously held and quickly crossed the wooden sill to enter the hut. She heard Mouric's footsteps only an instant later and tensed. Her explanation of the incident with Balor had not satisfied him—that, or his visit had yet another purpose.

She knew the latter was true as he silently took up a position just inside the door, leaning against the support post, his arms crossed over his chest. She cringed. She was left with no means of escape and no means to deny him voice.

"What more?" she asked, feigning a calm she did not feel. An unsettling sense of fear had come upon her. Indeed, there was a strange—yet somehow familiar—look in his eyes, and the smile fixed upon his face was one that held no humor.

Again his gaze went to her belly. "You have no one save yourself to blame," he stated slowly as if savoring each word. "By refusing to rid yourself of that bastard seed growing within you, by refusing to enter Cerrix's household . . . you have invited the shame you endure."

Her growing fear made her reckless. "Leave my house. There is no tie of blood between us. Your rights as kinsman died with Keir. I do not owe you explanation for my decisions."

She saw the glint of anger enter his eyes, yet discounted it, turning away from him.

"My brother would not have wanted this life for you."

"Your brother?" she shrieked, whirling to face him anew. "How dare you presume to know what he would have wanted? In life you did not understand him. I refuse to allow you to dictate his wishes in death. Hypocrite! You forced him from this village, and now you would evoke his name to wield influence over me—just as you have used his memory within the tribe as a sacred cause for personal vengeance. You know—and knew—nothing of him!"

His complacent smile grew cruel. "I know enough. I know he was incapable of being a husband to you, and in that I know the seed within you is not his. And as he could not give you a child, he could not give you pleasure. All those years . . . without a real man, your woman flesh void of what it craved . . . Is that why, Rhyca? Did the hunger of unfulfilled passion lead you to spread your thighs for his murderers? Did you take what they gave and enjoy it?"

"Get out!" she screamed, trembling under the onslaught of his accusations. Within her breast there burned at a white heat a pain she could not endure, a pain of combined despair and loathing.

But instead of leaving, he strode toward her, grabbing her arm viciously and pushing her back against the wall. He ignored her scream and held her fast with one hand, tight between the wall and his body, while with his other he fumbled between her legs. "Show me," he snarled. "Show me how much you struggled. How hard did you fight? Or did you? Perhaps that is why they let you live?"

Tears welled in her eyes and rolled down her face. Save that one outcry when first he had grabbed her she could not find her voice. Numb, she was unable to move, to fend off his attack.

Abruptly he removed his hand, yet maintained his hold. "I thought as much."

Through the pounding blood in her ears she heard a crash. Weakly she turned her head toward the doorway suddenly almost completely filled with a man's form.

"Release her."

A growllike sound served to break through the hazy terror that gripped her. She pulled away from Mouric as he released her—not in compliance to the Roman's demand, but in preparation to confront his enemy.

"Balor was right, Roman," he sneered. "You have not learned your place."

The Roman's lips curled in a cold smile of challenge. "Think you that you can teach it to me, Briton?"

"There is nothing that would give me greater pleasure. Do you forget I have already brought you once before to your knees to grovel at my feet? Now . . . you will bend your knee, slave." Mouric laid his hand upon the sword hilt at his waist. "Bend it—or I shall bend it for you."

The expression upon the bronzed face at first did not alter. And then, a single brow arched in mocking superiority. "I give you leave to try."

The defiant invitation was spoken so softly that it was barely audible. But for all its softness, it was unmistakably deadly.

The Roman took up a defensive stance. That he was unarmed seemed not to matter. "This time you have no unarmed boy to behead, Briton, no force to wield but your own. Let us see if it is mighty enough."

Rhyca stumbled forward, putting herself between the men. A will not of her own, a will she did not understand, compelled her to stop this battle ere it commenced. "Get out," she hissed, raising her eyes to lock with the Roman's steely stare. "Leave! I command it, slave!"

Why she prayed he would obey, she understood no more than her impulse to step forward. But for some unfathomable reason he *did* obey. Shedding the defensive poise of his body as he might a cloak, he inclined his dark head to her in a most reverent manner and stepped backward.

And suddenly she understood, though no words were uttered in explanation. In his eyes she perceived his thoughts as surely as if he had spoken them. And

142

in fact, he had—the day she confronted him as he cut the rotted tree for firewood. His respectful obedience now was not obedience but compliance by choice—his choice. To leave was of his choosing, just as to enter and intervene with Mouric upon her behalf was of his choosing. And that he had intervened was repayment in kind for what she had done with Balor for him. The debt between them had been repaid.

She watched his exit and waited until he was out of sight through the open doorway before she turned to face Mouric. The appearance of the Roman had given her time to collect her thoughts and to gather strength. As repulsed as she had been by Mouric's actions, she did not fear him any longer. His contempt of her would take no expression beyond the cruelty she had already endured. Still, she had to force herself to meet his scathing glare. His eyes were no more than twin slits of fiery rage and suspicion.

"You protect him," he accused. "I demand to know why."

"Protect him?" Her resultant laughter was a dead sound in the space. "I loathe him. What was done to me, I shall never forget, and with every breath I curse him and his kind."

He looked at her. "Should I learn differently . . ." The menacing glower riveted upon her precluded his need to complete the threat. He strode to the door, wheeling at the threshold to offer a final ultimatum. "For now I will believe it is need of his back and your woman's dearth of reason that has twice caused you foolishly to defend him. It will *not* occur again. And one thing else . . . if your slave dares so much as to lift his eyes in my presence again, I will see to it that

143

he is more worthless to you than that crippled boy you coddle."

As if rooted to where she stood, Rhyca watched him exit the hut and head across the yard to the opening in the palisade. Her breast heaved with the rapid beating of her heart, and only when it slowed, returning to normal rhythm, did she venture toward the doorway to reassure herself he was gone. She stumbled over a log lying in the passageway and in looking down realized the cause of the crashing noise she had heard earlier upon the Roman's entrance. Scattered at her feet was an armload of firewood. Whether he had purposely dropped the wood in preparation to do battle with his enemy or merely to capture Mouric's attention, she was not sure.

Nor was she sure how far his intervention might have proceeded without her interference. Certainly the enmity between him and Mouric was strong enough that any excuse—even that of defending her—would have provided him ample excuse to act upon it. And what of her own actions? Why had she attempted deliberately to avert a coming to blows?

Just as with the incident with Balor, she found herself without a ready answer. Then, however, she had not tried to examine her reasons. Now she must. Had she sought both times to protect the slave from injury—or the man from harm?

By day's end she had considered the question more times than she could count, and still had found no answer. She could not deny that in the time passed since his coming—nearly a fortnight now—her hatred of the Roman *had* yielded to grudging acceptance of his presence. Without conscious thought she had en-

144

tered into a truce with her enemy, and, in a curious way after Cerrix's visit, she had begun even to grow accustomed to him. The sight of him . . . the sound of his tools as he labored within the enclosure . . . they seemed so much a part of her life now that she could scarcely remember before he came. Each day began and ended in the same way—his knock that announced his arrival with wood for the fire.

Suddenly the doorway that had been lit with the fading sunlight of late afternoon darkened.

She knew him without his speaking and before the familiar knock sounded. She lifted her gaze from her loom to glare across the room at him as he entered. "Are you mad, Roman—or merely unbelievably dim-witted?" She rose awkwardly, brushing off her cheek a tendril of hair that had loosened itself from her braid. "He is dangerous."

What she saw in his black eyes—the fire that burned in the dark depths—needed no spoken expression. *So, too, was he dangerous.*

"I do not fear him," he stated at last, crossing the room and bending down beside the hearth to stack the firewood.

Where once she would have denied him mere entrance, now she watched his movements, realizing how familiar they—and he—had become. Disturbed by the thought, she averted her gaze and would have returned to her loom had his voice not stopped her.

"He wants you."

"What?" She snapped her head around and stared at him in disbelief and immediate anger. "What did you say?"

"Your hearing is also unimpaired, *domina.*" Clearly

145

he remembered and now made reference to a similar contention she had once made regarding his own auditory senses. He smiled ever so slightly, an unmistakably strained smile that carried neither his usual mocking amusement nor humor. "Mouric. He wants you. Today . . . when I intervened, I did so because I heard you scream. I have had the opportunity since to think, however. I am wondering if perhaps I interrupted. Perhaps you welcome his attentions?"

Rhyca gave a dry laugh. "Now I know you are dimwitted, Roman. Either that or it is your sight which is dim. You could not be more mistaken . . ." She let her voice trail, realizing that without the knowledge of Mouric that she herself possessed, what he had seen of Mouric's clawing and fumbling at her could only have appeared as he had perceived it. She shuddered in remembrance of the physical and verbal assault. "You do not understand what you saw, Roman."

The strange, hard look that had settled across his face remained. "Then, explain it to me." He rose slowly to dwarf her with his far greater size. "Tell me how what I witnessed could be seen as anything else."

That she owed him no explanation at all immediately entered her mind. Nor was this a subject she wished to discuss with him, and yet beneath his dark and penetrating stare she found herself searching for the words. "Very well . . . I can assure you Mouric does *not* want me. What you saw was not an acting upon his desire, but an expression of his contempt. You see, Roman . . ." She paused, hearing her voice begin to waver. She drew a deep and steadying breath. "My brother-in-law cannot look upon me without seeing a woman who allowed herself to be violated by

146

his enemies. Of course . . . you had already suspected as much, had you not, soldier of Rome? The fate of the women left alive . . . spoils of war you call it, yes?" She lifted her chin and forced him to look at her and acknowledge her unspoken accusation—and answer it.

"Yes."

Was there a tightness in his voice? She stared at him. A wry smile of triumph formed on her lips. "Yes," she whispered, twisting the blade of his guilt, *"soldier of Rome.* And even if Mouric could abide the sight of me . . . for your knowledge, for his nightly bed Mouric takes a man."

She paused, awaiting his reaction to her disclosure. She was disappointed to see a flicker of only the briefest amusement cross his features.

"So . . . for all his strutting arrogance and vanity, he neglects the primary duty of a good cockerel."

Rhyca regarded the man before her in thoughtful silence. This Roman knew of the lifestyle of the tribe's warriors—theirs being a society of man-to-man bonds—for he had betrayed no surprise in hearing of Mouric's choice. Or were the ways of his people the same?

Among her kind once a young boy of the warrior class had seen seventeen summers, the age of bearing arms, he lived almost exclusively among those of his own gender, learning fighting, swordsmanship, hunting and drinking—all feats to prove himself worthy of battle. It was not unusual that friendships between these men should turn sexual. Most often sleeping in their warrior huts with two companions in a bed, they were content with the embrace of one of their own sex, viewing women not as pleasurable pastimes, but objects suitable for breeding only. That practice and the accompanying belief that warriors should see their own as the only suitable company was accepted among her people as natural.

She studied the silent Roman. The world he had known had also been a world exclusively of men— soldiers, thousands in number, living together within the walls of their fortresses. It would make sense he should understand. Only his remark led her to believe he was not himself one who made such a choice. She was annoyed as well to realize the revelation of Mouric's sexual preference did not appear to have dissuaded the Roman. She could see it in the indulgent look he gave her, before he responded aloud.

"That he wallows among bed fellows is no indication he does not desire to possess you as well. I am not unacquainted with the ways and beliefs of the Ordovices. Many of your warriors find pleasure as readily in a woman's arms as a man's. Nor does this revelation of yours answer my original question. Do you—would you—requite or welcome his attentions?"

Her annoyance yielded to anger. "No. I do not. Not his—or any man's! You are mistaken, Roman," she concluded coldly, "you do *not* know our ways. For a woman, bed is not a place for pleasure, but for marital duty."

"If you truly believe that, *domina*—" at last his smile appeared genuine and gentle—"then you have not known the right man. You should not have to compete with another man to know either your own pleasure or a man's passion. You are more woman than that, and should be taught to know differently."

Rhyca could not deny the sensation that shot through her at his words. Inexplicable, it was a fearful sensation, yet one not of fear, but rather of a longing—somehow familiar, yet foreign. Heat rose instantly to her cheeks. "I would rather *never* to know another man than ever again to endure a Roman's touch!"

Spat in vehemence, her venomous response caused his dark brow to arch in sudden confusion. "I was merely stating fact, *domina.*" He looked at her with unnerving steadiness for a moment, then added quietly, "I was not offering."

Like a flame the heat within her heightened. But before she could respond, the dark and now silent man before her had turned and left.

Eight

What was said that late afternoon was never mentioned again either by Rhyca or her slave. What he had wanted to know, she had told him, and Galen saw no need to cross again the line between them that seemed with each passing day to become less defined. He knew the cause, and it was one neither of his choosing nor undoing. But two people—even mortal enemies—could not be so much with one another that their enmity did not either increase to the point of confrontation—or decrease.

He had seen much the same occur in war—strangers that became friends, defeated foes and captives that became with time and acquaintance allies. Much the same was happening with his own men here—though some had adjusted more quickly to their new life than others. After little more than a fortnight the blond youth, Gaius, had practically been adopted by the aged man and wife to whom he had been given. No longer was he kept with the others in the stockade at night. Facilis, too, had carved out a place for himself that made him more family than prisoner to his masters. Even Rufus Sita, the huge Thracian who was soldier to the core, looked at home in the fields. Of the six only Drausus still refused to accept his fate. The other youth, Valerius, seemed not to know in which world he lived, and so it did not matter.

Their commander, too, found memory of his former life faded. But what concerned Galen was not the ease of tension between himself and the woman, Rhyca. For that he was grateful. She had come at last to accept him. What gnawed at him was the knowledge of what could occur. Between men once enemies such familiarity and constant contact might cause a friendship to develop. But between a man and a woman it was not friendship that formed, but the bonds of a different tie.

Galen had recognized the risk that first time he had felt his body's instinctive response to her—he could desire this woman. And hence he had taken care never again to allow a similar confrontation between them to occur. But inasmuch as he could control his physical vulnerability to her, he was helpless to control an emotional one. A man could not labor for a woman, be tied to her in all manner save of the flesh, and *not* consider the possibility. Nor could he not feel possession. As much as he was hers, she was also his. He had realized that fact in his need to know what her bond to Mouric was and in his satisfaction upon learning there was none. In a way, however, it would have been easier had there been something between her and the warrior—a barrier or obstacle to halt the desire Galen knew he must not—and would not—allow himself to feel.

And so the days of summer passed, ever strengthening the tenuous bond sought by neither the Ordovician woman nor her Roman slave. The month his people named in honor of Augustus neared. . . .

Rhyca shaded her eyes and looked out across the field. Stripped of its first harvest and cross-ploughed to break up the soil for replanting, it lay barren and scored in rills awaiting the sowing of its second crop—barley—which would ripen before spring to be harvested just when winter supplies ran out.

From the corner of her eye she noted the others in the fields about her own. From left shoulder to right hip, the women and children all bore—as did she—sacks heavy with the seeds to be broadcast. In the wake of the sowers there followed men armed with wooden and antler rakes, who covered the seeds with soil.

She pressed her palms to her lower back and arched, trying to relieve the aching pressure caused by the weight of the filled sack. Sudden voices behind her—Dafydd's and the Roman's—caused her to straighten and turn.

"Across the field. There and back. And Rhyca will go up and down." Dafydd nodded in impatient understanding as he repeated the instruction just given him by the tall man who stood at his back.

Bent over the boy, the Roman adjusted the sack slung across the child's front while surreptitiously testing the bulky weight Dafydd had insisted he could carry. "Not too quickly now either," he cautioned firmly.

"I know." Heaving an aggrieved sigh, the child

152

darted a glance in Rhyca's direction. "The baby makes her slow . . . the baby makes her weak . . . the baby makes her cross . . ." Eyes rolling, the blond head bobbed from side to side in accompaniment to the sing-song recitation.

At once the Roman stepped in front of Dafydd and clamped his hands on the slender shoulders. "Watch your tongue, boy," he reprimanded sharply. "She cannot help the changes wrought by the life growing within her."

Clearly crestfallen at the scolding, the child hung his head.

"Look at me," the Roman commanded, his tone gentling.

In reluctant compliance Dafydd obeyed. "I just wish we had the old Rhyca back," he murmured, his lower lip quivering.

"You shall have her soon enough." The bronze face softened with a smile. Affectionately he tousled the blond head, and immediately Dafydd's face brightened, his injured feelings soothed. "Off with you now." A reassuring pat sent the boy off toward the field's uppermost corner.

Seeing the Roman then raise his dark gaze to seek her out, Rhyca averted her own. Watching the scene just played out, she had been struck with conflicting thoughts and emotions. Dafydd regarded the man with an admiration that approached awe. That he was Roman, a slave and an enemy captive, mattered not at all to the boy. The men of his own kind viewed him as a freak—or ignored him. Until the advent of this man there had been no male influence in his life, no father figure to mold the man he would become by caring enough to school or discipline him now. Indeed, she could see the change the Roman's attention wrought. Each time he visited her, Dafydd displayed more confidence, a happiness with himself previously absent.

How could she therefore in all good conscience resent the role her slave had assumed in the child's life? And did she really resent it? Truly, had not her first reaction been just the opposite? The pleasure she had felt in watching the interaction of child and man had been a comforting warmth—doused icy by the sudden remembrance of who this man was.

A shadow fell across her. "Would you prefer to return home? The sun is hot this day. Perhaps you should allow Dafydd and me to sow this field. It will go slower without you, but certainly we can manage—"

"As can I," she interrupted curtly. Though she saw the concern in his eyes, she refused to acknowledge it and stalked off toward one of the lower corners. From there her course up and down the field would be one perpendicular to Dafydd's crossward pattern—thus ensuring complete coverage of the plot.

Galen watched her retreat in silence. Until her sowing path and that of the boy's intercepted, there was nothing for him to do. He raked a hand through his hair. She did not look well. Her face was drawn and her brow furrowed with weariness. Clearly the growing child was sapping her strength.

Grimly, he followed her progress. Though purposely sized to allow a lone man to plough its entirety in a single day, the field still encompassed a respectable area, certainly more than what could—or should—be covered by a woman heavy with child. If she did not collapse mid-field, he would be surprised.

Despite his dire prediction, however, she did not falter. Steadily she walked the field's length and back, carefully timing the handfuls of seed she cast to match her measured steps. From the corner of his eye he spotted Dafydd haphazardly slinging fistfuls to the wind, the seeds to land where they might. He heard her voice call out an annoyed reproach and chuckled softly as one from among the boy's rather justified litany of complaints promptly echoed in his mind: *The baby makes her cross.*

That she could have heard his private laughter seemed hardly possible, yet there was no denying the cold gaze he suddenly felt leveled in his direction. Nor was there any mistaking the anger of her words.

"Intend you to stand there until the entire field is sown, slave, before you take rake in hand?"

By the time she reached the upper third of the field Rhyca was sure the sack hung about her had somehow come to be filled not with seeds but stones. For the third time in as many steps she stopped to arch her back, tilt her head and curse the sun blazing above her. Squinting against its rays, she did not see the man who had been watching her all along toss down the rake in his hands. With firm resolve he strode across the field and was upon her before she realized it, plucking the sack from her shoulder and lifting it over her head in one swift action.

"You need to rest."

She felt his hand on her arm and pulled instinctively

away, shaking her head and blinking as her vision seemed suddenly to blur. "No . . . I'll be all right." She lifted a shaking hand to her forehead and swept back the damp strands of hair that lay clinging to her brow.

"You are stubborn, *domina.*"

At his words the dizziness that had come so quickly upon her passed. She glanced around, noting the workers in the other fields. Many had paused in their labors and were watching her. "And *you* are attracting attention," she hissed, glaring furiously at the man beside her.

"I will attract more if you do not at least sit in the shade and rest." His dark head inclined in the direction of the onlookers. "What attention and gossip think you it would provoke should I bodily pick you up and put you there?"

She started at the wording of his threat. He knew. He knew of the talk she had tried to ignore, but could not, as it seemed to grow only more frequent with each passing day. "You would not dare."

"No?" The black brow lifted. "I should have thought you to know me better by now."

And so she did. She left his side, tramping back across the sown portion of her field toward its eastern boundary to where a huge oak stood. Its age and girth having precluded extraction and removal, its leafy crown cast a generous shadow of cool shade even now at midday. From behind she heard the Roman call Dafydd in to take rest as well.

Never would she have admitted it, but she was glad to sit. She propped her back against the tree's trunk

156

and leaned backward, closing her eyes. The solitude was short-lived.

"Look, Rhyca!" Dafydd called, his voice and laughter carrying across the field to her. "See what he's doing. There!"

She sat forward and followed the direction of his outstretched arm. In a field bordering her own a crowd of children swarmed about a man in their midst. He appeared to be tossing small, fist-sized rocks into the air. As they fell, he caught them and threw them back upward. What made the feat wondrous, though, was that he handled more rocks than he had hands. Yet he seemed to have judged just when to toss each so that they fell at different times in such a manner that he could catch and throw one before another needed to be caught.

"Facilis." The all too familiar voice was suddenly beside her. "He enjoys an audience for his tricks. Certainly the children are amused."

With the Roman's words Rhyca recognized the man in the field. Even at a distance his red hair proclaimed him—the captive with the protruding ears and spotted face. Before she could reply, Dafydd had joined them, limping forward and settling next to her once he had removed the sack hung from his shoulder.

"Galen, did you see?" he asked, pointing toward the red-haired slave.

"Indeed." The Roman smiled. "Perhaps some time he will show you how he eats fire."

"Truly?" The child's eyes widened with both awe and disbelief.

The Roman nodded, throwing his long length down

upon the ground and stretching out in a leisurely fashion at her feet, his hands clasped behind his head.

Annoyance rippled through Rhyca. That the others in their fields had also stopped in their labors to rest, including the handful of guards that seemed to pay their charges little if any heed, mattered not. She had not invited his presence or given him leave to rest. She was forming a sharp command with the intent to send him back to the field when Dafydd's voice again sounded.

"Can a man really and truly eat fire, Rhyca?"

She wondered as much herself. Certainly the expression on the Roman's face had been sincere enough. "I don't know that a *man* can," she answered, "but no doubt it is a power not beyond the ability of a *demon.*"

His soft chuckle increased her annoyance twofold. "Facilis is no demon, *domina.* Merely a man whose journeys have taken him to places where there are arts of trickery unknown to most."

" 'Journeys,' " she repeated in cold sarcasm. "So it is by that word you call your armies' conquests?"

"A soldier must go where he is ordered." Though the tone of his voice was still affable, he now sat up, bearing his weight on his elbows, and pinning her with a dark stare.

"He is funny-looking." Unaware of the change that had occurred in what had been only a moment earlier a lighthearted conversation, Dafydd continued merrily and innocently. "I've never seen hair such a color. Still, I prefer him to the one who has no hair at all!" He giggled. "That one is frightful-looking. And the small, dark one always looks angry. Why is it, Galen?"

"Why is what?" the Roman asked, at last turning his gaze from her and directing an easy smile toward the child.

"Why do they all look so different? Your men? And you?" The boy scrambled onto his knees and crawled next to the man. He held out his left arm and placed it against the Roman's massive one. "See. My flesh looks like milk while yours is like bronze. And your hair is black, yet the one who is not so very old has hair the same color as us. He even looks like us, save his clothing."

"That is because he comes from Gaul. There the people are very much like the Ordovices—in their appearance and in their customs and language as well. The others . . . Facilis, Sita, Valerius and Drausus . . . they come from different parts of the Empire. Unlike the legions of a hundred years ago, whose ranks were filled with men recruited mostly from Italia, a goodly half of their numbers now are men from the eastern and northern provinces."

A confused look from Dafydd sent Galen sitting upright. "Rome is really only a city, but its borders reach to the far ends of the world. It is that which is called the Empire of Rome. I will show you."

As Dafydd looked on in rapt curiosity, he smoothed with his hand an area of ground between them and began to scratch lines in the dirt. "This a picture of the world, called a map."

"The world?" Skepticism weighted the young voice.

"What we know of it. There is much beyond your mountains, Dafydd. You know how when you are in the hill fort, the village looks small?"

159

A mute nod from Dafydd was his only reply.

"Well then, if you were a bird and could fly high in the sky—"

"As high as the sun?"

"Yes. This is what you would see. No longer could you see people, villages or even mountains and forests. You would see only the outline of land and the sea. Now . . . this is the Empire."

Unable to contain her own curiosity, Rhyca looked over the boy's shoulder to see what the Roman had drawn. It was a strange-looking image, almost like that of a crouching animal with a round head on the left, a thin leg with a foot, a much thicker second leg very near it, then a body that grew thick to curve around like a great tail. How fitting their empire should look like a beast!

Despite her thought, she listened and watched, heeding the Roman's explanation.

"This, what looks like a boot, is Italia. It is here that"—he pointed to what she thought looked like the knee of the beast's first leg—"Rome, the city, is located. Facilis comes from this area here to the north. Drausus comes from Hispania."

The beast's head, she noted, her gaze fixed upon the Roman's "map" and his finger which moved on to the shoulder, then higher still.

"Gaius, the blond youth, calls Gallia his homeland. Valerius is a Frisian from the Low Countries. And Sita—" he smiled and glanced up at the boy—"the one without hair, is a Thracian. His homeland, Thracia, is here."

The heel of the second leg.

"And you? Where is your homeland?"

160

"My father came from a land across this sea." He drew another line beneath the beast. "Here, called Mauretania."

"Where am I?" Dafydd edged closer in obvious fascination. "Show me."

"You are an island here. The province is called Britannia, the most distant frontier of the Empire. As you are so far north, the sun does not shine so hotly, hence your skin is not dark and your hair is fair. Drausus and I, our people are from places where there is no winter, where the sun burns with great heat."

"The sun burns hotly here!" The boy sat back, rather indignant to think the sweat upon his brow was insignificant.

"Not so hotly as other places. Here and here," he said, pointing, "there are no rivers or forests, only great seas of sand stretching farther than a man could walk for many days."

"How do you know?" Again the skepticism returned to Dafydd's voice. Thus far he had been willing to accept what the Roman said as truth, but this description of a land without rivers and forests warred too much with what his young mind knew to be otherwise.

"Because I have seen it, have been there."

"Where? Where have you been? Show me."

It seemed to Rhyca that he pointed to all corners of what he called his map. To each place indicated, he gave its name: Judaea, Lusitania, Aegyptus, Dalmatia, Gallia.

"Gallia? That is Gaul—where you said the people are like us? That is why you know our language?"

"That—and my mother was a woman of Gaul."

161

"Truly?" Dafydd squealed in delight at this revelation. "Then, you are not so different from us?"

Her gruntlike expression of derision went unnoticed by either the man or the boy, who continued his questions.

"But the homeland of your father is separated from your mother's by this great sea, yes?" Dafydd pointed to the ground. "Was your father, then, also a soldier?"

The Roman nodded. Clearly he was pleased with the boy's quickness of mind. "My father was an auxiliary—a soldier recruited from an area whose people had not yet been awarded Roman citizenship. After twenty-five years of loyal service, an auxiliary is given, rather than the small amount of land and gold earned by a legionary, a more prized reward—Roman citizenship for himself and the right to legal marriage with the wife he then possesses. As such, his children, if they be born after his discharge and the issue of that legal marriage, are also granted citizenship. And their descendants are as well."

"So it is, Dafydd, with the armies of Rome, that with the bribe of Roman citizenship men of lands once conquered by the Eagles come together to be the conquerors of new lands." Her sarcastic comment, her attempt to have the boy see the man he so admired in a less favorable light, went unmarked by the child, who in his curiosity and desire to learn saw instead only another question.

"Why are your armies called the 'Eagles'?"

The Roman looked to her before replying. What Dafydd had failed to see had not escaped his note. "Perhaps another time—"

"No! Please, I want to know."

The boy's soulful protest and darting glance to Rhyca instantly raised guilt within her. She shrugged to indicate disinterest in whether the conversation continued or not. The dark brow lifted in amusement, and the explanation followed.

"Each legion possesses a sacred battle standard—a silver eagle surmounted upon a pole. That standard represents a kind of spirit which joins the men together. It is called *genius,* and for it men fight and die. When a legion's eagle is captured in battle by an enemy there is no greater disgrace. All that legion's spirit and good fortune and reputation are gone. There is nothing left to do but discharge or transfer any surviving men because the legion is no longer alive."

"So you fight for a silver bird?"

The Roman laughed. "When worded thusly it does sound rather foolish. But it is not the 'bird' itself, Dafydd, rather what it represents to us—honor, duty, loyalty. When you are grown these are things you will better understand."

Dafydd shrugged. He had no interest in what to him were merely words. "Tell me about your father and when you were a boy like me."

"There is not much to tell. Because there is the fear that an auxiliary might take it into his head to rebel, he is never stationed in his homeland but sent far away. Hence my father was garrisoned on the border with Gaul. There he met my mother. I was born in a village outside the gates of a legionary fortress. You see, a soldier is not permitted to marry until his service is finished. Many do marry, however, but their wives and children must live outside the camp. I grew up in the army, in army camps. My mother and I, more fool

163

she for she loved him, followed him from garrison to garrison. There is even a name for such sons of soldiers—*catris.*"

He paused for a moment and raked his hand through his hair, as though reflecting upon the past. "The life of a soldier and his family is hard, especially for an auxiliary who is garrisoned in forts on distant frontiers far from his homeland. Also he is worse paid, yet is the one to take the first assault in battle. My father was killed when I was twelve. My mother, because she knew no other life, found herself another to take his place. As soon as I was old enough I enlisted. I was sixteen. Because I was considered illegitimate by the army that did not recognize my parents' marriage, I was not entitled to the citizenship my father's nearly thirty years of service would have earned him upon discharge. Only by enlisting myself could I be granted it. Then, too, like my mother, I knew no other life."

"You have been a soldier a very long time," Dafydd commented softly, his voice lilting suddenly. "Perhaps you sometimes think of another life?"

Rhyca recognized the childish hope beneath his words. It was dangerous for him to grow too attached to this man, for she knew instinctively he was not one to long endure the yoke of slavery. Someday he would leave, escape or be traded to the Romans in exchange for Ordovician prisoners as was common practice.

He laughed quietly and shook his dark head. "All good things I have ever known—the loyalty of men, sense of purpose, pride, and honor—I have found in service to my Eagles. I grew to manhood in their shad-

164

ows to serve as my father served. I am not suited to any other life, Dafydd."

The look of disappointment upon the boy's face was unmistakable, and her heart wrenched with the sight of it. In his short life he had known only abandonment. "It . . . it is time to go back to work." She made a move to rise, pointedly ignoring the brown hand instantly extended to aid her.

"You should return home."

"I have rested. I am fine. I can continue." As soon as it was made, she regretted her assertion. The dizziness she thought gone had returned, and that he knew it was undeniable.

He looked at Dafydd. "The handle on the rake has become loose. And she is tired. I am going to take her back, then repair it. Are you strong enough to continue without me for a while?"

Dafydd's small chest swelled with pride. "I can work alone." He reached for his sack of seed, clearly delighted to have been entrusted with such a great responsibility. "Don't worry, Rhyca, I promise to be careful and not waste any seed."

She smiled, hearing the solemnness of his tone. "I know you will, Dafydd."

Without waiting for the Roman to retrieve the rake he said needed repair, she made her way toward the path. She did not relish being seen leaving with him. There was talk enough.

He caught up with her a few moments later and fell into a silent step beside her. Still, she could feel him looking at her and grew steadily more uncomfortable. "I will not faint if that is what you are waiting for," she declared, venting her irritation with his companionship.

To her annoyance he ignored her acerbic utterance, choosing instead to regard it as an initiation of conversation. "Dafydd's father died when he was quite young."

She was not sure if he asked or stated fact. Avoiding eye contact, she responded curtly. "He was two or three years of age. He does not remember him at all."

"It is unfortunate. To have had a father would have made a great difference. He is a bright boy, with a quick mind that compensates for his deformity."

She glanced at him from the corner of her eye. "He responds to attention and kindness. But then . . . you already know that."

Her thinly veiled accusation elicited a faint smile. "Do not look for a motive in my actions, *domina*. There is none. I simply like the boy and recognize his need. To teach and guide him every boy needs a father—or at least a man willing to assume that role. I was fortunate. In an army camp there are many men far from their homes and families, lonely men who will as readily adopt a fatherless youth as one might take in a homeless dog."

"You were older and unimpaired."

"It does not matter. Regardless of his age and deformity, his need is the same. He needs a father."

"Well, he does not have one!" The thoughts she had considered earlier returned. Dafydd's attachment to this man could only cause him pain. "The gods are not always merciful, Roman. Ofttimes we do not have what we want or need. Dafydd must learn that and not waste effort indulging in foolish and childish hopes." Coldly she regarded the man beside her. "Do not encourage his fantasies."

Galen watched the bitterness rise in her eyes and thought he realized its cause. Though he had spoken of the boy, she had taken his meaning to encompass another. In an effort to redirect her thoughts, he searched for a topic of conversation. "Tell me about my men," he stated, his even tone betraying nothing of his own thoughts which remained upon that other child who would be fatherless.

"Your men? What could I possibly know of them?"

"You know to whom they were given. I would like to know as well."

Her eyes narrowed in suspicion. "What you would like is to draw me into speech, Roman."

"And if that were so, would it be such a terrible thing?"

His simple question, coupled with the appearance of a sudden gentleness in his voice and face, made her suddenly and inexplicably uneasy. She looked away.

"Would it?" he repeated.

Refusing to answer his question, she responded instead to his request—for clearly he would not let both rest. "Myrddin . . . the Druid upon the platform that day . . . he is a wise man. The selections he made were both compassionate and just. The youth from Gaul was given to a man and wife who lost their only son to sickness last spring. His presence has filled that void in their lives. They treat him as their flesh-and-blood. But then—" she glanced back at him—"that is also something you already knew—for the youth is no longer kept in the slaves' enclosure at night."

167

He acknowledged her charge with no more than a slight nod. "Go on."

"The one in the field with the children, his master has been without a wife for nearly a year, hence he bears the burden of being both father and mother to his five children. Today you saw how it is with him—the one you call Facilis. He is less a slave to them than a plaything, a source of entertainment and amusement."

Abruptly she stopped. Though she did not understand its cause, she knew only she did not want to continue. "Enough."

"You have not finished."

"It is pointless."

"I would be the judge of that. My men are my responsibility. To know they are well treated and unabused is therefore of import to me."

"Then, you may rest easy," she retorted sharply, the wellspring of her latent loathing at last accessed. "They are better treated than they deserve! The Thracian was given as slave to a man very much like him, a man past his prime who, when a Roman blade took his arm, had to abandon sword for plough. With each having lived a life of war, there is mutual respect and understanding between them. The mute youth and the small, dark man, their lot—while not so ideal—is by no means harsh. They are slaves to their masters, yet they are not abused or mistreated."

She finished with an icy glare. "Cerrix would not permit such to happen."

Now at the entrance to her enclosure, she wheeled from his side, anxious to be free of him. She heard his footsteps behind her and ignored them. A few paces from the doorway to her hut he overtook her, stepping in front of her and blocking her path.

"There is something I want to say."

"Get out of my way."

"Not until I have said what I will."

"Then, say it!" She looked up at the bronzed face above hers, devoid of expression and so controlled. Only his eyes revealed the faintest hint of emotion, emotion she could not read.

"I want to apologize for my thoughtlessness earlier. The talk with Dafydd and about him, the talk of fathers and sons, I know it caused you pain. It was not my intent. I am truly sorry for what has happened to you, the wrong you have suffered. It is an added injustice that your child shall not know his father."

She responded instantly, the hurt and loathing rising within her like a tide that would drown her. "And why should he enjoy a privilege I did not? I knew him neither."

She marked his confusion and the control that fled his masklike features. Almost reveling now in the spate of venom released, she spat her final revelation. "The seed that spawned this life was *Roman*."

Nine

"Roman?" Galen repeated thickly. Shock and realization were twin blows, and for a moment he faltered. To what she had revealed, he could find no response. He could only stare at her in silence.

But within his mind there was no silence. His thoughts clamored with a dozen voices as logic—which should long since have told him what she had just uttered—now found its tongue: The depth of the hatred she bore his kind and the ostracism she suffered from her own made sense only when viewed through this truth's eyes—even Mouric's peculiar pairing of desire and disgust was now explained.

Despite her avowal that her brother-in-law bore her solely contempt, Galen had known the fallacy of that claim. The highest level of a man's aversion to a woman was apathy, but longing's dark twin was loathing. On that day Galen had been almost certain; now that he knew the truth, he was convinced: Mouric's contempt was but the cloaking of a desire to possess what he would despise.

Originally, knowing as he did of the Celtic suspicion

and fear of pregnant women which so warred with the Roman veneration of motherhood, Galen had attributed the man's contradictory emotions to the fact that she nurtured life. Now he knew it was the form of the life itself—a life planted by a Roman rape. Above all else an Ordovician warrior feared dishonor and ridicule. No man as prideful of his manhood as Mouric could accept the disgrace of having the object of his desire swell for public view with his enemy's seed. Therefore he had no choice but to loathe her outwardly and inwardly deny his longing.

"Would you stand there and gape, Roman? Surely you cannot be so overwhelmed by this revelation that speech has left you?"

Beneath the bitterness of her voice he heard its underlying pain. Men of his own kind had placed it within her, this pain and hatred, while her own had but added shame to the burden she already bore.

"I am sorry," he stated quietly, at last breaking his silence. As much as logic denied his responsibility, he did feel a commitment, a sense of obligation toward this woman which compelled him to ease her suffering.

The gray eyes trained upon him flashed with immediate rage. "I do not need your sympathy," she hissed. "My hatred serves me well enough, for it has deep and healthy roots."

"At what cost? You are poisoned by it. And because your hatred encompasses all men, you are alone." He saw the pain rekindle in her eyes. But he could not stop. No purulent wound could heal without being lanced. She needed to be shown the price exacted, and only the cruelty of his words could pierce the festered hatred within her. "Tell me, at what age does a boy become a man in your eyes? When will Dafydd feel your love turn to loathing for the simple reason that his gender is male?"

She slapped him hard.

When he stood unmoving, unresponsive to the blow, she moved to strike again. "Roman dog!"

He caught her wrist in midair, checking the second blow before it met his cheek. His grasp of the one hand firm, he seized the other. As he transferred her left wrist into the hold he still maintained upon her right, his one large hand easily captured both. With his freed hand upon her shoulder he propelled her backward against the hut's outer wall. Pressed flat to the mud and reed surface, she glared up at him. There was no pain in her eyes now and no fear—only the fury of her hatred.

Without knowing why, he stepped closer and moved his hand from her shoulder to her neck, then higher to cradle her cheek. He could feel her body trembling against him, yet she did not twist her head or waver the gray stare that was both fire and ice.

Suddenly he was aware of his own body's response to this contact between them. The stirring within him of physical need he could ignore and master. What he could not ignore was that which defied his iron control—the stirring of emotions wrought within him first by the knowledge of her suffering, and now by the feel of her heaving breast against his chest, the softness of her skin beneath his fingertips and the sight of the hatred frozen in her eyes. He would take that hatred from her. . . .

The thoughts he silently formed rose unbidden to

172

voice. "You should know differently . . . that a man's touch can be gentle and his passion a source not of pain but of pleasure."

The hand along her cheek moved in response to his words. With his thumb he traced the outline of her mouth. The lips were parted and quivering. The wanting to claim them was like a raw ache within him—born not of lust, but rather a longing he had never before felt. His confusion and inner conflict increased. Why did she not pull away? If she would struggle, he could seize control. He released her hands and waited.

She stood in silence, never blinking, and his confusion grew stronger yet. He could kiss her, and she would not fight him. Nor would she respond. His gentleness and his desire to comfort her would be no different than the cruelty of others and their desire to possess her. He still would be taking what she would not give. It would be as she had always known, and he would succeed in showing her nothing but that he was as every other man.

And then he understood. That was what she wanted! Of course she would not fight. Therein lay her victory.

"I am more man than that, Rhyca." He smiled as a glint of understanding came to her eyes. "I am neither one that violated you then nor one who scorns you now. From you I will take only what is given freely. The hatred within you may have deep roots—too deep to pull—but even the deepest and strongest of roots must still find nourishment if the plant is to thrive. I will not feed your hatred."

He stepped back and laid his clenched fist upon his chest, over his heart. The barbarian *Celtae* believed a man's soul—and hence his power—was in his head, hence she would not understand the gesture. Still, he made it, compelled by his own beliefs. It was a man's heart that gave him might, including the power of speech. He bowed and issued his solemn pledge. "Be prepared, *domina*. Once a Roman legionary makes the vow to do battle, only death can defeat him. I will see your hatred wither and die."

He turned, giving her no opportunity to respond, and headed for the enclosure's exit. He stopped only to retrieve the rake he had dropped in the yard. That it needed repair had been a lie, a pretense to escort her to the farmstead because he had worried for her physical well-being.

But what concern had prompted the occurrence of a moment ago? What force had guided his hand and inspired his words? He was not a man to act carelessly nor one to succumb to an instant of weakness, least of all an impulse of the flesh. Moreover, he knew it could not be lust. Lust did not touch with comfort or speak of commitment. What motive, then? What motive had caused him to reach out to her when he knew the danger—both from without and within?

Or was it that very element of danger that stirred his blood? He was after all a soldier. To break through her defense, her hatred, challenged him as might a rampart surrounding any military objective. Surely therein lay the answer. There could be no other. What he might have been to this woman, he could not be. He could not be the husband taken from her, nor the man to love her as she needed to be loved and possessed as she should be possessed. He could labor for her and protect her—no more.

The voices of the farmers afield, along with their

slaves and laborers, came to ear. He put aside his thoughts, turning his concentration instead to the plots of land lying left of the pathway. With a single sweeping glance he noted the location of his men and the placement of the guards, whose number had increased in his absence. Three others had joined the four of that morning. Two he recognized only as having been part of the war band that had brought the Romans to the hill fort over a month ago. The third, however, he knew by more than mere sight or even name. And that the man now stood before Dafydd, his hand clamped upon the boy's shoulder, caused a muscle in Galen's jaw to jerk. His fingers' grasp of the rake handle he carried on his right shoulder tightened. Still, the control that was discipline's legacy reared to suppress rash emotion.

Ignoring an indignant shout from its owner, he cut across the middle of a newly sown field to come up behind the unsuspecting warrior. As he drew near he could hear Dafydd's voice, tearful and stammering with fear.

"She . . . she was sick and . . . and the rake was broken. I said I could do it, and I pr-pr-promised not to waste any seed. And I didn't. I was c-c-careful."

A snarl of disgust issued from his assailant. "Are you lame of mind as well, boy? Think you I care about seed?"

"N-n-no, Balor." A sob broke free.

"Dim-witted cripple!" the warrior shouted. He shook the boy hard, deaf to his outcry of pain. "Where is the Roman?"

"Here."

Balor whirled, dragging the terrified child with him.

His gaze locked instantly with Galen's, and a contemptuous sneer formed as he beheld his opponent. "One day I'll cut that arrogance from you, slave." His eyes darted from side to side. His sneer widened. "Perhaps this day—seeing as she that protected you before is not here." In accompaniment to his threat his sword hand moved to the sheathed blade at his side. "Tell me, Roman, do you stand as bravely without the shield of a woman's skirts?"

From the corner of his eye Galen saw the two warriors from the war band draw nearer. A farmer and his wife who had been laboring in a neighboring field also edged closer. His thoughts as one with his actions, Galen lifted the rake from his shoulder and slowly set the pronged end on the ground. The handle was old, the wood dry and brittle. One well-aimed stroke of his foot would break off the antler. With any luck at all he could parry a blow or two of the warrior's sword before the rake handle cracked; with a little more he could drive the splintered end into the bastard's belly. He readied himself while appraising his jeering opponent with purposeful disdain. "I would be far more inclined, Briton, to feel the sting of the taunt did it not come from a braggart hiding behind a *child.*"

For a moment the complacent smile wavered. But Balor clearly was a man as well skilled in the art of insult as swordplay. To demonstrate his scorn he laughed and shoved the boy from him.

Galen did not let his focus leave the man's face. This confrontation was not over, and he would see first in the other's eyes when he would strike.

"I did not harm the boy." Still grinning, Balor

stepped back. Clearly he did not intend to make the first move.

Without relaxing his guard, Galen watched him. He readied himself. Balor would have to force Galen to initiate the attack if he was both to save face and avoid Cerrix's retribution. His voice harsher than he intended, he spoke to the cowering form standing carefully out of Balor's reach. "Dafydd, go to Rhyca."

"I want to stay with you."

"Go!" He broke his stare long enough to look at the boy. "Now."

Balor laughed a second time. "You've carved out a place for yourself, haven't you, Roman? The boy . . . the woman. Of course a crippled child and a whore already known to have spread her thighs willingly for a Roman shaft are hardly great conquests for a mighty soldier of the legions."

Fury slammed into Galen. Before reason could grasp hold, he had taken a step forward. Too late he knew his error.

The pale eyes trained upon him glinted in immediate triumph. Balor recognized his victory. Inadvertently he had found what had until this moment evaded him—his foe's weakness and the flaw in his armor of iron control. The mouth beneath the long mustache curled into a smile, and he stepped forward with a taunting leer. "You know . . . I've been tempted, though . . . to ignore the belly and take a turn at her myself. After all . . . what's one more man between her legs when there have been so many?"

He laughed in perverse pleasure as he grabbed hold of himself, thrusting his hips as he had that time before. "What's a scream or two, eh, Roman? And a bit of struggle—that only makes it tighter."

Galen felt the rage within him rise. Knowing his target, Balor had driven the knife. Encountering soft flesh, he would now twist the blade yet deeper until the wound was mortal.

"But maybe she doesn't scream . . . Maybe since she got a taste of Roman meat, she needs a diet of it now. Tell me, Roman, how does it feel to travel a road so well paved by your own k—"

In the crack of splintering wood the final word was lost. The rigid discipline of a lifetime snapped as the fury Galen could no longer contain exploded within him. Training honed to instinct now took control. Before the jeering bastard in front of him could react, the broken shaft of the rake had met his jaw and torn across his cheek. Galen felt the bone break, saw the blood spurt from the jagged tear. Savage, icy satisfaction flowed through his veins as the man went down in a crumpled, crimson heap.

She heard the terrified scream that carried her name and raced from the hut. Like a hand that would choke the breath from her, fear clutched at her throat. *Dafydd.* Through the pounding of her heart she heard him call out to her again—the same piercing, frantic shriek of urgency that sent her trembling limbs to cover the ground between them in utter disregard of all else save the need to reach the white-faced child stumbling toward the enclosure's entrance.

"Rhyca! Quick! You have to come."

At some subconscious level she looked for blood

or sign of injury as her shaking hands extended to him. But he pulled away, evading her grasp and snatching her sleeve. Again his tearful plea sounded, and he tugged at her fiercely. "Come! You have to come! Hurry!"

Relief that the boy appeared unharmed rose within her and was dashed in the same heart-pounding instant. His terror infected her, and she staggered forward in response to his unrelenting urging. "What, Dafydd? What? Tell me what's wrong!"

"It's Galen," he sobbed. "Oh, please, hurry!"

His words slammed into her like a fist. She stopped dead.

"No!" he screamed, clutching at her with both hands. "You have to come!"

She shook her head numbly. Suddenly she was more afraid than she had been before she knew the cause of the boy's hysterics. The fear locked her limbs and rooted her to the pathway. She could not move.

"Please, Rhyca!" Dafydd pulled at her wildly. "You don't understand! He hit Balor—they'll *kill him!*"

His head was starting to clear. Cognizant now of the blurry sights and muffled sounds around him, Galen slowly lifted his cheek from the rough bark. Though his bonds allowed him to turn his head from side to side, he realized there was little need. Only out of his right eye could he see clearly. The left was swollen nearly shut. . . .

More of the veil of semi-unconsciousness lifted, and he remembered. He remembered the countless blows delivered by the pair of warriors from the war band who had taken turns at him while two others from the fields had restrained him.

Yet the brutal beating meted out by his comrades had not satisfied Balor, who had been brought to his feet to witness the retaliatory battery. Crazed with pain and rage, he had refused any attempt to minister to his broken jaw other than to accept a cloth to hold against the bleeding wound. When Galen had been beaten nearly senseless, he had ordered the thrashing stopped—but not for mercy's sake. The clusters of curious farmers and laborers drawn by the confrontation between slave and guards had inspired him to a different course, one that served both his blood lust and his need for personal vengeance.

At his command a short-handled whip with a long, plaited leather tail was taken from a farmer with oxen afield and placed into his eager hand. Then, again under his direction, Galen was dragged to the huge oak, where he was stripped to the waist before being shoved against the tree's trunk.

Balor knew the contact of bare skin against the coarse, jagged bark would cause a scraping of flesh. Even that insignificant pain he had relished his enemy suffering as ropes were tied to his wrists. Then his arms were wrapped around the oak's girth, and the ropes knotted together. It had been then that Galen had lost consciousness. When the ropes had been pulled so tightly as to nearly yank his arms from their sockets, pain exploded in his right shoulder. . . .

Now in unwitting memory his facial muscles twitched, and his wrists fought their restraints as he relived the agony. The last of the haze lifted, and his full senses returned, sharp and clear. It was this moment for which Balor obviously had been waiting.

He stepped into Galen's line of vision. The lash he wielded cut through the air with a sadistic hiss. He stood, glaring venomously at his victim; then he stepped out of Galen's view.

Galen turned his head, not to follow the warrior's movement, but to look at the crowd gathering about him in morbid curiosity and anticipation. He had seen men flogged—the punishment was a common one in the army. He had seen men faint from sheer fear of the leather's bite, or whimper and sob after only the first stroke. Others had borne the first dozen lashes in silence only to scream in agony as the first cruel welts raised were then laid open. But he knew, too, that his pride would not let him cry out. He would bite off his tongue first, and that silence would only enrage his tormentor.

Mithras god! This would be no sight for a child to witness! Where was Dafydd? Had the boy obeyed his command and left the field? He could not see him.

And what of his men? Were they to attempt interfering with his punishment, they would suffer the same. Drausus, the hotheaded Spaniard, he would be the first to react—if he had not already—out of pure hatred for his captors. Then Facilis. He would know any action upon their part would be foolhardy and futile, yet loyalty might force him to respond. Only Sita, the grizzled veteran, would possess the presence of mind to know that Galen, in having made the choice to strike Balor, had also made the choice to suffer the punishment.

A wry smile tugged at his split and swollen lips.

He winced, but the smile remained. Under the same circumstances, he would do it again. The only thing he might have done differently was to have first commanded his men's restraint.

Suddenly he was aware of the crowd's growing restlessness. They awaited the first strike of the whip. But since this anticipation in and of itself should be a torment for him, Galen knew Balor would prolong it as long as possible. Painstakingly he searched the growing ranks of spectators.

A movement, a jostling for a better view, caught his eye, and he found the faces he sought: one red with rage, another white with dread, the third inscrutable beneath its heavy bearding—but all surrounded by their Ordovician masters and guards. With his focus upon Drausus, whose right eye—true to Galen's expectations—was already purpling with an ugly bruise, he gave the command that would bind all three. "Nothing. You will do nothing to intervene. The act was mine alone, as will be the reckoning."

Purposely he had not spoken in Latin. Their time among the mountain tribe had taught his men the Celtic tongue. For their safety it was as important for their captors to understand his order of nonaggression as it was for the Romans to heed it.

Reaction rippled through the crowd, and a low hum of appreciation sounded as they recognized and acknowledged his courage. This was a rare man, and a man endowed as equally with honor as with valor. But one who heard the murmurs was incensed by the admiration his enemy had earned.

Balor maneuvered into position and furiously snapped the whip into the air, hoping the sound of its crack would evoke at least an instinctive flinch or a sharp intake of breath. This slave would not make a fool of him as he had of Mouric that first day upon the platform! But even as he made the silent vow, he knew what every person watching knew. He would kill the Roman before he broke him, and the centurion would die, in all likelihood, as he was now preparing to suffer the lash—in stoic silence and acceptance.

Galen braced himself. He focused upon the distant hills. His jaw locked, his body rigid, he awaited the first true strike of the whip.

And then it came. . . . Like a white-hot iron laid flat across his back, the plaited leather landed, beating agony into his flesh. He jerked in response to the fiery pain, clenched his teeth to hold back any sound that might be taken for an outcry, and curled his fingers.

Again the whip snapped, descended and slashed. And then again. A fourth time. A fifth. The thin lines of agony spread. His back was on fire. With the sixth lash the taut bronze flesh split open.

At first she saw only the farmers, their families and laborers massed in a half circle around the great oak. For a gathering of so many, though, their silence was strangely incongruous—as if they either feared to speak or stood intently rapt in hushed expectation. But expectation of what?

Her answer came in the sudden crack that cut the air to be echoed in the crowd's collective shudder. The sound was unmistakable, and her throat constricted with the horrifying knowledge of what it was that they had so reverently awaited.

She looked down at the boy whose frantic grasp of her hand had tightened instantly at the sound. Dafydd knew, too. She saw it in his eyes. Wide with terror and filled with tears, they beseeched her to act.

"Stay here," she ordered, tearing his hand from hers. She could not let him see what lay beyond the ring of spectators. "Do you hear me? You must not try to come closer. Promise me, Dafydd!"

The sharp snap of leather sounded again.

He nodded, tears spilling down his cheeks. "Balor made him hit him. Make them stop. Oh, please, Rhyca—make them stop!"

She did not know how she could do what he asked. She knew only that whatever fear had frozen her steps earlier now melted away beneath his tears. "Just stay here!" she commanded, turning from him.

She managed to push her way into the onlookers' midst before another crack heralded yet another strike. She flinched as if the whip had struck her and staggered forward—deaf to the wave of whispers that surged through the crowd as she was recognized.

Drawn as they were to watch the grisly flogging, the staring spectators were nonetheless equally compelled to watch her. They craned their necks for even a glimpse of the woman for the defense of whose nonexistent honor the Roman now paid. With the diversion of their focus, a narrow break opened in their tight ranks.

Rhyca reeled at the sight revealed. That every eye had now turned from the man bound to the tree, she did not know. She saw only him. Stripped to the waist, his arms encircling the trunk of the great oak, he still stood defiantly erect, although his back was red and pulped, crossed with welts and cruel raw wales that trickled blood. Tensed against the agony to which he would give no voice, his every muscle and sinew stood out in sculpted detail.

Again the lash descended. His body heaved against the tree, his head jerking back. Her stomach twisted in revulsion as she saw the fresh crimson tear cut into his flesh by the leather's savage bite. And still he stood silent and unyielding.

Not so the man who wielded the whip. His curse of bellowed fury cut into her as had the plaited strip the Roman's proud back. In chilling horror she beheld Balor's mutilated face. From deep within her a silent voice screamed, and she thrust herself forward. But before she could break through to the forefront of the crowd she was stopped, restrained by an unseen hand and an unfamiliar voice.

"You cannot help him. You will only put yourself at risk."

She stared down at the hand that held her arm. Covered with a matting of dark hair, only its knuckles were bare. She raised her gaze. Blinking away the tears she had not realized had formed, she recognized the bearded face before her.

Again the whip cracked. She saw the man flinch as she had, saw the latent fury in his eyes and stared at him in confusion. Why did he stop her from trying to intervene? Angrily she yanked her arm free. A child's cry sounded, and she turned to see Dafydd struggling to push his way toward her.

She reached out and pulled the boy to her. Wrapping her arms protectively about him, she took care that her body blocked his view of the tree. His small form, pressed tightly to her, trembled. His sobs tore into her as did his plea.

"Please, Rhyca. Make him stop! Make him stop!" He flailed wildly with his fists, then pushed her away, breaking free.

The Thracian immediately snatched him back, thrusting him into her startled grasp and seizing her arm once again.

"Take the boy and leave—or you will only make it worse for yourself."

"No!" she cried, trying both to fight off his hold and restrain Dafydd. But the crowd was pressed too tightly all around. In helpless fury she stared up into the eyes of the man who should have been trying to aid her, not stop her. "If we do not stop this, who will?"

"He will." With a sudden excitement in his voice the Thracian pointed. "Look."

Rhyca followed the direction of his outstretched hand to where a white-robed figure effortlessly cleaved a path through the crowd.

Whispers of awe followed in his wake, with many of those he passed actually drawing back in fearful reverence. It seemed that the Druid had appeared from nowhere.

Without hesitation he glided to where Balor stood paused, watching his approach. In mute command he held out his hand for the whip. "Enough, Balor. As he has suffered for his arrogance, now let him be spared for his courage."

Rhyca sagged against the sturdy bulk of the Thracian in relief. Myrddin's will was law. Balor had no choice but to obey. Wheeling furiously from the priest, the bloodied warrior barreled into the crowd, which hastened to open a pathway to him.

The surrendered whip now in hand, Myrddin lifted his arms skyward, recapturing the focus of the staring spectators. "You have seen a slave justly punished for striking his guard. From this flogging let him learn his place, and let the sight of him now be a warning to others. Until the sun sets he is to remain bound. But no man will touch him further. Now it is the gods' turn to mete their punishment as they see fit—be it in the form of the flies that will settle upon his tortured flesh or the sun's heat that will parch his throat. Return to your fields now. I command it."

The crowd dispersed until Rhyca stood alone with Dafydd. How she had known that she was excluded from the Druid's command, she did not know. She knew only that he intended her to remain. And so she did, nervously stroking Dafydd's hair while maintaining a firm hold to prevent him either looking upon the Roman or going to him.

At last Myrddin approached. Bending down, he put himself at eye level with the child and laid a comforting hand upon his shoulder. "I want you to go to the sacred oak grove and look for the plant always green—the mistletoe, whose leaves will ease your friend's pain. I will join you shortly."

As Dafydd nodded in understanding, the man rose. He watched the boy head toward the field's boundary in the direction of the forest before turning his focus to her.

She felt an unwelcome rush of heat and lowered her gaze beneath his which was one of all knowing and all seeing.

"Look at me," he commanded firmly but not unkindly. "If you bow your head in shame now, your Roman has suffered for nothing."

Rhyca looked up in immediate confusion. "I do not understand."

He smiled. "Do you know why he struck Balor?" Without giving her a chance to reply, he answered for her. "He was provoked, Rhyca, provoked by Balor's insults of you that suggested he might be providing more service to you than that of a mere slave."

The accusation—unanticipated and shocking—made the breath leave her body in a gasp of disbelief and fury. "That is a lie!"

"The truth or falsity of the taunt is of little import. What matters is his defense of you. And know this as well, a man does not suffer such a beating as a mere gesture."

She reeled beneath the intensity of his gaze and the import of his message. But Myrddin would allow her no opportunity to either dispute or deny his perceptions.

He laid a gentle arm about her shoulders. "Go to him. Let him look upon you. For what he has endured he has earned the sight of the compassion that now fills your eyes."

Rhyca watched the Druid walk away, then numbly moved toward the tree. She stood to the side where the Roman could see her if he opened his eyes. But they remained shut—in blessed unconsciousness? She stared at his face, pallid beneath the bronze skin, and at his back—so cruelly marked by Balor's vengeance.

"Why?" she whispered. "What did you think you were defending? My shame allows me no honor. I am

188

not worth this." With a shuddering sigh, she turned. "You *are* dim-witted, Roman."

"Galen."

"What?" She whirled, but could detect no movement. His eyes were still closed. Had he spoken?

"My name . . ." His eyes slowly opened. "Say it."

"Galen."

Her whispered obedience was so low she thought he might not have heard it.

But he had. He nodded ever so slightly, and his eyes drifted closed.

She stared at him for several moments. Finally, sure that he had to have lapsed into unconsciousness, she turned again. She had taken but a single step when she heard his voice once more.

"You are wrong. You *are* worth this."

Ten

Cerrix looked up at the man standing in solemn silence before him. "He will recover?"

"Yes. He survived the flogging well enough. However, it will be several days before he is of much use."

Cerrix nodded, then motioned to the several warriors sitting on either side of him. "Bring the Roman to me. I would see for myself the ravages of Balor's lash." As his men rose in immediate obedience, he gestured for the priest to be seated.

Judiciously, Myrddin waited until they were alone to speak further. "As evidenced by the events of this day, it would appear that the seed you planted has sprouted life, Cerrix the King."

Cerrix noted the Druid's furrowed brow. "I have heard that she had to be restrained by one of his men. Is this true?"

"Yes. Had I not stopped the flogging when I did, I fear she might have put herself between him and the lash."

Cerrix nodded in unabashed satisfaction. "This bodes well."

"Does it?" Myrddin stared at him. The furrows etched into his prominent brow had deepened. "You know this will feed the gossip, serving to make idle talk credible. At considerable cost he defended her—both her name and her honor. Speculation is sure to be more open now."

A derisive snort, accompanied by a scoffing, dissuasive wave was Cerrix's reply. "Idle talk and gossip is just that. The woman is with child."

"A child, it is rumored, *not* fathered by her dead husband."

"If true, this only gives her further reason to hate him."

"Or turn to him, since her own people have spurned her. Your intent from the beginning?"

Cerrix avoided answering the question, averting his gaze toward the screen that divided the hut's interior. There, in the murky glow cast by the oil lamps that were lighted each twilight, a shadow of movement had caught his eye. "Come."

At his command a small form edged around the partition to stand hesitantly in view. Cerrix extended his arms, and his youngest son toddled immediately forward. Casting a cautious glance to the Druid, the child crawled into the security of his father's embrace and contentedly laid his head upon the broad chest.

Fully aware that the accusing stare emanating from the man seated across from him had not wavered, Cerrix shifted the boy's weight to a more comfortable position. "Proceed, Myrddin."

"That first day on the platform I remember thinking your choice odd—that your giving her this particular slave was no accident. At the time I presumed your motive to be no more complex than the desire to anger Mouric. Later, when you hinted that there was something more, I doubted the possibility of this scheme's success. I believed you might have chosen the right man, but I was convinced you had the wrong woman. I did not believe her hatred could be breached."

"And now?" Cerrix asked, affectionately stroking the small blond head nestled in the hollow of his neck.

"I concede victory to you. However . . . I caution you to withhold celebration and to exercise restraint. Do not be so ready to embrace him into your trust. The Roman's actions—as noble and brave as they might have been—were still solely at personal cost. There has been nothing that might suggest his loyalty to his empire has been compromised or even tempered."

"I do not agree. This man has previously shown us his manner of control. He does not act without forethought. He knew that to strike Balor would put him at personal risk—and any risk to him is also risk to his governor's plan. Still he acted. That says much to me, Myrddin. Between the woman and him there has formed a bond, and the tie he feels to her must also encompass our people—for the fate of one is the fate of all. When he returns to his legions, he will return with a personal—and far stronger—commitment to peace. His unwavering loyalty to his empire *has* been tempered, and his blind faith in its legions given new sight. 'Victory at all cost' has come to hold meaning beyond the words. And that cost may be one he is no longer willing to pay."

Cerrix looked down at the child in his arms. "Not as a king, but as a father and a man, I have learned two lessons, Myrddin. When the lives to be lost hold value, one does not so readily sacrifice them. The other truth is that once an act worthy of trust and faith has been proffered, it must be answered in kind, else what has been gained is lost."

The priest's deeply set eyes widened in sudden understanding. "You intend to tell him."

"Yes."

"Are you sure this is wise?"

"This I will discover only in his reaction."

"Why? Before, when it was only rumor, you were adamant about keeping the news from him. Now that it is fact, you will tell him?"

"Before, the time was not right. He would easily have been able to choose his stand and his course. Whatever words he spoke would have been tainted by his unflagging loyalty to Rome. Now, because of what he feels for her, I know his words will be pure."

Before Cerrix could say more the sound of footsteps announced the return of the warriors sent to bring the Roman. He set his son on his feet, and, with a steadying hand at the child's backside, propelled him toward the partition. "To bed, Brychan."

As the boy skulked reluctantly from the company of his father back to the quarters relegated to the women and children, Cerrix looked toward the dark figures emerging through the open doorway into the lamplight.

The Roman, flanked by his escorts, strode forward. He inclined his head in greeting to the Druid, then focused upon Cerrix. "Lord Cerrix."

Cerrix dismissed his waiting men with a wave. Myrddin rose to take his leave as well. After casting his king a glance that advised caution, he directed his attention to the bare-chested man standing before him. "Should you have need of my ministrations further, know that the guards have been instructed to send for me immediately. Your pride may dull pain, Centurion, but no manner of dignity, however strong, can stop a wound from festering."

The Roman nodded in acknowledgement of both the aid offered and the admonition against refusing it.

Still seated, Cerrix tilted his head and studied the man's face. The ordeal had left its mark—shadowy bruises beneath and above the left eye, a split and swollen lip. . . . Cerrix's gaze lowered. The Roman's naked chest bore several raw scrapes, while blows landed to his belly had left a deep coloration on the taut skin. Still, in affirmation of far more than mere survival, the set of the shoulders was square—proclaiming the strength of his will. The Druid's poultices and herbal concoctions aside, he must be in pain, his back feeling as if it were in flames. Yet there was nothing in the man's posture or in the stoic gaze that so evenly met Cerrix's to betray it.

"Turn," Cerrix commanded quietly.

With an almost bored gesture of patronizing indulgence, the Roman complied.

Cerrix noted the cruel welts, many encrusted with dried blood, that crossed the broad back. "You are an uncommon man, Centurion," he stated matter-of-factly, indicating that he had finished his examination.

The Roman turned again to face him, his dark brow lifting sardonically. "And is my 'uncommonness,' Lord Cerrix, the reason I was given as slave to a woman you knew had been raped and impregnated by

194

soldiers of my army? Was that trait somehow intended to make my intrusion into her life more palatable—a less vivid reminder to her of all she has suffered?"

The blunt accusation did not catch Cerrix off guard. He had long anticipated this conversation. His only surprise was the Roman's clear knowledge of that which he himself had known only to be conjecture until this moment. "She admitted, then, that the child she carries was bred of the rape?"

"She did. And my question remains unanswered, Cerrix the King. Why? Why would you deliberately choose to force me upon her knowing what she had endured—and continues to endure? The price of her survival has been not only shame, but public defilement—with my presence now serving most handily as further fuel for the fires of vulgar speculation."

Calmly Cerrix lifted his eyes to intercept and hold the unrelenting stare. "I might ask *you,* Centurion, why you would deliberately choose today to defend her against that speculation and defilement."

The two men glared at one another, neither willing to reveal to the other the reasons for his actions. At last the silence between them was broken by a single word.

"Sit."

Galen ground his teeth. The movement, the pulling of muscles beneath his tortured flesh, would cause more than discomfort. He preferred to stand. But to decline the invitation would be to reveal weakness. The man behind the blue eyes that now watched speculatively knew it as well, hence he had purposely issued the challenge.

With a mustering of the same pride that had kept

him from crying out in response to the burning agony of the lash, Galen sat stiffly, his jaw locked and his pain therefore mute.

"You are a stubborn man, Galen Mauricius." The blond head across from him dipped in respect. "But then, so am I." With a disarming smile Cerrix reached for an elaborately worked bronze flagon on the low table beside him. "Wine?"

Galen declined the offered drink. Whatever the Druid had forced upon him earlier had rendered him dizzy. Only now was his head reasonably clear, and he was not about to risk the wine inducing a return of dulled senses. There was more cause for this audience with the Ordovician king, their first formal meeting since his arrival, than Cerrix's desire to assess his physical condition.

He knew he was correct in his thoughts as the man seated across from him replaced the flagon—also without partaking.

"Word has reached me of your governor's arrival," Cerrix stated abruptly. "Nine days ago Agricola landed at the channel port you call Rutupiae."

Galen acknowledged the information with a nod, and Cerrix continued.

"I am, however, curious . . . you and I know the true cause for his late arrival—to allow you additional time among us and also to ensure that your legions remained in garrison, thereby discouraging hostilities while this plan of ours commenced. What reason, though, was given to the generals of those armies who were forced, for lack of a supreme commander, to sit idle as their campaign season passed?"

Galen silently smiled. The man seated across from

him was shrewd, indeed, to have recognized that without a plausible excuse for Agricola's delayed arrival, more than complaints would have been raised by the legates of the four legions currently stationed in Britain. "His departure from Rome was delayed to allow his daughter's marriage ceremony to take place at a most propitious time in our calendar."

"Very fortuitous." Suddenly Cerrix's previously relaxed demeanor became less so.

Galen sensed rather than saw the subtle change. In warning response his body tensed.

"The tribes expected him sooner, of course. In fact, they had planned a welcome of sorts to coincide with his landing in Britain. His late arrival, though, has resulted in that gesture occurring prematurely."

Galen felt a muscle twitch in his jaw as his instincts were alerted further. "What welcome?"

Cerrix met his penetrating gaze without flinching. "Factions rival to mine, along with others as yet unaligned with our cause of peace, have joined forces. At the beginning of this moon they ambushed a Roman cavalry unit in garrison on the fringes of Ordovician territory. You should know this as well . . . the unit they attacked was the one that massacred the village of Brithdir last spring. As you are aware, Rhyca was the only survivor of that attack."

"I presume the action was successful."

"Completely."

As he noted Cerrix's grim nod of affirmation, Galen struggled with the conflicting thoughts that assailed him. As an officer of the Eagles his first reaction to this revelation of the slaughter of Roman troops was outrage. On the other hand, as a soldier Galen under-

197

stood retaliation. From earliest times it had been the unswerving policy of Rome that no attack upon its civilians would go unanswered by its legions; defeat and destruction must be avenged. To that call he had raised his own sword and seen its blade bloodied in the name of revenge.

Still, there was more to his reaction now to this news of the Ordovician reprisal than either his soldier's reaction to defeat or a warrior's respect for an enemy's retribution for an attack upon women and children. Through him flowed an iciness that cooled his heated outrage, an iciness not unlike that which he had experienced after striking Balor. He knew the feeling—it was the cold, savage satisfaction of vengeance taken. The men that had violated her were dead.

Cerrix's voice sounded in the silence. "Your reaction is slow in coming, Galen Mauricius. Perhaps it is mixed—as was my own upon learning of this. On the one hand I see avenged the deaths of those farmers and their children. On the other I see a threat to the peace to which I am committed. Yet it is neither your nor my response which matters, but Agricola's. Tell me, emissary of Britain's governor, how will he respond?"

Unwaveringly Galen met the man's questioning stare. "His course can follow one of two paths. As you stated, the campaign season is at an end, the roads unfit for travel until spring. Auxiliary units are scattered throughout the province. All things combined hinder a new campaign. For the sake of expediency alone he may decide the attack was justified, a final legacy of his predecessor. Before acting himself, he may wait and watch the points where danger threatens to see if the fires of revolt will indeed take flame from this spark."

He paused to see the effect—if any—of his words, and then continued. "I would be lying, Lord Cerrix, if I professed to know in certainty what his response would be. This attack could just as likely escalate hostilities. Among us there are factions as well, some that hold fast to the need for total conquest, and who will view this action as proof that the Ordovician desire for peace is hollow. However, there are others who have realized conquests are more easily made than kept. Of late there have been rumblings."

"What of your emperor?" Cerrix asked. "Is not his the will to be followed?"

"His and the senate's. Imperial policy adheres now more than ever to the principles of our great Augustus—frontiers should be maintained but not extended. In addition, there is very much alive in the Roman Senate a faction that holds Frontinus has been rashly ambitious of military glory. It was through their clamoring for a new governor, one who was free from feelings of hostility or triumph and who could deal fairly with our conquered enemies, that Agricola was selected. Certainly, I have heard his critics say that because his blood is Galli he feels too deeply for the peoples he would rule. Yet, it was for this very reputation public opinion insisted that the province of Britain be offered to him. As a man known for his compassion, it is unlikely he will follow war's path—at least without further provocation."

"Unlikely?" Cerrix repeated the word, his brows arching sharply.

Galen found it impossible to read his thoughts, and so waited for him to speak further.

"I would hear more of this man 'known for his compassion.'"

"He is a youthful man. With only forty-one years, that he should have reached so high a position as the governorship of Britain and command of four legions is clear proof of the high confidence placed in him by Vespasian. Gnaeus Julius Agricola is austere of character, known for moderation, and not greedy for fame. While legate under Cerialis's governorship, he claimed no credit for his successes. Some find him prone to lose his temper. Others claim he possesses no sense of humor. But he has no difficulty in recognizing a good man—"

"That proof sits before me. But I would know of him as a soldier."

Galen guarded his expression and answered evenly. "He can be a formidable enemy, Lord Cerrix. No fort or military site of his choosing has ever been taken by storm, has ever capitulated or ever been abandoned. When he takes field against Rome's enemies, he takes it in person. He marches in front of the column himself in full sight of his foe so as to impart his courage to his men by sharing in their danger. But his military ability is united with statesmanlike justice and the belief that little is gained by conquest if that conquest is followed by oppression. He understands the feelings of a conquered people and has learned from the experience of others. Arms can effect nothing if injustice follows in their wake. Therefore, while he is a man resolved to root out both cause and camp of rebellion, when finished he will seek peace."

"You believe this?"

"I do. I would not have come here otherwise."

Cerrix fingered the thick gold neck ring at the base of his throat. The *torc,* symbol of his kingship, lay suddenly heavy upon him. How fully could he trust this man before him? Myrddin's warnings echoed in his mind. Did he heed them or his own instincts? Was the path he would take the right one?

Almost as if he were able to know Cerrix's thoughts, the Roman spoke. "You have chosen your course, Cerrix the King. I implore you to follow it. A man can find in Agricola an honest witness to his merit. As formidable as he can be as an enemy, so, too, can he be as an ally. I would ask you to give him the opportunity to prove himself."

Suddenly Cerrix felt a weariness beyond his years. What rested upon his shoulders—the fate of his people—was a burden no single man should bear. "That may not be possible, my friend."

He saw the light of suspicion mingle with the shadow of confusion in the dark eyes, and reluctantly explained, "Agricola has made his choice. The dispersal of your troops appears to be irrelevant, the lateness of season as well. My scouts tell me that he has departed Londinium and travels west to Viroconium—"

"The legionary fortress there is the permanent base for his old command, the Twentieth *Valeria Victrix,*" the Roman interrupted. "It could mean nothing."

Cerrix shook his head. "Rumor says he intends to order his 'old command' into action and within this moon will take field against the attackers of the cavalry unit."

Both suspicion and confusion vanished. Yet what

had been disclosed elicited no true surprise from the Roman. He simply bowed his head as though to gather his thoughts. Then Cerrix heard a long, drawn-in breath and a soft curse of frustration—and he knew it was his emotions that the centurion restrained. Indeed, when the man finally looked up, his eyes were clear of the anger and grief he could not allow himself as a soldier and emissary of Rome to feel.

"I still implore you to wait. If Agricola takes field, he does so against those who dispute Roman authority, who fight without seeking truce or mercy. Your desire for peace is known, as will be your actions now. Join those factions that rise in revolt, and your people are doomed. Stay with the course you have chosen. Lead your warriors not into war, but keep them here, safe in these mountains. Beyond that, exert the influence you hold over other chieftains who waver still. Be the Great King who will at last unite the Ordovices—not under a banner of war, but under a bough of peace!"

"And for what reason should I heed your words?" Cerrix shook his head. "In truth, can I even be sure that *you* have not been sent here for this very purpose—to keep the tribes divided? I am not a fool. Far more harm can be done by one who cloaks himself as a friend and ally, than by one who is openly a foe. Nothing has helped your legions more in their fighting against my kind than the tribes' petty rivalries and steadfast refusal to cooperate and unite. If, by your counsel, I delay or do not join my brothers in their fight, they will surely fall more easily to your legions. Then, when the Eagles' eye turns toward my mountains, there shall be none left to stand by me."

With the steadfast calm of a man who knew his

soul and hence did not fear truth but saw in it a friend, the Roman smiled. "Believed you that, I would have died this day under Balor's whip—never having learned of Agricola's intent to march. Nor is it too late. If you fear the knowledge I have gleaned in my time among your people or doubt the honesty of my counsel—kill me now. At your waist you wear a dagger. And should you not be fit to the task, your warriors are but a summons away."

Galen watched the man's eyes brighten with fury as he rose to the challenges to both his manhood and his judgment.

"Should there come a time, Roman, when I doubt your honesty, distrust your motives or see in you a threat to my people, I will not need to call my men. Know this—and know it well—I *will* end your life."

Galen inclined his head in mute acknowledgement. "With that agreed, Cerrix the King, would you listen further and hear my advice?"

"Proceed."

With a silent sigh of satisfaction Galen faced off against a different objective. To some degree he had convinced Cerrix of his trustworthiness. Now he had to convince the warrior king to wait in order for Agricola to have the opportunity to convince the Ordovices of his. As disturbing as was the news of Agricola's rapid action against the rebellious tribesmen, Cerrix had to realize the response was justified. Agricola had seen the attack as he was meant to see it—as a test. Were Britain's new governor to ignore the challenge, he would command no respect among the eastern tribes already under Roman rule. If he did not strike immediately to put down this rebellion in the west, he risked all-out civil war.

What Galen had told Cerrix he believed, and his belief now took voice in a plea for patience. "Agricola is devoted and committed to bringing peace to Britain. To that end he must deal firmly with those who not only prefer war, but embrace it. Delay your response and wait for the outcome of this first enterprise. That it occurs during the month we have named for the great Augustus, a man who favored peace above conquest, can be seen as a favorable sign, a good omen. Wait, too, that you may truly know the manner of man Agricola is."

"And if I decide to wait and then learn he is a man no different than his predecessors . . . If the campaign he leads does not end with the destruction of those who openly war, but extends to those who have raised no arms against Rome—what then?"

"Then you must follow one path and I the other. Once more we shall be enemies, Lord Cerrix."

"I would prefer you as friend."

"As I would you."

"At least we are honest." Cerrix laughed dryly. "Very well, Galen Mauricius. I will wait until such time as your governor either proves or disproves your faith." Indicating the audience was hereby ended, he leaned back and summoned forth the men who were waiting outside to escort their captive back to the prisoners' compound.

Galen rose to his feet, wincing with the effort. This time he did not bother to conceal his pain. Nor did he care to, for such was the trust born between them this night—he owed Cerrix the seeing of it.

"Before you go . . ." Watching him, the Ordovician king suddenly raised a hand in a halting gesture. "There is one thing else. In all matters you have been forthright save one. But because it is a private one, I will respect your reserve and say only this. There is risk and danger if you remain with her. Like a summer's rain sprouts mushrooms on the forest floor, what occurred today will spawn more suspicion. Your own men may now see cause to question your loyalty. Do you want me to rescind my order and have you taken from her?"

The question sent a shock through Galen. And yet before any thought or logic could stop it, his answer was made. "No."

"Are you certain?" Cerrix regarded him in penetrating silence. "For I will offer you that choice now— and only now."

"I have given my answer," Galen replied coldly, feeling the control that had momentarily fled return. The reasons for his response were his own. He would make no explanations.

"So be it." Cerrix nodded. When he had seen the Roman's pain revealed, he had understood the gesture—the proffer of trust it represented, as well as the honesty between them. He could do no less than respond in kind, especially in knowing what was to come. Honor had demanded that he make the offer. But the Roman had declined. Nonetheless Cerrix's debt was paid, his conscience eased.

He stood, signaling forward the three men who had taken up deferential postures just within the doorway. "Return this slave to the prisoners' compound."

But as two of the guards led the Roman from him,

he beckoned back the third, motioning for silence until his companions and their charge had exited.

"See that he is kept in the stockade for the next several days and given no labor—not even the lightest of tasks. I want him healed and ready to be moved with the others."

"Moved?" the warrior repeated, his brows drawing together in confusion. "To where, lord?"

Cerrix eyed him keenly before he answered, "The farmsteads. Summer is quickly ending, and warriors can no longer be spared from hunting and scouting parties to guard a handful of slaves. Tomorrow you will go to their masters and tell them that with the new moon they must assume the responsibility themselves. See that chains and shackles are provided. Each may make the choice whether or not to use them, but should his slave escape it will mean that farmer's head."

"*All* of the Romans, lord? Even that one—the woman's?"

While Cerrix understood immediately the concerns prompting his man's inquiry, he chose to address none of them. Calmly he reassumed his earlier seat beside the table and the flagon of wine for which he suddenly thirsted. "All of them," he stated firmly. "Now go."

Barely had the welcomed sweetness of the wine passed his lips, when Cerrix heard the footsteps of the evening's last expected visitor. He motioned the silent figure forward.

Bowing his cloaked head, the man avoided the fire's illumination, thereby effectively keeping his face in shadow. He did not speak, but awaited Cerrix's command.

206

"The time has come. Do whatever must be done—and report to me his every move. Now more than ever he must be watched, for not since this plan's inception has it been so imperiled."

While the draped head nodded in understanding, a clenched fist rose to the man's forehead in a warrior's vow of obedience.

As he then withdrew, Cerrix returned his attention to his drink. He was confident he had done all he could—he only prayed it was enough.

Eleven

"He's no longer fit to command!" Black eyes blazing, the wiry man at last ceased his pacing, whirling to glare at his comrades. The light cast by the burning torches affixed to the stockade's timbered walls bathed him in a fiery glow that only heightened the appearance of a man consumed by inner rage. "Why can the two of you not see, when it's as plain as the ears on Facilis's head?"

"I didn't say I couldn't see it." Facilis, his broad face coloring to a hue similar to his hair, returned the Spaniard's angry stare in full measure. "What I said was that I was not fool enough to challenge him. You tried that already and where did it get you, except on your knees, holding your gut?"

The goading reminder of his humiliation a month earlier brought an immediate response. It was Drausus's turn to color in anger. But he recovered quickly, the stain beneath his olive skin receding even as he commenced a new direction of attack. "My mistake was in confronting him alone. We must stand together in this—united." He looked over to the large man casually leaning against the stockade wall. "What say you, Sita? There are still three of us to his one, even without Gaius and Valerius."

The reference to the absent recruits, both of whom were now kept upon their masters' farmsteads instead of in the prisoners' stockade, brought an instant and sobering silence as each of the men sought to deny the indisputable truth. With the passage of time they were gradually being assimilated one by one—finding new lives among their Ordovician captors.

Facilis especially looked away, seeking to hide his guilt. He found himself most at home with his *Celtae* masters. It was only out of loyalty to his comrades that he had declined to leave the slaves' compound.

"What say you, Sita?"

That it was Drausus who finally broke the silence came as no surprise.

"Well?" he prompted again, his concentration now fully fixed upon the burly veteran of the trio.

"I say your hot blood has finally boiled away your reason." The Thracian's bald head, its shiny surface acting as a mirror to catch and reflect the torchlight, shook from side to side. "Have you ever seen a man stoned to death, Drausus? It's a sight to make even a battle-hardened warrior spew up his guts. And the last I heard, stoning was still the penalty for mutiny— which is what you're talking about."

In subtle threat he pushed his bulk from the wall and folded his arms across his barrel chest. The blue eyes that were normally almost lost in the large, fleshy face grew even smaller as he pinned both younger men with a warning look. "I will hear no more of this. We are soldiers. Ours is a duty to obey, and we have been given our orders."

"To remain slaves? To learn what we can of their terrain and number of men under arms—all in the foolish hope we will one day leave this place and put that knowledge to use?" Drausus hissed in disgust, "Do you really believe that is our duty as *soldiers*— rather than trying to escape?"

"Those were the orders we received," the older man repeated, anger at last entering his voice. "As I believe he did also."

"What are you saying?" Drausus glared at him suspiciously.

"I am saying our coming to this hill fort was no mischance. Mauricius was ordered to Britain by Vespasian himself. Ordered, I am convinced, to do exactly what he has—infiltrate the enemy camp. Falling into that ambush was no error in judgment, but a calculated scheme."

Clearly, Drausus recognized the possibility that this reconstruction of events might be true. His dark eyes filled with grudging hesitation. "Then, why we were not told?"

"Told what? That we were going out on patrol for the purpose of being captured?" The large man emitted a snort of derision. "How long have you served under the standards, Drausus? Orders are given—not explained."

But Drausus was undaunted. Having learned that their capture might have been deliberate seemed only to reinforce his ire. Of all the Roman prisoners, only he seemed able to continually bank the fire of hatred against their captors. "And so we stay, and with each passing day we become more Celt than Roman? Already this buffoon finds it easier to speak their tongue than ours."

"That is not true!" Fists clenched, Facilis strode forward from the shadows into which he had withdrawn. "Unlike you, Spaniard, Latin *is* my mother tongue."

"Then, what else can explain your reluctance to speak out against Mauricius?" Drausus taunted further as he took up a fighting stance against his comrade. "Or is it a question of courage?"

Rufus Sita shook his head in exasperation. He had hoped that by revealing his surmise as to the true cause of their circumstance he might unite them in purpose and lessen their divisions. Clearly, however, the ploy had failed. Still, it was time to end this. In that one matter the hot-tempered Spaniard was right— they must stand together. "Enough!" he growled.

"It's *not* enough." Drausus whipped his head around to glare at the veteran. "And it is because I *am* a soldier that I can no longer keep silent. Unlike you, old man, the fight has not been drained from me, nor am I blind to what I see. Whether he was sent here by design or not, he now collaborates with the enemy, and in so doing he betrays Rome."

"Your eyes see what your hatred would have them see." Rufus countered, feeling the anger within him rise and knowing he must control it. "If his mission is to learn what he can of the enemy's strengths, he must win their confidence even if that means to side— at least outwardly—against his own. I see no collaboration and no compromise of his loyalty."

"No? What of his attachment to the woman? Would you also claim his actions with respect to her are

211

solely for the 'mission's' sake?" He spat, wiping away a lingering trickle of spittle from his chin with a furious swipe of his hand. "You are blind *and* a fool. He risked his life for her this day, and you yourself held her back from rushing to his side. Yet you do not see what grows between them or see the threat in it?" In disgust he shook his head. "You speak of my reason being 'boiled away.' Have you never seen what the fire in a man's loins can do to his reason? I tell you, Mauricius is thinking with his cock. What he was sent here to do he has forgotten. It's only a matter of time before he completely turns his back on Rome, on the Eagles—and on us."

"You're wrong, Drausus. I know him. He is not one whose judgment can be seduced along with his flesh. In Palestine I saw him have his pick of willing harlots ready to part him from his pay. With his rank and youth they swarmed about him like flies on a dung heap. And yet he showed so little enthusiasm for what was his for the taking that there were many who speculated his interest must run to young boys. But there were enough of us to take his leavings to know there was no truth to that claim. His was simply an unwillingness to attach himself."

"Camp whores." The dark man sneered. "A willing mouth and open legs. What manner of fool *would* do more than spill his seed? And if in the past his bed has been filled so regularly, maybe that is what drives him now. I have known men for whom the hunger for a woman was as a sickness, a consuming need to be sated at all cost."

"Would such a man—by choice—leave the orgy couches of Rome?" Rufus challenged with a knowing

212

smile. "For he did exactly that. When he returned briefly with Vespasian to Rome, he was welcomed in the homes of the finest families. The hospitality of our grateful Empire knows not continence, nor gossip the deterrent of distance. Even in Palestine we heard the tales of promiscuous wives and virginal daughters alike, all clamoring for the privilege of being bedded by the hero of the Judaean campaign. Yet he took it all as his due. When he'd had enough he returned to his posting—unchanged from the man who had left."

Unrelenting, Drausus shrugged in smug arrogance. "A man can change in ten years."

"Not this one." Rufus shook his head. "I served under him for three years in that accursed desert. I saw him fight and watch his men die that Rome could possess the land and call it Judaea. Do not speak to me of questioning his loyalty. I *saw* his loyalty—to Rome, to the Eagles *and* to his men. No, I don't understand his actions with this woman. But I know the manner of man he is, and he is still in command. Until his deeds show me that he has clearly abandoned the oath he swore to serve Rome, I will continue to obey him. I will also stand against any man who would oppose him."

"As will I," Facilis abruptly joined in, stepping forward to stand at Rufus's side.

Rufus looked at him in surprise. Indeed, he had forgotten the younger man's presence—so fixed had been his attentions upon the wiry Spaniard. But clearly Facilis had listened to his words and been persuaded by them.

"Then, you are both fools!" Drausus spat a final time. If he intended to say any more, however, his

213

opportunity to do so was precluded by the sudden telltale rattle of chains.

In knowing silence the three men turned their eyes toward the timbered gate that now scraped across the ground as it was pulled open from the outside.

Galen felt the tension at once. Like a colorless cloud, heavy and dense, it emanated from the three men standing near the wall opposite the stockade's gate. He could almost reach out and touch it. Still, as he preceded his warrior escort into the compound, he gave no reaction that might have alerted the Ordovicians at his back to the dissension among his men. It must not be revealed to the enemy, for they must detect no weakness in their captives.

He strode forward. Once he was well within the perimeter, his guards ceased to follow. He heard them withdraw, pushing the gate closed. Only then did he direct his attention to his men. Indeed, upon his entrance he had needed no more than a glance to know what had occurred here in his absence. Shoulder to shoulder, Sita and Facilis now stood in silent and united opposition to Drausus.

Galen allowed himself a secret and wry smile. He had chosen well. Each of the men selected to accompany him had acted as he had anticipated, each playing a specific part to guarantee the success of this mission.

Early on, during the ambush itself, Facilis had fulfilled his purpose. Surprisingly, despite his comical physical appearance, he was the best swordsman at Deva. Without the unerring accuracy of his blade their casualties would surely have been greater. Too, he possessed a nature that allowed him to accept this current circumstance without undue complaint. Not so Drausus.

Galen met the Spaniard's wary gaze, holding it until the small man finally looked away. Wordlessly, Drausus stepped apart from his comrades, retreating to the spot of ground that served as his bed. Sita and Facilis did the same. Galen watched the three for a moment longer. Once they all had bedded down, he stiffly sat. Bringing his knees to his chest and hunching forward, he blocked the fiery pain in his back with thoughts of the man who had thus far walked a fine line between obedience and rebellion.

Drausus's hatred for his Ordovician enslavers remained still unassuaged by this time among them—and for that he had been chosen. Should Agricola's plan fail and Galen need escape, he would need a man such as Drausus, one who could kill his captors without hesitation. In addition, the Spaniard had been stationed the longest in Britain. In flight through the rugged mountains, an Ordovician war band at their heels, his knowledge of the mountainous terrain would be indispensable.

"Centurion."

Galen lifted his head and beheld the burly Thracian. In his hands he held Galen's cloak. "If you can bear the feel of this against your back, you'll need its warmth."

Galen nodded. Despite Sita's gentleness in placing the garment about him, he gritted his teeth in pain as the rough wool came in contact with his raw flesh.

"If the welts break open in the night, I'll have to soak this off you in the morning. Try not to move."

The advice brought a smile to Galen's lips. "I recall

215

having once spoken those last words to you. It still took six men to hold you down as the surgeon dug that arrow out of your thigh."

The bearded face split into a grin. Squatting down beside his commander, the large man rubbed the inside of his leg. "Too close to my manhood, it was. I didn't trust that Greek not to slip with his knife."

Galen watched as the old memory was relived in the veteran's eyes. But when it faded, it took with it Sita's grin.

He rose to his feet. "Is there anything more I can do?"

Galen shook his head. "You have done more than enough." He glanced toward Facilis and Drausus and quietly added, "Thank you."

Sita followed the direction of his gaze. "You know, don't you?"

"Yes."

For an instant the older man looked as though he would say more. Indeed, Galen could read the need for reassurance in his eyes. Sometimes faith alone was not enough to quell the doubts that twisted a man's guts. But then he blinked, and the questioning look was gone.

"Sleep well, Centurion."

Galen watched his departing back, and for the first time noticed a slump to the massive shoulders. The years had taken their toll. Sita was weary, and for all his experience upon the battlefield, this time of peace had only further weakened a body already undermined by age. Still, what had made Rufus Sita's inclusion in this mission imperative were those same boons of age and experience. He held the respect and trust of his

216

comrades: his was a voice they would hear, his a wisdom they would heed. And because he was one of them, he would hold them together should the time come that Galen could not. . . .

He quelled the thoughts he was not prepared to examine before they could rise. His future and his men's would be determined by forces over which he held no control. It was for the gods to decide their destiny. He raked his fingers through his hair and turned his gaze to stare up into the night. He was weary, too. He closed his eyes, and as the soft sounds of his men's snoring filled the silence, he willed the advent of sleep that would ease his pain and clear his mind.

She gently brushed to the side the shock of straight blond hair that always fell across his forehead. A tug and a tuck of the fur around his slender shoulders completed the ritual. Kneeling forward, Rhyca brushed her lips against his cheek. "You must try and sleep now."

But the bright eyes staring up at her held no trace of sleepiness. Too much had occurred this day to accord the child a peaceful repose. Indeed, it was the agitated state of Dafydd's emotions that had prompted Myrddin to return him to her for the night. The Druid knew—as did she—that the boy's true mother would give her son neither comfort nor compassion.

Almost in response to her thoughts Dafydd spoke. "He'll be all right, won't he, Rhyca?"

"Of course he will," she reassured calmly. "You know how very strong he is."

"And brave, too?"

With a soft smile and an assenting nod she dutifully repeated the words. "And brave, too."

"Myrddin said I could see him tomorrow."

"And so you shall. But now you must sleep, Dafydd." Once more she smoothed the wayward lock of hair, then stroked his forehead in the slow, rhythmic movements that usually lulled the boy to close his eyes. This night, however, they would not close. Fiercely, his blue stare held hers. Then, suddenly, he spoke.

"Rhyca . . . why do Balor and the others think you wanted what happened to you?"

A soft gasp rose and escaped before she could stop it. In shocked silence she looked down at the boy's questioning face, realizing what he must have overheard. "Why do you think that is what they believe?" she asked, striving to keep her tone even.

"That's what they said to Galen. Balor even told him you liked it, too. He said you . . ." His voice trailed as tears of confusion and embarrassment slowly welled in his eyes. "But you d . . . d . . . didn't—did you?"

His beseeching whisper begged for answers, and like a knife his pain twisted inside her. "No, Dafydd. No. I did not want what happened."

She reached for him, pulling him to a sitting position that allowed her to gather him into her arms. "You are too young to understand," she murmured helplessly as she rubbed his back in an effort to comfort him.

"But I want to understand!" Almost angrily he lifted his head. Again his gaze held hers. "Please, Rhyca."

She drew a deep breath and searched for the words. How did she explain to a child the belief of their people—that she should have died rather than survive an enemy's violation of her body? "It is because I lived, Dafydd, that Balor and others like him think as they do. They do not believe I fought hard enough to stop the soldiers from . . . from hurting me. You see, sometimes it is better to suffer death than dishonor, and what those men did . . ." Her voice broke as the words failed her.

"I know." He pulled away and looked at her with eyes that were no longer a child's. "I know what they did," he repeated. *"He* does it to my mother. Sometimes in the night I hear her cry out. And if the fire has not died, I can see." The bitterness in his voice reflected more than his hatred of his stepfather. It held the hurt of a child who could not resolve in his mind his mother's betrayal. "She likes him to do it. Even when he hurts her, she begs him not to stop." He turned his head and blinked fiercely, trying not to let his tears fall.

"Dafydd . . ." Rhyca reached out and laid her palm along his cheek, forcing him to look at her. "It is what is supposed to happen between a husband and wife. When you are older, you will understand. Your mother does nothing wrong. The vows of marriage give a man the right, and so the woman is not dishonored by his taking of her. With what happened to me, it is different. They had no right. They took from me what I did not give. But no one who was not there will ever believe that."

The scars formed by time were not as thick as she thought. As the old pain threatened, she fought against feeling it and drew a deep breath. "There will always be talk of the kind you heard today."

"But it's not true!"

"It does not matter. Balor and the others shall believe as they will."

"*I* believe you." He slipped his hand into hers.

Rhyca felt the rise of tears. The trusting innocence of the child's faith was as a balm applied to a stinging wound. Yet it was she who should soothe his pain, not he hers. "I know you believe me." She squeezed his hand and released it, taking hold of his shoulders. "But I want you to believe everything I have told you—about your mother as well."

Again he looked away to avoid her gaze.

"Dafydd, look at me," she demanded gently. When he obeyed, she continued. "What you have seen with your mother and her husband is not bad or wrong. It is good. It is how a baby is made, how the man's seed comes to be in the woman. As we sowed seeds today in the earth for the goddess to nurture, that is how a father sows his seed in the mother's womb. Only the seed grows to be a child."

"Always?"

"No, but sometimes . . ." She saw the blond head tilt in contemplative silence and wondered as to the thoughts within. With Dafydd it was difficult to know. At times he was very much a child, but at others his perceptions were frightfully intuitive.

He looked at her suddenly and pointed to her swollen belly. "Was your baby planted by a Roman?"

She swallowed hard, and yet could not deny him the truth. "Yes, Dafydd," she whispered, removing her hands from his shoulders and leaning back.

He nodded almost in satisfaction, as though he had solved for himself a puzzling question. "Then, that is why Galen protects you."

The matter-of-fact statement of such utter certainty caught her off guard, and at first she had no reply. She had tried very hard not to think of the man and what he had said before losing consciousness. Now Dafydd would have her confront exactly what she was loath to consider—the cause for Galen's actions and words. "What do you mean?" she finally asked, knowing her emotions were betrayed by the trembling in her voice.

"Because he is Roman and the baby is Roman." Dafydd looked at her in confusion. "Don't you see, Rhyca? It's like he is the baby's father."

"He isn't the father!" she snapped. Assailed by sudden and inexplicable emotions, she was unable to indulge the child's foolish logic and his idealistic thoughts of what a father was—or should be.

"I said it was *like* he was." His lower lip caught between his teeth. Yet despite his injured feelings, he did not desist. "That's why he hit Balor for saying those things, and that's why he was whipped."

"No!" Denial sharpened her voice. Too much of what Dafydd said was rooted in the possibility of a truth she simply could not accept. There could be no bond between her and this Roman! And that her womb nurtured life planted by a Roman did not entitle him to weave one and call it his responsibility. She neither wanted nor needed his protection. She had, in fact, refused it!

In her private torment she was powerless to soften the stern gaze she leveled at the child. "Listen to me,

Dafydd. You must see him as he is—not as you would like him to be. He was whipped because he struck his guard. Myrddin said as much—he must learn his place. A slave cannot show such disobedience and not be punished as an example to the others."

"A man can truly be a slave only if he lets himself be."

She tensed. "Where did you hear that?" She knew the answer before he gave it.

"Galen told me." Eyeing her cautiously, he seemed to know he should say no more. He wriggled down beneath the fur and settled back in his bed, closing his eyes. His soft whisper was almost to himself. "Maybe that is why they whipped him . . . because he will not be a slave. I think they are afraid of him."

In spite of herself she smiled wryly at the clarity of the small boy's insight. "I think so, too," she murmured, without understanding why the thought of the Roman's strength of will should give her a sense of comfort. "Now you must go to sleep."

"Rhyca?"

"Yes?"

Once again the blue eyes were wide open. "If Galen had not hit Balor for saying those things about you, I would have."

She blinked back the tears that would form. "I know you would have." She patted his small hand and leaned forward to kiss his cheek. "That is why you are so dear to me, Dafydd. You would protect me and defend my honor. Yours is the courage not of a boy, but a great warrior."

He colored instantly, yet the look that came to his features was more than pleasure at her praise. Unmis-

222

takably it was a look of hope. "Then, you truly do not hate him. I did not think you did. You tried to help him today, so you must like him now."

"It . . . it is not so simple as that, Dafydd." She looked away.

"You tried to help him," he insisted.

"Yes, but—"

"Then, you must like him. You cannot hate him anymore."

"It is not that easy."

"Yes, it is. It is easy to know if you like or hate someone. I hate Balor because he is cruel and hurts others. Myrddin is kind, so I like him. I think I like the Roman with the red hair also—because he makes me laugh. The very large one with no hair . . . I did not think I liked him before. But today he wanted to protect you, too, in a different way. I think I shall like him now as well . . ."

She stared, unseeing, at the hearth fire, listening to his innocent child's chatter. It was so simple in his mind whether to like or hate. . . .

I would see your hatred whither and die. Suddenly the words Galen had spoken echoed within her. She felt the taste of tears rise in her throat.

She heard Dafydd sit up. "Rhyca, why are you crying?"

"I'm not."

"Yes, you are." His hand reached out, and a finger touched her cheek, then withdrew. "See. It's wet."

"Oh, Dafydd . . ." She sighed. "You ask too many questions for which I have no answers. Go to sleep now, and perhaps tomorrow will bring those answers."

She kissed his cheek a final time and rose. If only

she could believe that the light of dawn would indeed bring a resolution to the turmoil within her.

"Rhyca?" a sleepy voice murmured.

She did not turn to face him. "Yes?"

"Perhaps it is you who needs to see him as he is . . ."

Mouric sat cross-legged on his pallet of bracken covered with hides. With a still-steady hand he raised to his lips the wooden tankard that had already been filled and drained enough times that he had lost count. Tipping back his head, he drank deeply. While no quantity of wine could douse the churning fury that had consumed him since his return to the hill fort, he was nevertheless determined to try—for he could do nothing else.

Only in hindsight did he now realize the error he had made by absenting himself these past three days. Indeed, even the glow of his hunt's success had tarnished upon his learning of this day's events. Had he been present, he could have changed them. The confrontation between Balor and the Roman would have ended far differently!

His throat constricted in renewed anger, and he choked on the wine coursing down his gullet. Coughing, he swore a silent oath: A *ban-sidhe* curse upon Balor! The shortsighted fool should have killed the dark bastard outright and taken his head. Instead, while attempting to restore his lost honor, he had succeeded only in enhancing his enemy's. For the rest of his days Balor would bear the Roman's mark: the jagged scar upon his cheek, his face—that part of a man held by the Ordovices to be the very seat of honor—would forever proclaim his shame. The Roman, on the other hand, could wear his scars proudly. He had borne the lash in silence, and to all who had witnessed his flogging his courage had been proved.

It was the last thing Mouric needed—to have Cerrix's slave-centurion elevated yet higher in the eyes of their people. The Council of Elders would be more inclined than ever to consider this cowardly plan for peace.

Belching in disgust, Mouric threw the empty tankard aside.

The sound of the heavy cup hitting the clay floor appeared to waken one of the hut's sleeping warriors, for he rose from his bed and crossed over to the hearth.

Finally feeling the wine's effect, Mouric leaned forward and watched the play of firelight upon the naked figure. Pride in one's own body provoked appreciation of others', and Mouric assessed the muscular physique and lithe movement of the young warrior now poised at the hearth, tossing a few lengths of wood onto the flames.

His name was Ynyr, Mouric recalled—as he raised his gaze to take in the youth's decidedly feminine features. Surely the delicate brow, fine cheekbones and flawless skin rivaled any woman's for beauty. A familiar quickening sensation settled into Mouric's loins, and he shifted restlessly to recline on his side, propping his chin in his hand.

The sound drew the younger man's attention, and he turned his head toward it. His gaze met Mouric's, then broke away. A moment later, his right hand, which rested easily upon the naked breast over his heart, moved slowly across the breadth of muscle. Palm to skin, the hand languidly slid up his throat, then along the line of smooth jaw until the long fingers lost themselves in a tangle of tawny locks. Giving his head a careless scratch, the youth yawned. Once again his eyes, lazily half-lidded, met Mouric's. This time he did not look away.

The invitation was unmistakable.

At once Mouric felt himself stir in response to it. The prospect of having the graceful youth as bed fellow was an appealing one.

Ynyr appeared to sense his thoughts, for he turned slightly, according Mouric a fuller view of him. When the older man's gaze had traveled the scalloped muscles of the younger's belly, Ynyr turned again toward the fire, revealing to Mouric's receptive eye the sleek flanks and smooth curves of his buttocks.

With this mute statement of consent Mouric was most pleased, for his first choice of bedmates always ran to his fellow warriors. Like many of them, he believed that a man—despite his potency—was conquered in the act of love, and the sapping of his strength after climax was a form of temporary death. Thus, if he were with a woman, his attainment of final release accorded her the triumph. Because she was still capable of further response, she was the victor— and he the vanquished. This Mouric had never been able to reconcile with his pride. Therefore, unlike other warriors of his tribe who enjoyed equally either men or women, he found no satisfaction with a woman if she opened her legs to him willingly. With a woman he needed to fight for that which he ultimately took.

And yet, even then, in the wake of his pleasure a sense of capitulation and defeat gnawed. Hence, by choice he took to his bed only those with whom pleasure—and defeat—would be mutual.

That the sleekly muscled warrior beside the hearth intended such mutual pleasure was indisputable. Again he turned and faced Mouric, repeating his hand's earlier journey, this time in a downward direction.

Seeing the now visible evidence of the youth's lust, Mouric's own mounted. He rose to his knees and beckoned Ynyr to him.

Ynyr lay down upon the pallet and looked up. The face he saw and the voice he heard, however, were not those of the man he was about to accept as his lover—but of the man he had long ago taken as his king. *Do whatever must be done . . . now more than ever he must be watched. . . .*

Several moments later, through the door on the other side of the hut, a trio of warriors entered. They took no notice that in a darkened corner two of their spear brothers were making love.

Twelve

He was inside, pouring water from the filled buckets into the vessel beside the hearth, when she entered. Rhyca knew he had to have heard her footsteps, yet he did not turn or acknowledge her presence. Still, she was not surprised by his ignoring her now.

Earlier, when they had both been at the river—she to bathe and he to haul the day's needed supply of water—he had not spoken either. It mattered not that they had encountered one another quite by accident, or that the stretch of rock-strewn bank which had separated them had been but a few yards in length and that there had been no others about the secluded bend, shaded by overhanging limbs and tall reeds. As soon as he had seen her, he had turned away to fill the buckets, leaving soon afterward without even so much as a grunted greeting. Ever since his removal six days ago from the prisoners' stockade, he had been so—taciturn and distant. . . .

At first she had welcomed his demeanor of detachment and felt a sense of relief. His return to her service had evoked too many feelings within her, feelings she was unwilling to sort out just yet. The words he had spoken in semi-consciousness—indeed the entire incident of the flogging—were best forgotten. The less contact there was between them now, the better.

This seemed the best and only feasible response to the proximity imposed upon them by Cerrix's command that the Romans be resettled on the farmsteads: As his sole purpose was to provide labor, the slave thrust upon her would be regarded no differently than any other beast of burden.

In unspoken agreement and with mutual understanding the conditions for their forced cohabitation were set. He slept with the oxen and spent his days in the field. He entered her hut only to bring wood or water. His food was left outside the door. Unless there was need, they did not speak.

But his maintaining of a physical distance between them could not countermand what had previously formed. With each setting sun it became more and more evident to her. She felt it every time she saw him or heard his voice. And when Dafydd visited and she beheld his gentleness with the boy, her heart ached with an irrefutable knowledge—Dafydd had been right.

. . . *see him as he is—not as you want him to be.* . . . Those words had haunted her since the night she had spoken them and Dafydd had echoed them. Outwardly, she could profess differently and deny the truth. Yet to herself, she could lie no longer.

This she realized the day Galen was brought back to her. Looking upon the bronzed face, marred with its vicious bruises, she had felt the strangest mix of relief and confusion. And when the silent strength he embodied for her seemed to wrap her in a warmth of comfort and security the likes of which she had not believed possible to feel, she had known. She could conjure no loathing for this man.

The lash that had torn into his flesh had torn into her hatred as well. But could she let the tattered strips fall? Once removed, that armor of hatred could never again be donned. Could she stand before him so vulnerable? Yet vulnerable to what? For nothing did she know with as absolute a certainty as this—that from him no harm would come.

From the very beginning the dark Roman had refused to don the cloak in which she would wrap him. No matter how often and persistently she had sought to garb him as her enemy, he had each time defiantly torn off and tossed aside that guise—at first daring her only to look upon him, and then, finally forcing her to see him for the man he truly was. Those of her own kind and kin had cast her out, yet this man, this *Roman,* had sheltered and protected her. Unlike any man she had ever known, his strength was cause for faith—not fear. . . .

Nervously Rhyca brushed back the tendrils of damp hair that clung to her forehead. Waiting for him to complete his task, she stood and studied him.

It had been nearly a fortnight now since the beating. The bruises on his face had completely disappeared, she noted. She wondered as to the welts on his back. To heal, they should have been left open to the air. Yet not once since his return had she seen him bared to the waist. She considered the long, sleeveless tunic he wore and pondered what might lie beneath.

A crisscrossing of leather laces closed the neck

opening that ended mid-chest. The garment, which had belonged to her father, was a deep reddish brown in color and of a heavy woolen weave. Therefore, it might not show the seepage of blood as easily as might a paler color or thinner fabric.

"I . . . I want to look at your back," she stated suddenly, quietly.

She saw his dark brow lift in what might be either surprise or displeasure.

Whatever the emotion, he recovered from it quickly. Masklike and calm, his features now revealed nothing. "It is not necessary," he answered. Still avoiding looking at her, he took up the emptied buckets and stepped forward to pass her.

She placed herself directly in his path, blocking his exit to repeat her request. This time her voice was firm. "I want to see your back."

He looked down at her, meeting her gaze at last. His own narrowed into a scowl of anger that twisted into a mocking leer. "Why? Would you see the damage wrought by Balor's lash, *domina?*"

At once she knew the purpose for the arrogant taunt. He hoped she would rail in response to it and forget her request, sending him from her without sight of what he clearly did not want to reveal. She held his stare. "I would see what you would conceal."

An unfathomable look descended across the bronze features. With an intensity that was both hot and cold, his dark eyes bored into her. "Some things are better left concealed, *domina.* As long as they are hidden from perception, they can be denied."

She had the strangest feeling he was not talking

231

about the scars upon his back. "Please. I . . . I need to see—to know."

His mouth thinned. Though she could see the refusal steadfast in his eyes (a part of him would still deny her), he set down the buckets. His eyes never leaving hers, he began with slow and deliberate movements not merely to open the laces, but to unthread them.

When he had finished, he discarded the leather thong on the floor and took hold of each side of the opening, ripping the garment to the hem with one tug.

She flinched both at the sound of the tearing fabric and at the anger she could feel emanating from him. Pointedly he turned and pulled the cloth downward, baring to her sight what she had wanted to see.

The once smooth skin was marred with a slashing pattern of raised scabs. Several of the welts which had not cut so deeply into the flesh had already healed completely—their pinkish color and tender appearance stark in contrast to the sun-bronzed skin untouched by the whip. A fine sheen covered his entire back, and she realized someone had applied a coating of oil to the wounds.

"Dafydd," she whispered, and he nodded.

Not knowing why, she reached out and carefully traced one of the wales scarred over with new skin.

Galen's reaction was instantaneous. Though her fingertips upon him were gentle, he tensed and fought the urge to pull away. Gladly he would have suffered the cruelest stroke of any whip rather than to endure the silent agony now evoked by her willing touch of him.

Purposely, to avoid what he was feeling—and had

232

known he would feel should there be any physical contact between them—he had asked Dafydd rather than Rhyca to apply the healing oil the Druid had provided. Never had he considered the possibility she would demand to view Balor's handiwork. . . .

Again, he felt the warmth of her fingertips, this time upon flesh that had escaped the lash's bite. He clenched his teeth and swallowed a groan. He felt as if he were balanced upon the narrow rim of a dark and gaping chasm. One small push and he would tumble over the edge. . . .

He whirled and seized her wrist to keep her touch from again descending, then fought to take hold of himself. What he would feel for this woman, he could not feel! "If my choices must be your hatred or your pity, *domina* . . . ," he gritted out with deliberately cruel sarcasm, "I would prefer your hatred. What I did, I did willingly, and not one lash do I regret."

But the anger he had hoped to stoke refused to kindle. There was no reaction from her.

In silence Rhyca stared up into the face she had once despised. Try as she might, she could see in the handsome features no trace of the enemy he had once been. She felt the tears form, then fall. She was helpless to stop them—and helpless to understand the swell of emotions within her. Anger, guilt, compassion, confusion—all rendered her numb.

"I have never known such a man as you," she murmured. "When first you were forced upon me, I saw in you the representation of all I have loathed. I looked upon you and I hated you. Now . . . now I look at you and . . ." She trailed off, aghast at the thought silently forming. . . . *and feel safe.*

Suddenly she felt his hold of her wrist tighten, and there came with the iron grip a pain that served to penetrate the numbness. Sensation returned, and with it strength. When he relaxed his grip slightly, she jerked her wrist free. Furiously she swiped at the tears rolling down her cheeks.

Galen released a silent sigh. As quickly as it had opened, the chasm had closed. He stood again on solid ground, his control restored.

But to test himself, he reached out and threaded his fingers into the silken strands of hair that fell forward across her left shoulder to brush against her cheek. Forcing himself to feel nothing, to prove the rule of will over want, he watched her eyes. Almost at once he saw in the blue-gray stare a questioning anger which displaced her unnerving confusion of a moment earlier.

"Wha—?"

"Your hair is still wet from your bath," he explained evenly. As he rubbed the damp strands between his fingertips, he permitted himself a satisfied smile. "You should stand outside and let the sun's warmth dry it."

Rhyca blinked, taken aback by the peculiar remark.

But he said no more. He withdrew his hand, took up the buckets and stepped around her. She stood in silence, staring at the tunic he had left discarded on the floor.

Dafydd shifted his weight to his good foot. Shading his eyes with his hand, he watched the man laboring a short distance from him.

With each powerful, consecutive blow of his ax Galen deepened the split he had begun near the smaller end of the thick oaken log lying braced between his feet. Aided by a second ax imbedded in the fissure to keep it open, he was about to reach the heartwood. At that point Dafydd knew that the huge log, the girth of a man and almost his height in length, would crack and split into near even halves. He had watched enough of the hill fort's carpenters and builders at work to know how it was done, and to know, too, the force and accuracy of Galen's blade now. What the boy did not know, however, was the reason for the man's moody silence of late.

Perhaps his back pained him still, Dafydd thought. But as he watched the movement of hard muscle beneath the scarred flesh, and saw the ax arc smoothly into the air above the dark head in prelude to a mighty downward swing, he doubted that cause. Galen's strange reserve had its source in something—or someone—else. While he was the same around Dafydd, talking to him as he had before the beating, whenever Rhyca was near he was different. He did not laugh anymore, and he hardly smiled. Most often he simply found excuse to be elsewhere.

It was not that he was unkind, Dafydd had realized soon after the initial awareness of a change in Galen's behavior toward her. He was neither rude nor actually unpleasant. He was just different. Dafydd was sure Rhyca had noticed the change as well. He was sure, too, it bothered her, even if she tried not to show it. More than once, after Galen had been almost curt with her, Dafydd had seen her wipe away tears when she thought no one was watching.

And yet it was not only Galen who seemed changed. Between him and Rhyca it was not as it had been before. Together they were different, and their behavior odd. Once Dafydd had seen them stand and look at one another for the longest time. They had not spoken—only stared.

Dafydd released a frustrated sigh that was lost instantly in the loud crack made by the straining wood as the log was cloven in two. He did not bother to watch the halves roll apart. With his gaze still focused upon Galen's bare back, his thoughts turned to a second enigma: the man's refusal to let Rhyca tend to his wounds.

He had said he wanted to spare her the sight of the bloody welts and ripped flesh.

"But she has already seen your back and what Balor did," Dafydd had pointed out.

"Then I could not prevent it. Now I have the choice." The intensity and hardness in Galen's face had been suddenly softened by an indulgent smile. As he always did when he was either about to discipline or school him, he had crouched down in front of Dafydd and placed his large hands upon the boy's shoulders. "Among my father's people if a warrior's wound must be sealed with a heated blade or if an arrow is to be dug from his flesh, a woman is always brought forth to hold him still. In her presence he will neither struggle nor cry out. It is a matter of training and pride. Because he is protector and provider, he must be strong. Never may a man reveal to his woman his pain—his weakness."

At the time Dafydd had accepted the explanation without question. He had seen no reason to doubt

Galen's motive or even to wonder at his choice of words. ". . . never may a man reveal to his woman his pain . . ." But now two of those words flitted about inside Dafydd's head like a pesky gnat he could not slap away: *his woman*.

Might it be? Was it possible—despite what Rhyca had said—that Galen *did* think of the baby she carried as his? And hence, Rhyca to be his as well—for why else would he have wanted to hide his pain from her?

Once it was realized, this solution—along with its twisted logic—were to his child's reasoning as straight as an arrow's flight. That Galen's behavior toward Rhyca after his return should therefore have been less reserved and detached rather than more so, was now but a detail that did not merit Dafydd's consideration. He was after all a small boy. Hope and faith outweighed fact and reality, and the explanation he had just conjured was one in whose truth he wanted desperately to believe.

In frantic thought his head bobbed as he excitedly stepped forward to verify his conviction.

"Galen . . . how does a man become a father?"

Impatiently he waited for a response while Galen labored to lift up an end of one of the halved logs and lay it, flat side down, onto a smaller supporting log he had kicked into a crosswise position. As he went to the log's opposite end to repeat the process, he finally responded. "He sires a child."

"You mean he plants the seed in the mother that grows into a baby?"

"Yes." He set the log into place upon the second support and straightened. Raking his fingers through his hair, he at last looked at Dafydd directly. The slightest hint of amusement shone in his eyes. "Why do you ask?"

Dafydd shrugged. This was not going as he had wanted. "Is . . . is that the . . . the only way? I mean, there is no other to make of a man a father?"

A smile he clearly struggled to hold back instantly tipped the corners of Galen's mouth. "It is the only way that *I* know of, Dafydd. A man—" he bent to retrieve his ax as he spoke—"and a woman join and—"

He broke off and looked up sharply as though in sudden understanding. All traces of his earlier amusement had been wiped from his face.

Dafydd stiffened in anxious dread. Had he said something wrong?

Galen thought for a moment before speaking. If the boy were truly questioning what happened intimately between a man and a woman, the matter was not one to be made light of. "Perhaps what you are really wanting to know is *how* a man plants that seed?" he prompted gently.

To his surprise Dafydd's eyes did not lower in embarrassment. "I know how it is done," he replied, his voice containing a prideful sort of bitterness. "What I want to know is if a man can be father to a child who does not grow from his seed."

Galen rubbed a hand along his jaw. Rhyca had warned that Dafydd might come to see him as the father he did not have. Her fervent insistence that he therefore not encourage the boy's fanciful expectations now pricked at his conscience. He wondered if the "boy" in Dafydd's question was Dafydd and himself the "man." Was Dafydd attempting to pursue his fantasy—or did his question have a different impetus?

Certainly it was also possible he might merely be questioning the right to the authority over him held by his mother's husband.

Until Galen knew with surety what the boy was truly questioning, he knew he must be cautious with his answer. "If the mother of the child is his woman, and the man so chooses, he can assume the role of father and call the child his. Also, among the Romans there is a practice called adoption, a legal means whereby a man may make of any male, whether of his flesh or not, his son, and thereby his lawful heir."

As he heard his own words, Galen stiffened—for with this mention of adoption he suddenly realized the subconscious turn that had been taken by his thoughts. That he had probably sired children he had no doubt, but never before had he contemplated the idea of fatherhood. Now, looking down into Dafydd's trusting eyes, he found himself actually considering as reality the child's fantasy and wondering. . . . Was there still time and room in his life for a son?

As quickly as the thought rose, he dismissed it. He was a soldier, and soldiers were not permitted to honor the bond of family. That lesson he had learned all too well from his own father and at an age younger than Dafydd's. The army of Rome was a selfish mistress; she allowed her lovers no other ties.

"What . . . what if the man wanted to be father to a child, but the child's mother was *not* his woman?" Voicing yet another question, Dafydd spoke again. "Could he make her his, and then be the child's father?"

At once—and with a peculiar sense of loss—Galen realized he had been wrong. Dafydd was not talking about himself and Galen—but neither was he asking about his mother or personal circumstance. Galen was now utterly perplexed. "Customs and laws can be different," he answered slowly. "Among one people how a man may lay claim to a woman and make her his might not be done in the same way among others. But among my kind . . . yes. If a man provides for a woman, shelters and protects her, this makes her his woman. Her child could then become his."

Immediately a wide grin claimed the boy's face. "I had thought as much!" he declared happily.

Galen understood Dafydd's reaction no more than he had the purpose for his questions. But since from the corner of his eye he suddenly caught sight of Rhyca exiting the hut, he knew he could now delve into the matter no further. He ran his palms down his thighs, wiping his hands upon the woolen cloth of the *bracae* which early on in his captivity had come to replace the soldier's tunic as his normal attire.

Then, without looking at the approaching figure, he picked up his ax and returned to his work.

Never had Rhyca been more aware that she was the focus of another's thoughts. That his broad, naked back was now to her mattered not. He could have stood, turned and stared directly at her, and she would have felt no differently than she did at this moment. Crossing the yard, she felt as if she had been stripped bare beneath an unseen stare.

Twice she nearly changed her mind and returned to the hut—for even as the distance that separated them narrowed, she was yet to invent a reason or plausible excuse for this contact. She knew only she could not leave it between them as it had ended yesterday—with none of her questions answered, and more confusion added to her welter of emotions.

Ultimately, however, it was Dafydd who made the choice for her. Spotting her approach, the boy waved, shouting out her name in greeting. "Come see," he beckoned.

He started to clamber across a large half log lying on the ground, but Galen called him back to where he worked on the log's mate which rested across two smaller logs.

Rhyca looked about as the man straddled the split tree trunk. He must have used one of the oxen to pull it from the forest, she thought, noting the drag marks and hoof prints in the dirt. Her curiosity aroused, she stepped closer to watch.

On either side of the end of the half log, Galen cut a small notch into the bark. Down into the first notch he then wedged what looked to her to be a piece of dark cord he had wrapped around a thick stick. Walking the length of the log, he unraveled the cord as he went. At the log's opposite end he squatted down, eyed the point at which the cord was secured into the bark and pulled his end of the cord taut. "Now, Dafydd . . . as I showed you. Snap it."

Intrigued, Rhyca stepped closer still. Dafydd went to the middle of the log, pinched the cord, lifted it slightly and suddenly released it. Because of the tension of the cord, it did indeed "snap" against the surface of the bark, and where it struck there was left a blue line. She knew at once what had been applied to the cord. Only crushed woad leaves made such a color.

Galen and Dafydd repeated their actions upon the log's other side. When they were finished, the pair of blue lines appeared to mark off the broad middle portion of the split log.

"What are the lines for?" she asked.

Crouched and studying his efforts, Galen did not reply.

"To use as a guide . . . ," Dafydd answered as he limped over to her, "to make out of a round log a square timber." Clearly he was proud to show off the knowledge he had no doubt just acquired himself.

"But for what purpose?"

Though she looked to Dafydd for the answer, it was Galen who unexpectedly gave it. "A square timber is more easily split into boards."

"And what will you make—once you have your boards?"

Ax now in hand, he ignored her question and stepped up to stand atop the log. Dafydd edged closer to stand in the circle of the arm she unconsciously draped across his shoulders. Together they watched in silence as Galen swung the ax, directing its blade into the side of the log at an angle. He did not deepen or widen the cut with a second stroke, but instead moved down the log to make another and then another.

Watching his efforts, Rhyca did not doubt that his eye was experienced. The series of notches he cut into the half log were even in depth and equally distanced. The boast he had made months earlier that he could do the job of carpenter had not been an idle one. In the hill fort she had seen timbers hewn and squared for use in building, and recognized this process. Once the log had been scored, the wood between the notches would be cut away to leave a flat surface. Still, for any use of wood about the farmstead this preparation seemed too complex—and indeed unnecessary. "What are these boards to be used for?" she asked again.

It happened that she spoke at the same instant his ax bit into the log. Now when he did not respond, she was not sure if she had been heard, or if he was ignoring her as before and purposely avoided answering her question. If that were so, she was loath to speak it again, and thus lowered her gaze.

Without warning, his voice sounded. "A cradle."

Rhyca's head snapped up, and she stared at the man poised atop the log. Her sight of him blurred beneath a veil of sudden tears. Her heart hammered in her chest, and she struggled for composure—but could find footing only in anger. "Then, leave it, lest your efforts be wasted, Roman. I do not want it."

She heard Dafydd's sharp intake of breath and was barely cognizant of the boy moving away from her. Her attention remained fixed upon the man before her. She felt lost in the potency of his dark stare—helpless to deny the knowledge she saw reflected there.

"Which, *domina?* The child or the bed?"

"Damn you," she hissed, at last finding the strength to look away. The faint thought trickled through her mind that this was the first time he had spoken of the child since his learning of its Roman siring. But before she could react further, he spoke again—this time to the wide-eyed boy at her side.

"Dafydd . . ." His voice was calm and reassuring, and in that moment when her own emotions raged, she loathed him for his control. "I need you to go

243

back to the hut and fetch the sharpening stone. Will you do that for me?"

Mutely the boy nodded and started toward the hut. She heard Galen's ax bite into the log, then an instant later his footsteps. Rooted where she stood, she could not move, not even knowing that he came toward her.

He stopped in front of her, his greater height shadowing her. She could smell the dampness of the forest on him, the scent of tree sap and of freshly hewn wood. He was less than an arm's length from her, and still stepped closer.

"Which do you reject?" he repeated. "The bed or the child?"

With her face turned she could avoid the sight of him. But his voice still sounded, and the truth it carried tore through her like a jagged blade.

"Or is it both?"

"You have no right," she whispered, forcing herself to raise her gaze. "You cannot know . . . know what I feel."

He grasped her hand and forced it to her swollen belly. He held it there, covering it with his own. "Touch it," he demanded, his voice uncompromising and yet strangely gentle. "Inside you a new life grows strong and healthy—and utterly innocent of the circumstance of its conception. You cannot deny it for the crime of merely being. You must accept this baby."

"How?" she countered bitterly. "How can I accept it, when each time I think of it I remember how it came to be? I remember everything . . ." Her voice cracked, yet she continued, forcing tears and emotions to remain at bay. "Hatred comes to my heart and

244

shame to my soul. No man in knowing what was done to me can look upon me without averting his eyes."

"For any man to look upon you and not know therein lies courage and beauty, he is either fool or blind." The unexpected tenderness of his smile was matched by his sudden touch as he laid his hand along the side of her face. "And *my* eyes are not averted."

Rhyca stared at him. She was being drawn to him by word and deed as surely as if he had clutched her. "But would they be—if this child were *not* of Roman seed? Would you be building it a cradle?"

Suddenly fear ran through her like an icy wave. She could not allow herself to believe in this man. She had to push him away before it was too late. "Or perhaps it is not truly a cradle that you build? Perhaps it is a shrine . . . a cradle meant to glorify *all* of the bastards bred of Roman rape. Like an animal leaves its droppings to mark its territory, so does the mighty army of Rome leave its form of dung—in the swollen bellies of women. Tell me, Centurion of the Eagles, were you to build a cradle for every life spawned by *your* seed, how many would you have to build?"

"Perhaps more than you could count," he answered coldly.

She saw the anger enter and narrow his eyes, and felt safe. In his anger she felt no threat. It was his gentleness she feared, for it touched a vulnerability within her she could neither admit nor reveal.

"But now you tell me, woman of the Ordovices . . ." he continued with the same icy edge to his voice, "who is the true target of your spite?" He grabbed her, his fingers biting into the flesh of her upper arms like talons. "Is it the handful of men who violated you or the *one* man who let you be? Or the men who have since forced upon you a shame of which you are undeserving?"

His hold relaxed slightly, but his tone remained stern. "Look at me. I am none of those men, Rhyca. I have sought to prove it to you with more than words, and now I also say it: I will not harm you—or let you be harmed."

"You are the fool, Roman." She twisted from his touch. She could not—would not—take his pity! "You speak of my courage . . . Well, I tell you now, it is hatred for your kind that sustains it—hatred that burns within me like a flame."

"No flame can burn without fuel."

There was no warning, no betrayal of his intent in the bronze features. Before she knew what was happening, his mouth came down upon hers with a force that crushed her lips between his. He sought from her a response, an answer to a question only her soul perceived. And perceive it, it did.

Her mouth opened beneath his. She would accept what he offered.

Instead he shoved her from him. "Now . . ." His voice was hoarse, his breathing labored. "Now you have fuel for your hatred."

For a brief moment Rhyca had no response. Her reaction to his kiss had horrified and confused her. But worse—far worse—was his subsequent rejection and the resultant shame that now burned within her more hotly than her hatred ever had.

"Curse you, Roman!" Readily the condemnation

came to her lips as she found her voice at last. Then, because she tasted him still, she turned her head and spat into the dirt. Defiantly she raised her chin.

No further testament was needed to know his aim had been achieved. Galen took a half step backward, turned and walked away. The gods had been generous. He could as easily have failed—and would have deserved to.

He had broken one of the most elementary rules of combat: He had acted not only without thought, but out of a tumult of emotion: spite, anger, frustration. For months he had offered her comfort, respect and protection, but in return she had only thrown up higher defenses. With her refusal to accept him—or even to accept his gift of the simple gesture of the cradle—he had lost all patience. Would she cling so steadfastly to her hatred of Romans, he would give her cause to hate one more!

His kiss had been a stratagem meant to evoke her loathing. But a part of him had wanted her, and that she *would* have accepted him in that manner had aroused in him what no enemy on any battlefield had ever provoked—fear.

He could almost hear the gods laughing. In trying to goad her fury, he had stumbled upon what he had not known he even wanted—only to realize he could not have it. Even as he put needed distance between them, the truth remained undeniable. He could be her protector, but not her lover.

Yet were he to compare the feelings invoked by this woman to a situation of impending warfare, he knew he would be visiting the legionary stonecutter and ordering his gravestone. Though now firmly in place, his own line of defense was at best tenuous. It would hold—but only against an attack that were seen coming.

Thirteen

He looked to the jagged horizon where the distant mountains stood black against the graying sky. Only a few moments earlier there had been an abundance of brilliant hues behind the rugged crests. Gathering clouds, looking as though they were catching fire, had burned crimson and gold, dominating the sky. But the sun's light was gone now, taking with it the heavens' color. Darkness would fall soon. Already a blurred moon hung low, and a growing wind held the possibility of storm.

Galen pushed back from the palisade, the top rail upon which he had been leaning creaking with the release of his weight. For a moment he paused and looked about the farmstead and its surrounding area. The habits and training of a lifetime were hard to break. He had stood too many sentry watches to go to his bed without a final look.

He turned and headed for the oxen's stall. Despite the weariness of his body, his mind refused to rest. Unwillingly he found himself reconstructing the morning's events. Dafydd's persistent questions, the confrontation with Rhyca . . . each had seemed at the time unrelated. Yet each had aroused in him the same manner of response—acknowledgement of a longing and then denial. Were they therefore somehow connected—the irrational consideration of fatherhood and the precipitous kiss?

The unconscious gesture that always betrayed a deep confusion of his soul surfaced. He passed his right hand through his hair. Its length served to distract his thoughts and to call up a reckoning of the amount of time since his mission's onset.

It was two months since the forage patrol had departed Deva's walls, two months since his arrival to the Ordovician hill fort. Yet in that time what had he accomplished? He had been sent to learn the mind and manner of the man who would be the tribes' Great King. His convincing Cerrix to delay action against Agricola constituted only a partial success. Whether Cerrix could hold the Ordovices together and force them to honor the desired peace with Rome still remained an unanswered question. All that Galen had truly learned was how, with time and distance from the familiar, a man could change—and inwardly far more than in outward ways.

Before he had come to this place Galen had never believed himself to be a man lured by comfort, or one to be seduced by peace. But his time in this place had shown him differently. He, who had known no life but that of soldiering and war, had begun to consider as home the mountain farmstead to which he had come in chains. Over the land he worked as slave he had come to feel ownership, and for the woman he protected and the crippled boy that seemed to bind the three of them together, the longing for possession. . . .

The thoughts that suddenly crowded his mind were disturbing ones, and Galen stopped short. The impossibility of what he had just admitted disconcerted him far less than did the admission itself. Indeed, he felt as if a foe, sword in hand and at the ready, had just emerged from the shadows.

But the moment of vulnerability was only that. As he lay down upon his bed of hay, he was already formulating his response. Whether against an enemy of flesh and blood from without or one of thought and emotion from within, he knew how to effect victory. The training that had made deadly his blade had also taught him how to defy his heart.

The boy he would keep at arm's length, and her even farther. Whatever his personal wants or unrealized longings, they would yield to his oath to Rome. He had lived his life thus far—and well enough, too—without either a child's love or a woman's comfort. But honor, duty, loyalty? Without them he was nothing!

In his need he was nothing without her. The realization was one that mortal man failed to acknowledge. But for a god, whose power was omnipotent, recognition of want was not weakness—rather the necessary prelude to fulfillment.

He shifted in his bed. As the heavens rumbled, the night became charged with a prickling force that gave fair warning to the earth's denizens—and to their god-

dess. Beware and heed, for he would come in awesome fury.

And then he called out.

Claps of thunder rolled along the valley bottoms. Bolts of lightning threw themselves upon the hills. The god of the sky summoned forth his mate to awaken and rise to sate his need.

Galen pulled his cloak tighter to him against the cooled air and sharpening wind. Despite that wind, there was an uneasy stillness to the night. He looked up at the moon, now high in the sky, but obscured by dark thunderclouds that had amassed unheeded by sleeping man or slumbering beast.

Alerted only by an unknown instinct, he shifted restlessly in his bed.

All at once the night exploded with din and light.

Rhyca awoke screaming. Her dreams had returned her to the attack upon her village, but the terror that consumed her was real. Now, as on that night, she could hear the thunder's crash and see the lightning's flash. And just as then, she felt the penetration of a dagger-sharp pain that ran through her body, seemingly to slice her in two.

She clutched her midsection and rolled onto her side, drawing her knees in as much as the girth of her swollen belly would allow. Curled up, she tried to protect herself from the assault. After a moment the pain subsided . . . then she fought the fear.

It was not time for what she suspected was coming—not until the passing of two more moons and the dark of a third. Had she eaten something spoiled or performed some labor too strenuous? There must be another cause for the pain which was now gone. Perhaps she had only dreamed it after all.

Using both hands, she gingerly pushed her cumbersome body into a sitting position. Almost at once there was a warm gushing from between her legs. The bed beneath her was soaked. She had heard women speak of it, and knew. Her water had broken.

"In the name of the goddess, no." Her whispered cry echoed in the dark hut. But there was no one to hear it. Dafydd had returned to the hill fort before dusk. She was alone. As she had been when the life was put into her womb, she would be as that life issued forth.

Suddenly another wave of pain washed over her as if to confirm what she knew: This night the baby would be born.

A cry of denial left her body—only to be swept away by the howling wind.

Galen was on his feet and running toward the hut before the cry died on the wind. He had felt more than heard her scream. Somehow he sensed her fear and knew her need.

Dimly through the sounds of the raging storm her voice now came to him: *Galen!*

She could not straighten completely. The cramping in her belly hunched her forward. Heavily she leaned against the wall of the passageway, waiting for the pain of the contraction to pass. When it did, she straightened and fumbled in the darkness for the latch of the outer door.

Just as she released it and the door swung inward, a strike of lightning splintered the black sky. To eyes accustomed to night, the brightness was blinding. Rhyca instinctively threw up her arm to protect her sight. When she lowered her arm, he was there as if materialized out of the storm itself, not a mere man but a force of nature sent to her.

And, as the wind whipped her unbound hair and pressed the thin shift she wore so tightly to her swollen form that her body might as well have been naked to his stare, she acquiesced to the will of the gods. Finally and forever she accepted this man, this *Roman,* and sank into the refuge of his arms.

Galen saw the spasm of pain rake her body as she lay stretched upon the pallet. At Moguntiacum, his posting before Deva, he had been present when the woman of one of the men in his cohort had given birth. It had been the dead of winter, in a snow-covered army camp. The father had roused him out of bed in a state of terror: The baby was coming out feet first. Galen had summoned the legion's surgeon. With twenty years of experience in delivering the illegitimate offspring of Rome's army, the man had managed to save both child and mother.

Nonetheless, for this birth Galen did not hold such optimistic expectations. He was not a surgeon, and having assisted in but a single birth hardly gave him the credentials of midwife. Too, he knew this baby was coming much too early. But early or late it *was* coming. . . .

Her fingers clawed at the cloak that covered her. She clenched the woolen fabric and balled her fists at her sides. She would not give voice to her pain. She felt wetness seep from beneath her lashes.

"Cry out, Rhyca. It will help you to bear the pain.

She shook her head—but then another contraction came. The pain tightened and turned within her. She moaned aloud. Her back arched against the floor, and her eyes flew open in terror.

"I cannot do this," she gasped.

"Yes, you can." Kneeling beside her, he took her hand into his own. Gently he wiped the tears from her face. "When it is worst, squeeze."

At once her hold tightened until her nails dug into his palm. He continued to speak, "It will crest in a moment. Hold on. Hold on to me."

She did and instinctively began to breathe in quick rhythm with the pain. After a moment it was over. She lay back, spent and terrified because she knew it would come again.

And it did.

Closer together and ever stronger, the contractions came, one barely ending before the next commenced. Sometimes the agony was so unbearable it was all she could feel of her body. It filled her mind. She tossed her head from side to side, but could not displace it. "I cannot do this," she sobbed.

"You must and you *will*." He moved to take both hands. "Look at me."

When she obeyed she found the gentleness in his eyes a stark contrast to the firmness of his grasp and the sternness of his voice.

"Listen to me, Rhyca. Do not think of the pain. You have no choice but to bear it."

Once more she was swept up in the throes of a contraction. She gasped and looked away, her eyes darting wildly about. Though he had built a fire and its glow was sufficient to light the hut, nothing in the familiar space captured her mad gaze.

His implacable voice brought her focus back to him. *Me. Look at me. Only me.*

"Damn you," she cried. The pain was all there was. She began to weep openly and closed her eyes. "Let me go. I want to die!"

"No. No, you do not." Again his voice forced her concentration. Only this time he soothed her brow with his hand as well. "Did you hold so lightly to life, you would not have survived that night. Now open your eyes."

She felt one of his hands carefully take hers. As she opened her eyes, he tightened his hold.

"This night you are *not* alone."

The labor continued throughout the night while the storm outside the hut's walls raged. Often his face and voice were hazy in a red mist of pain, yet she never lost her way. He never let her go. She held fast to his hand, unaware of the crescent-shaped wounds her nails cut into his flesh.

It was just after dawn, when the darkness that had gathered around the dying fire began to give way to gray, that she delivered the child. Stillborn. In the womb its neck had become wrapped by the cord. Birth had strangled the baby.

As she slept the blessed sleep of exhaustion, Galen wrapped the tiny body in his cloak. The scarlet mantle of a Roman centurion was the only link to the identity of its paternity that he could provide the unborn soul. At sunset he would bury the corpse.

He laid the wrapped bundle aside and turned his attentions to the living. Pale and still, she lay upon a fresh bed of bracken. She had not spoken, not even to ask about the baby. He was certain she must know it was dead. No doubt to her thinking no more did she need—or want—to know.

He went to her and knelt at her side. The storm had ended before dawn. A brisk wind still blew, however, rustling the roof thatch overhead and entering the smoke hole to make the flames of the newly banked fire dance. He knew their heat would soon warm her pale flesh, so pale as to be almost translucent—like alabaster and just as cold to the touch. Purposely he had let the fire die earlier, hoping to discourage a fever from setting in. Now he realized there was no danger of that. What unsettled and concerned him was her pallor and the piercing luminousness of her eyes. She seemed to look right at him without seeing him.

Rhyca gritted her teeth and stared up at the smoke-blackened ceiling. Why did everything sound like a baby crying? The wind in the thatch . . . the morning birds. . . .

Tears stung the corners of her eyes, and she blinked fiercely. Suddenly she could bear it no longer. She struggled to sit up, turning toward the silent figure at her side, and collapsed into his arms. She buried her face in the hard muscles of his right forearm and clung to him, seeking the strength he had always embodied for her.

If he were caught off guard by her actions, he did not show it. He brought a hand to her hair. "Weep, Rhyca," he murmured as he began to stroke her head tenderly. "Grieve your loss."

She pulled away instantly and leveled a cold and fierce gaze. "I have no loss to grieve," she hissed. "Or have you forgotten the life lost was Roman?"

"But of *your* womb," he answered quietly. She saw his hand reach out and felt his fingertips upon her wet cheeks and trembling mouth. "He was *your* son."

"Curse and damn you!" She screamed and tried ineffectually to push him from her. She had not wanted to know whether it—the being that had been inside her—were boy or girl. Without a gender or name she had not lost a child, but an unwanted burden.

He refused to loose his hold, yet allowed her to give vent to her heart's pain. When she had finished, he folded her more deeply into his embrace.

"Weep, *domina*."

Rhyca closed her eyes and helplessly began to sob, the deep inner sobbing that somehow cleanses the soul.

When she at last ceased, she felt emptied of strength and the will to fight. Though the pain was still within her, her body could endure no more. She surrendered to exhaustion and a blessed unconsciousness that finally released her from pain and gave her rest.

Galen held her to his chest, her heart against his. His hand stroked her hair. For the first time in his life Galen Mauricius, Cohort Centurion and warrior of

258

Rome, knew helplessness. What he felt for this woman was no bond of need or circumstance, nor was it guilt or lust. Though he held her, it was he who felt enclosed, overwhelmed by something that was taking his breath away.

He lifted her head from his chest, laid her back down upon her bed, and rose. For now he could not concern himself with the knowledge that gnawed at him. While she slept and could be left alone he had a task to perform.

Silhouetted against an orange and purple sky, he buried the tiny body in a box made of the planks that would have formed its cradle. Upon one board he had carved the words *Dis Manibus*—to the gods of the dead. Before setting the lid in place he removed the wide leather band worn as a bracelet about his left wrist. It was a legionary's purse, able to be opened only when off the wearer's wrist. With valuables then inserted or removed through a folded slit on the inside, the purse made it difficult for a thief. Too, its nondescript appearance usually escaped attention, as it had his Ordovician captors' months earlier.

From it he removed a gold coin. The dead must be ferried across the River Styx to Hades. In the mouth that had uttered neither cry nor drawn breath he put the coin with which Charon, the boatman, could be paid by the soul of Rhyca's son.

Her head hurt . . . behind her eyes . . . a burning pain. . . . Even to draw simple breath was an effort.

She wanted to sink back into the darkness . . . but knew she could not.

Rhyca forced herself to open her eyes. In the murky glow of a single oil lamp she saw someone hunched at the hearth, setting wood to build a fire. She tried to sit up, and promptly discovered she possessed no strength. It was as if her limbs had turned to lead. Helplessly she lay back upon her bed to watch the shadowy form nurse the fire.

His head was turned from her, and so she could not see his face. Yet she had no doubt who he was. In the storm he had come to her, and had been with her when—

Suddenly memory returned. A sickening pain filled her. She swallowed hurriedly and hard—lest she spew openly on the floor. Squeezing her eyes tightly shut, she willed for the return of the sleep that had before delivered her from suffering, granting her peace.

A moment passed, and she heard his approach. She intended to feign sleep, but his touch upon her forehead startled her. Her eyes flew open, and she found herself looking up into his face.

"I did not mean to wake you." He withdrew his hand, sitting back on his heels as he continued. "I merely wanted to be certain there was no fever."

She stared at him, hearing his words, but ignoring them. It was in the weariness of his eyes that she saw all that he had done. Self-consciously she ran her hand across her flattened belly. Beneath the furs that covered her she was naked, and yet she felt no sense of shame. She knew the hands that had tended her had touched her only with tenderness. "You are a rare man, Roman," she whispered.

He shook his head in mute denial and slipped an arm beneath her shoulders to help her sit forward enough that she could drink from the gourd he put to her lips.

After a tentative sip she tried to turn her head. She had no hunger and no will to swallow the warm barley and leek broth.

His insistence that she do so was as firm as his support of her shoulders. "Whether you want to or not . . . you will eat."

Self-pity welled within her. "For what purpose?"

His brow arched sharply. "Survival, *domina*. Or has it become your intent now to *give* your violators what they then could not take?"

She stiffened and glared at him. She wanted to take a mouthful of the broth and spit it in his face!

As if he could hear her thoughts, he smiled, the corners of his eyes crinkling in amusement. "Do it," he taunted softly, pressing the bowl again to her lips. "But know that for every mouthful you spit out, I will pour a like amount down your throat and force you to live."

Through the anger that gripped her there slipped reason's gentling touch: Of all men this one least deserved her fury. Feeling suddenly very tired, she sank back against him and drank.

When the bowl had been drained, he placed her carefully down upon the bed. "Tonight I will sleep just outside the door. If you need me, you have only to call out."

Rhyca watched him stand. But as he turned to walk away, she realized a sense of fear she had not felt when he was near. "What . . . what if I did not want

261

you to go? What if I wanted you to stay . . . with me?"

"Then I would stay."

In the silence that fell between them no sound could be heard save that of the fire burning in the hearth. Then, almost lost in the hiss of the flames, a single word was softly spoken.

"Stay."

In the days that followed Rhyca's strength steadily returned. Outwardly she would soon be as she had been before the rape. Inside, however, she was changed forever. Her womb had nurtured a child, yet her arms were empty. That scar upon her heart would not heal as quickly as had her body.

On the third day, strong enough now to do so, she went to the site where Galen had buried her son. A few strides back from the farmstead's clearing just within the tree line, the grave lay nestled between a pair of tall pines.

She stood for a long time looking down at the small mound of freshly turned earth. It all seemed without meaning: That a life destined not to be born should even have been formed; and that she should have endured these months of anguish only to have it all become meaningless. Or had the goddess purposely taken her child before he could know mortal life? And if so, why? Was hers designed to be a punitive or merciful act?

Against a chill that did not exist, Rhyca wrapped her mantle more tightly about her. Suddenly she knew she was not alone. Though no sound had betrayed him, she felt his presence. She looked up and saw him watching her from a respectful distance. From his cross-armed stance it was evident he had been there for a while. Now that she was aware of him, however, he came forward.

She avoided his eyes, unwilling for him to see the tears in hers. "Dafydd told me where . . . where it was," she explained, stepping away from the grave.

"I was not certain you wanted to know."

"I did not—until now." Despite the warmth of the morning's sun and the weight of her mantle, she shivered. She knew he had to see it. Then, too, in the last several days there had formed a bond, an understanding between them that required no words. He seemed to know her thoughts and emotions . . . her needs. "I have not thanked you for what you did . . . and for the burial," she stated quietly.

"It is not necessary."

"Yes. Yes, it is." Suddenly the thin thread of pride to which she still would cling seemed to snap. "It hurts," she whispered, at last lifting her gaze to meet his. "I did not expect it to—at least not this much."

"The pain is still fresh. It will dull with time."

She nodded, but only in acknowledgement of his reply. She stared at him. His features had not changed. The square-cut jaw was no less chiseled or the lean hardness of his face any more softened. And yet as she looked upon him now, she saw his gentleness—as much a part of him as his strength.

"You should go back now."

She shook her head numbly and set her thoughts upon a different course. "No. I want to talk to Dafydd." She pointed toward the boy listlessly dragging a stick through the thick mud left by a puddle of rainwater near the oxen's stall. "He is worse today . . . withdrawn and sullen. Earlier when I tried to talk to him, he barely spoke. He told me where to find the grave, then walked away."

The dark eyes turned in the direction she indicated. For a long moment he silently watched the small figure now squatting down beside the pool of mud. He then returned his attention to her. "You must remember, Dafydd only learned of it yesterday. The conditions of the path after the storm kept him from coming that first day. And though he seemed to understand when I explained what had happened, surely now he has questions and is confused. After all, he is a small boy facing his first true meeting with death."

Rhyca shook her head again. "No. It is something more. I know Dafydd. Yesterday afternoon, when you brought him inside to see me after you had told him, I could sense it. He is confused, yes, but he is also angry, bitter—and a part of him blames me for what happened . . . for the stillbirth."

Galen saw pain shadow her features. The instinct to protect her reared, yet he resisted the urge to comfort her. "Dafydd does not blame you. He knows what happened was the gods' will. But perhaps he, too, feels a loss?"

Fully aware that he was relaxing his recently imposed boundaries upon his emotions, he still continued. Compassion and gentleness resonated in his voice as he lightly touched her shoulder. "You are more mother to him, Rhyca, than his own. It would make sense that he feels in a way that he has lost a brother. Go back to the hut. I will talk to him."

She looked at him without responding. From the quizzical expression on her face he thought she intended to question his motive. He was not prepared to offer an explanation and so turned, walking away. Not hearing any following footsteps, he was satisfied she would return to the hut and bed. He gave his concentration over to the matter of the small boy still hunkered down next to the mud. The questions Dafydd had posed several days earlier now suddenly held possible new meaning. Galen hoped he was wrong.

All the while he crossed the compound, however, an inner voice warned him he was not.

He came up from behind the boy and was nearly upon him when the blond head whipped around. Piercing blue eyes, burning with rage, were trained instantly upon him.

"You're not going to stay—are you? You're going to leave!"

Surprised by both the accusation and the vehemence with which it was made, Galen was not immediately sure how to respond to either. He squatted down beside the boy. Purposely he avoided eye contact and stared at his loosely clasped hands. "Why do you say that, Dafydd?" he prompted gently.

"Because I know," the child spat back without hesitation. "I heard. I heard some of the warriors in the hill fort talking. They don't pay much attention when I'm around. If I hear, they don't think it matters. *I* don't matter . . ."

Without turning his head Galen glanced at the boy. Dafydd was blinking, fighting back tears as he also struggled to hold on to his anger and continue. "They . . . they said you g-gave your word to Cerrix—you and the others would not try to escape until spring. That's why you don't have a g-guard anymore."

While the boy's statement revealed nothing that should not have been common knowledge among the Ordovices, Galen felt a sense of unease. The threat to the success of Agricola's plan was very real if other details of the agreement with Cerrix were being as casually discussed about the hill fort. "Did the warriors say anything more?" he asked, keeping his tone even as he raised his gaze.

The boy shook his head. "Is it true? Did you promise not to leave only until spring?"

"Yes. When first I was brought here, I believed it was important for the safety of my men to remove the chance of escape and recapture. I ordered their obedience and made a vow to Cerrix. As long as the legions were in winter quarters it was pointless . . ." He stopped, realizing the boy was not listening to his explanation. "Dafydd, listen to me. I never—"

"What about her?" The blue eyes flashed with renewed fury and accusation. A grubby hand came up to wipe an errant tear. Instead, a muddy streak was left upon the pale cheek. "What about Rhyca? Who will protect her and take care of her when you go? Or don't you care anymore b-because her baby was born dead?" Quavering with emotion, the child's voice finally broke. He gulped a needed breath. "You just wanted *it*—not us!"

The boy's words were like a barb entering his flesh. Galen clenched his hands into fists. The inner voice had been right! So had Rhyca. She had warned him of the boy's growing attachment. And yet how could he fault the child for this secret want when he himself

266

had conjured the same? However briefly or fleetingly—he, too, had thought of the three of them as a family.

Ironically Galen had seen Dafydd as the bond that brought them together while the boy had instead seen Rhyca's child as that link. Hence his questions of fatherhood and how a man might make a woman his. Everything that had been asked that day all made sense now. But how to repair the damage done, the false hopes given and now dashed?

"Dafydd . . ." He winced as the boy lowered his head, pretending not to hear. "Even if Rhyca's baby were alive, it would change nothing. I told you a long time ago, I am a soldier. A family and home are not choices I can make. I have my duty, my orders . . . When it is time, I must go."

Without raising his head, Dafydd responded tearfully, "What about us? Don't you care?"

Galen sucked in his breath. The barb ripped and twisted within. "Yes, I care. But I do not have the right to act upon those feelings. My first responsibility must be to the oath I swore—"

"To a stupid silver bird!" the child spat, his head at last coming up. His eyes brimmed with tears. "It's not fair."

Galen tried to reach out, but Dafydd pulled away and stumbled to his feet. Galen allowed him the gesture of independence and assertion, remaining seated on his heels. He hoped at least to get the boy to speak his thoughts further. Mere expression might serve somehow to show the infeasibility of his longing and the foolishness of his fantasy. "What is not fair?" he asked gently.

"Everything!" With a balled fist Dafydd swiped at the tears rolling down his cheeks. He hobbled away and was a half dozen meters from where Galen still squatted when he uttered his final words. *"I hate you."*

Galen rose to his feet, intending to follow. He was stopped by her voice.

"Let him go. It is time he saw the truth."

Caught off guard by her approach, he turned and stared at her. In full sunlight the strain and weariness he had noted earlier at the grave site were now even more evident. The shade and filtered light beneath the pines had kindly concealed the lines about her eyes and the gauntness of her face. Still, there was no shadow deep enough to hide her sorrow.

"I thought you had returned to your bed," he stated with unintended harshness. He nodded toward the boy crossing the yard. "How much did you hear?"

She clutched her mantle to her as she followed Dafydd's movement. "Enough."

Galen flinched as he then saw in her unblinking stare the shimmer of tears. "You know I never meant to hurt him, Rhyca."

"I know." A sad smile touched her lips. "I was told by someone who has been very kind to me that time will dull pain. Give him time, Galen. He will be all right. He will understand."

"What about you?"

The intimacy in his voice sent a shudder through her. Rhyca drew a deep breath and forced herself to meet his gaze. Staring into the dark depths, she felt the same sense of awakening awareness she had felt when she would have accepted his kiss. A part of her was terrified, and yet there was another part of her that recognized the rightness of what she felt.

"I need time as well," she whispered in reply to him—and to herself.

Fourteen

In the sunlight that streamed into the hut through the opened doors her hair shone like pale gold. She was wearing it loose, rather than plaited in the single braid she usually wore, and he wondered as to the reason for the change. Unbraided, its length cascaded nearly to her knees and each time she bowed her head, a heavy wave of flaxen tresses would fall forward over her shoulders.

She knelt down to adjust a sandal strap, and, as her face disappeared from his view beneath the silken veiling of her hair, he had his answer.

This trip to market was her first appearance in the hill fort since the stillbirth. Knowing she would be a target for both attention and gossip, she would do the little she could to shield herself from probing eyes.

His thoughts were confirmed as she straightened and ran a nervous hand over the front of her. Her gown was one he had not seen her wear before. Red, of the color of the sunset sky, its knee-length overtunic was patterned with small checks containing the same red, added to a soft pink that matched the dawn, and gold the color of the sun at midday. Even ungirted and left to drape loosely, the tunic did not disguise her slim figure with its now narrow waist and flat belly. Those who had not already heard of the loss would need only to look upon her to know she was no longer with child.

She stood up, and he took her arm gently, steadying her balance.

"Are you certain you are strong enough?" he asked. He brushed aside an errant strand of hair from her cheek while studying the oval face and the flawless ivory skin for signs of fatigue or pallor.

Rhyca stared up at him without answering. Each time now that they occurred—that warmth in his voice coupled with a gentle touch of innocent physical contact—her reaction was the same. It felt as if a surge of light were penetrating the darkness of her very soul. Instinctively she was as afraid of this sensation she could not name as she was in want of it.

She backed away and moved to take up a basket lying by the doorway. Galen reached for the two heavier ones filled with vegetables and cloth-wrapped gourds of butter cheese. She balanced her basket upon her hip and smoothed the front of her tunic. "We should go," she said quietly, avoiding both his question and his eyes.

The silence that had greeted his disclosure dissolved into a rush of angry voices. Mouric concealed a complacent smile, reveling in the discord and strife that now filled the room. The faces of the men seated around him revealed all manner of disbelief, shock and outrage. In many a furrowed brow he saw the contemplation of vengeance, while fury clenched blue-veined hands into fists of rage.

From his speaker's position, standing in the council's midst an equal distance from each member seated cross-legged in the circle, he turned an eye to the only one whose features retained a masklike appearance of calm. "Your silence is noteworthy, my king," he offered with a veiled sneer. "Might it be that what I have imparted has caused you at last to see the ruinous outcome of this scheme—and our people's fate should you not abandon this folly?"

Without detectable emotion the man he addressed slowly lifted his gaze. "From the beginning, Mouric, you have stood in opposition to this plan for peace. I ask *you* . . . might it be possible that your personal feelings have caused you to offer a reporting which is less than objective?"

Mouric ground his teeth against the release of a heated oath. He knew Cerrix's tactic. With this shrouded accusation he would goad Mouric into a loss of temper, thereby exhibiting to the council his rival's quickness to anger and loose control, proving once again the younger man's unsuitability for leadership.

"Surely I have misheard you, Cerrix," he gritted, swallowing hard, "for only a fool would cast suspicion upon my deed or question my honor when the truth of what I have said can be so readily attested. Eight other men scouted the same terrain as I. They, too, saw the burned villages and charred fields. The mountain lairs of our brothers to the east are now inhabited only by old men, wailing women and fatherless children. The entire fighting force of the tribes along the river valley of the Severn has been cut to pieces—massacred by an army of Rome led by the very man—" he gathered spittle in his mouth and spat—"with whom you believe peace is possible!"

Cerrix glanced over at the glob of spit darkening the clay floor near his right knee. As a father might dismiss the tantrum of a petulant child, he shrugged in amusement, dismissing the pointed gesture. "Agricola did not strike the first blow." He looked up and responded evenly. Then, lowering his gaze from the man before him, he focused upon the circle of seated men. If the council sensed in him the slightest doubt or apprehension, they could withdraw their sanction of the plan. Hence he could not waver in his outward confidence.

One by one he sought the eyes of each member. All the while he spoke in a cool and purposeful tone. "Nor does the news of this action by Rome's governor come as unexpected. With the advent of the last moon we heard rumblings of a possible Roman reprisal against those tribes who had lent either men or support to the attack upon the cavalry outpost. Moreover, we knew when Agricola left the plains and marched into the hills to undertake that action. It was, in fact, word of that campaign's completion which dispatched Mouric and his scouting party into the Severn valley a fortnight and a half ago."

"*Reprisal . . . action . . . campaign's completion . . .*" One of the council members spoke out in a soft, chiding manner. "I caution you, Cerrix, do not continue to disguise the invaders' deeds with words that are purposely less distasteful to the ear. Your choice of rhetoric is a deceptive cloaking—like a hag

273

wrapped in a mantle of golden threads. What the eye perceives outwardly may be pleasing indeed, but what lies beneath the finery remains ugly."

There issued from the council an immediate murmur of approval for the elder's admonition.

Cerrix nodded in respectful acknowledgement. "My apologies, Berec. Such was not my intent to mask the loathsomeness of Rome's revenge. And yet I must remember and remind that our brothers' fate was one of their making. With their attack upon his cavalry, those federations sent a clear message of challenge to Agricola. Hence, for them the path of war was a course of choice."

"And what of *our* choice—for peace?" asked another voice. "We must be as certain of the motive behind our choice as we are of the rightness of that choice." The white-haired figure seated across from Cerrix then opened his arms in an encompassing gesture as he looked from side to side at his fellow council members. "Is what dictates our decision the cowardice of old men whose hearts have ceased to beat with youth's valor? Do we cling to this hope like a babe to its mother's teat because therein we find comfort? Or do we truly believe within this plan there lies the only hope for our people's survival—and the preservation of our honor as well?"

"Enough!" rasped a third voice with marked impatience. "This has already been debated and decided. As Cerrix has stated . . . we knew by Agricola's own declaration that he would move against those who raised the banner of revolt. The question is now whether we shall allow emotion to eclipse reason. Shall our outrage over the slaughter of our brothers in the east dissuade us from pursuing peace with Rome?"

"I disagree. The question is whether or not it is prudent that we continue to believe in Agricola's commitment to that peace." Aware of the eyes turned swiftly upon him and the surprise his unexpected response had elicited—for with these words he appeared to be entertaining the idea of war—Cerrix rose to his feet, facing Mouric across the open space in the middle of the circle. He held the kingship and must therefore act as a king. The council might advise and caution, but only he could rule.

"Do I hear you correctly, Cerrix?" Berec, the elder who had criticized him only moments earlier, tilted back his head and pinned him with a penetrating stare. Thirty years ago Berec had been a great warrior, and while his body had succumbed to the ravages of time, his mind was still sharp and his counsel wise. There was no other member whose words held as much sway. "Are you expressing doubt? Or are you suggesting that if Agricola intends to break his word by launching an offensive against the tribes who had no part in the rebellion, we should strike first?"

"No. But not to consider all possibilities would be the course of a fool." Cerrix turned to look at Mouric. "Where are the armies of Agricola now?"

An unmistakable gleam entered his rival's eyes as he answered. "We followed the wake of their destruction to the fortress that lies at the head of the Dee Estuary."

"Deva . . ."

". . . from whence the captured patrol came," elaborated the voice of a second elder.

275

Cerrix knew that in the wake of those bitter utterances there echoed a silent chorus of suspicion. There was not a man among them who did not know of the significance of that particular Roman encampment. It was at the foothills of their own mountains that Deva lay. With careful reconnaissance and advance scouting, only five days would separate Agricola's legions from the Ordovician hill fort. And with knowledge of the terrain, such as that acquired by a small, specially trained group of men who had previously forded the secret river crossings and traveled the hidden mountain passes, that same march could be made in three.

"Perhaps your unfailing trust in the bronze-skinned centurion has been misplaced," offered one of the elders almost snidely. "Perhaps this was Agricola's intent from the beginning. While his soldiers now clean their swords and shields of Ordovician blood in preparation for the next slaughter, he awaits his 'emissary's' escape and return."

Before Cerrix could respond, Berec spoke again. "In light of the facts presented this, too, is a possibility which must be considered—that the Roman officer is not here for the purpose we believed. But first, there is another thought which gnaws at me." The eyes of the aged warrior returned to the pair of standing men. "Mouric, this time it is *your* silence that I find noteworthy. Your brevity in answering Cerrix's last question contrasts greatly with the profusion of vivid details you were so willing to offer only moments ago. Indeed, I find it strange that you have not attempted to fan the flames of suspicion now burning among us. Nothing would support a path of war more—and your bid for the kingship—than evidence of an impending assault by Agricola into our mountains. Of course . . . that evidence cannot be offered—if it does not exist."

"What are you saying, Berec?" Mouric's snarling reply resounded loudly in the sudden quiet of the room.

Cerrix smiled. He knew what the old man was asking of the younger. He turned to face his rival. "I believe what he is saying is that you have not finished your report. I ask you again, Mouric. Where *are* Agricola and his legions now?"

Hatred filled Mouric's eyes. "I would not be so smug, my king, for the truth does not vindicate him wholly. Five days ago Agricola departed Deva's walls, leading an army of horse and foot soldiers."

"In what direction?"

"Northwest, following the river to the sea. When he reached the coast, he turned southward. By keeping to the ravines and cliffs, we were able to follow without being detected by their scouts. We tracked them for a day to be certain. He is headed for the Menai Strait and the Isle of Mona."

Thoughtful for a moment, Cerrix considered the information Mouric had revealed. The Isle of Mona had long been a stronghold of resistance to Roman rule, with the islanders making good use of their isolation and resultant freedom. While Mona's priests instigated revolt and provided spiritual support, the island's granaries fed the mouths of those who raised their swords in rebellion against Rome. It was therefore not surprising that Agricola should now marshal his legions for an attack upon the druidic sanctuary. Yet, as disturbing as this news was, it was also strangely comforting. Clearly Agricola was adhering to his vow, striking out only against the forces of insurrection.

"If that be his direction and the target of his attack, then he has broken neither his word nor the terms of the agreement which I swore a blood oath to honor." Cerrix paused to allow his next words to ring clearly, intending their meaning to linger long after they had voiced his conviction and will. "Nothing that has been learned this day has convinced me otherwise. As long as I am king—or until Agricola breaches *his* oath—our course shall not be altered."

In the descending silence Mouric carefully watched for the council's response. It was quickly obvious that none of the elders was prepared to challenge Cerrix's decision outright.

No matter, he thought with a grim smile. The garrote was around the king's neck, and Cerrix would tighten it himself with this insistence upon pursuing peace! It would not be long before Agricola's battle fleet joined with his army and crossed the Menai Strait. Once the island lay devastated, its warriors butchered, the sacred oak groves put to ax and the granaries to torch, Rome's governor would cast his eye back to the mountains. He would feel the prick of the single remaining thorn of armed and organized resistance. Oath or no, with less thought than he might give the scratching of a bothersome itch, he would move to pluck out that thorn.

Bowing his head to hide his widening smile, Mouric assumed a posture of humility. With opened hands he gestured helplessness. "With this thereby decreed . . . I have nothing else to offer the council, save my sword. Unless—or until—it is needed, my presence here is unwelcome. Too ardently do I remind you of what you dread to face. Therefore, I will take my leave to fill my empty belly and find my bed."

Without waiting for a dismissal, he exited the circle and made his way toward the door. None spoke out to stop him, nor did he expect any to. Fools! If it would require the actual sight of dust clouds kicked up by Agricola's marching soldiers upon their own horizon to prove the threat and need for war—so be it! The battle would be brought to them soon enough.

Outside, with his eyes not yet accustomed to the bright sunlight, he paused to blink and decide upon his next course of action. A full moon had allowed him and his band to travel throughout the night. Their dawn return to the hill fort and his immediate summons to appear before the council had precluded obtaining any sleep. He was bone-weary, and while there was much to which he should first attend, the temptation of the physical comforts awaiting him in his hut tugged at him strongly. Even at this moment his belly rumbled with the need to be filled. . . .

"I had heard you were returned."

He turned toward the approaching figure. With the rising sun at the man's back combined with its glint off the bronze and gold bands about his throat and forearms, Mouric did not at first see the face clearly. When he did, he needed to force himself from staring.

There had been a hope that with time and healing Balor's facial injuries might have become less disfiguring. But while nearly a moon had passed since their infliction, the broken jaw and slashed cheek seemed little improved. The bone had not mended cleanly, and the resulting misalignment and protrusion in the jaw line caused a distortion of Balor's lower features. Pulled toward the red and jagged scar that ran from chin to ear, his mouth looked to be frozen in a grotesque and permanent half leer.

"Yes . . ." Mouric rubbed his own jaw self-consciously as he finally mustered a response to the greeting given. "We returned at first light."

If Balor had either detected his unease or surmised its cause, he did not reveal it. In fact, his only emotion seemed to be one of excitement. "How was it . . . with the council?" he asked in a low voice, casting a cautious glance about him. "Your new bedmate, the youth Ynyr, says that Berec and the others demanded a reporting almost upon your first steps through the gate."

His sarcastic laugh followed, and the warrior stepped closer, lowering his voice still further. "You know Cerrix expected the news you brought back to support his cowardly cause—this path of peace. Ah, to have been an insect in the roof thatch and had the opportunity to view his face when he heard Agricola and his Eagles were on the march!"

Mouric looked at the man in sudden irritation. "Do not sharpen your war spear yet, my brother. The council has not withdrawn their support of Cerrix's kingship, nor has our king abandoned his path of peace. Because Agricola marches on the Isle of Mona, he sees no threat or cause to take up the banner of revolt. By his decree we shall continue to wait—like sheep—for the wolf to leap out from the thicket and strike."

Balor reached out and clamped his hand upon his comrade's shoulder in reassurance. "But when he does strike—this wolf of Rome—then the elders shall know

280

of their error in allowing Cerrix to wear the *torc* of king. Heed my words, brother. It will be around the neck of a warrior that they next place it, the neck of a warrior with the courage to face the dark ones in battle—your neck, Mouric. Your neck will wear the boars' head *torc!*"

"Would that the eyes of others saw so clearly!" Mouric answered. He did not bother even to try to conceal his delight. Balor had put to voice the thoughts that would be soon upon the lips of many.

Then, in imitation of Balor's action, he clasped his hand upon the man's shoulder in an embracing gesture. "But soon. Soon all shall see what fools these pursuers of peace be!"

Balor nodded. "The swords that have been sheathed shall clear their scabbards and then . . ." He removed his hand from Mouric's shoulder. But instead of dropping the arm to his side, he brought his hand to his face and traced the ridged scar. "And then those who have thus far been shielded shall know the stroke of naked blades."

Mouric knew instantly of whom he spoke. He tightened his grip, digging his fingers into the warrior's shoulder. "This promise I make. When I am king, my brother, I shall command it—the cur that scarred your face and dishonored your soul shall be yours and yours alone."

Balor stared at him in intensity and silence. Slowly he shook his head and removed Mouric's hand, clasping it for a moment with his own. "No. He shall be *ours*. We shall share him, for he has dishonored you as well. By what he now does, he vilifies your name and disparages your manhood as can no other deed."

"What are you saying?" Mouric stiffened. Suspicion washed over him like an icy wave. "In my absence what has occurred?"

"Much. Your brother's widow . . ." Pausing and turning his head, Balor looked out toward the hill fort's southern perimeter where in the cold sunshine farmers and inhabitants of the settlement alike were now amassing around the wares and goods of market displayed upon the dew-wet ground. "Let your eyes seek her out, and then tell me if you do not see what all have seen—and whispered behind your absent back for a fortnight now."

Immediately Mouric looked in the direction indicated. His gaze swept across the small clusters of gossiping women. He knew Rhyca would not be among them. Nor was she likely to be found anywhere near the large fires or pits, in which meat either roasted on spits or boiled in the ground from heated stones dropped into the water. These were the places that drew the warriors, sitting in groups and passing a large wooden tankard of mead to be refilled the day long from a close by vat.

At the edge of the market area a woman dressed in red captured his eye, but her back was to him. Yet there was something gnawingly familiar about her . . . something in the way she stood . . . with her head held high. She was talking to a man Mouric recognized as a herder, one of twenty or so who took the tribe's flocks and herds to high summer pastures. When autumn approached they brought the animals down, returning them to their owners.

"Do you not see her yet?" Balor asked.

Mouric heard the sneer in the other's voice and resumed his search. From the corner of his eye he then caught sight of an all too recognizable form. There could be no mistaking the size and darkness of him for any other's—nor the arrogance.

Without looking right or left the slave centurion passed through the marketgoers. He made his way toward the woman in red. In the same instant three separate actions coalesced as one: The Roman reached her side, she turned to look at him, and Mouric was at last afforded a full view of her face and form.

Barely had he made this recognition, when a second realization struck. "The child she carried . . ."

He spun his head to look at Balor.

"Dead," the man responded with an accompanying nod that answered the unvoiced question. "A fortnight ago. They say it was stillborn."

Mouric's mind raced. While it had been speculated that the rape might have bred her child, no one had known with certainty the babe was not her husband's—save he. Mouric alone had known of his brother's impotence. With this knowledge he had dreaded the birthing of the bastard as the time when all would know from its coloring the truth of its fathering. But if the child were now dead, could not the secret of its siring have died as well—thereby sparing him any added humiliation? It was dishonor enough that his kinswoman had been violated by his enemies without having it known that she had nurtured and nearly given life to their putrid seed!

He looked back at the woman whose survival had caused him so much disgrace. "Who attended her?" he asked, forcing a casual tone to his voice as his gaze again traveled her slender form.

Balor's derisive snort and harsh laugh told him the answer before it was given.

"Her Roman lover—who else? For what man would do that manner of thing unless the woman *were* his? Look at him," Balor goaded. "Look where he stands— at her shoulder. Watch him long enough and you will see his hands upon her. I tell you . . . he has made her his—and he cares not who knows it. In fact, since your absence he has come to flaunt it openly—his possession of your kinswoman."

The fury surged from his testicles into his gut like molten fire. Mouric knew his spear brother's words were true. Yet he also knew that until he held the kingship, he must suffer this new outrage in silence.

He turned his sight from the couple—he would see no more—and fixed his stare pointedly upon the scar on Balor's face. "You alone know and understand the want for vengeance that burns in my heart, for you alone have suffered as greatly. Yet you are right to have spoken of delayed revenge. Now is not the time—but soon."

Though Galen kept his eyes focused upon the skin-clad herder, he only half listened as Rhyca negotiated with him. At the moment the man's price to bring her cattle down from summer pasture, and to see to the sale or slaughter of surplus animals not required for breeding in the spring, was of far less import than the pair of warriors Galen had spotted near Cerrix's hut. Balor and Mouric together were a dangerous combination. Too, he could not help but wonder what news Mouric and his scouting patrol had brought the council. Since Rhyca's and his arrival this morning in the hill fort, he had hardly heard another subject upon the tribesmen's lips save that of this unprecedented dawn assemblage of their elders and king.

"A word with you, Centurion."

The entreaty, faintly spoken and uttered in Latin, drew Galen's attention immediately from his thoughts. Moving only his eyes, he looked about him. A half dozen meters off to his left he spied Sita's bald head and massive shoulders bobbing behind a cart laden with tall pottery jars. Beyond the Thracian and the wine cart he was unloading there was an open area in which a score of boys, some of an age with Dafydd and others nearly at the edge of manhood, were playing *baine,* a Celtic ball and stick game. Later, once they were fueled by drink, the warriors of the hill fort would show off their own skill and prowess upon the playing field. For now, however, it belonged to their sons.

Discreetly Galen waited for a break in Rhyca's conversation with the herder before he bowed his head to signal his intent to depart. She nodded, and he withdrew from her side, making his way slowly toward the game in progress—and the man who had beckoned him.

He hoped the ruse would be effective. Certainly he knew it was necessary. Since their dispersal among their Ordovician masters, he and his men had been denied almost all contact. Communication had been reduced to a few guarded statements or surreptitious glances in passing. While his men's isolation from one another had aided Galen's mission by lessening the possibility of a conspiracy among themselves and against him, his separation from them had also made it impossible for him to know each man's temperament and mood. He was very much aware of the fact, as well, that he had no control over their actions and must put his faith in the belief they would continue to obey their orders.

A few feet from the cart he halted. Legs planted apart, his arms crossed over his chest and his eye on the game, his was the relaxed stance of an interested spectator. To anyone watching him he looked merely to be engrossed in the boys' sport—oblivious to the presence of the bearded slave on his left who lifted wine-filled *amphorae* over the side of a cart.

After a moment he heard Sita's voice. "Have you heard that the bastard, Mouric, is returned?"

Galen raised a hand to his mouth and feigned a quick cough, thereby nodding in response.

He heard Sita release a loud groan of exertion followed by thudding and sloshing sounds which would indicate the lowering of yet another heavy wine jar to the ground. From the corner of his eye he then saw the man lean forward, resting his hands upon his knees and hanging his head as though to catch his breath.

"Rumor has it that he and his band were sent to verify reports that Agricola has marched against the eastern federations. The same rumor says those hill forts are now piles of smoldering charcoal and that Mouric tracked our new governor and his army to Deva, then down the coast."

Galen was careful in his reaction—and not just for the benefit of any possible onlookers. How much of the plan Sita might have guessed at—and how far the Thracian would actually support it—were both questions whose answers he now did not have the time to determine. "The truth of rumors cannot always be trusted," he responded, cocking his head nonchalantly to one side. "However . . ." He brought a hand up to scratch his jaw. "If this one *were* true, why the coast? What would be Agricola's objective—his target?"

"Mona."

As Sita straightened and returned to his labors, Galen watched the ball of hide and straw being batted down the playing field. His thoughts, though, were not upon the game.

It was not unfamiliar to him—Mona—the name Sita had spoken. Before his departure for Britain Galen had been instructed in the province's geography. But while he knew of the existence of the island sanctuary and its long-standing function as a supply base for those in open rebellion against Roman occupation, he did not know enough.

"How long?" he asked. In his voice he heard a hoarseness he knew had nothing to do with any effort to speak furtively. He cleared his throat. "How long," he repeated, "before Agricola's legions would be ready to march again . . . against their next target?"

An eruption of cheers and shouts from the crowd of boys drowned out the beginning of the Thracian's answer. Galen strained to listen.

". . . a week to traverse the coastline. Then if the fleet is not there—weather is always a factor—he must dig in and await the ships to ferry his troops across the strait. Once the fleet arrives, however, it should be no more than a matter of another week or so before the entire island lies wasted. Therefore, while it is difficult to say with certainty, Centurion . . ."

Once more the thud of pottery and the slosh of wine sounded.

". . . my guess would be less than a month."

. . . *less than a month.* . . . As real as that effected by a fist driven into his belly, Galen experienced the sudden sensation of having had the wind knocked out of him. As he sucked in a lungful of air, a silent oath formed. Time had nearly run out—and it was the eastern tribes' attack upon the cavalry outpost that was to blame.

Not one of the plan's creators—not Agricola, Vespasian or even Cerrix—had foreseen the possibility that the nonaligned tribes would delay their reprisal for Frontinus's spring massacre until his successor's arrival in Britain. Yet once that blow to Roman dominance had been struck, Agricola had been left with no other choice. Not even to provide the six months of truce agreed upon by the proponents of the plan could he ignore open rebellion.

And so, instead of having until spring to accomplish his mission, Galen now had less than a month. Again he swore silently. He felt cheated. Had he had the time initially promised, peace would have been obtainable. He was sure of it. But now he was sure of nothing, except that he would be leaving this place soon.

Soon. The thought was like a hammer smashing through his thoughts and battering at his defenses, releasing emotions he was unprepared to face. He pushed them aside to consider the tangible reality of his leaving. Under what conditions was he fated to go—and in what capacity to return? Would it be emissary come back as friend, or escaped slave as conqueror?

The emotions he had denied wrenched in his gut. And yet he knew it was for the gods to decide man's destiny, not man. When it was time, he must be guided by their hand.

Suddenly from the playing field a second outburst of voices and laughter served to wrest him from his thoughts. Different from before, these were neither the light, carefree tones of play nor the heated yet innocent flare-ups born of competition.

"Hear you what he says? He wants to play!"

"Play? When he cannot even walk?"

More laughter erupted, followed by a chorus of jeers and mocking taunts: "How can *you* play, cripple? You must run to play. Yes, *run*—not hobble!"

"Hobble, hobble, hobble."

Inwardly Galen winced as the crowd of youths then began to trickle one by one or in pairs off the playing field. He knew for what manner of new sport they abandoned the old. Such was the way of boys on the path to manhood. To feel strength they sought out the weak among them, the one who was different—the one who presently stood at the farthest edge of the field, alone.

To his chest the small figure clutched his pitiful semblance of the curved playing sticks the others brandished. He had meant no harm. He had only wanted to play, to join in the fun. But in his desire to be no different than his peers, Dafydd had forgotten that he was. Now their cruel contempt would punish him for his forgetfulness and foolish presumption of acceptance.

Galen frowned. He had endured the same. However, for him it had been his dark coloring and his father's inferior auxiliary status which had set him apart. And he would have suffered worse than he had, but for his height and brawn. But Dafydd did not possess those attributes of strength.

He possessed another.

The thought formed instantaneously as Galen, watching the youths converging upon the small boy, clearly realized what he witnessed. Despite his confusion and fear, Dafydd clearly intended to hold his ground. Pride swelled Galen's heart. The stoicism and detachment that had been drilled into him for more than two decades was swept away as he whispered unwitting encouragement. "Yes, Dafydd. Do not run. Face them!"

Amid clouds of dust, stirred up by their earlier play and still hovering in the windless air, the amassing line of threatening youths encircled their target.

"Away with you, cripple!" cursed one of the leaders. "You're not wanted here."

His followers joined in at once in a singsong chant of spiteful voices:

> *"Hobble, hobble,*
> *cripple, cripple.*
> *Away! Away!"*

Galen clenched his jaw until the muscles ached. That he recognized what he was witnessing as a rite of passage—meant to humiliate more than hurt—did not make it any easier to watch.

From within the circle several thuds, a grunt, and then an outcry of pain sounded. There was another wave of laughter, and the boys stepped back. Given the quick boredom of youth, their sport suddenly lacked novelty. The tight cluster of bodies broke apart to reveal a solitary form balled up upon the ground.

Though he wanted to go to him immediately, Galen remained where he was, watching in relief as he sat up. After several moments had passed and the game was resumed, he skirted the playing field and noiselessly approached the child.

Dusty, his tunic torn, Dafydd sat in the dirt, wiping his bloodied nose on his sleeve.

"You did well to stand up to them. Now you must learn to fight them."

The blond head slowly swiveled. As Dafydd looked up at him, Galen was afforded a full view of his face. Large tears rolled down his dirty cheeks as his quivering lips fought to remain together—no easy feat as his thin chest heaved with both exertion and emotion, and he could not catch his breath.

"I c . . . c . . . can't," he finally stammered. A shaking sob rose within him and escaped, and he lowered his gaze in shame.

Galen squatted down beside him. "If a man does not learn to stand, he will forever be forced to crawl."

"That's what cripples do—crawl!"

Dafydd's swift retort contained enough anger that Galen knew the will to fight was still within. "No," he answered quietly. "That is what cowards do."

Dafydd shook his head. "You don't understand," he whispered almost to himself. "It's easy for you to have courage. You have strength. I have this!" He clenched his hand into a fist and pounded his deformed foot. Then, as if to dare Galen to deny his truth, he lifted his gaze and stared straight at him.

Galen snared the boy's wrist. His own gaze never

wavering from the blue stare, he forced Dafydd's hand back to his chest. He could feel the racing heartbeat through the child's clothing. "You also have this—a heart that does not recognize the limitations of this." He wrapped the fingers of his free hand around the misshapen foot. "The choice is yours, Dafydd. If you want to learn, I will teach you how to fight."

He released his hold and stood, waiting for a response.

But the boy's head never lifted. Blankly he stared straight ahead.

"Very well." Galen shrugged and turned to step away. He had taken only a few strides, however, when he heard a small voice.

"When? When would you teach me?"

The same sensation that had struck him earlier, when Sita had given his estimation of time remaining, occurred again. Galen drew a deep breath. Once again he ignored the tug of emotions.

"Tomorrow." Without looking back, he walked away.

Fifteen

It was not a sudden or strange noise, but the absence of a faint and familiar one, that roused her from sleep. Rhyca sat up. So used had she grown to the rhythm of his breathing that not to hear it had wakened her. She looked across the hut's darkened gray interior. Since that night after the storm—and her request that he remain—Galen had made his bed there, in front of the doorway.

At first the arrangement had been for practicality's sake; he would be near should she have need of him. And yet, with her strength's return and her recovery from the stillbirth, he did not go back to the oxen's stall. Perhaps he merely waited for her to make the decision that she needed his presence no longer. Or perhaps he had realized what she had: There was a rightness in his nearness that did not recognize any unseemliness in their sharing a common roof. Too much else had they shared to be ever again as they had been before.

She strained to see his empty pallet and started as she heard dull, thudding sounds—not like the ringing strikes of an ax, but similar in the rhythm and repetition of the blows.

Her curiosity aroused, Rhyca grabbed and donned the linen undershift lying folded neatly atop her gown and tunic on the floor beside her bed. She scrambled to her feet and padded barefoot to the door. Almost as an afterthought she snatched her striped cloak from its peg before heading outside. There she paused beneath the shelter of the doorway's lintel to toss the woolen wrap about her shoulders.

A fine mist shrouded the morning, making more dark and mystical those scarce and brief moments that occurred between the night's end and the sun's ascent. She shivered and directed her gaze left, toward the source of the sounds which had lured her from her warm bed.

There, in an area between the hut and the palisade, an area Galen had reclaimed from the encroaching woods and in which she had considered planting a second garden in the spring, he attacked the earth with pick and spade. It was not furrows for later cultivation of crops that he dug, however, but a single hole for what purpose she had no inkling, as its width was much too small for a storage pit.

Unwilling to alert him to her presence, she remained in the doorway. Despite the bone-chilling damp that made her glad for the cloak wrapped around her, she noted that he labored clad only in *bracae*. Whether the exertion heated his blood sufficiently or he did not feel the cold as did other men, she was not sure.

For several moments more she watched him. She could not help but be reminded of the larger pit he had dug—not so long ago if one counted time by each fall of night, but a lifetime ago if one measured that same time by events and change.

Finally she stepped forward and crossed to where he now sat on his heels seemingly gauging the depth of the hole. "I could ask what you are doing . . . ," she stated by way of announcing herself, "but as the answer is obvious, I shall instead ask why."

His head turned, and he looked up at her. She found the tension in his features impossible to understand. In fact, since their return from market the previous day, he had been of a peculiar temperament, reserved as though somehow distracted by private thoughts. Without responding, he looked back at the excavation. Apparently its depth satisfied him, for he then rose to stand upright. "The hole is for a post, a post that will act as a target for arms training."

"Target? Training? I do not understand."

A deep breath lifted his bare chest as the fingers of his right hand stabbed through his hair in an impatient gesture. "It is not very complicated. I am going to give Dafydd the training in arms which Ordovician law would deny him because of his deformity."

The bluntness of his response coupled with the actual meaning of his words took her aback. She could manage only a strangled reply. "Why?"

He scowled. And for a brief moment, she was certain he would refuse an explanation. But then he answered, his tone terse. "Yesterday Dafydd was beaten by a group of older boys. He had the courage not to run, even when they were through with him, but it will happen again. He must learn to fight and defend himself."

Rhyca heard only part of what he had said. Her mind had filled with horrifying images of the small boy facing a pack of attackers. She leveled an incredulous and accusing stare at the man before her. "Are you saying that you watched this attack occur—and yet did nothing to stop it?"

The muscles in his jaw tensed instantly. "It was not my place."

She felt a surge of anger. But where a month ago she would have acted immediately upon it, lashing out at him without second thought, ready to believe the worst of him, now she could not. He had waged too fierce a battle for her faith. She knew of his capacity for compassion and the genuineness of his feelings for the boy, and so her anger was tempered with confusion.

She drew a calming breath. "Not once in the time I have known you, has that iron collar about your neck meant anything more than a discomfort. Hence I cannot believe it was to maintain your slave's status which kept you from going to his aid."

He appeared to allow himself a small smile. "Indeed, that was not what I meant." He then grew serious once again. "I say it was not my place, for to have interfered would have tainted him with greater shame than that of having suffered a beating."

"Better that he be shamed than hurt!"

"Such would be a woman's response. A man's reality, however, is far different."

Her first instinct was to bristle at his cocksure arrogance. Then she realized that the matter-of-factness of his words carried neither judgment nor derogation. "It matters little . . . ," she retorted coolly, "woman's

296

belief or man's. Dafydd is neither. He is a boy—a crippled boy."

A sudden and inexplicable anger flashed across his features. "If he is continued to be treated as such, he will never be anything else!"

She flinched at the harshness in his voice and wondered what force had served to strip away his normally inexorable control over his emotions. "Why are you doing this?" she asked.

"Because it must be done." Without warning he reached out and took hold of her arm, drawing her to him. In contrast to the firmness of his grasp, his gaze was almost beseeching as it sought and held hers. "Listen to me, Rhyca, and try to understand. He cannot cling to your skirts any longer. Nor can you continue to watch over him, protecting him. Yes—he is a boy. But one day he will be a man. He has to learn to fight . . . and he has to learn to kill."

"No!" The word escaped before she could stop it. Revulsion swept over her, and she would have staggered backward had it not been for his hold upon her. Yet even as she struggled to refute his truth, she felt a draining sense of resignation overwhelm her. Helplessly she met his hard stare. "By what right do you make that decision for him?"

He shook his head. "I did not make the decision. The choice was his. Once he made it, I only offered to teach him."

"But by what right?" she asked again, suddenly trembling. Unnoticed, her cloak had slipped from her shoulders, and it now lay at her bare feet upon the cold, wet ground.

"A self-imposed one." He bent and retrieved her

cloak. Upon straightening, he met her gaze once again. In his dark eyes there was that same strange look of unyielding resolve melded with an unspoken request for understanding. "He has no father, and no warrior of the tribe will claim him. Therefore, as long as I am here—I shall. I hereby claim him, and henceforth do I exert that right of possession to teach him what he must be taught to be a man."

She blinked back sudden, unbidden tears. "You are not an Ordovician warrior, Roman. And whether you acknowledge it or not, the collar of slave still binds your neck. You can make no claim of possession."

The dark eyes seemed both to harden and heat. "I told you once before . . . I am no slave. As a soldier I will lay claim to whatever I desire to possess—as a man, I will maintain my possession over whatever I hold dear and have chosen to protect."

She swallowed hard. The ardor of his words was unmistakable. But might she be wrong in what she sensed in his stare—and heard in his words? "I did not know 'protection' was a means to possession," she offered stiffly as she attempted to regain her composure.

He stepped behind her to settle the cloak about her shoulders. She felt his warm breath against her ear. "Then, you know no more of armies than you know of men, *domina*."

Heat rose to her cheeks, and she spun to face him. But the question she would ask remained mute upon her lips. Was it the asking she dreaded—or his answer? Or was it the questions she must first ask of herself that stilled her voice?

He had stirred something in her no other man had

ever touched, something she had not known even existed. Yet it was there, deep within the wellspring of her being. When he had kissed her, she had felt it—briefly, but undeniably—the sensation of more than mere need. She feared to name it, and still . . . she knew. Could it be that what she felt for this man before her might be the farthest emotion from hatred?

She diverted her eyes, frightened and ashamed of the madness of her thoughts. "Tell me," she finally whispered. Nervously she pushed a wave of sleep-tangled hair from her face and steadied her gaze. If what she believed he was saying was true, she needed to understand his actions. "Of what possible purpose, or worth, is possession—without ownership?"

His brow arched ever so slightly. "Some would say they are one and the same."

Rhyca shook her head. "Such would be a man's belief. A woman's is far different."

As he no doubt recognized his words returned to him, a hint of amusement softened his features. But then it was gone, replaced by a look of sharp intensity. "In what manner?"

Without hesitation she answered. "Possession is but taken."

"And ownership?"

"Ownership must be—" Suddenly she stopped, realizing what she was about to say. No, not yet. Not yet was she ready to make that admission even to herself.

"What must ownership be?" he prompted.

Once again she shook her head, this time in a gesture of dismissal. "It does not matter . . . not now."

Just for a moment he looked at her so intently she

was certain he intended to press her for an answer. But he did not. "What about Dafydd?" he asked instead.

She knew instantly this was to be his price. She fought to affect a demeanor of deceptive calm while looking pointedly past his right shoulder to where a halo of light above the horizon now signaled the imminent dawn. As soon as the sun had risen, the hill fort's gates would be opened, and Dafydd would make his way down the steep shale path.

"You know how he is . . . ," she began slowly, "once he has set his mind upon a thought or course of action. Nor does he wait well. When he wants something, he wants it at once."

As she listened to her own words, she realized she had already made her decision. She had less right to deny Dafydd this path than Galen had to set him upon it. She gathered the folds of her cloak to her, intent upon heading back to her hut. "You should return to your labors," she suggested quietly. "Complete your preparations that you may be ready when he comes."

"Then, you accept this?"

She felt the tears gather as she stopped midturn. "No. But neither will I resist it. Dafydd has made his decision, and I shall respect it. I ask only one thing of you."

His dark head inclined in grave respect. "If it is in my power—"

"It is." This time it was she who initiated the unwavering stare between them. "He is all I have, Galen. If he must learn these things, teach him well."

* * *

"No! Do not swing. A slashing blow not only wastes effort, it announces your intent. Always thrust . . . low and direct. Two inches in the right place and the blow is always fatal. And make sure that when you withdraw, you stay behind your shield and keep yourself covered. Thus."

With his instruction and demonstration given, Galen stepped back from the post and passed into Dafydd's eager hands the wooden sword and wicker shield he had fashioned for the boy.

Watching this handing over of weapons, Rhyca felt a succession of conflicting emotions. On one hand she felt a sense of solemn reverence for a timeless ritual of manhood—the knowledge and skill of the father imparted to the son. On the other hand, however, she felt sorrow and a sense of loss. Even now Dafydd's young face mirrored the expression of methodical concentration she saw in Galen's. How long before she saw in the child the hardness and cold detachment as well?

She winced in pain and looked away. Had she erred by allowing this? Whether the weapons were of wood or steel, in his learning to wield them, the boy was being taught to kill. *Kill or be killed.* Over the past several days, those words had gnawed at her persistently; they added the unwanted ballast of reality to her turmoil and made her even more uncertain. What was disturbing her, the events happening outside her door—or the changes occurring inside her heart?

Amid the reservations and incertitudes that had of late entered and left her mind with the ease of the autumn breeze through the now baring trees, one agonizing constant remained: How could she—for the

301

sake of this mere emotion, which she feared even to name—have so easily disregarded what this man had been before he had entered their lives? Despite these past months with her and Dafydd, by his own admission his had been a life of only soldiering and war. Surely one would not have to scratch the sun-bronzed flesh very deeply to find the Roman soldier still within. Indeed, she could see and hear evidence of that stranger each time she witnessed these training sessions with Dafydd. His clothing, speech and pupil might be for the moment Ordovician, but this man who was now such an integral part of their lives was still Roman. And yet as each day passed, that fact seemed to matter less and less—or not at all.

She looked back to the post, to where Dafydd now clumsily feinted and lunged in practice attacks against the stake.

"You are trying too hard," Galen admonished, as he paced behind the child, watching him.

Dafydd stopped and lowered his sword. Rhyca recognized at once the dejected, defeated slump of his shoulders.

"I can't do it." The bitter proclamation was then punctuated by the thud of his sword and shield hitting the ground.

Rhyca held her breath in anxious anticipation. While half of her rejoiced, the other half looked for Galen's response. In watching him these past days she had realized his intent was twofold. Dafydd's deformity had precluded him from participating in the games and normal play that served to develop in his peers their coordination and confidence. Galen strove to instill in him both. Still, he was a man accustomed to training soldiers. How would he react now to a child who simply recognized his physical limitations and thus wanted to quit?

Fearing the worst, she stepped away from the palisade where she had been unobtrusively watching.

Galen waved her back immediately. "You know, Dafydd . . . ," he stated evenly, "agility and speed are offensive strengths. But in the matter of defense neither is as important as good judgment and careful, deliberate reaction."

As he spoke, he unlaced the neck closure of the close-fitting leather tunic he wore. Pulling it off over his head, he then threw the garment aside. As it was without sleeves, and the late afternoon's temperature now cooled rather than heated, she questioned the reason for its removal.

"It is not necessary to outfight an opponent in order to win," he continued. "You merely need to outthink him. By watching your attacker closely and correctly anticipating his actions, you do not have to move more quickly—just first. In effect, his own size and speed will then work against him."

Though he had been feigning not listening, Dafydd's squint of disbelief betrayed him. Rhyca saw Galen's own gaze narrow in recognition of the pretense.

"Come here," he ordered, beckoning the boy toward him. "Face me."

In that instant she knew why Galen first had stripped. It could not have been greater—the contrast between this half-naked man, his body hardened and well muscled by years of training, and the small, thin boy.

To Dafydd's credit, however, there was no fear in his step as he approached the man. His eye traveled the other's length, sizing up the far greater height and weight, with a look of wary disdain. "This is stupid," he declared.

"Watch and listen," Galen countered. For the first time sharpness had entered his voice. He moved to stand opposite the boy. "If a foe charges at you, he has but one course of direction—straight toward you. You, however, have a choice. You can try to stand fast—which is what most opponents will expect. Or you can move. That action alone—moving—will double the likelihood of your staving off the first attack. But because you can move right or left, your odds improve again. Your attacker not only has to anticipate that you will move, he has to correctly guess in which direction. Too, the faster he is coming toward you and the larger he is, the more difficult it will be for him to alter his attack in mid-approach."

Rhyca saw the light of sudden understanding ignite in Dafydd's eyes. She saw the eagerness as well.

"C . . . can we try it?" he asked.

Galen nodded. "Remember to wait until the last possible moment before you act. And concentrate. Do not let there be anything in either your expression or posture which might provide me a clue as to your intent."

If she had not seen herself what happened next, Rhyca might not have believed it. Yet exactly what Galen had predicted would happen occurred. He lunged at the boy and just as he was nearly upon him, Dafydd pivoted on his left foot and stepped backward. The choice of his direction—to the left—was made more unexpected by the fact that to move thusly he had to utilize his bad foot.

Only with effort (and she suspected an exaggerated bit of show) did Galen avoid landing on his face. There was, however, no need to exaggerate his pleasure as he returned to where Dafydd stood—also grinning.

"Well done." He tousled the blond head in affection and pride.

"Can we do it again?"

Galen shook his head. "The point has been proven. Perhaps now, though, you will heed my words, Dafydd, and believe in yourself. Strength comes in many forms, from many sources. From pure physical size, yes. But also from love and courage."

Bending down on one knee, he drew the boy into arm's length. "And while there are many forms of love—a soldier's love for his empire; or a king's for his people; or a man's for his family, his children, his woman—courage comes from a single source."

He laid his large hand upon the child's thin chest. "Here. From within. It is not a courageous man who has no fear, but a fool. A man with courage is one who *is* afraid. Yet for the love of what he holds dear he will face his fear and confront it. That, Dafydd, is the truest test of bravery . . . and the ultimate measure of a man."

Rhyca strangled a cry and clutched at her breast as she averted her gaze. She could watch no longer—but not only because her eyes burned with blinding tears at the sight of this man of such strength and might now on bended knee before the crippled child. She could not watch because she had seen enough—and heard too much.

Like the sharpest of blades his words to Dafydd had sliced through to the core of her being where they had shattered the darkness there into a thousand shards of agonizing truth and brilliant joy. The goddess forgive her! *She loved him.*

A shower of sparks shot upward from the hearth. But none of the gathered warriors, including the one who had just now carelessly tossed the heavy log onto the brittle embers, paid the arcing fire storm any mind. Despite the quantity of drink consumed this night, the senses of the six were not so dulled as to miss the clear affront contained in the offhand remark of an instant ago. The eyes of all were upon the one who had uttered the careless comment—and he who had taken rightful offense at it.

The speaker now sat in stone silence, his every instinct alerted. Above the dagger hilt at his waist his right hand hovered. While his hesitation indicated that he was not prepared to be the first to seize his weapon, and hence to kill for the sake of his mistake, neither was he prepared to die for it.

Mouric glared at the man seated across from him. Scornfully he eyed the poised hand. "Complete your thought," he growled in a slow, sneering challenge. "You began it, now finish it."

The other shook his head. "I would rather offer my apologies. This subject was ill-chosen. It was not my intent to shadow your honor, Mouric, but to bring to light the dark gossip of others. Allow me to dismiss the matter."

Mouric's answer was a definitive shake of his own lime-stiffened locks. Casually he fingered the hilt of his blade. "I shall instead take you at your word and reputation, Llewen, and believe that the thoughts you voiced are those of others."

Relief instantly eased the tension in the man's round face, and its previously ruddy color subsided. Those who knew him also knew of his fondness for rumor and gossip. He was worse than a woman, yet his penchant served a purpose. Little occurred within the hill fort that escaped his note. Hence when he spoke he was listened to.

Mouric then smiled balefully. "And I shall believe that you are now speaking as a loyal friend, so that I might know what those who are without the courage to speak to my face are whispering behind my back."

In ready consent Llewen nodded. "Theirs is an indulgence in ribald humor, Mouric," he promptly offered. "They say your sister-in-law's preference is for the thrust of a Roman spear, and that he who wields this particular spear relishes the duty—for in its performance it is you he pricks. After all, it was you who hung the collar of slave about his proud neck. Too, whatever else may be said of this dark bastard, he follows a warrior's code ever to seek out the most formidable foe. He knows it is you—not Cerrix—who commands the respect of the tribe's warriors. Hence it is in you that this officer of Rome's army sees his worthiest adversary."

He paused to permit an outburst of spirited agreement from the others to be heard.

Heartened by this flattery and his comrades' quick expression of faith and loyalty, Mouric was able, with the aid of a mouthful of wine, to rinse away the taste of bile that had risen in bitter response to the initial portion of Llewen's speech. He nodded for the man to continue, confident more praise was yet to come.

He was wrong—and nearly spewed his next swallow.

"And yet for your part, Mouric, it appears that you intend to do nothing as this Roman centurion now wages a most guileful manner of battle against you. He is doing it through her—or should I say *in* her . . ." Llewen paused, laughing softly at the clever turn of his words. Upon realizing, however, that none of the others appeared to share his humor, he hastened to return to his previously somber tone. "Each time he buries his shaft within her, he conjures your face. With every thrust your manhood is thereby diminished and his enhanced, your honor disparaged and his affirmed. But it is not only your manhood and honor that he mocks. It is ours as well."

"Llewen is right," a voice agreed angrily. "This Roman slave is making fools of us all—and seemingly with impunity! First he is allowed to walk about in near total freedom. Now he dares to bed one of our women. Where will it stop?"

"And *who* will stop it?" Llewen peered at Mouric. "Many say it should be you. They say even that you should have already acted and wonder why you have not. You are the one he has most assailed."

"And what would these cowardly purveyors of lies and gossip have my brother do?" From his favored position, a darkened corner beyond the reach of the fire's light, Balor's voice exploded with the force of his outrage. "The dark-skinned bastard enjoys Cerrix's full protection, with the council's blessing!"

Llewen shrugged as he squinted in the direction of the shadowy form. Rather than argue with him, he appeared to patronize Balor instead, conceding. "You are right. Perhaps . . . presently . . . nothing *can* be done to or against him. But what of her?"

His gaze slid back to Mouric. "She *is* your kinswoman, and with no other male to claim dominion, she is solely your responsibility. She possesses some wealth in property. Certainly that rare occurrence—a woman with land—would pose to most men an enticement. Too, with her belly gone and her brat stillborn, she is not at all unpleasing, to either the eye or the flesh. Some would wonder why you do not at least take her from this slave—for yourself."

"Do they forget what shame she represents?" Mouric snorted in disgust as he tossed his head proudly. "To take my enemy's leavings . . . I think not!"

"Some say you do not, because you *can*not."

At this retort Mouric's eyes narrowed into slits. He leveled a furious gaze, his fingers wrapping about the knife hilt. "What are you saying, Llewen?"

"*I* am saying nothing. *They* are saying—they are saying that for all his cowardice, your brother may have been in some ways *more* of a man than you. After all, he took a woman to wife and seeded her."

Mouric nearly choked on the bile and ire that rose in him. Nothing that had been said to this point enraged him as did this last remark. And yet despite the molten fury heating his blood, he possessed the presence of mind to know that this erroneous belief as to the siring of Rhyca's child was preferable to the truth. And yet, how could he allow the belief to stand, that Keir had been—in any manner—more man than he? No matter which posture he chose, he was damned!

"Since when does a warrior of proven courage need to defend himself against such prattle?"

With Balor's question eliciting only a few weak nods of agreement, Mouric realized the seeds of doubt had been planted. To even these men—his spear brothers and comrades-in-arms—his manhood would lie in question without proof through demonstration.

"What you do with your sister-in-law, Mouric, is your decision," Llewen continued. "But as the brother of her husband, and her only living kinsman, you have rights. Indeed, in the time of our grandsires, a man shared his wife freely among his male kin. Take what is yours by right of ancient law. At least you will have proven yourself able. Then toss it aside, thereby exhibiting to all your pride in refusing to accept the 'leavings of your enemy!' And, you would be showing this arrogant Roman his place. Make him watch as you take what he thinks is his. And if he dares try to stop you . . . Regardless of Cerrix's grant of protection or the council's support, you have every right to kill a rebellious slave."

Like dry tinder touched by flame, there was an immediate and fervid reaction to Llewen's prodding. An instantaneous chorus of shouts and crude encouragements erupted from the gathering of men whose sensibilities—and urges—had been fired by drink and talk.

"It is time he paid for his pride," Balor acknowledged. He looked toward Mouric.

Mouric knew his brother's unvoiced thoughts. Whatever the oath Mouric had sworn to keep the Roman alive, it would indeed be nullified in such an instance. But there was much more benefit to this plan than any of these men could imagine! Were Mouric able to kill Rome's emissary, Cerrix's entire scheme for peace would unravel like the threads of a rotten cloth.

"Perhaps it is time she felt the thrust of an *Ordovician* spear—and he the vengeance of Ordovician steel."

As one low voice spoke aloud the thoughts upon the tongue and mind of each man, Mouric's own loins stirred—not at the images provoked by the drunken suggestion, rather the anticipation of Cerrix's defeat. He looked at the faces of the men about him.

Beneath the questioning stares and furtive glances being exchanged there was an unmistakable consensus. In choosing to lie with a Roman, Mouric's kinswoman had not only forfeited all rights to respect and protection, but she had committed a crime for which this was but a meting out of just punishment. And as for her lover, a slave whose insolence mocked the manhood of the entire tribe, death was just punishment indeed.

In fact, of the five men either reclined or seated around the hearth, Mouric noted that only the features of one man retained a neutral countenance. Off to the left, just within Mouric's field of vision, a sleek recumbent form rolled leisurely from his back over onto his belly. Ynyr cupped his chin in his hand. He was attentive but also unmoved. Given his own preference, he would not feel the outrage the others felt. It hardly mattered to him whom the Roman bedded. If he felt any emotion at all, it was no doubt mild amusement at the need of other men to prove between a woman's thighs their own manhood. Behind his palm and splayed fingers the handsome youth then appeared actually to hide a yawn.

Mouric returned his attentions to the others. Like the trumpeting of a war horn his next words would clearly signal his intent to those men awaiting his decision. He smiled in anticipation as he looked back over his right shoulder at Balor's shadowed face. "Tell me, my brother, who holds the gate watch this night?"

Sixteen

As he had so many nights of late, Galen lay awake. Tonight, though, his restiveness was worse than usual. No matter how he tried to empty his thoughts—to reach for sleep—she filled them. He could not leave off thinking of her and what had occurred this day.

During the training session with Dafydd she had seen something that had caused her to flee rather than to continue watching. And though she had attempted later to discount her reaction by acting no differently toward him, she had failed. He knew what it was that she had seen and fled from.

The knowledge that she still could not accept that which he was filled him with regret. There were things decreed by the gods that a man could not change—the course of a river, the direction of the wind, the blood that ran in his veins. He was, and would always be, Roman. And yet a part of him also felt relief.

His presence in this place was for but a single purpose: to serve the needs of Rome. Never, from the day he had sworn his oath to serve and obey, had he ever hesitated or wavered in regard to the performance

313

of any duty. He could not afford any more entanglement than he already had! First and foremost, he must keep in mind his purpose in this place and the fact that his time in it was growing short.

From across the space that separated them he suddenly heard her stir. Turning over onto his side, he rose up on an elbow and looked to where she slept. She lay on her belly, her head pillowed on her arm. Like a cascade of moonlight beneath a night sky her flaxen hair spilled about her bare body.

Immediately he rolled over again on his back and stared at the ceiling. Where once to live without the nakedness of a woman had been simple, to deny himself this woman was more agonizing than any blow or blade he had ever known.

The irony struck him then. By pure definition and circumstance he had been a slave since his capture—but it was only now that he felt enslaved. Enslaved not by the restraint of the iron collar that had been placed about his neck, but by the restraint of iron will he had placed upon himself! Damp with his own sweat he lay beneath this roof, his body alive with the want of a woman he could not have and would not take.

Swearing softly, he rose from his bed. For him there would be no sleep this night.

Rhyca lifted her head and looked to the room's center, to where he squatted before the hearth. Elbows on knees, weight balanced on the balls of his bare feet, he sat hunched forward with his dark head bowed, staring down at his loosely clasped hands.

Noiselessly she sat up, gathering and pulling the fur

about her shoulders. As if she were seeing him for the first time, she studied him, watching the reflection of the hearth's flames as their orange light danced across his naked torso.

Even in this state of utter repose he embodied absolute strength and power. None could look upon him and fail to see the warrior he was. But it was not with force of might that he had broken down her walls to instill love in hatred's place. It was with gentleness, in the form of what she had seen this day with Dafydd, that he had placed in her heart the feeling that now dwelled there.

Suddenly, though she knew she had made no sound, his head lifted and he looked at her. "Did I wake you?"

"No." She stared at his face. The play of flickering shadow and light across the chiseled features made his expression impossible to discern. Nor could she find clue in the tone of his voice. It seemed strained . . . but perhaps that was only in contrast to the broken quiet.

"You should lie down and go back to sleep."

She nodded, yet made no move to obey. The beating of her heart seemed suddenly to quicken, thudding loudly in her chest. As emotion swelled within, a desperate courage seized her. "Lie with me," she whispered.

Instantly the fingers that had been loosely laced twined and tightened. He stared at her for the longest time without response. At last he spoke. "Do you know what you ask?"

As she nodded wordlessly, an inner voice spoke to

315

her. He was surprised by her request, but not confused by it.

She rose to her feet. Clutching the fur to her, she crossed to where he remained motionless, watching her. He was like a graven image. Only the rise and fall of his chest betrayed life. Slowly she knelt before him and looked deeply into the dark eyes leveled at hers. "Yes, I know what I ask," she repeated softly.

He shook his head. "I cannot."

"Cannot or will not?" Her lips trembled as they formed the words. She knew she could not be wrong in what she sensed in him, for what she felt in him was twin to the ache within her. Why did he then refuse her? Why, too, when he had done so much to strip away her hatred, would he now reject her love?

Again he stared without reply. At last he spoke. But the sounds he uttered were foreign to her ear.

"I do not understand," she murmured helplessly.

"Yes, you do."

His accusation was like a cold fist about her heart, but he held her eyes so fiercely she could not look away.

"Within each of us there are many voices, Rhyca. Listen to the one that tells you this is not possible."

She shook her head. "That voice no longer speaks to me. The one I hear now speaks only of my want."

The line of his jaw tightened. "Think you I do not hear that voice as well?"

Almost angrily he looked away. "I desired you when your eyes were still hard with hatred, *domina.* While loathing burned in your soul, longing burned in mine. I have never wanted a woman as I have wanted you. Yet I have ignored that want. And now so must you."

At once she felt a flood of both joy and relief. But before she could even attempt to understand the feelings assailing her, he returned his gaze to her and continued to speak. Now, however, his voice was level and toneless—as if he had forced all expression and emotion from it.

"There can be nothing between us . . . not this night or any night."

Tears of pain gathered in her eyes. Still, she would hold fast to what she felt. The clamor of newly found love would not be denied. "Your command comes too late. There is already something between us."

"But it will not be acted upon. Believe me, one day you will look back upon this night and understand. And you will be glad for what now seems to be unfeeling harshness." He bowed his head as though to dismiss her. "Go back to your bed, Rhyca."

Disbelieving, she stared at the stalwart figure. She had admired and even envied his strength of will, but in it now she suddenly confronted an invincible enemy. "Is your conviction so strong?" she asked in angry bewilderment.

He raised his head. "No, *domina*. But my control is—strong enough for both of us. Some day you will see your weakness for what it is, and be grateful I did not permit you to act upon it."

She bit into the flesh of her lower lip to stifle the cry of shame and rage that filled her anguished soul. Then, as burning tears obliterated her vision, she struck out blindly. She did not know that she lost hold of her robe or care that its draping slid from her shoulders to her hips just as her right palm connected with the side of his face.

The stinging slap was followed by another. Her pain and anger spilled forth. "Curse your control!"

He withstood the pair of blows without flinching— as if he welcomed them.

That he did not react frustrated her even more. She moved to strike again, and at last he moved. In the same action he seized her wrist and pulled her with him as he rose.

"Enough," he whispered, his voice thick with emotion.

She stared up at him in an impotent rage. "Curse and damn you, Roman!"

"Yes, *Roman,*" he repeated. By the manner in which he spoke the name he seemed purposely to make of it an echo to her own curse of many months ago. "Remember it . . ." Suddenly his face became cruel. She would look away, but he cupped her chin, thereby forcing her to look at him. "And then remember when last a Roman touched you and fouled you with his possession."

"No!" She glared at him in denial of his truth and tried to shake her head. "I will not listen. You are not like those others—"

"I am," he hissed. The pressure of his hold upon her wrist increased. "I am *exactly* like those men who attacked your village, murdered your husband and violated you. I am a Roman soldier. In the name of my Empire I have conquered, killed and raped."

He then removed both hands from her and stood back. His eyes were confident and cold. Callously he

318

stared at her. "Is this the manner of man you want in your bed? The truth, Rhyca. Is it?"

The viciousness in his voice slammed into her with the force of a fist. Yet as she fought for breath, her fury did not rise—but fall. Like a single star shining in a black sky, the spark within her heart that was love's flame refused submission to the darkness.

"How dare you," she whispered, reveling in the look of surprise that seized his obdurate smile. "How dare you dictate what is to be or not be between us! And how dare you attempt to resurrect my hatred to suit your needs. You ask for the truth . . . it is this . . . I love you! That is the only truth I know—save one other: I do not see a Roman before me."

She took a half step forward and softened her voice. "I see only a man, a man of gentleness and kindness. When none of my own tribe would look upon me without disgust, this man bestowed upon me his respect and protection. My hatred he returned with compassion. He was with me when the life that was forced upon me was lost, and it was in his arms that I wept."

She reached out with her hand to touch his chest. "And it is in his arms I would know what I have never known—the pleasure of a man's possession."

He caught her hand. As his fingers closed around hers, he looked down at her strangely, deeply. There was a light, a look in his eyes, that made her tremble. His dark head bent lower, and she felt his lips brush hers. "I am sorry, Rhyca. I will not."

Mad instinct prompted her action. What she had seen in his eyes had been love. She pressed her mouth to his and threw her arms around his neck.

"Lie with me, Galen. Love me."

Whether she had actually whispered her plea or he had felt it in her kiss, it echoed now within him. His desire for her surged. Mithras god! He wanted her. He wanted her so fiercely that the sensation nearly sent him reeling. Still, there was his control which would not yield to mere emotion. . . .

Intent upon breaking her hold and setting her from him, he reached for her hands locked behind his head. But suddenly he felt something let go . . . slip away. . . .

It was odd—for he had always thought that if his control were ever broken, it would snap, like a rusted blade bent beyond endurance. . . .

He kissed her. Lightly at first, then harder. Her mouth parted beneath his, and the longing took hold. He tasted her, savored her. Like a starving man who is suddenly presented a feast, he wanted every bit of what was now his for the taking.

He slid his hand down to cup her breast. He knew she must feel the desire in his touch, for an answering shudder ran through the length of her warm, silken body. He entwined the fingers of his other hand in her hair to hold her steady as he deepened his kiss yet more. Fierce, fraught with need, it was almost punishing.

Yet she responded, opening her mouth to his tongue's seeking and pressing herself closer to him. Allowed easy access by her lack of any resistance, he slipped his hand softly between her thighs. Reining in his own desire now, he resolved to make sure this time for her would be different. He stroked her there gently. In giving herself to this Roman, she would feel no pain or shame.

Rhyca felt a rush of heat at his most intimate touch. An ache for completion and an instinct as old as the gods and goddesses guided her. She grasped his forearm and urged him down with her onto the floor. He leaned over her as she reclined beneath him. His body covered hers, and when his head bent down that he might suckle her breasts, she felt as if she had drunk a draught of one of Myrddin's magical potions.

Her arms lifted in an embrace, her hands sliding across the hard muscles of his chest. She did not care who this man had been or who he might become. For now she was drunk with desire and need—a woman's need for the man she had chosen to be her lover.

He ran his hand down over her belly, and down once again between her legs. Slowly his fingers worked their way up her inner thighs. As he stroked her woman flesh and then entered her opening, her body seemed to rise on the wave of a new and desperate desire. Her back arched against the floor, and she reveled in the sensations he elicited from deep within her—wet, hot, filled with light. . . .

Galen heard her soft outcry for him, a moan that both bespoke her pleasure and begged for fulfillment.

Suddenly he could not bridle his own need. He had readied her for his lovemaking and would delay that consummation no longer. He knelt between her thighs. Resisting the urge to thrust into her, he penetrated her slowly. Then, with his shaft sheathed in her heat, he took her hands from him and held them to the floor at either side of her head. He wanted to cry out at the exquisite torture of holding back his release. Instead he concentrated upon her.

"Open your eyes, Rhyca," he commanded softly.

"Look at me. I want you to know the man inside you, to know who it is that you give yourself to."

Beneath him she looked up. Her eyes were filled with passion, and her words came thickly. "I know him to be the man I love. There is nothing else I need to know."

With her declaration he was a man no longer in possession of any control. She was his only need. He thrust inside her, taking her hungrily, moving within her madly.

Her legs closed around him, and he released her hands. Her arms slid around his neck. Tentatively at first, and then surely, she began to match his motions. Each time he withdrew, he felt her thrust upward and toward him until he returned, filling her. She urged him deeper, and he answered. He leaned in, swelling and moving faster as the desire mounted and built in him.

Rhyca did not know what impulse guided her. She knew only that she needed what he gave. Her whole body quivered and throbbed with an enraptured desperation. She felt a sensation like fire at the bottoms of her feet. She arched up against him. With every impaling lunge she rose higher and higher. At the moment of his entry she had closed her eyes. Now she opened them.

The look of ultimate possession on his face told her what her body already knew: She was utterly, completely—and forever—his!

She closed her eyes again, surrendering to his mastery. Both physically and emotionally she strained upward to meet his passion.

Suddenly his maddened rhythm started to abate. His

frenzied, lustful jabs became a slow and sensuous tempo of deep thrusts. She tightened instinctively around him, and they were as one, their limbs entwined, their bodies grinding against each other. With her arms encircling his neck and her legs wrapped around his hips, she sought to pull him even deeper into the swirling heat of her loins.

And then it started . . . a white fire, intense and rolling, spreading through her. She clutched at him, and he stilled within her, allowing her passion to crest. A moan filled her throat and escaped her lips. But then, just as the waves of pleasure began to ebb, he thrust again. This new feeling, built on the fringes of the first, carried her yet higher. The sensation was nearly unendurable. Her head tossed wildly from side to side. Breathless and shaking, heaving in helpless passion, she clung to him.

For the sake of her pleasure, Galen had delayed his own. Now hearing her cry of completion, his own climax erupted. In burning need he groaned as his seed spilled into her. Whether with this act he defied fate or fulfilled it, he knew only that he had met his destiny—and it was she.

Fearful to move lest she somehow spoil or undo what had occurred between them, Rhyca lay utterly motionless. Eyes closed, she let herself float upon the unaccountable sensation that rippled through her in quivering waves. She reveled in the feel of him still inside her, and moaned softly when she felt him finally withdraw to roll over and lie beside her. But before her body might protest too loudly the loss of his, his arm reached across to slip round her and bring her to him so that she lay in his embrace, her head upon his chest.

Beneath her cheek she could feel his heart, its beating still quickened by passion's rhythm. Suddenly diffident in this intimacy that now existed between them, she wanted to see his face, needing to know what emotion might be betrayed there.

She started to rise up. But his free hand promptly laid her head back down upon his chest. While the accompanying low growl of displeasure left her little doubt as to his wishes, she was uncertain if he merely desired the continued closeness and feel of her against him—or whether he knew his vulnerability and would guard against her seeing it.

Regardless of his intent, she found that her momentary sense of shyness had vanished. She shifted onto her side to snuggle closer, bending and bringing her left knee up to rest atop his thigh. Despite the glow of the hearth's fire that bathed them both in a golden wash of warmth and color, the contrast of her pale flesh against his darkness was as great as that between the pair of naked bodies themselves. Where she was soft, rounded and curved, he was hard, sculpted and lean. And yet as different as they were to sight or feel, they were halves of the same whole—for surely no other explanation could account for the feeling of utter completeness she had felt when they had been joined.

Unconsciously she traced with her fingertips the path taken by her gaze across the bare length of him. By touch she followed the contours of taut flesh and thick muscle. Just beneath the nipple of his right breast there extended a faint scar that ran downward and around his side. A second scar, twin to the first, traversed his belly in a nearly parallel course.

She traced the smooth lines, wincing as she thought of the pain their infliction must have caused. For some reason, with her having accepted the man, she now wanted to know of the soldier as well. "Tell me about these," she whispered.

"The scars?" He tilted his head to look where she gestured.

"From where did they come?"

His low laugh sounded. "From where? From a sword point, *domina*—the sword of a Jewish rebel in Judaea."

She ignored his use of the now familiar title instead of her name, yet made memory to ask later why he would still persist in its usage. "What of this one?" She reached across his chest and pointed to a jagged, indented scar that ran much of the length of the inside of his upper right arm.

"A Batavian spear . . . hurled during a minor conflict along the bank of a river called the Rhine." He brought up and into her view his left arm, which had been draped around her shoulder. "Here . . ." He rotated his wrist to expose first the outside and then the inside of his forearm. The pair of small round scars he thereby exhibited appeared to mark the entrance and exit points of a wound that had penetrated his forearm. "This was a Rhoxolani arrow . . . in Moesia."

She raised her head to look at him. Strangely, his voice contained no trace of anger or animosity toward the men who had wielded their weapons against him. If she heard any emotion at all, it was of pride in the service he had rendered to his "Eagles." She remembered what she had overheard of his conversation with Dafydd, what he had said about a soldier's love for his empire. Did a love so strong preclude all others?

She pushed back the sudden and nagging thought, refusing to allow doubt to form more fully into truth.

"These odd and curious names that roll with ease off your tongue—Batavian, Rhoxolani, Moesia—they are of places?"

He nodded. "Of places and peoples." He then smiled resignedly before pulling her head back down upon his chest. "Such are the bodies of Rome's soldiers—those who survive. They are living maps of the Empire. With their scars they can chart each battle and war. No one knows better than they the price paid for conquest and the cost of victory . . . save those they conquer."

At once she sat up to stare at him. In his voice there had been a tone of such undisguised sorrow. . . . "Do you question it—or regret it—this manner of life you have lived?"

His dark eyes captured her gaze. Yet not with anger did he respond, but with a forceful, deliberate tone. "Regret is not a luxury a soldier may enjoy. To survive he must be disciplined and controlled, hard—not just in body, but in heart and mind. When he has been such long enough, there comes a time when he can be no other way."

Then he reached up to sweep the hair back from her face in a tender gesture of familiarity. She laid her cheek in his palm, and his voice softened as he continued.

"But sometimes in the dark of night, when weariness sets in, a soldier's control lessens—just a bit. Memories creep in. Memories of the endless miles he has marched in mud and snow and in blistering heat. He thinks of comrades he has lost, and lives he has taken . . ."

He paused and drew a breath which he let out almost as a sigh. "But then the control returns—and with it the discipline which has enabled him to survive. He remembers, too, the sense of purpose and pride that he has known only in service to the Eagles. For me it was home as well. Many said I was overly ambitious, driven to rise above the circumstance of my birth—the bastard son of an auxiliary. To possess Roman citizenship I had to enlist. But it was more than that. The army was all I had ever known . . . or desired."

"And now?" she whispered.

Galen drew her to him, clasping her to his heart as his mouth sought and found hers. Her voice, her question, lingered inside him: *Now?*

But for now he had no answer; for now he had only this moment. For whatever reason, the hands of fate had guided him into this woman's arms. He would accept—no, take—take and hold on to whatever amount of time he was to be granted with her.

"Now I know much differently," he whispered, hungrily taking possession of her mouth again, wanting to silence with his kiss her questions—and his own doubts.

Rhyca rejoiced in his words. He took her a second time then. Slowly, more gently than before, but with an underlying sense of urgency. . . .

She did not understand fully, yet knew—in the dark

pit of her reason, where rational thought resided to mock the flight of emotion—the words and feelings wafting about them were for a time and a life they would never have together. For them there could be no future, but only the present. Yet for this moment he would love her, he would give to her all he had to give. And for this moment that was enough. It was enough to know that as much as she wanted him, that much he wanted her.

Seventeen

"Are you certain?"

With an impact like a blow, full comprehension struck. Cerrix tossed back the hair from his forehead to look intently upon the cloaked figure standing before him. The loyalty and trustworthiness of this man were beyond reproach; still he needed to ask once more. "There can be no doubt?"

"None, my king." Careful not to displace the draping that concealed his face from full view, the warrior shook his head. "I delayed as long as I dared. But save for my own participation in their plot tonight, I could not be any more certain of his intent. He has gone too far and said too much to turn back. Whatever manner of control he desires to have over these men can only be ensured by his acting upon his threats."

Cerrix nodded in understanding, then barked a sharp command which brought almost instantly from an adjacent room two of his household warriors. "I want ten men at the gate awaiting my command," he ordered the sleepy-eyed pair.

Neither offered so much as a raised brow as they hastened to obey. Upon their exit Cerrix returned his attention to the cloaked warrior who, at the others' appearance, had stealthily retreated into the shadows. "You have done well."

Cat-footed, the man stepped back into view and bowed his head in acknowledgement of the commendation. While a squaring of his shoulders indicated his pride and pleasure at the praise, his words remained modest, almost deprecating. "I have merely obeyed my king's command to report the actions of one who may be the enemy of his peace. For this I am undeserving of distinction."

Cerrix tugged thoughtfully at the corner of his mustache as he considered the naked sincerity of this response. He had forgotten the zeal that was youth's—and youth's alone. But then, years and life's experiences did that to a man. Like a polished blade that has not been overly used, but merely utilized as needed, the keen edge of a man's spirit was blunted and the purity of his soul sullied by time and deed.

"Would that I had a thousand warriors who were your equal in honor and devotion, Ynyr; I would have no need to seek this peace with Rome . . ." For the briefest instant the Ordovician king allowed himself to mourn the inevitability of his decision. Then he returned his thoughts to the present. "Go . . . before your absence is noted. Mouric must be given no reason to suspect it is anything but ill fortune and a watchful gatekeeper which have served to thwart his pursuit of vengeance this night."

* * *

Through the smoke hole in the roof there showed the flawless black of a night sky bereft of either moon-light or starglint. Within the hut the embers of a dying fire cast but a small circle of illumination. Yet to eyes accustomed to the outside darkness, the red glow of that firepit was as a sun in whose scarlet incandescence there were betrayed two sleeping figures entwined in a lovers' repose.

The woman slept deeply, safe and cherished in her mate's embrace. The man, however, slept lightly, his the disciplined sleep of a soldier.

It was for that habit and training that he sensed more than heard the near noiseless steps made by the small party of stalkers as they advanced upon the small hut. Thus before slumber had wholly left him, he was crouched, waiting and ready, as the door was thrust open. . . .

Unarmed, with only instinct and training to gird him, Galen caught and seized the first intruder by the throat. A glimpse of pale hair crossed his range of vision as he flung the would-be assailant toward the clay floor, oblivious to the dagger in the man's hand. He heard the dull crack of the skull hitting the raised hearth, yet did not slow in his response.

He straddled his enemy's half-conscious body and grasped the wrist of the hand that held the knife. In suddenly wakened blood lust he reveled in the feel and the sickening sound of the bone snapping beneath his fingers' savage pressure. As the tribesman heaved beneath him in pain, he drove his fist into the warrior's face. The man convulsed and lay still. . . .

Rhyca thought at first the crashing noise was of her dreams. She sat up, eyes open wide, frozen with the terror of a previous night—a night she had prayed never would be repeated. But the voices and shadowy figures that filled the hut were not of those demons from the past reconjured in her mind. These apparitions spoke in her own tongue as they called out to one another by names she knew!

Shock and fright clutched at her. Questions tore through her—with answers that terrified. Why were they here? And how had they known? A single thought then broke free. With the knowledge of their identities came the realization that her fear could no longer be for herself. She scrambled to her knees, frantically searching for Galen.

But the light cast by the glowing hearth embers was too weak to reach the perimeter of the room or to clearly illuminate the four or five indistinct forms dispersing about it. In the open doorway there was only blackness. Against her bare skin she felt the chill of night air. She pulled the bedrobes to her and clung to hope. *He must not be found with her!* Goddess, please, she prayed. Her willingness would mean nothing. It was a matter of honor. For his having bedded her these men would kill him!

"The fire," a muffled voice commanded.

Casting eerie, elongated shadows upon the hut's walls, one of the dark figures darted immediately forward. In the next moment flames rose from the hearth. Despite the sudden light, though, everything still seemed muted and gray, as though she were peering through a thick fog while fighting for balance on the fringe of a nightmare.

"Seize him!"

Mouric's hiss dissipated the opaque silence, and her

numbed senses awakened to the vivid images before her.

There were four of them reeking of wine and ale: By the hearth's farthest side the one who had fed the fire; another near the doorway; Balor, evenly spaced in between the two—and Mouric, several feet from him on his right.

The eyes and focus of all, however, were upon the dark man who stood slightly to her left, half-crouched above the prone body of one who had been with them. In his right hand he held the unconscious warrior's dagger.

Balor's voice sounded, jeering. "You cannot kill the four of us, Roman."

The fire illuminated an answering smile of cold confidence and challenge which formed instantly upon the chiseled features. "If you knew that for certain, Briton, yours would be actions and not words."

Arrogantly he faced his enemy like a warrior of old, naked, his bare body gleaming. In this perfection of strength and power incarnate, he might have been the image of a war god cast from burnished bronze and suddenly come to life. For then, knife in hand and poised to strike, he took a step forward. And another.

His words, like his body's movements, came slowly and deliberately. His silken tone both taunted and challenged. "From the beginning you have wondered . . . the question has gnawed at you. . . . Let us answer it . . . you and I, Briton . . . now. Let us see who is the better man."

Rhyca realized his intent. Even as he dared Balor to act by moving toward him, he was also attempting to put himself squarely between her and her tribesmen.

Balor bared his teeth. As with a wild beast the mocking provocation from his hated adversary brought a white foam to the corners of his twisted mouth. He fisted it away and then slowly closed his grip on the hilt of his own dagger. A mordant laugh rolled from his throat as he advanced. "I shall relish as nothing else the feel of my blade as it rips into your guts, Roman. I will disembowel you—and offer up your entrails to the gods in a thanksgiving sacrifice!"

Dread held Rhyca still as she watched Galen crouch into an attack stance—left leg forward, knees bent. He lowered the hand holding the dagger and held it close to the side of his right leg. His left hand was extended, the fingers spread.

She feared to move or breathe. She forgot about the others in the room. In this moment only the two men poised at the edge of mortal combat mattered. . . .

Balor lunged forward. The Roman was ready—as Mouric had known he would be. Indeed, the centurion's prowess had been of prime consideration in determining their strategy. Still, he was one against many, with a vulnerability that needed only to be seized and turned as a weapon against him.

In flawless execution the Roman's left forearm smashed down on that of Balor's knife hand, diverting the thrust which should have gone deep into his belly. With a sidewise step he twisted away. The slashing blow that otherwise would have then caught his thigh encountered instead only air.

As Balor stumbled to regain his balance and footing, the two remaining warriors attacked, their daggers sheathed. As much as Mouric wanted the bastard dead, he was not willing to take foolish risks. It would be better to find another way to subdue him. . . .

Rhyca felt the touch of cold steel upon her shoulder. Without turning her head and before she heard his gloating threat, she knew the man who wielded the sword behind her.

"Drop the knife, Roman—or she bleeds."

The dagger clattered to the floor. At once Balor leaped forward, but the pair of warriors had already seized Galen, one capturing and holding each arm locked behind his back. He did not struggle to escape their grip, rather twisted to turn and face what he now must realize to be his true enemy. Every sinew, tendon and muscle of his naked body tensed in readiness. A raw savagery flowed from him—the savagery of an animal protecting its mate.

"Touch her, and I will kill you," he growled, his words heavy with the pure venom of hatred.

"You are in no position to fulfill that threat," Mouric sneered. "But know if you try, she will bear the cost for your efforts."

Wanting to savor fully this triumph over his rival, Mouric turned his complete focus upon her. Leering, he stepped back to sheath his sword. Like a mask removed and tossed aside, he discarded the control he had been compelled until now to maintain. He allowed the molten fury that had been dammed within to break free. It coursed through his veins with a force that caused his limbs to shake. More intoxicating than the strongest of drinks was the exhilaration left in the rush's wake.

Mouric enjoyed it as he advanced on her—the helplessness of the Roman's rage as he now stood with

Balor's blade at his throat, knowing that did he attempt any struggle she would be punished. Tenfold the bastard would pay for the insults Mouric had endured—the smear upon his honor and the derogation of his manhood.

"Whore!" he spat. "Wanton slut!" With each step he spewed a different aspersion, gloating at her fear and the rise of understanding he saw in her eyes. "Defiler of my brother's memory!"

Rhyca recoiled in horror. What loomed before her was not man but demon, a hazy shadow with eyes that burned blood-red with the fire of his fury.

Suddenly she felt his crushing grip clutch her arm, and he jerked her to her feet.

"Look at me," he hissed. "You shall not lower your eyes to escape the revulsion and disgust you have reaped. May it sear your soul like a heated blade, whore, and brand you for what you are!"

Indeed, her soul burned at a white heat under the combined forces of her fear and humiliation. But Mouric was not finished with her.

"Roman bitch! Barely is your womb empty of one of their spawn when you would open your thighs to have another plant his rank seed in you!"

She realized the madness upon him then, that he would blurt out what he had so long striven to conceal—the fact that it had been a Roman child she had carried.

Suddenly Galen's roar of fury sounded. "Loose her, you vile coward! It is me that you want. I am the one who has defiled your brother's memory by bedding his widow. Defend his honor and his name with your sword—or do you fear to try lest it be shown that the impotence that was his in bed is yours in battle?"

Mouric turned his head to look at him. His lip curled in contempt, and then he looked back at her. "Tell me, kinswoman," he sneered, "is the wetness of your thighs reserved only for Roman cock—or might I find as ready a welcome?"

She went numb with icy terror. Seemingly from far away she heard Galen bellow. His voice came dimly to her through stupefied senses.

"I will kill you, Briton. By the land, the sky, the flame, and the water, I will take your head!"

The scuffling sounds of a struggle—fists pounding flesh and grunted oaths—burst forth.

From the corner of her eye she could see him fighting to escape his captors' hold. But he was one pitted against three. Seeing Balor drive his fist into his belly, she sobbed.

He slumped forward, only to be wrested straight backward by the grasp one of his captors retained on his hair. Again Balor struck him viciously, this time in the lower abdomen.

"No, stop it!" It was her voice she heard, though she was not aware of having formed the words or of having screamed when the cruel blow landed. She turned a tear-filled gaze to the man gripping her arm. "Leave him . . . please."

That she would beseech him to stop the brutal beating clearly amused Mouric. Derisive laughter exploded from him, but ceased as quickly. He smiled fiendishly. *"Beg* me to spare him."

As he forced her to her knees, Mouric watched the fear spread across her face. He drew his dagger, laying the keen edge against her throat. Realization surfaced in her eyes, feeding the madness now upon him.

"Oh, yes," he taunted, "I could kill you both, and none would condemn me for it." He slid his left hand into her hair, seizing a fistful and yanking her head back. He leaned his face in close to hers. "But he shall not die just yet. Such would be too swift and merciful a death. Instead he shall live long enough to witness *your* punishment—a punishment worthy of your sin."

Straightening and stepping back, he slowly replaced the knife in its sheath at his waist. Then he reached out and delivered a stinging slap that caught her on the side of the face. When he pulled her to her feet, she did not try to break his grip, but swayed unsteadily, clutching at the fur that covered the front of her. He shoved her against the wall and pressed himself close as he ran his hand down her side. Grabbing at the fur, he ripped it from her.

Rhyca bit her lip to stop a cry of pain and shame. Dizzy, her head ringing, she shut her eyes. She could smell the odor of sour ale about him, could feel his hardness against her. Her throat constricted in revulsion and terror.

He ran a hand over her naked breast. But there was not even lust in his loathsome caress, only the desire to degrade and humiliate. She then felt his hot breath against her ear.

"Dare to fight me, and I *will* let Balor kill him now."

The threat was unneeded. She had already fled to that place within her mind that freed her from feeling any more pain. Nothing he could do would touch her. . . .

With one glance Cerrix knew what had occurred. He knew, too, what else would have transpired had but a few more moments elapsed.

Anger that the peace plan had almost been undone by this self-serving coward mingled with disgust and thickened his voice as he commanded his men to remove Balor and the other three. It was Mouric who had led them. The burdens of guilt and responsibility were therefore his and his alone.

Cerrix gestured then for one of his men to cloak the woman, who had suffered enough shame and did not deserve to have her nakedness on display. Indeed, he found himself tempted to let the Roman have her tormentor.

Noncommittally his gaze flickered to where the dark warrior stood to the side. At their arrival he had broken free from Balor and the pair of warriors restraining him. It had taken three of Cerrix's men to pull him off Mouric, but now the fury that had been upon him appeared to be gone—or at least so tightly leashed that there was no outward sign of it. His features were masklike as he rubbed the knuckles of his right hand against the palm of his left, opening and closing the fist as though to work the fingers.

Cerrix dismissed his remaining men and drew a deep breath to rein in his own emotions. There would be some who, without knowing the true yet treacherous reasons behind them, would be of the opinion that Mouric's actions were warranted, at least in part. If he had discovered his brother's widow in the arms of her Roman slave, it would be understandable to many that he had gone mad with rage, a viable excuse for his attacking and murdering the centurion.

For that reason, and because he could not betray either the Roman's real purpose or identity—nor that of Ynyr, who was the source of his own knowledge—Cerrix knew his rendering must appear to be both just and impartial. It must not look as though he acted out of personal animosity against this man known to be his rival.

He turned slowly to face him. "Have we become no better than our enemies?" he asked, his voice measured and low. "Do we also rape our own women now?"

Mouric glared at him. "This is not your concern. The matter is one of family."

"Matters of *family* do not cause alarmed guards to roust me from my bed because a party of armed warriors has slipped out over the fortress walls." Cerrix inclined his head in the woman's direction. "Nor should *family* scream in terror and cower in fear of one of their own."

"I am warning you, Cerrix," Mouric snarled. "Leave it."

"No, I am warning *you*." His calmness waning, Cerrix responded with an answering guttural growl. "I can guess at what brought you here in the dead of night, for my ears are open to the same gossip. Too, I can guess at how it would have ended. And that does concern me, Mouric. I need him alive! I will not have *my* plans destroyed and the future of our people jeopardized for the sake of *your* pride—because you have perceived your honor to be somehow besmirched by what was discovered here."

"*Somehow* besmirched?" Mouric's face mottled with immediate indignation. "My brother's wife lies with an enemy slave—and this does not dishonor *me?* There is not a warrior among us who would not have felt the same rage."

"I doubt, however, that many would have acted upon it as you intended to." With his tone Cerrix made clear his disdain for the thwarted rape.

Mouric's rejoinder was a confident smirk. "As her kinsman I am well within my rights, by law, to lay claim to her. In this you have no say."

"But *I* do."

Cerrix turned and looked in surprise at the woman stepping forward. Her face was ashen, her walk unsteady, and yet there was also a strange look of strength about her.

Tightening the folds of the borrowed cloak, she unwaveringly faced her detractor. There was almost defiance in the way she met his heated glower. "I have a say. And I, too, have rights. The right of choice— which I have made, and which, once openly declared, you may not by law disallow."

Understanding flashed across Mouric's face. "What are you saying?"

"That your claim, Briton, is hereby forfeit . . . and mine intact."

As the Roman strode forward, Cerrix could not help but witness the look exchanged between him and the woman. Her eyes were misted with an emotion that could be none but a woman's unconditional faith, while in his there burned the conviction of a man whose right to possession had just been confirmed. Had Cerrix any lingering doubt before this moment, it now vanished. What bound this man to this woman was stronger than any chain or shackle. From the flames of hatred, the ashes of war and the seeds of hope there had grown love.

Mouric's scornful laugh sounded. "Slave, you may make no claim."

"A challenge, then," the Roman countered swiftly. He came up on her left, laid his hand upon her shoulder and pulled her back to stand behind him. "Fight me for her in single combat."

"I do not need to fight you to have her."

"No, you do not." Agreement came with a facile grin. "But it surely will be wondered why you would not. Do you fear the outcome?"

Mouric's hand twitched for his sword, yet the Roman never flinched. Cerrix had seen enough. "Accept his challenge, Mouric."

Mouric wheeled on him. "Are you serious?"

"Very. You profess to want satisfaction. This is how you get it—in honorable combat. While by tradition neither of you dies, the better man will persevere through his prowess. Defeat him, Mouric, and you will have redressed the disgrace to your honor. She will remain under your dominion, and what you do with her is your choice. If he wins, however, your claim upon her is forever severed. She shall be free to exercise her right to offer herself to the man of her choosing."

With smug delight Cerrix watched as his rival weighed his alternatives, only to realize what Cerrix already had: Mouric had no other recourse. He could

342

not ignore the challenge; he must fight or be called coward. Yet single combat against an opponent so evenly matched would entail the very real risk of defeat. Nothing would serve Cerrix's purposes better than to have his challenger for the kingship suffer additional humiliation at the hands of the Roman.

But should Mouric, by chance or the gods' will, emerge the victor, Cerrix would have lost nothing. Rome's emissary was still alive and the peace plan viable. Granted, Cerrix preferred the centurion to win. After all, he had placed him with the woman for the purpose of forming the very bond that now compelled him to fight for her. It would be regrettable to see her go instead to Mouric.

"Your answer, Briton."

The Roman's prompt to Mouric elicited an oath and his snarled acceptance. "Dawn. As soon as it is light enough for me to see your dark hide." He turned and stalked from the hut.

Speculatively, with an eye upon Mouric's departing back, Cerrix regarded the Roman. "Were I you, I would kill him. But I ask you not to. Not for the sake of abiding by our rules of single combat, but rather because dead he would be far more dangerous to our aim. The cause he espouses needs no martyrs, Centurion."

"I understand."

Cerrix smiled. "Dress then." Pointedly he looked toward her. "I will wait for you outside."

Rhyca stood with her eyes downcast. Now alone with Galen, she suddenly feared to meet his gaze. She felt his touch upon her chin. He raised it and wiped

343

gently with his knuckle at the blood trickling from the corner of her mouth.

"Are you all right?"

She nodded, still without looking at him. "I am sorry."

"For what?"

Her heart wrenched. What she had so wanted not to confront—and would have continued in darkness to deny—had been brought to light. She must acknowledge the truth. She met his eyes. "This commitment," she answered softly, "I know it is not what you wanted, and now I have put you in the position of—"

"Of fighting to protect you?" He smiled gently. "I have done so before, *domina,* and would do so again."

"This time is different. A declaration was forced from you which I know you would not otherwise have made."

He shook his head. "The choice to covet you was mine. I knew the consequences of that decision, but I also know what I have made mine, shall remain mine."

"But for how long?" She saw the line of his jaw tighten. The betrayal of emotion only confirmed what she knew; still, it hurt. "It is not a question I want answered, Galen. I have always known that your being here was not happenstance, from that first day on the platform when I overheard Cerrix and Mouric speak of a 'plan.' Then later, when I saw the freedom and trust you were granted, I knew you were more than a war captive made slave."

She smiled in poignant memory. "How often I have heard echoing in my mind your avowal, 'I am no slave.' And you never were. Somehow that collar about

344

your neck serves as a badge of distinction and not a mark of slavery."

"Are you asking me, Rhyca, to tell you the purpose for my presence?"

"No. The purpose does not matter. All I must know is what I have always felt. You will not stay. And while a part of me therefore now resents the forces that have brought you here—and into my life—there is a stronger part that accepts what is to be. After this I want never to discuss it again. I do not want forced declarations between us, Galen, or foolish attempts to believe in what can never be. Nor do I want to know how much time has been granted us or is remaining. I want only what I have thus far had from you: your honesty—and the feeling that for the few moments that I am in your arms, you are with me and not with your Eagles."

Silently he folded her into his embrace. She did not know if she was meant to hear the lamentation then whispered into her hair. But if it were possible for words to comfort and still anguish, his did.

"Would that I could change destiny, *domina*—my love."

Eighteen

Rufus Sita made his way through the thickening crowd. His face was a common enough sight in the hill fort that only a few curious and cautious glances were cast in his direction. For the most part, therefore, he remained unconcerned. It was unlikely that any of the assembling warriors would sacrifice their forthcoming entertainment for the purpose of preventing him from also witnessing the event. Neither were they likely to give up their privileged positions at the forefront of the circle of spectators now forming, merely to stand watch over him at its outermost edge. Still, he proceeded carefully.

Running his palm over the top of his smooth head and scratching at his beard, he searched the sea of faces and forms, morphean in both mood and appearance in the steel-colored light of dawn. Word of the single combat must have spread like a wind-driven wildfire. In spite of the early hour the crowd gathered in the center of the hill fort seemed to include most of its inhabitants, along with a goodly number of farmers from outside the fortress walls. He knew she must be here: the cause for the combat—and its prize.

Resentment and a sense of angry betrayal knotted in his gut. This Ordovician woman of pale beauty, what spell had she cast upon Mauricius? What was it she possessed that the dozens of whores and daughters of Rome who had come before her had not? Indeed, what allure, what force, could be so compelling that a man would knowingly yield to it, defying all that he was and risking all that he had?

The answers eluded him, and so, with his soldier's discipline, the grizzled veteran pushed the questions and his personal emotions aside. He turned his concentration back upon the crowd. This time his eye found her. She stood apart from the others with the clubfoot at her side.

Rufus wended his way toward her. Without attracting her notice, he took up a protective but unobtrusive position several meters at her back. Another might not have done so, given the resentment he bore her. Yet loyalty did that to a man. It bound him and made him feel obliged to serve. Right or wrong—and unless the outcome of this combat made it otherwise—she was his commander's woman. This was, therefore, where he belonged.

Arms crossed and head bowed, he watched the convening spectators beneath half-lowered lids. He listened as well to their conjectures and lewd comments.

Guilt for the brazen act appeared to be evenly divided between the woman and her slave lover. Perhaps that explained the nonviolent mood of the crowd, who had clearly amassed not for cruelty or blood lust's sake, but rather for entertainment and the satisfaction of simple curiosity. While there were a few jeers and oaths against the Roman made in defense of tribal honor, there also appeared to be considerable speculation that the bronze-skinned outsider just might emerge the victor. It would seem, judging from the heated wagers tossed about, that tribal honor lost some of its luster in the face of hard betting and even odds.

That thought provoked a softening of Rufus's stern countenance. He did not care to count the months' pay he had diced away in the past. Smiling, he brought his left hand to his chin and rubbed the thumb along the jaw line. His good humor, however, was short-lived—for in the very next moment a great uproar went up from the crowd, signaling the arrival of the combatants.

Unarmed, stripped to the waist and clad only in *bracae,* each man was accompanied by a pair of warriors. From opposing directions they passed through the ranks of excited onlookers to enter the circle's center, their field of conflict. As they faced one another at arm's length, the crowd stilled to assess the attributes of both fighters. Though akin in size and strength, with their dissimilar colorings the men were like two different breeds of wildcats—equally deadly, but impossible to judge. The Briton's limed locks lent him the look of a desert lion, while Mauricius's sleek darkness conjured the image of a panther. From the hands of their respective escorts each man then accepted his weapons.

At the sight of the round shield and leather-tipped sword given his commander, Rufus frowned. The Moor was as skilled a swordsman as any he had ever seen—but with the Roman short sword. Mauricius would be at a decided disadvantage with the Celtic long blade, nor was he accustomed to this smaller shield.

A second clamor sounded. The cause, Rufus realized, looking to the rear, was the approach of the Ordovices' king, who was accompanied by the Druid priest. The men cut a swath through the crowd and entered the circle.

The warriors escorting the combatants withdrew. The Druid then raised his hands to quiet the now impatient spectators. An uneasy silence descended. Like the moments before a storm, the sultry tension suddenly in the air was almost palpable.

From the corner of his eye Rufus saw the woman clutch the boy closer to her. He pushed back an instinctive urge to reassure her. He could not; he blamed her for what was about to occur.

"Soldier of Rome . . ." With his voice elevated so as to reach the farthest fringes of the crowd, the white-robed priest spoke out, "Do you make formal challenge of this warrior?"

"I do."

"And you, Mouric, do you accept his challenge, agreeing as well to abide by the outcome of this battle as decreed by Cerrix?"

As if to do so would be to dignify his challenger in some manner, the Briton did not make a verbal response. Instead he looked to his king and nodded. Then, jutting his chin toward his opponent in contemptuous invitation, he crouched into a feral position. The look of vindictive hatred upon his face was unequivocal.

Mauricius's features were wiped clean of any expression, but there was a set to his shoulders Rufus recognized all too well. This was what the Moor knew, that for which he had been trained and for which he had trained countless others. Slowly he lowered into a battle stance: shield low and to the front, body turned to present a smaller target, left foot leading, and sword held to the side—the point slightly up.

At command from the Druid the combat commenced. At first the two men circled in deadly silence, each making short, tentative lunges to assess the other's strength and skill.

Rufus noted that the Briton moved quickly with the rash, innate instincts of a born fighter. Repeatedly he struck, almost in confident disdain, searching out an opening in his adversary's guard. Mauricius's movements on the other hand were wary and thought-out—the honed instincts of a trained soldier.

The veteran nodded in silent approval. Despite a personal stake in the battle's outcome, the Moor was focused and clear-eyed. Unawed by his opponent, he would bide his time and wait for the moment to strike.

Now the Briton no longer feinted with his sword. He swung, his blade coming down hard upon his opponents. The clang of steel meeting steel echoed, and the first true blows drew a receptive roar from the crowd.

With his shield Mauricius pushed the tribesman from him. The move was unanticipated. Caught off guard, the warrior faltered. Helpless under the sheer strength of the shove, he stumbled several steps backward.

Several of the spectators shouted their approval. Once more the men circled. Again it was the Briton who lunged and swung, and again the Roman's sword came up to intercept and stop the dangerous blade.

Rufus knew that despite the swords' leather-tipped points their razor-sharp edges could slice a man's arm or shoulder to the bone. And still Mauricius merely maintained a defensive stance, parrying each slashing blow without initiating a counter attack. Suddenly his opponent swung his blade in a wide downward arc. Mauricius caught the blow with his sword, but then his right arm seemed to lose all strength and fall limp to his side.

Rufus cursed aloud. Until this moment he had never seen any proof to support the rumor, yet for years there had been talk. On the Danube frontier an army surgeon, so as to not impair use of the arm, had left rather than cut out a Dalmatian arrowhead imbedded in that shoulder.

Anxiously he held his breath. If, at this distance, Mauricius's vulnerability was obvious to him, surely it was evident to the Briton as well.

. Indeed, the Ordovician immediately raised his sword to strike, dropping his guard completely. It was then that Mauricius struck out. Surprised, the man was barely able to dodge the slashing blow. Mauricius slammed his shield into him, knocking him to the ground. Stunned, he lay without moving. Blood gushed from his nose. He had taken the blow full face.

Making no move to advance upon his foe, Mauricius looked to where the Ordovices' king stood.

With a verifying glance first to the Druid, the king nodded and stepped forward. "It has been decided," he proclaimed, turning his head from side to side to address the crowd. "It is over. Return to your huts and

351

your farms. By our own laws a victor has been decreed. This is finished."

"No!" Mauricius's vanquished adversary crawled onto his knees. Staggering and swaying, he rose, spitting blood. "This is *not* finished!"

The Druid came forward. "Yes, it is," he asserted calmly. "Accept your loss, Mouric. Leave while your legs can still carry you, and before you dishonor yourself further."

A wave of grumbled assent rippled through the crowd. For those who esteemed honor there was nothing worse than defeat, save whiningly to deny it. In obedience to the command already given they began to disperse.

Rufus then lost sight of Mauricius in the scattering throng. He glanced at the woman. The boy was tugging on her hand in an effort to draw her forward. Yet she was holding back. Obviously she had no intention of satisfying the prurient expectations of those who had hoped to see her rush into the arms of her victorious lover. What was between them was private and not for public exhibition.

As a twinge of guilt threatened to loosen the knot of resentment in his belly, Rufus turned away. He had no doubt Mauricius would come to her. He could therefore wait. After all, what further harm could be done if he were to allow them a few moments together? He owed his commander at least that much before he confronted him.

Hauntingly and without warning, his words to Drausus that one night in the stockade returned: *Until his deeds show me that he has clearly abandoned the oath he swore to serve Rome, I will continue to obey him.* That time had come. None could fault him; Rufus Sita had been as loyal as any man could be. But now, with this event just transpired, faith must cease and blind trust end.

He turned to look where the woman had been. Indeed, she and the boy were no longer alone. The man who had fought to possess her stood at her side. Even were his back not to Rufus, he would not have known of the Thracian's nearness, for his attention was solely upon her.

The child, however, was not so captivated. With his bright eyes darting about he had obviously noted the large man's prudent approach and now smiled in shy recognition. "Did you see?" he called out. "How well he fought?" Clearly his pride in Mauricius's victory outweighed his timidity.

Rufus nodded, returning his smile. "Indeed. He fought with much courage."

While the boy bobbed his head in emphatic agreement, Rufus glanced over at his commander. "Centurion," he offered in greeting.

"Sita." Slowly Mauricius turned his gaze from the woman and looked at him in mute reproach. "You rise early."

Rufus nodded. "A habit too long instilled by the *bucina* to break simply because its call does not sound in my ears. Too, I did not want to miss the entertainment."

A dark look seemed to enter the man's eyes. Yet before Rufus could identify it, the woman had recaptured his attention.

"You have matters to discuss," he heard her state

rather firmly as she beckoned the boy to her. "Come, Dafydd."

Her perceptiveness surprised Rufus, and he bowed his head to her in unwitting and unintended respect.

When she had stepped out of earshot, taking the child with her, Mauricius gave a curt nod. "All right, Sita . . . what else?"

Rufus forced a smile. "The years since Palestine have not seen your skill with a sword diminished, Centurion. Nor your prowess." He paused. He needed to know whether he was right in his assumption. "You read the bastard well," he continued calmly, watching the other's eyes closely, "knowing he would strike at the first and slightest sign of weakness . . . I congratulate you on your victory."

The stoic Moor looked at him wryly. "To show weakness where there is strength and strength where there is weakness is an old ploy, Sita. Think what you will. Now . . . spare me your further attempts at tact. We have known one another too long for me to believe it was in want of entertainment that you woke before dawn to view this combat. And certainly you do not now engage me in conversation for the purpose of bestowing compliments. There is something within that bald head that would be given voice. Speak."

Despite the leave given, Rufus hesitated. The charge he was about to level was no minor infraction of military code. He squared his massive shoulders and proceeded with slow caution. "Once I knew you as I know myself. At your command, Galen Mauricius, I would have followed you to Hades and back without question or hesitation, for you were a rare man among officers, one untainted by either personal ambition or

354

greed—or emotion. Your loyalty to the Eagles and to Rome was without equal. But in the time that has passed in this place I have seen actions which from any other I would not hesitate to call treasonous. Yet I have stood fast, believing in you—until today when I saw you place this woman and your attachment to her above the mission you were sent here to perform."

"And what mission would that be?" While a trace of amusement appeared upon the bronzed features, the timbre of the voice retained its sharp edge. "You presume much, soldier, without basis in either fact or understanding."

"I understand what I see," Rufus countered in swift and disappointed anger. Mauricius had not even attempted to deny the allegation! "And I know what I know. When the best officer I have ever served under made an error in judgment beneath even a smooth-faced recruit, I knew the cause was deliberate. We were *led* into that ambush as surely as I stand before you now."

He paused. He did not expect the man to deny the charge outright, but he did expect some reaction.

He received none, save a single word reply.

"Continue."

"I believe that just as Vespasian ordered you to Britain, he also ordered you here—to this hill fort. Drausus, Facilis, all of the rest of us . . . we were needed only to make the plan believable. From the very beginning it was you who was to be the spy as Agricola's advance scout."

Again Rufus hoped, as he watched for denial and saw none. Then, suddenly, the dark head moved slightly from side to side.

"Not spy. Emissary." In a colorless tone, Mauricius continued, his words curiously clipped as though the brevity might somehow serve to distance him from their meaning. "Dispatched by Julius Agricola to the mountain fastness of Cerrix the King. Purpose, to foster trust and peace between Britain's new governor and the lone Ordovician chieftain uncommitted to war. Only in the event of the plan's failure was I to escape, bringing back strategic information for an immediate counteroffensive."

In instinctive shock Rufus drew back. The ramifications of what had just been confessed were almost too staggering to comprehend. "Your mission was peace?" he finally managed to form the response. "Not war?"

Mauricius nodded.

"What about the woman? What part does she play in this?"

Suddenly, and for the first time, Rufus detected in the impassive features the uneasiness of a man at odds with himself.

"She has no bearing on this," came then the terse reply. "My reasons for my actions in regard to her are personal."

Rufus looked at him. "You know as well as I, Centurion, that is a luxury no soldier can afford. A legionary's heart has room for only one mistress—Rome."

The Moor's answering gaze was as ice. "I had no choice but to fight. There was nothing else I could have done."

"You could have lost," Rufus offered quietly. "Then there would have been no pull upon your heart, no temptation—"

"No!" the man answered, his response defiant and resolute. "I could *not* make that choice and let that bastard have her."

"I understand." Rufus nodded, for indeed he did. In his life he, too, had known the all-consuming need to defeat an avowed enemy in whom there dwelled only evil and for whom there could exist no mercy. "But I must ask this, Centurion. You are still a cohort commander of the Imperial Legions of Rome. What if it comes to pass that you must make the choice between this woman and the oath you have sworn to serve? Should this plan for fostering peace fail, and the orders come, could you lead an attack upon this hill fort?"

He saw the strangest look enter the man's eyes. It was a look as black as Erebus—the darkness through which only the souls of the dead traveled.

"Yes."

In that moment—with that single utterance—Rufus felt a shiver pass through him. He knew he had seen in the man both the presence of death and the essence of duty. In fear and reverence he turned away his gaze. "I believe you."

Galen stood in silence, unresponsive to the Thracian's declaration of faith. The poets were wrong. The taste of victory was not always sweet. What rose in his throat to fill his mouth was bitter, and even if he were to spit, the bitterness would linger.

Sita had seen the inner battle between the two halves of his whole—the man and the soldier. Only one could rule him, and Sita had forced him to choose. Yet, for one such as he, could there truly be a choice?

Since long before the woman called Rhyca had ever been born, the army had been the core of his life.

Courage, honor, loyalty. The words resounded in his mind; a chorus of voices spoke them—his father's and his emperor's among them. *Obligation to duty, obedience to command.* Their meanings had been drilled into him: to follow orders without question or hesitation—or any compromise to emotion or personal desires. What had been awakened within the man by this woman was irrelevant. The soldier must—and would—prevail.

For what had to be the fourth or fifth time in as many moments, Rhyca glanced up. His tall form still filled the doorway. She lowered her gaze and tried once again to concentrate upon her meal preparations. She knew she waged a lost battle when she felt the burning cut of the knife blade as it slipped and sliced into the meaty part of her palm.

She rose up from where she had been kneeling beside the hearth and turned toward the wall behind her. In several places the daub had cracked and crumbled off to expose the woven slats of cane beneath. There in the small chinks cobwebs abounded.

Cursing her carelessness, she swept her fingers through the strands, then rolled the sticky threads collected in her fingertips to form a mass. This she pressed against the cut which was neither deep nor long. It stung a bit, and perhaps that was good. The pain might force her thoughts from the quiet man staring out into the night.

Since the morning's combat Galen had barely spoken. Even Dafydd had not been able to draw him out of the somber mood that had seemed suddenly to settle upon him after his conversation with the bearded Thracian. In fact, he had rebuked the boy's overtures by callously suggesting that Dafydd not come to the farmstead for a few days. While the child had pretended to accept the explanation offered—that some time should be given for the tension in the hill fort over Galen's victory to abate—Rhyca had seen the hurt and disappointment evoked by the rejection.

She fared no better. Upon their return from the hill fort he had occupied himself with tasks about the farmstead until the darkening sky had forced him to cease his labors. Even now, though he was but a few feet from her, he seemed no less inclined to avoid her.

The questions mounting in her mind beset her with fearful doubts. Was it the commitment she suddenly represented that he would shun? Or did he now, in having had the time to reflect upon his actions, regret his rashness all together?

Finally, no longer able to bear the uncertainty, she went to him, her bare feet noiseless on the clay floor.

Painfully she was aware of the ache and longing that came upon her as she approached to stand close enough behind him that they could touch. "You have been very quiet," she said.

At the sound of her voice, he immediately turned. Given his aloofness the entire day, she was surprised with his next action. Without a word he drew her to him, slipped his arm about her shoulders, and moved her into the doorway, facing outward. Without relinquishing his hold, he stepped close behind her and reached over her shoulder with his other hand to gesture at the night sky.

"Your nights are lighter than those to which I am used," he stated, his response no answer at all to her unasked question. "Indeed, it is strange . . . by blood I am the son of a desert people. To think that I could come to accept rain, fog, and cold sunlight . . ."

Reveling in his closeness and lulled by the rhythm of his voice at her ear, Rhyca found the questions she would ask fleeing from her thoughts. Whatever had passed between him and the bald, bearlike Roman did not matter now. Contentedly she leaned back against him, turning her head to the side so that her cheek rested upon his hard chest.

"I have seen many lands, Rhyca, and gazed up at many skies. Skies that stretched over sun-baked seas of sand, rain-drenched mud holes, and frozen mountains. Skies which at night were so black and dark that I felt dwarfed by the nearness of my gods. But never beneath any sky of any land have I felt the contentment and sense of completeness I have known here in this place . . . with you. I want you to know . . . I wish I *could* be the man you would have me be."

Rhyca was not certain of what he was attempting to say. But before they had gone to the hill fort, when Cerrix had granted them a few private moments, she had spoken her heart. Was it now his turn? Was he confessing his want? Or was he apologizing because nothing for them could change? In spite of his victory this day which granted them the right to be together, he was still bound to Rome and hence could make no commitment to her.

Yet she had always known that, so therein was no

new loss to be suffered—save that of her fear and anxiety that perhaps he did not want her now.

She turned to face him. "Galen . . . do you want me?"

His answer was one not of words. He grasped her shoulders and brought his mouth down to hers.

Without hesitation her mouth opened to his tongue as her hands slipped about his neck. "My heart, my love."

Galen groaned with the desire she roused in him, yet pulled away. If ever there were a woman to whom he would cleave himself, it was this one! But he had to rid himself of this emotion. He had to think clearly, to remember the purpose for which he had been sent.

Once Cerrix had asked him if he were one of those fools blindly convinced of the invincibility of Rome. No, he was not. Sixteen years in service under the standards had shown him the terrible price that must be paid to ensure that Rome would endure, a price paid with the lives of men who would fight, kill and die. But never had he known that there was this manner of sacrifice as well.

He stared down at her. It was no different now than it had been the first time: Her eyes still possessed the power to move his blood as the moon pulled the sea.

The thoughts and considerations that had retreated earlier to perch abidingly just beyond his ken now gathered and assaulted him. His need for this woman was much more than physical lust. She had become necessary to him, as necessary as food and drink and air. Sita would contend that even to acknowledge this truth was to betray Rome. But was it really betrayal if Rome did not suffer by his actions? What difference could it make—or harm be done—if just for now he was first a man and then a soldier? He had given so much. Surely it was not too much to ask in return to be allowed to love her for the time remaining?

In his heart he knew the answer and pushed it deliberately from his mind. He had made his decision.

He reached out and slowly untied the neck closure of her gown. Very tenderly, almost in reverence, he eased the sides open, baring to his sight and touch his lover's body. It was a gesture as old as the gods and goddesses—this unveiling of woman by man. He slipped his hands beneath the cloth to caress the soft flesh of her breasts. He brushed a thumb over each nipple and felt in the immediate hardening of the buds a surge of desire akin to his own.

He paused to watch the love rise in her eyes—as brilliant as the star-streaked sky.

Trembling, she then stepped back and slid the gown down over her shoulders and arms, letting it fall to the floor.

"Mithras god," he breathed, his voice hoarse with the depth of his longing. "I wish I could give you more than what I can."

"It is enough," she whispered, stepping into his embrace.

He reveled in the feel of her beneath his hands. He was helpless to overcome the need and desire she elicited from him. He swept her up into his arms.

Just for tonight, he vowed, as his honor was engulfed by the swelling passion of his love. Just for tonight he was not a soldier of Rome.

Nineteen

The trio of warriors that had tracked him from the hill fort maintained their silent positions in a thicket some fifteen yards away, watching. His actions were those of a man who clearly thought himself to be unobserved.

Nonetheless, from time to time the wiry slave raised his dark head and glanced about before returning his concentration to the small pile of ash and oak saplings he had gathered and was now sorting through.

Mere force of habit and training, Mouric suspected. He signaled for continued vigilance, squinting as a bright flash suddenly assailed his gaze.

Wordlessly the warrior on his left nudged him. He nodded in acknowledgement. He had seen it also. The slave had some kind of blade in his hands. Hunkered down, he was working at cutting the ash and oak poles into spiked stakes.

Again Balor prodded him. He pointed toward the several round-handled baskets filled with elm leaves that lay on the ground next to the man.

Mouric understood his spear brother's meaning. The

Roman slave had obviously been sent into the forest by the farmer who owned him—the moron! But then, what else could be expected from a no-witted earth tiller? Concerned only that his storage pits be filled with winter feed for his cattle, he would see no danger in allowing a trained enemy soldier to wander the woods unguarded!

Beneath Mouric's mustache his pointed teeth slowly bared in a smile of pleasure. Actually . . . this was too perfect . . . to find the dark little bastard here like this, squatting beside a pile of makeshift weapons. It had to be an omen, a sign from the gods that his plot for vengeance was indeed their will!

At that instant a warm flood of certitude flowed through him, infusing him with confidence. For three drunken days and two sleepless nights past, his had been a singular course of thought: how to exact revenge not only upon the Roman who had publicly humiliated him, but upon the man who had contrived the entire farce—and its outcome—for the purpose of ensuring his own tenuous hold of power!

And while the answer had come easily—to wait no longer and to seize from that coward, who did not deserve to wear the *torc* of king, his right to do so— the method by which Mouric could achieve that aim had required far more deliberation. His plan, like the antlers of a buck deer, must branch out to meet three objectives: First, no blame could fall to him, no suspicion. Next, it must look to all that it was by Cerrix's own hand that he had toppled. His errors in judgment and mistaken trusts must be the very weapons of his destruction. And last, the tribe must see in his fate their own, unless they departed immediately from this shameful path of peace!

Mouric had no doubt that the instrument of his revenge was now but a good spear's toss from him—the Roman slave the others called Drausus.

Having seen enough, and convinced more than ever of the righteousness of his course, Mouric rose. Ynyr and Balor followed.

They came perhaps within twenty feet of him—certainly far closer than any Ordovician warrior would have let an enemy approach—before the man finally appeared to hear them. He quickly shoved what Mouric now saw to be a broken scythe blade into one of the baskets. Another he tipped over—seemingly in an awkward haste to rise. Like an animal's the man's black, beadlike eyes darted from Mouric to the men standing at his sides. He appeared to calculate the odds and not like his chances of escape, for he held his ground.

Mouric smiled scornfully, watching the nervous shuffling of the bare feet. The little ferret! Did he think them fools—that they would not see the fresh shavings and sharpened sticks he was attempting to cover over with the spilled leaves?

Even Ynyr perceived the feeble attempt at concealment. The youth shoved the man aside and knelt, brushing at the pile of leaves. He then lifted one of the stakes to peer more closely at its sharpened point. "Crude, but effective." With his handsome features betraying amusement, he extended the makeshift spear for Mouric's inspection.

Mouric took hold of the shaft. "Tell me . . ." He looked the slave up and down as though he had need

365

to refamiliarize himself with his face. "One they call 'Drausus the Spaniard,' what prey would a slave hunt with such a weapon?"

The Roman glared at him in hate-filled silence. Mouric laughed and tossed the spear to Balor. "Make a fire and harden the point."

It was difficult to say which was the stronger emotion leaping then into the Spaniard's dark eyes—surprise or fear. He was self-controlled enough, however, to assume a posture of blatant indifference. "Torture first," he sneered, "or do you intend just to kill me outright, Briton?"

"Neither, Roman. What I intend is to offer you a proposition. One that would be mutually pleasing and beneficial."

With no effort made to disguise his loathing, the wiry man spat. "What would 'please' me would be the sight of your head, Briton, rolling along the ground as once did that of an unarmed boy you butchered."

Mouric clenched his teeth. Though his hand itched for his sword, he forced a semblance of calm. He needed this man. Among the Roman captives he alone harbored a hatred for his captors deep enough to act in defiance of the tall one's orders. Hence, he was the only one who could accomplish Mouric's aim. "Make no mistake, Roman. I would kill you as much look at you—did I not have need of you."

For just an instant the light of hatred and arrogance in the other's eyes seemed to dim. "What 'need,' " he asked, suspicion coloring both his tone and features.

Mouric ignored the question. "Tell me . . . Drausus . . . would you take your freedom were it offered? Would you leave this place, returning to your legions? In doing so, would you disobey the tall one's orders?"

The Roman made no reaction to the sound of his name. Even the question about his freedom elicited little response. What snapped his head up and wiped the sneer from his face was Mouric's mention of the man who was his commander. "Mauricius commands me no longer! Let the others—who are little better than he in their collaboration—look away in the face of his treachery, but not me. No man may serve himself *and* Rome. He has made his choice—and it is not to the Eagles that his loyalty now lies, but to the whore he beds."

With the clicking sound of Balor striking a flint faint in his ears, Mouric continued with the execution of his plan. It should serve him well, this slave's unabashed disdain for his former comrades. "The hatred that burns in your eyes, Roman, is pure. For that I respect you. The hatred in my heart is as bright. But there are those who would see a peace grow between our peoples. Indeed, they planted it many months ago. You have been betrayed by your leaders, as I have been by mine."

Interest sparked in the beady eyes. A slight nod followed, indicating agreement perhaps?

Mouric took a half step closer. "Your patrol was led into a planned ambush, Drausus. I knew not only where to attack, but how many there would be. I had even been promised little to no resistance. You see . . . your centurion was willing to sacrifice your life and those of your comrades so that *he* might be brought here—to nurture that seed of peace, along with cowards of my own kind."

367

"Why would you tell me these things?"

Mouric knew the dark slave believed him, for he did not question what had been disclosed, only why it had been revealed. "I want to see that peace fail— and for that I need your help."

"You must be mad, Briton." He snorted in disbelief. "What has this to do with me?"

"Hear me out. I want you to kill Cerrix, or at least wound him. Our law forbids a maimed or injured man from holding the kingship. The leadership of the tribe must be held by one unblemished, for a diminishment of his powers is a diminishment of the tribe. With Cerrix removed from power, the peace he supports will die."

The Roman looked at him and then at Ynyr and Balor, who were crouched a few feet away, hardening the points of the spiked stakes over a small fire. For a moment he seemed confused, as if he doubted that what he was hearing was reality. Then he laughed aloud. "As much as I have no compunction for ending a Celt life, kingly or otherwise, I am no assassin. If you want him 'removed,' Briton, do it yourself."

"I cannot, for did the slightest suspicion exist that I had anything to do with this, I could not wear the *torc* of king."

A snide grin appeared. "So . . . it is not in support of your beliefs that you plot, eh, brave warrior—but in support of your own ambitions!" He laughed again and shook his head. "Find yourself another Roman. No sooner would my spear enter your king's heart than yours would find mine."

It was no easy feat to hold his tongue still and his sword hand fast. Mouric doubted he had ever before held such contempt for a man he intended to let live. "You need not fear for your life," he managed at last to grit out. "I need you alive, escaped, and on the way back to your legions. Only then is the threat believed; only then can I raise the banner of war."

A new light glimmered in the slave's eyes. "For your own ambition, you would decree the destruction of your people?"

Mouric's control threatened to slip, but then an inner voice seemed to speak: While he still held the little Spaniard's attention, hope was alive. "You are arrogant, indeed, to think that victory would be yours, Roman."

"And you are a self-serving fool to think yours can do what no other people has done—face the legions of Imperial Rome and live!"

"At least we will have died like men and not been slaughtered like sheep beneath the swords of Roman slavery!"

Silence suddenly descended. The two men glared at one another. As strange as it was, Mouric knew that in their common hatred they had found a tenuous bond and even a manner of respect.

"Why should I trust you?" the Roman at last asked.

"I have told you. I need you alive. Your death would serve me only in half measure."

"So say you. But experience has taught me that a man who'll betray once, won't hesitate to betray twice. I've no reason to believe you, Briton." He spat. "And less to trust you."

Mouric was not surprised by this reaction. He had, in fact, anticipated just such a response and had formulated one of his own. All the same, it was not with-

369

out misgiving that he took the gold band from his right forearm and pressed it into the man's grasp. "Take this to Cerrix. He'll know it is mine, and he'll know there is no other way you could have obtained it save did I give it to you. Then tell him what I have plotted. I can promise you that he'll see the truth of it even if you do not. I will die, and his peace will live. Is that what you want? Your legions following your centurion's example and trading their swords and manhood for the comforts of peace found between our women's thighs?"

Mouric waited for his answer. Would the weasel be clever enough to know that if he did try to go to Cerrix, he would never make it through the hill fort's gates?

The man's dark gaze narrowed, then lowered to the armlet in his hand. He turned the golden band slowly in his fingers. "Did I agree to this—and I have not *yet*—how would I get close enough to kill him?"

Drausus listened carefully to what spilled next from the Briton's mouth. Each detail he committed to memory. Yes, he nodded, he knew where the deer trail crossed the small stream—inwardly he grinned—and he *would* be ready. He would have his long-awaited vengeance—and more. If but half of what this lime-haired Celt bastard had spouted were true, he was about to seize back his own future! By Cerberus's heads, he vowed, evoking the name of the three-headed watchdog of Hades, he would emerge from these mountains a hero—for he would see to it, by whatever means necessary, that there would be none to dispute *his* telling of the tale!

* * *

They left the hill fort at sunrise, twelve men, with swords at their hips and carrying either light javelins or stout boar spears. The air was crisp and cool, clear above the tops of the pines and oaks, though a blanketing of ground mist remaining from the heavy night fog still lay in the hollows and gullies. It was not, however, a source of concern for any in the hunting party that the morning murk might make tracking prey difficult. That was what the dogs were for.

Mouric kept his own pack of three close at heel. This was not a day for the great grays to take off crashing through the brush. . . . An inadvertent discovery of the slave before the little ferret had fulfilled his purpose would doom much more than the plan for Cerrix's demise!

Lest mere thought give it viability, Mouric refused to consider the disturbing possibility further and reflected instead upon his conviction of divine favor—a conviction that was in that very instant fatefully affirmed by the sudden appearance of three birds swooping in startled flight above Cerrix's head.

While the others in the hunting party attempted to make light of the occurrence with humor—as is often the wont of frightened men—Mouric cast off the final vestiges of doubt. That the omen of three birds could as easily portend restored life as imminent death was not to be considered by the man who now basked in his knowledge of what was to be.

At last—and certainly not soon enough for one who had so much to anticipate—the dawn became day. The climbing sun had burned off the lingering ground mist. Like hazy blades, rays of sunshine penetrated between the trees, and the dark, dank forest enjoyed a semblance of light and warmth.

Now the dozen men separated into two parties. Cerrix would lead one, Mouric the other. From this point, in a "V" direction, each party would move opposite but parallel the other through the woods for several miles before altering course and working their way back to rejoin as one. Any boar or deer flushed out and caught between the two flanks would then be driven by the dogs toward the center.

With the smell of damp greenery in their nostrils and the rustling sounds of small, scurrying animals in their ears, the warriors set out. Cerrix's party, following a narrow deer trail, moved south, Mouric's north, then both turned west. They would meet up again where the deer trail crossed a rivulet and where there was a natural wall formed by the upward slope of a craggy hill, along the crest of which was strung a particularly dense growth of underbrush which overlooked the streambed below. Here the hunters would trap their prey.

The sudden silence of the forest birds alerted him to the hunters' approach. Drausus shifted his weight and position. He was ready. Since before dawn he had been waiting in the copse of bramble, waiting to take hold of his destiny. Now it was at hand—in the form of the spear he raised and leveled.

With the infinite patience unique to a man with the sweet taste of vengeance in his mouth, he watched the two lines of men from opposing directions draw closer. There was no mistaking his target. Indeed, with the warrior's pale mane thonged at the neck for hunting, Drausus could not miss sight of the identifying gold *torc* that hung round his neck, shining in the sunlight.

He aimed at a spot a splayed hand's width beneath that glint of light. Left arm extended for balance, he drew back his right.

"There!" He heard a shout ring out. "The slave!"

In less time than the space between the two outcries, four spears were hurled toward him into the thicket. Two found their deadly marks.

The pain screamed through him. He collapsed to his knees. Mouth gaping open in almost embarrassed surprise, the would-be assassin looked down at the pair of shafts jutting from his lower chest and abdomen.

He was a soldier. He knew. One of the spear heads had penetrated the lung; the other had severed the great artery that runs along a man's backbone behind the stomach. Blood was filling up the inside of him.

He called for the Boatman to take him. Then, through blood-flecked lips, Drausus the Spaniard drew his final breath.

Below, at the streambed, Mouric stared up at the thicket. Like a spark, realization flared to burning flame. Through the thick cane and bramble there might have been—especially to a sharp eye expecting it—some slight sound or sight of movement betrayed, perhaps even enough to have divulged a man's presence in the underbrush. But specific shape and form, enough to reveal the actual *identity* of the man hidden there? No! That was not possible. To have been able to shout such a warning, the warrior who had given the alarm had to have known more than he had seen. For that there was but one explanation.

Like a man sleep-walking, Mouric was unaware of what came next, of heading back to the hill fort. Fortunately the killing of the slave so occupied the minds and tongues of his fellow hunters that none seemed to note as strange or suspicious his almost stuporous state. And so he was able, once the initial shock had passed, to deliberate his next course of action.

From what Mouric was now overhearing it appeared obvious that Cerrix must have revealed to only a handful of men in his closest confidence his knowledge of a probable attempt on his life, but no other details. And while it was possible he did not know who had masterminded the plot, Mouric doubted that were so. Most assuredly Cerrix knew and was merely biding his time, waiting to use the knowledge of Mouric's treason to his own best advantage. Too, the arrogant bastard just might think that the seemingly accidental manner by which his assassin had been dispatched might conceal the fact of advance warning of a plot. Perhaps he even hoped to use his spy further.

Mouric ground his teeth in an effort to contain his rekindled rage. Only one man could have betrayed him, a man whom he had trusted as far more than friend! But the time for revenge was not now.

Through his silent deliberations the voices of the other hunters filtered into his awareness. Mouric listened to the conversations around him, which though rampant with speculation, still managed to follow a single path of reasoning.

The wiry Roman had never made any pretense of having accepted his capture and enslavement. Hence, none could truly be surprised by this attempted escape. A search of the farmstead would be made, and the likely discovery of his master's body should serve to confirm what most already suspected. This had been a desperate bid for freedom. Upon spotting the approaching hunters, he had no doubt mistaken them for a search party and decided, as he was about to lose his own, to take a few Ordovician lives with him.

Mouric felt revitalized. There were, after all, still warriors with honor enough to chafe under the benevolent treatment shown to these captives who were their enemies! If he could exploit this attempted escape by one Roman slave, using it as example of the untrustworthiness of all Romans and proof of the irrefutable danger they posed to innocent lives, he might actually increase the number of his supporters. Before he was exposed, he must take those loyal to him and leave. Perhaps *this* was the gods' intent all along!

Confident once more, Mouric returned his deliberations to the one other matter he would see resolved before his leaving.

As he entered, Mouric rose up to his knees and beckoned him.

Smiling, Ynyr approached. If he thought it odd for the older man to be abed at midday, his expression did not reveal it. Almost coyly he waited for Mouric to gesture his request before undressing and kneeling before him.

Once facing his bedmate, however, he required no further invitation. With his loins pushed provocatively forward, he reached out to stroke Mouric's chest.

Skilled as he was in the arts of male love, he deliberately avoided an intimate touch, allowing anticipatory desire to build.

Mouric closed his eyes. He felt himself lean closer, seeking the younger man's caressing hands. Ynyr fisted him deftly and began to work him to full arousal. Mouric groaned in pleasure, and as he slid his hands over the youth's shoulders and down his back over the curve of his buttocks, he felt the tug of regret mixed with anticipation.

For several moments he continued to enjoy the sensations, foretasting his gratification. Finally stimulated to readiness, he moved away from the youth and urged him forward on his hands and knees. He laid his chest over the broad back, and as the length of his body came in contact with the smooth skin and hard muscle of another man, there was an immediate surge in his loins. It was with thought of his lover so unprepared and unsuspecting, that his desire crested. He was ready.

With his left hand he reached up to grasp Ynyr's shoulder as if preparing to position himself against the youth's buttocks. Rising up, he reached down behind him for the knife lying atop the pile of his discarded clothing. His fingers closed about the hilt as he slipped the dagger from its sheath.

Then he lunged forward and thrust, burying the naked knife blade in his betrayer's back.

Twenty

Above the sound of Dafydd's chatter Rhyca heard the voices of men. They were not loud voices, but rather indistinct. She thought they might even have been deliberately lowered, for in the quiet of inactivity which came at dusk, words carried easily on the evening wind. In fact, if her door were open and the breeze just right, it was not unusual for smatterings of conversations taking place beyond the palisade to reach inside her hut.

Out of curiosity more than anything else she rose up from where she had been sitting on her heels beside Dafydd, watching as he milked the cow. Looking over the animal's rump in the direction of the voices, she saw the two men—one fair, the other dark—standing at the palisade's entrance.

A sudden sense of uneasiness came over her. There was no tangible reason for the feeling, nothing in either man's expression or stance which should have unnerved her, yet in seeing Cerrix and Galen together she felt fear. Not the dark, weighty sort of fear that frightens as when one is in danger. This was light, skittering, the kind that warned something was wrong.

"Why is Cerrix here?"

Dafydd's question echoed her own. "I . . . I do not know," she murmured in utter honesty. She glanced down at the boy who was looking underneath the cow's belly in order to view the men across the yard. "Perhaps it is some matter concerning one of the other Romans . . ."

Dafydd immediately turned his head to squint up at her in skepticism. "He's never come here before."

"Perhaps there was never this sort of problem before," she answered, forcing a light and comic lilt to her voice. She reached down and tousled his hair. "You think too much and work too slowly. Finish. I need to see to supper, or we shall be eating in the dark of night."

Only when she heard the rhythmic hiss and splash of Dafydd's resumed milking did she look back toward the men. They had moved from the entrance and were now inside the compound, sitting on their haunches in the shade of a scrub pine. Watching them so deeply engrossed in their conversation, Rhyca felt her heart start to hammer in her chest. She drew quick, shallow breaths. With a feeling of dread penetrating her mind, she looked away.

As Cerrix spoke, he watched the face of the man before him. The Roman listened without reaction. Even the news of his man's death failed to provoke any change of expression in the bronze features disciplined never to show weakness.

When Cerrix had finished, his dark listener then casually shifted his weight as though he were merely endeavoring to relieve a cramping thigh muscle.

"What of your informant?" he asked. His voice, every bit as trained as his countenance, also betrayed no presence of emotion.

"Dead," Cerrix answered tersely. He noted that the slight change in the other's body position now allowed him to watch more easily the woman and boy across the compound. With a furtive sense of satisfaction he wondered if Rome's stalwart soldier realized how much that seemingly insignificant action had served to reveal.

"A rational man would have never taken the risk . . . the time," the Roman mused, almost as if to himself.

Cerrix knew of whom he spoke. "Mouric is beyond the reach of law or reason. His honor has been diluted by the bile of frustrated ambition. However, for many his royal blood alone legitimizes his actions."

"How many do you estimate left with him?"

As blunt as was the question, so came its answer.

"Close to forty. A small number." For just an instant Cerrix hesitated. Yet it must be his full measure of trust that he gave—or none at all. He continued. "But there are too many other such rogue bands with whom he can unite forces. He has only to spark a small war, then have your legions retaliate against an innocent village, and he will have succeeded in inflaming a total rebellion—for then thousands would join his cause and gather under his banner."

The Roman did not reply immediately. He picked up a small stick and toyed with it. Finally, without lifting his gaze from the twig, he spoke. "You know that would sign the death order of every Ordovician man, woman and child in these mountains. Not a living being, unto the beasts in their stalls, would be spared. Your people—" he snapped the twig, tossed aside the pieces, and raised his head—"would cease to exist, Cerrix the King."

The meaning of the small demonstration was not lost upon its audience. Cerrix's pride and anger flared. "We are not dried twigs, Roman, to be broken so easily beneath the heel of Rome. We are as the sacred oak—mighty and indomitable. To rid these mountains of us, you will have to put to the torch every forest, wood, grove and covert. And even then, from the flames we shall vilify your name and fight unto our final breath!"

"I know you shall," the other replied, his voice nearly inaudible.

The hollowness of his tone took Cerrix aback. Holding his own tongue, he watched as under the pretense of looking where the discarded halves of the twig had landed, the dark gaze drifted to the woman and boy.

It was said that a man's eyes could betray the contents of his soul. Perhaps it was true—for in the obsidianlike depths of the Roman's eyes Cerrix saw a flicker of something he knew had never been there before. The impassive soldier of Rome had just experienced terror—not for his own life, which meant very little to him, but for the lives of the two people he had come to love.

The centurion blinked, and the look was gone, the emotion suppressed. He spat into the dirt.

Cerrix wanted to tell him it would not help. How

well he knew! A man could spit until his mouth was dry as dust. But that bitter, coppery taste would remain—a constant and irrefutable reminder to him of his fear.

Galen forced from his mind all thoughts save one. From this point on nothing could ever again be as it had been. Now he must—for their sakes—be what he was and live the life his destiny demanded. He pinned Cerrix with a piercing gaze. The time for half-truth, conditional trust and withheld knowledge was past. From this point forward there must be between them absolute and unmitigated faith and truthfulness. "It is too late to stop Mouric from amassing an attack force." The confidence of command edged his tone with a razor-sharp preciseness. "You know there is but one way now to prevent an all-out war."

The Ordovices' king nodded. "I would not be here otherwise. As we speak, the preparations are being made. Four warriors from my own household will accompany you. But first . . ."

He paused. Reaching beneath his tunic, he withdrew a red cylinder-shaped object made of leather. "Two days ago my scouts took this from a captured Roman courier. I want you to tell me what is the message inside."

Galen recognized at once the unbroken seal affixed to the scroll case and wondered why the man had chosen to show it to him now. "You know it bears Agricola's seal?" he asked.

Cerrix nodded.

"Most likely it contains his report to Vespasian, an accounting of the assault launched against the island known as Mona."

"You knew of the attack—beforehand?" Immediate suspicion narrowed the blues eyes trained upon him. "You knew of the attack—beforehand?"

Galen shook his head. "No sooner than you. A fortnight ago, when Mouric and his scouts returned with the news that Agricola was marching toward the coast, I suspected then that the island might be his target." He gestured nonchalantly toward the scroll case. "You should know, it is his wont to send duplicate dispatches, usually three. Unless your scouts have also intercepted the other two, that message is well on its way to Rome. And I shall tell you this as well. Since not even the fastest courier can make that journey in less than two months, the one thing that dispatch does *not* contain is Agricola's request for permission from Vespasian upon a course of action. He has made his decisions, and that missive is merely his reporting of it to his emperor. But how do you know I will not lie? I could tell you that he is returning to Deva to wait out the remaining months promised, when in fact he is planning just the opposite."

Beneath his mustache Cerrix smiled. "I must trust you, Roman. Also, you possess too much honor to lie on your own behalf. And now, I think you have two compelling reasons not to lie even on Rome's behalf." He handed him the case. "Read it. You and I both have lives we want to safeguard."

Galen felt a muscle twitch in his jaw. He did not need to be reminded that what he cherished could be lost! He opened the cylinder, breaking the seal, and removed the scroll. He leveled a final probing stare at the man across from him. "One final question, Lord Cerrix. What if Agricola has wearied of waiting or

382

has learned of those rogue bands you spoke of? What if he is intending to attack?"

"Then, we should know of it, Centurion, that we may pray to our respective gods that you reach him first and persuade him otherwise."

Galen unrolled the papyrus sheet. What seized his attention immediately was not what was contained in the dispatch, but what had been omitted: the laurel. "The inhabitants of Mona have surrendered the island and sued for peace," he stated, summarizing for Cerrix the beginning few lines.

He saw no need to offer the actual details of the assault. It hardly mattered, after the fact, how Agricola had achieved his victory—that he had not waited for his fleet to cross the strait, but instead had utilized his auxiliary cavalry who were trained to swim in full armor while carrying their weapons and keeping their horses under control. Besides, he suspected Cerrix's scouts would already have informed him of the unusual feat—noteworthy even by legionary standards. What mattered now and most was how Rome's military governor had chosen to announce his achievement.

Raising his eyes from the scroll, he looked at Cerrix. "This dispatch is not laurel-wreathed. What that means is that Agricola has chosen deliberately *not* to represent this action to Vespasian and the senate as a campaign of conquest. Instead he states that he has merely acted to keep a defeated tribe under control."

The significance of that distinction might or might not have been apparent to the proud Briton chieftain, who clearly bristled at the words "defeated" and "control." He gestured toward the scroll. "I would hear the voice of him who would 'control' me, Centurion. Read it as it is written."

Galen complied, translating the Latin as best he could. " 'I understand the feelings of this province. Perhaps it is as my detractors and critics would claim: my Galli blood causes me to feel a sense of kinship with these island people, an appreciation of their innate love of freedom. And while there can be no doubt that their subjugation to Rome must be complete enough to ensure obedience, it should not imply slavery. In the past there have been errors made in Rome's name. Injustices have been meted by officials in positions of power who acted solely for their own good, and not the good of those they had been sent to rule. These mistakes and acts of injustice have contributed to revolt. Perhaps I am arrogant to make this claim, yet I do so candidly. I will not repeat the past, but learn from it. I have done enough to inspire fear; now I will try the effect of clemency. I intend to show these Britons the advantages of the *Pax Romana*—which through the negligence or arbitrariness of previous governors has been as much feared as war. I have had no word from the Ordovices' king. I go now into his mountains proffering peace, but prepared for war. By my honor, this province shall have the latter if not the former. I shall present my terms of surrender. The choice is his.' "

Galen rolled the sheet of papyrus, replaced it in the case and handed it back to the silent man before him. "You must decide, my friend. Peace or war. Even did Mouric not threaten the truce, the time for watching and waiting is passed. Agricola comes for your answer."

"Go to him. Tell him I will hear his terms."

Across the yard Rhyca watched as the two men stood and clasped forearms. A few more words passed between them. Cerrix then nodded, and they parted.

Rhyca looked away. The drumming in her ears that was her heartbeat quickened so that it nearly drowned out the sound of Galen's approach. Still, she heard his footsteps, and stiffened as they neared.

"Dafydd . . ." She forced a taut smile and tried to speak calmly. She must be rational. There was no tangible reason for what she felt. "Why don't you take the milk inside, and I will see to the cow."

"But I want to ask Galen why Cerrix—"

"Dafydd, please! Don't argue. Take the milk inside." She knew the brittle tone with which she snapped at the child betrayed her fear.

"Do as Rhyca asks you, Dafydd." His voice sounded at her back.

Wordlessly the boy obeyed him. With her eyes she followed his progress across the yard. A trailing of spilled milk marked his wake. Not until he was almost at the hut's threshold did she finally turn to face the man behind her. "You are leaving?"

It was not truly a question. She knew he was.

"Yes."

Suddenly there was no moisture in her mouth. She could not swallow. For a frantic, fleeting instant she thought she might actually choke on her own tongue. "When?" she finally managed to rasp.

"As soon as Cerrix's warriors arrive."

A cold numbness enveloped her. She wanted to look away, but his eyes would not let her. They held her own and kept her where she stood just as inextricably as his grasp might have. And then she felt herself nodding—as though she understood! She heard her voice. "I need to see to Dafydd."

The spell broken, she took a half step.

His hand darted out, and he seized her arm, checking her retreat. "Do you not want to know why?"

The anger in his tone was unmistakable. She looked up in bewilderment but avoided his eyes. Blinking fiercely to quell the rise of stinging tears, she repeated his question. *"Why?* It does not matter why." Her own tone was hushed and even—but with an underlying harshness to it she could not purge. As she spoke, it strengthened. "But I can guess. What you came here to accomplish has been achieved. Now Cerrix is sending you back to your Eagles."

"Yes, Cerrix is sending me back," he retorted sharply, "but not because what I was sent here to achieve has been won. If anything, it can all be lost if I do not go."

He was not making sense. She shrugged, indicating her confusion. But he must have taken it for indifference—or even dismissal—for he grasped her other arm as well and dug his fingers into her flesh, forcing a soft cry that was born more of surprise at his roughness than of pain.

In his own language he cursed, words she could not understand. She tried to pull back, frightened by the rage she felt in him.

His hold loosened, but not sufficiently that she could break free. "Listen to me, Rhyca. This morning one of my men tried to kill Cerrix. He was acting not as a soldier of Rome, but rather as Mouric's assassin.

Now Mouric has left the hill fort, taking with him nearly forty warriors who either did not know of his treachery—or who supported him in it."

Her confusion increased. "I don't understand. How does this involve you? Even if it were one of your soldiers who tried to kill Cerrix, for what reason would he now send you back to your army?"

"For the same reason that I left it and came to this hill fort nearly three months ago." Suddenly his voice was quiet and weary. He sighed. "I was sent here, Rhyca, by Britain's new governor, a man named Agricola. With Cerrix's full knowledge and cooperation, I was to be Agricola's eyes and ears, his emissary, acting to advance the cause of peace between our peoples."

A voice inside her head whispered in immediate response to what he had just confessed: *This was "the plan," the purpose for his presence!*

Aloud, she asked for confirmation of the silent surmise. "When Cerrix told Mouric that he needed you alive, else his plans would be destroyed and the future of the tribe jeopardized, this peace was what he meant, wasn't it?"

He nodded.

"It still does not explain your leaving now. You said everything could be lost did you not go. But if you mean the peace you have made with Cerrix, how can that be lost by Mouric's treachery?"

"Because Mouric's hatred and thirst for vengeance have taken him beyond the constraints of honor and law. He is like a rabid wolf that would attack even its own pack to sate its madness. To destroy Cerrix he will destroy the peace. Even now Agricola's army is headed here to negotiate that peace. But Mouric and those who follow him are on a path of war. If they reach Agricola and his legion before I do, and attack, Agricola will have no way of knowing that the strike comes without sanction and in violation of Cerrix's command. He will retaliate immediately and without mercy. He will not bother to distinguish between those who have revolted and those who have not. Even did I reach him then, it would be too late. The fires of war will rage between our peoples until one has destroyed the other."

He paused as if expecting a response from her. "Now do you understand why I must go?" He released his hold of her arm, and laid his hand along the side of her face. "Rhyca, look at me."

Only then, hearing his command, did she realize that in all this time she had been looking at him without letting herself see him, and listening without actually hearing what he said. It was as if he had been standing behind a veil. So that the impact of her pain might be bearable, she had seen him obscured and heard his words blurred. But now he would strip away the barrier, baring her heart to the full agony of the truth of his leaving.

Why then could she not feel it? She could not feel anything at all inside! Was this some manner of death? For surely if the heart died, the body could not live!

The sound of footsteps and a male voice calling out thundered into her thoughts. She knew without looking. Cerrix's warriors had come.

"You must go," she heard herself say. "You must stop Mouric."

He glanced over his shoulder at the waiting men,

388

then back to her. "Explain to Dafydd. Tell him why I left and tell him I will come back."

"No." She closed her teeth on her lower lip to still its quivering and looked into his face, his proud and handsome features which had not so very long ago been strange to her. Now she knew every line and plane. She lowered her gaze. Gently she slipped her fingers beneath the slave collar about his neck and fingered the hammered metal. Where it had lain against his skin the iron was warm.

"You will not be back," she said quietly, lifting her eyes to his. "You and I both know this to be true, Galen. Once he leaves, the man who stands before me can never return as what he was. *You* will leave, yes. But the one who might come back—though he will have your face and voice—will not be you. *He* will be a Roman soldier."

He did not offer denial or protest. There was no reason to. It was as they both had always known it must be.

"Roman! We go—now!"

She lowered her hand and her gaze. "I . . . I have to see to Dafydd. May . . . may the gods guide you." She turned toward the hut and did not look back.

"No!"

Rhyca understood his sense of betrayal, his anger. She reached out and put her hand upon his shoulder. "Dafydd . . ."

Immediately he gave a sharp jerk to remove her touch, turning his back to her fully and hunching his shoulders. "Leave me alone."

389

She took a half step backward. "We always knew, Dafydd . . ." Though no tone could gentle the brutal truth she must speak, she spoke softly. "We always knew that he could not stay, that he would one day leave us—"

"He is coming back!" The blond head whipped around, and tear-filled eyes met hers. "If he said it, it is so!"

"Yes, that is what he said. But he cannot know that for certain, nor can we. Much can happen to change—"

"He will come back. I know he will!" He brushed away his tears with a balled fist. Swallowing several times, he rolled his shoulders and jutted his chin—as though daring her to dispute his truth. "I know. And when he comes back, everything will be as it was before."

Rhyca sighed. At times Dafydd could be stubbornly devoted to reality—only accepting as real that which could be confirmed by his senses. But at other times he could be extremely fanciful. This was not the time for him to refuse to listen to reason. "Dafydd, it can never be again as it was. You might be right—he may come back. But he won't be the Galen you knew. He will be marching with his army, wearing armor and a helmet. You may not even be able to recognize him. And he may not be allowed to recognize you."

"Yes he will!" Anger burst across his face. "Don't say that!"

She knelt down before him. Taking hold of him, she turned his rigid form to face her. "I'm sorry, Dafydd. I do not say this to be cruel, but if he does come back, what then? Do you really believe he can just stay when his army goes? He told you a Roman soldier must serve for twenty-five years. Before Galen is allowed to leave his army, he will be a graybeard like the one he calls Sita. Dafydd, please. Listen to me."

She swept a hand across his forehead to brush the hair from his eyes. "He is not a man of peace destined to grow bent with age and to die in his sleep. He is a warrior. You heard his tales—of places and people far from here. Did he remain here with us, do you think he would be content—ploughing fields and harvesting grain?"

She softened her voice almost to a whisper. "I know you love him; I love him as well."

"Then, how can you let him go?" Disbelief mounted in the blue eyes filled with angry bewilderment. "Why won't you make him stay? At least ask him to!"

"Because he is not a farmer or a slave, Dafydd. He never was. And for me to try to force him to be is not love."

He shook off her hold. "Galen told me a man will fight for what he loves."

She blinked back sudden tears. "Dafydd, I was also there and heard his words. He meant that in the name of love a man will fight, not that he will fight to *keep* love."

He looked at her strangely. "You are a woman; you do not understand," he said quietly, turning from her. "But it does not matter. *I* know . . ."

As it was his child's way to dismiss what he could

not understand, she took this odd response to mean acceptance. Except then she heard the rest of it.

"Because he was talking about what a *man* would do."

Twenty-one

Against the brightness of the midday sun Cerrix shaded his eyes and watched the seemingly endless procession of soldiers moving through the narrow mouth of the valley below.

"One cannot help but wonder. If this army is a token force—as his message stated it would be—what must the sight of his *entire* legion look like?"

Cerrix did not respond to the question quietly voiced by the man who stood beside him on the fortress's high catwalk. He knew Myrddin did not ask it for the purpose of hearing an answer. The Druid merely expressed aloud for his king's benefit the thoughts, fears, and doubts of their people—who were also watching Agricola's army as it advanced in armored formation across the valley floor like some dark shadow creeping over the land.

"The scouting parties have reported seeing thousands," he stated at last. "The four warriors who actually entered his camp with the centurion were awe-struck. They claim the number of men he has under arms is as countless as the trees in the forest.

Therefore, I accept the truth of his words and believe that Rome's new governor *has* come into my sight with only a token force. And yet, while this gesture of his goodwill may be sincere, it is not without a self-serving purpose as well."

He turned his head to look to the priest. "It is not necessary to feel a fist close in order to recognize its might, Myrddin. This——" he gestured over the top of the timbered wall in the direction of the ever-advancing army——"may be only a tenth of his force, yet Agricola knows it is enough for me to realize his superior strength. Even did I order an attack, he has sufficient men to withstand it until his reinforcements arrive. In two days' time—or less—his entire legion would be in my valley. Against so massive a force we would have no chance at all."

"Are you certain?" the Druid asked.

"You know I am." With a rueful smile Cerrix looked back over the wall. Although the scouts had seen hundreds of mounted men among the body of Agricola's main force, he counted now only a handful on horseback. Those of the highest rank, he guessed, for all but one wore the scarlet colors he knew belonged to men of authority. Supreme authority, however, appeared to be held by the man who rode at the column's head. He was wrapped in purple.

Cerrix watched him for a moment, but the distance was too great to ascertain anything of the man he knew must be Agricola. And so he turned his attention back to the man's army.

In addition to the mounted officers there were a half dozen centurions who marched beside their men. Unlike those on horseback, whose helmets bore plumes of color, the helmets of these men bore distinctive red crests set athwart. Strangest to Cerrix's sight, though, were the men who carried aloft the eagle and legionary standards. They wore animal skins as headdresses. According to the scouts who had seen them up close, it appeared as if the man's head had been swallowed by the beast and the man was looking out the open jaws. The animal was one unknown to Cerrix's men. They had said it was like a great mountain cat, but with long, thick, tawny-colored hair about its neck.

Suddenly the man in purple raised his hand, and a signal issued by some manner of horn sounded. Agricola's army halted, broke formation and began to regroup, seemingly without command or effort.

In awe Cerrix watched the emerging pattern of men. His eyes scanned these new lines of soldiers who now stood stiffly with their tall, oblong shields resting on end upon the ground, the side edges almost touching. There was a symbol painted upon the shield faces. He was too far to see, yet it had been told to him by those who had that it was the image of a wild boar. Wondering as to the irony of the omen—that a beast revered by the Ordovices for its courage and ferocity should prove to be the symbol of the army that would subjugate them—he turned from the parapet to descend a ladder.

On the ground immediately below, the members of the council awaited him. Behind the elders stood his entire contingent of warriors, save those few standing watch at strategic points around the wall.

Halfway down the ladder, Cerrix stopped and looked out over the sea of bodies. With word of the

Roman army's approach hundreds had sought the protection of the hill fort's walls. There were too many people crowded into too small an area. The unnatural closeness made them restless, but there was more to their unease. It was a taut mood of fear and curiosity both that permeated the settlement. All were anxiously assembled in anticipation of learning their king's decision—and ultimately their fate.

Berec, apparently speaking for the council, came forward as Cerrix's feet touched solid earth. "Do we sue for peace?"

"We do." For a moment Cerrix's gaze locked with that of the old warrior. In the eyes clouded by age he saw tears, and yet the gray head nodded in assent.

"It is time. The dark night of Roman rule cannot be broken by the dawn of an Ordovician rebellion. Proceed, my king."

Cerrix threw back his head and called out to the men atop the walls. "Open the gates and display the branches." He then turned his attention toward a waiting group comprised of six of his best warriors. At his beckoning they stepped forward.

Under the force of a dozen men the massive fortress gates creaked open. Cerrix and his escort passed through and waited there, a few steps into the open. From the gateway's huge crossbeam above their heads there hung bundles of evergreen branches, the symbol of a Celtic truce and a signal to the Romans below.

A few moments passed, and then the horn sounded again—a different tone this time. The solid phalanx of soldiers opened up, and from within its midst nine Romans emerged. The purple-cloaked horseman, now afoot, and two others in scarlet were accompanied by

396

six common soldiers. The group proceeded toward the foot of the shale pathway that led up to the hilltop fortress.

Cerrix motioned his men forward. They made their way down the steep slope at a slow and measured pace which placed them and the group of Romans at the base of the mountain simultaneously. Both groups halted some ten yards apart, each eyeing the other warily. At a silent command from one of the red-cloaked officers the Roman soldiers set their shields down onto the rocky ground, edges locked. They held their spears upright, point end toward the flawless sky.

Two men then broke away from the group of nine and strode forward. Cerrix noted that the man cloaked in purple wore eagle feathers in his helmet. The other man he would have known even without the centurion's sideways crest which served to proclaim his rank.

Cerrix gestured to his own escort to remain where they stood. Alone, he took the final dozen steps to put him in arm's reach of the Romans. At his approach both men symbolically removed their helmets. Cerrix acknowledged the gesture with a deliberate nod—only in the presence of a friend did a helmed warrior bare his head. He then spoke to the taller of the pair, as it would have been unseemly to address Agricola before he had been formally presented.

"I think I prefer you as you left, Galen Mauricius. This iron shell gives you the look of a tortoise."

Although the bronze features maintained a proper masklike expression of disciplined control, for a brief instant the black eyes warmed before the sleek, dark head bowed. "Lord Cerrix, may I present Gnaeus

397

Julius Agricola, military governor of the Province of Britannia."

Silence descended then as Cerrix turned his full attention upon the stranger who from a distance had appeared rather unassuming. Even now with a close, cursory look Rome's governor was still less than what Cerrix had expected. With a thatch of brown hair, a strong-boned face, wide at the forehead and narrow at the chin, and thick, heavy brows, Agricola was pleasant enough in appearance. But overall there was a surprising lack of forcefulness to the features.

In studying him further, however, Cerrix saw a charm of expression and sincerity in the eyes that shone intently from beneath the dark brows. There was strength as well—not of outward physical might, but rather some inner force. Though a good head shorter than either the centurion or Cerrix, Agricola portrayed not the slightest trace of self-consciousness in his lesser stature. Quite obviously here was a man who knew his own worth. Nor was he uncomfortable under Cerrix's scrutiny—also the mark of a man of strong will and confidence. He simply used the opportunity presented to make his own examination.

Appraising, without being judgmental, he allowed his gaze to travel the length of the tribesmen before him. When finished he smiled and bowed his head in respect. "A man is judged by the qualities of his enemies even more than by those he calls his friends. In the name of Vespasian Caesar, Emperor of Rome, I am truly honored to greet you, Cerrix, Great King of the Hammer Fighters."

For a moment Cerrix was surprised at having been addressed in his own language. Then he remembered what the centurion had told him. By blood this governor of Rome was not a Roman, but a Gaul.

Pleased he would be able to talk to the man directly, he now found it easy to return his smile. "I am equally honored to make the acquaintance of Rome's new governor. Since first I heard your name and learned of your plan from that Pict trader these many months passed, I have wondered about you. I relish the opportunity now to satisfy my curiosity about a man who, with the authority to command tens of thousands into war, would prefer instead to scheme for peace. For I must question his motive."

"Then, we have something in common, King Cerrix. I have been every bit as curious about you and likewise have wondered. Does this king truly possess the unselfish wisdom to see that in war his people have no future, or does he have a motive other than peace?"

"My motive is the welfare of my people. What is yours, Governor of Rome's Emperor?"

"Logic. War brings only a waste of lives and resources, and the feeding of a few men's need for glory. Peace on the other hand brings a prosperity which can feed the mouths of an entire nation. And in that there is a far greater and more lasting eminence."

Cerrix laughed aloud. He shifted his focus then to the dark and silent man at Agricola's side. "You were right, my friend. He *is* a worthy adversary. I can now understand in part the steadfast faith you place in him. But I thought you had said he was not greedy of fame."

Suspecting that in his commander's presence the centurion would not speak freely, he returned his gaze to Agricola. "Yours is a high ambition indeed, yet it is somehow tempered by your sincerity. I believe you, but more importantly I may come to trust you. Set up your camp, Governor. The boughs of truce shall remain hanging over our gates. Tonight you and the centurion will accept my hospitality, and we shall take the first steps upon this path of yours to 'greater and lasting eminence.' "

By dusk an entrenched camp had been dug. Sixty tents stood erected upon the valley floor.

Vine wood staff in hand Galen patrolled the southern perimeter of the encampment, ostensibly to inspect the work done on the ramparts—deep V-shaped ditches, lined with sharpened stakes set slantwise into the dirt, and banked turf walls, formed from the excavated earth.

He could not see her hut, but a thin trail of smoke above the tree line indicated her presence. Somehow he had known that she would not be one of those to seek the protection of the hill fort, and her nearness now gave him a sense of both comfort and frustration.

Two days earlier, upon intercepting Agricola and rejoining his legion, he had slipped back into army life as easily as he had into uniform. By day the routine, duty, and responsibility of his rank provided him a haven from his thoughts and memories. But at night thoughts and recollections of the life he had lived here for nearly three months slid unbidden into his mind. At times he could almost feel her beside him, or hear her voice. He told himself these were wishful longings for pleasures once tasted and now gone. With time they would fade. He was a soldier; the army was where he belonged. And yet. . . .

"Centurion Mauricius."

The sound of his name jolted Galen back to the present. He turned around to see a junior officer from Agricola's staff approaching.

The man stopped and saluted. "The governor requests your presence in his tent. If you would follow me, please, sir."

Galen acknowledged the order with a curt nod and twinge of irritation. It was hardly necessary for him to have an escort. Every Roman army camp, whether erected from leather tents or built with stone and timber, was laid out in the exact same manner: with four gates, two intersecting avenues, and the headquarters in the center—in this case Agricola's tent. However, to appease his commander's rather nervous-looking adjutant, he mutely followed him.

Treading a dirt pathway already packed firm beneath the sandals of four hundred and eighty soldiers, they passed rows of tents so perfectly aligned a man could measure and find not a single tent out of line.

Only its location at the camp's center distinguished Agricola's tent from the others. The man sent to fetch Galen ducked his head inside, announcing to the tent's occupant the arrival of his requested visitor. He then waved for Galen to enter.

Galen pushed aside the leather flaps that formed the door and stepped inside, bowing his head to clear the low opening. He was about to straighten and remove his helmet as decorum dictated, when a small bundle of blond hair and bright colors came hurtling straight at him.

"Galen!" Dafydd flung his arms about him and hung on. "I told Rhyca! I told Rhyca you would be back! I was right. I knew you would. I just knew!"

"Dafydd." His voice tight with sudden emotion, Galen could manage no more than the boy's name. His heart seemed to want to turn over beneath the plates of his *lorica.*

"Ahem."

The rather innocuous cough from across the tent knelled reality. As reason struck with a dull ache, Galen gently disentangled himself from the child and pushed him to stand at his side, slightly behind him and out of the direct view of the man seated at a desk on the far side of the tent. He saluted, tapping the knuckles of his right fist lightly to his chest. "Your pardon, Governor."

Though he was known to possess little if any sense of humor, Agricola's mouth twitched into a half smile. "Rest at ease, Centurion. I do believe, after all, that your orders did include attempting to gain a measure of these people's trust. To show them, if you would, that Romans are not some race of demons with long tails and eyes that glow red in the night. It would therefore appear that in this one particularly *small* aspect—" his gaze drifted pointedly toward the boy— "you have accomplished your mission exceedingly well. However . . ."

The heavy-browed gaze returned to him. "You were given other orders as well. Your degree of success with the primary aim of your mission does not appear as clear." Stern-faced now, the man stared at him. "It was the Emperor's contention, as well as mine, that a man who had so well distinguished himself upon the

402

battlefields of Judaea could persevere through any situation. Hence the turn this mission appears to have taken is all the more unexpected and disturbing."

"I am afraid you have me at a disadvantage, sir. If the governor would perhaps care to explain—"

His voice died in mid-statement as Agricola lifted a hand and waved him silent. As if remembering Dafydd's presence, he lowered his eyes to the child's level and gestured to him. "Come here, boy. Our business is not concluded. Sit and be still."

At once Dafydd hopped over to the chair Agricola indicated, beside his own. He scrambled awkwardly into it with his legs hanging free, feet dangling a good foot above the dirt floor.

Galen removed his helmet, tucked it beneath his left arm along with his vine staff, and stood at rigid attention, awaiting Agricola's further acknowledgement.

It was warm in the tent, and he could feel the sweat trickling down his back. Agricola had removed his own cloak, and it lay draped across a small chest behind him. He sat in his tunic before a well-worn camp table rummaging for a stylus amid several sheaves of rolled scrolls and wax tablets. Dafydd sat quietly, kicking his feet to and fro, his hands resting flat on the chair's seat. Periodically he looked over at Galen and grinned—as if he were privy to some wondrous secret. What the boy was doing in Agricola's tent suddenly loomed as far less important than what he might have done—or said.

The stylus located, Agricola scratched something on a wax tablet. Closing the wooden leaves, he handed the tablet to Dafydd. "Take this to one of the men guarding the horses and you'll have your ride."

Dafydd's eyes shone with pleasure as he took the tablet. He pushed a shock of hair from his forehead. "Truly?"

Agricola nodded. "Now be off with you."

His face still lit with excitement, the boy slid down from the chair and started for the doorway. He stopped abruptly, looking back over his shoulder. "I really do want to ride one of the horses, but I would trade it for . . . you . . . you know . . . that other thing."

"Some things are not as easily arranged as others, Dafydd. An honest man does not promise what he may not be able to deliver. Now go."

Dafydd slipped past Galen, but before he stepped outside he paused to whisper, somewhat loudly, "For such an important man, he's not so very scary."

The noise that resounded from across the tent might have been a stifled laugh or a strangled snort of irritation. Galen was not certain. "Sir, about the boy . . ."

"A most beguiling child." Agricola finished for him. "I was making an 'inspection' of the latrine when he approached me, bold as Jupiter's balls. He said the eagle feathers atop my helmet must mean I was the leader of the Eagle soldiers, and asked if I was the one who had sent you here before. Then he told me he needed to talk to me about you. Quite a one-man delegation, he is— and rather adept at seizing an opportunity and exploiting it to his advantage."

Galen bit down hard and looked away. One did not burst into laughter in the presence of the military governor of Britain. Still, the picture suddenly presented in his mind's eye of the most powerful man in the province being confronted while relieving himself— and by a small boy—was not an easy one to overlook.

If Agricola was aware of his effort to suppress his amusement, he did not show it. Crossing his hands on his stomach, he leaned back in his chair. "His affection for you borders on love, Centurion. The mite actually had the mettle to challenge the decisions of an Imperial Governor."

"Sir?"

"He does not want you to leave. He wants you to stay here with his people . . . and some woman he called 'Rhyca.' " He paused and slowly sat forward. "Apparently there were a few details inadvertently omitted from your initial report, Centurion."

"Nothing that affects the final outcome, sir." Galen knew his emotions were effectively masked behind the impassive military stare fixed upon his features. Still, his thoughts raced. How much *had* Dafydd told him?

Agricola gave him a long, thoughtful stare. "I have served in Britain before and have more than a fair knowledge of these people, Centurion Mauricius. Nor am I blind. It was most evident earlier today that some form of a bond exists between you and their king, whence did I begin to wonder. Then this crippled child walks out of the woods as I am taking a piss and begs me to let you stay . . . and moreover, tells me there is a woman . . . now I have to wonder still further. I have to wonder if your recommendation that a peace with these people would be enduring is a recommendation made free of personal prejudice."

He spoke briskly now, with the tone of a man whose patience had been expended. "To be perfectly truthful, I have to question whether or not you are capable of making any judgment in regard to these people that *is* unbiased."

Galen gritted his teeth. "I can assure you, Governor, that my personal feelings have not affected my recommendations. I am very much aware of the conflict which exists between what I have come to feel for this woman and child and my oath to serve. However, it is a battle I have already waged."

"And the victor, Centurion?"

"I doubt I would be standing here, Governor, if you did not already know the answer to that question."

"You are right." The twitching half smile suddenly returned. "But I did want to see your face when you said it. Very well, then. I shall take your recommendations under consideration when we meet with Cerrix tonight. Until then you are dismissed."

Galen saluted and started to turn toward the tent flap. Agricola's voice stopped him.

"There is one thing more, Centurion Mauricius. You have rendered to Rome a great service." He tossed at him a red leather bag tied with a thong, which when Galen caught it made a distinctive chinking sound. "With the Emperor's compliments and my personal gratitude."

Galen bowed his head, conveying acceptance. He knew inside the bag he would find a silver gilt medal with the likeness of the Emperor Vespasian—a decoration to hang on his harness. He did not feel entitled. Men very often died in attempting to earn such honors. But then again, perhaps he was entitled. In this place a part of him *had* died.

"To all your terms we are agreeable—save one."

With Cerrix's resolute declaration echoing ominously in the large hut, Galen's focus shifted immediately from the Ordovices' king to his own commander. His concern was justified. Agricola did not look pleased.

"May I remind you that what we are building is a bridge between our peoples," he responded, his voice somewhat strained. "I ask you to consider carefully. Which plank do you want removed?"

Cerrix's eyes narrowed, and Galen knew the warrior had recognized the underlying threat contained in Agricola's response. "I am not removing a plank, Governor of Rome. I am adding the crossbeam—for without it, this bridge will surely collapse. We will allow the construction of roads and fortresses through our lands, and supply men for military service in your auxiliary armies. We will even pay your taxes and tribute provided there is no abuse. But we must be allowed to prevail in our way of life. In this one thing we are immovable: My people *must* be granted the right to govern themselves and to hold power over their own."

While the members of the Council of Elders seated in a circle along with Agricola and their king murmured their concurrence, Agricola deliberated in silence. Several times his eyes drifted to Galen. Enough times, in fact, that Galen began to grow uneasy. The glances were not going undetected by the dozen warriors with whom he stood along the hut's walls. Four days ago these men had known him as a captive slave. Now it was beginning to appear as though he were right hand to the man dictating the terms of their surrender. This blow to their pride was almost a deliberate insult, and he could hardly blame them did they recognize it as such.

"Very well." At last Agricola spoke. "This can be done—as long as it is done under Rome's eye. Your tribe may be granted its own governance. However, you will not be allowed to continue to hold this site which can be defended against Rome. The ramparts of this hill fort must be dismantled. A permanent garrison of Roman troops will provide defense against marauders."

There issued forth an immediate rumbling of discord from the elders and the warriors.

"What of our arms, our weapons?" demanded one of the elders.

Agricola looked directly to the man who had asked the question. "Under my governorship you may keep them," he answered. "Though it is under Roman law a capital offense to bear arms without imperial authority, I understand what my predecessors did not. To take away a warrior's weapons is to take away his manhood."

Agricola waited patiently as the council lords spoke in low tones. Finally there was a murmur of assent, and Cerrix stood.

"It is agreed. We accept your terms. In the morning you shall have our surrender, as well as the return of the four soldiers who remain among us. We ask that you grant us this night to grieve for our freedom and to assuage our pride."

"The four shall be returned tonight. They have been held long enough. However, the time you have asked for is granted. The night is yours."

Nodding, Cerrix rose to his feet.

Escorted by a handful of Cerrix's warriors, Agricola and Galen exited the hut.

Only the thin shred of a waning moon hung in the sky. Where there were torches set into the ground or mounted into the walls of the huts, there were circles of smoky light. Everywhere else there was blind darkness, and yet their escort led them unerringly to the gate and down the pathway toward the Roman camp. Somewhere in the distance a fox called. It was a soulful cry.

"In the end of a people's freedom there is a loss to all men's," Agricola stated softly. "It can be no other way, and yet to see so proud and noble a spirit fettered . . ." He did not complete his thought, letting his voice merely die in the silence of the night.

He did not speak again, and so Galen found himself left to his thoughts: The treaty had been negotiated. There would be peace. And yet this was not ended. Something else lay unfinished. He could not leave without seeing her.

Near the perimeter to the camp the Ordovician warriors left them without a word, melting into the blackness. Agricola called out to the sentry watch to announce their approach.

But Galen had no intention of entering the camp. "Governor, there is someone I must see."

The darkness hid Agricola's face. Yet his tone while firm was also compassionate. "See that you are returned by first light, Centurion."

She was not asleep, yet the knocking on her door still wrenched her brutally from a half-dream state.

Her eyes flew open, and she sat bolt upright. She expected to hear a voice identifying itself, but the only sound save that of the fire was the rasping of her own breath.

Again several knocks sounded. This time there was more anger or insistence behind the pounding. Slipping on her undergown, she stumbled to the door. Upon opening it, she went still and cold at the sight of the Roman soldier standing there beneath the lintel. A scream rose in her throat, then died with recognition of him as he pulled the helmet from his head. He was more smoothly shaven than she had ever seen him, but then he had always claimed that no Ordovician blade could take an edge like a Roman razor. And his hair was cropped close, as when he had first come to the hill fort.

He seemed to know her thoughts, for he raised a hand to run the fingers through his shorn hair. "I . . . I was not certain . . ." He spoke with uncharacteristic hesitancy. There was almost a nervousness about him. He tucked his helmet under his arm. "I was not sure I should come. You need only to say the word and I will leave. But I—"

Whatever more Galen had wanted to say never found voice, for she was then in his arms. His helmet clattered to the floor. With both hands he seized her. His mouth was upon hers with a crushing, bruising intensity. His tongue found entry. Deeply he kissed her. Within him there was no thought save of her and no need save for her. What drove him was not his longing to possess this woman, but the knowledge of his belonging to her.

He felt her hands fumble to unbuckle the fastenings

of his armor as her tongue for the first time ever slipped inside his mouth.

He carried her across the room and laid her upon the furs where, for only a few nights, they had made their bed together. Now each knew this would be their last night. She whispered his name, reached out to him, and he was lost.

He stripped the shift from her body. On bended knee he finished unbuckling his *lorica*. He dragged the armor over his head, flinging it to the floor. His tunic and undervest followed, stripped over his head and tossed aside. He knelt between her legs and leaned forward. He ran his broad hands over her body, her thighs, her breasts, her face. This night he would learn each curve and hollow of her and memorize every line.

Rhyca reached for him, the familiar places she knew—the hard knots of muscle behind his upper arms, the thick column of his neck. By touch she remembered the scars across his belly and then explored places she had before been too timid to learn. She ran her hands over his naked chest and downward to that part of him that proclaimed his need of her.

He was hard and heavy in her hand, and yet she knew no trace of apprehension, only the anticipation of fulfillment. None but this man could ever satisfy what he had awakened in her. With some new-found boldness she guided him and then watched as his body joined with hers, crying out as he entered her. Slowly he slid himself into her until he was completely sheathed. Now he leaned forward and reached for her again.

His passion surged. The desire to go slowly, to savor

and preserve each moment, warred with the desperate need to thrust deep inside her, to feel her heat sheath him and her arms hold him, to have her as his. As if though she knew his thoughts, she pulled him down to her, her legs closing tightly around him. He was almost brutal as he took possession of her mouth once more and then thrust.

Rhyca gasped as he drove himself into her, paining her with the swiftness and depth of his penetration. But she did not care. She knew only that she wanted him, all of him. She swung her hips up, pulling her knees back toward her. After a moment her woman's fluid wetted her passage, easing his way. And then there was only the feel of him inside her drawing out a sensation that was like no other that she had ever known.

She grasped his upper arms and pulled herself upward to take him deeper into her. She cried out for him, and as he made love to her with a savage desperation, she surrendered herself, understanding his primal need to take her almost violently. She was not his enemy; she was his prize. He would fight to have her—in fierce defiance of all that would keep them apart. For this one and final night together they would deny the gods and their fates alike—and even the army of Rome.

Galen plunged into her, abandoning himself to his body's need until it fulminated into climax like a burning sunburst. Though spent, he did not immediately withdraw from her, but instead remained buried within her.

Finally he heaved himself up and rolled over beside her. He gathered her close, stroking her hair, feeling its fineness between his fingers. She stirred, took a deep breath, held it for a moment, then released it slowly. He looked at her face, but she kept her eyes tightly closed, her head resting on his chest. Her hair like some silken blanket covered them both.

They did not speak. They had no need, not for words. Between them there was that manner of communication granted only to those whose souls are one. Nor did they sleep, but merely rested until renewed, for they would pass the night making love.

Awake, propped on his right elbow, her soft warmth beside him, he watched her. In this instant he knew his mind would never erase her beauty. In his memory she would never fade or be forgotten. Within him a dull ache twisted and knotted. The prospect of her gone from his life left him empty inside, hollow and cold. He shifted his weight to take the strain off his right shoulder. Wrapping an arm about her, he pulled her close and cradled her. She ran her hands down his bare back and pressed her face against his throat.

For a moment he buried his face in her hair and tried to sort his thoughts. Finally he lifted her from him, turned her face to his and pushed the tangled hair from her eyes. "Rhyca, after the treaty with Cerrix is signed tomorrow, I have been ordered back to Deva."

She stiffened in his embrace, yet said nothing, merely nodding to indicate she had heard.

"Would you leave this place and go with me?"

"Go with you?" So many emotions flashed across

413

her face he could not read even one. "As what? Your whore?"

"No." He sat up, pulling her with him. "As my wife."

Her gaze locked on his. He could tell she was struggling against it, but her eyes were welling with tears. "You know that can never be," she whispered. "You told me yourself that your army will not allow its soldiers to marry."

"They cannot prevent a marriage—only refuse to recognize it. As long as I can pay for you to live outside the gates and to follow me as I am transferred—"

"Transferred? To where? Those strange places you have spoken of, with names that I cannot even speak?" She laughed a soft and sad laugh. "No, Galen. I am not so strong. Though I have loved you as I have never loved anyone or anything, I cannot live my life watching you march to and from battle, all the while knowing that one day you may not come back. And should you not, what then? Do I, for survival's sake, find another to take your place as did your mother when her man did not return? And then another after him and still others, until I am so old that none would have me?"

She paused, her face intent, and then she continued. "As you cannot escape your fate, I cannot escape mine. This is where I belong . . . with Dafydd. I fear it is only a matter of time before Luned's husband forces her to cast him out. If I were not here, there would be none to take him. Since you left he has been with me nearly continually. Indeed, I was surprised he agreed to leave me this morning when I insisted he go back to the hill fort for safety. Surely you must see that I cannot go."

Rhyca shook her head. Her grief threatened to overwhelm her. She heard a rushing in her ears and feared for an instant all would go black. She wanted this man, she needed him, but always she had known she could never have him. She squeezed her eyes shut. Mustering the last of her strength, she pushed back the darkness and leaned forward to place a soft kiss upon his mouth. "You ask out of guilt, Galen, but I think you really knew before you asked what my answer would be. You cannot stay. And where you go I cannot follow. Here and now it must end between us."

He took her into his arms. She was right—in all that she had said. He *had* known her answer, but he had also needed to ask.

He lay with her then for the last time and took her with a gentleness that before he had known her would never have been possible. He took her not as man takes woman—out of lust—but as a husband takes his wife—in love. With all the intensity of his soul he made love to her.

Afterward he kissed her tenderly, eased from her side and rose to dress. He heard her go to the hearth and stir the embers, adding kindling and wood to build a fire to stave off the cold damp of dawn.

He finished buckling his armor and donned the shoulder belt from which the scabbard of his sword hung. He fastened his cloak into place, and lastly picked up his helmet from the floor. She was still kneeling before the fire, staring into the flames. He went to her. "Rhyca . . ."

She looked up. For just an instant the sight of him

armed and in uniform, towering above her, took her breath. She had always recognized his strength, his devotion to honor and sense of duty—they were traits inseparable from the man. Yet seeing him now as he stood before her, a soldier, she knew this was who and what he truly was. Her words to Dafydd the day Galen had left came flooding back: *He is not a farmer . . . he is a warrior.* Were he not, she realized suddenly, she could not have loved him as she did. But he belonged to war—as much as anyone had ever belonged to anything.

She did not understand how there could be comfort in this sudden knowledge, yet there was. In returning him to his destiny, she had bestowed upon him her greatest gift.

Standing, she tried to force a smile. "You must go. How will it appear to your governor if you are late?" She lifted her hand to smooth the folds of his cloak where they lay over his heart. It was an excuse to touch him, just once more.

He caught her hand, turned it over and brought the palm to his lips. With untold tenderness the fingers of his other hand followed the contours of her cheek.

"You know what you mean to me."

"I know," she whispered, feeling the tears quicken, tears she had vowed not to shed. "Now go, my love—while I still can find the strength to say leave me. Go freely, but please do not ever come back, for I cannot live in the constant and cruel hope that one day you might return. I must know it is finished. Promise me. Please, Galen."

"You will forever hold my heart enslaved."

"Mine is no more free. But you must promise me, Galen. Please."

As he nodded, she felt the tears quicken and fought them back by sheer dint of will. He had given her the fullest measure of his love.

"Go!" It was a cry from the depths of her heart. He put a hand to her hair, and then turned.

Twenty-two

The sun rose from behind the dusky hills like a molten ball. In bolts of piercing light its rays reflected off the polished armor and weaponry of the assembled cohort.

Galen squinted and kept his gaze steady. Then, out of the corner of his eye he saw a movement, a shadow cast upon the ground by something overhead. Lifting his eyes skyward he watched as an eagle, with a scarcely discernible flap of its wings, circled above then tilted its flight toward the forest. Had they witnessed it, the legionary priests would no doubt have proclaimed the bird a favorable omen. With a wry inner smile Galen returned his focus from the heavens to what lay earthbound before him.

In front of the Roman encampment, upon neutral ground, a ceremonial pavilion had been erected. Streamers of gold and crimson fluttered from its dozen stanchions. Beneath the billowing awning of imperial purple Britain's new governor sat calmly in a curule chair. He was flanked by a trio of his senior staff officers resplendent in their bronze-trimmed dress armor and gold-bordered scarlet cloaks.

Earlier Galen had respectfully declined Agricola's invitation to stand with those officers of the Twentieth Legion *Valeria Victrix,* for he had no place among them. His legion was still in garrison at Deva. Besides, he preferred to remain among the body of the army, where he would be far less conspicuous to the Ordovices. He saw no reason to rub so sharply into their skins the fact that he had played a part in their final subjugation to Rome. He also favored the more unobstructed view accorded to a man standing in the open, and therefore chose a position to the far left and slightly behind the front ranks.

While he believed Cerrix would honor the truce, he could not ignore the persistent and even increasing sense of unease settling upon him. There were some feelings a man learned to trust. The instinct of impending danger was one, and that tight feeling deep in his gut warning that all was not right was another. But whether there was a real, external cause for his restlessness now, or whether it was rooted within his own personal turmoil, he could not distinguish.

Too, old habits and training fell hard before change. Emotions aside, he was still a soldier—and still capable of recognizing a sorry defensive situation when he saw one.

Assembled as Agricola's army was, positioned with one century on either side of the pavilion and the remaining four ranked solidly behind it, their backs—though to their own camp—were still unguarded. Moreover, this parade ground deployment of close ranks made each square of eighty men the perfect target to an assault of arrows or spears. It would be almost impossible to launch either weapon into one of the tight formations and *not* hit a man. If it were large enough, a single well-aimed volley could take out a third of Agricola's force.

Slowly Galen cast his gaze over the rows of soldiers on his left. Each man stood stock-still, sword and dagger in their sheaths, *pilum* and shield held at attention. At least these were battle-seasoned troops, he reckoned, recalculating the odds.

His inspection did not appear to have escaped the heed of the man who stood directly beside him. Sita glanced over at him knowingly, shifting only his eyes. The veteran shared his thoughts concerning this gilt and purple pomp. But both sides required it; without it the vanquished did not feel vanquished, nor the victors victorious.

Galen had not spied the bald Thracian until just before the order to assemble had been called. He would like to have spoken with him. In fact, he would like to have questioned the other released captives as well: Facilis and the youth Gaius, both of whom now stood in ranks; and even the half-mute Valerius, who had been given over to the surgeon's care and would most likely be discharged. The sight of his friend's beheading had broken something inside the youth no splint or salve could mend.

Galen cursed himself for his oversight. He should have insisted upon talking to his men either before or after the meeting with Cerrix and the council. Rumors were sometimes founded in fact, and they always reached a man's ear first. It was possible the Romans could have overheard from their Ordovician masters

420

some talk they had simply discounted at the time as idle gossip.

Four days had passed since Mouric's disappearance. Cerrix's scouts had been unable to locate any sign of him or his band, nor had Galen and the warriors who had escorted him to Agricola seen evidence of the renegades. Still, Galen knew the man would not abandon his bid for power. He and perhaps hundreds of rebels who might have joined him by now were biding their time. Indeed, if Mouric were waiting for the right moment to strike, this day—on the morning of a treaty-signing between Rome and the last unconquered tribe in western Britain—would seem to be the perfect one.

More uneasy than ever, Galen turned his focus to the hill fort. No less than fifty warriors were now descending the shale path. They were led by the elders of the council and the white-robed Druid priest.

Galen watched the reactions of the men around him. While the sight of the lime-haired Britons drew no sound from the well-disciplined troops, the tension evoked by the Ordovices' approach was patent in every face. Grips tightened on spear shafts, and shields raised ever so slightly. However, to the credit of the centurions who commanded them, the men never moved—not even when the warriors took up positions facing the pavilion and directly opposite their front ranks. Less than fifty yards separated the two armed forces. This nearness gave the Romans, with their close arms fighting tactics, the strategic advantage. Yet Galen doubted the nervous legionaries either recognized or appreciated that fact.

He kept a wary eye on the forward line of centuries

especially, while periodically looking over toward the Ordovices. Fingering the sword hilts at their waists, they ranged impatiently behind their council and the Druid priest, stopping frequently to glare across the open area. In mutual distrust the Romans glared back.

At last Cerrix appeared alone in the hill fort's open gateway seated upon a caparisoned horse. His surefooted mount made its way upon the steep shale pathway with slow care. The sun glinted off his gold arm bands and *torc*.

As he drew nearer, Galen noted that his copious cloak was of blue and green squares signifying the heavens and earth, while his tunic was black threaded with gold denoting the night and the sun. At his waist, beneath his girdle, there was a branch of evergreen. Similar boughs adorned the horse's bridle.

Once descended from the trail he rode toward the pavilion. He made a ritual sunwise circle around it before halting his mount before its entrance. A moment passed, and then a solitary figure emerged from beneath the canopy. Cerrix dismounted. He flung down his weapons and knelt in silent submission at the feet of his conqueror.

Galen felt a muscle twitch in his jaw. He knew what this wordless act had cost Cerrix in terms of his pride and manhood.

Agricola bade his vanquished foe rise. "I have known you as an honorable adversary, Cerrix, Great King of the Hammer Fighters. Hereafter may I greet you as a friend." He extended his arm, which Cerrix grasped just above the wrist, and raised his voice that his words might carry to all. In the Celtic tongue he solemnly intoned, "Let our peoples dwell no longer under the dark cloud of war. Let there rise from this day forth in the skies over Britain the glorious dawn of peace." Then he repeated this declaration in Latin.

In Latin and Celtice the terms of the treaty were read aloud. At Agricola's beckon Myrddin came forward to stand before them and officiate during the ceremony. With the dagger he removed from his belt the priest carefully pricked the tip of the fourth finger on the left hand of each man. A small amount of blood was then squeezed from both into a bowl and mixed with wine. To seal the treaty Agricola and Cerrix would drink a blood covenant. But the rite would do more than make the treaty of peace official and binding. With each man drinking the blood of the other, the same blood would now run in the veins of both rulers, thereby creating a kinship between them and an inviolable peace between the peoples they ruled.

With the blood-letting completed and the bowl now cupped in both hands, Myrddin tipped it from side to side and front to back, toward each of the four winds. He then offered the vessel to Cerrix. As he who had been vanquished, his would be the more bitter swallow.

Cerrix raised the bowl to his lips. He drank without hesitation, then passed it to the victor. Agricola drained it.

As Rome's governor lowered the bowl, a resonant sound quivered through the still air. It almost seemed an intended part of the ceremony, except that Galen and more than a hundred others immediately recognized it for what it was—the bay of a Celtic war horn.

For Galen all thoughts and memories of the past months fled, as the soldier in him came to the fore.

He, as well as the six centurions of the Second Cohort, looked immediately to their commander for response.

As Agricola's order rang out, his army sprang into action, accompanied by the answering tones of a Roman trumpet. Men who only an instant earlier had been standing at rigid attention for a ceremony honoring peace were commanded into fighting positions. The pavilion was instantly encircled by a large ring of soldiers, four deep. Agricola's life must be protected at any cost. The remainder of his army formed a battle line between the pavilion and the forest with their backs to the hill fort.

Cerrix's warriors had been caught even more by surprise than the Romans, and before they could react, the Ordovices found themselves surrounded by shield-bearing soldiers leveling spears. Their king and priest, inside the protected circle with Agricola, were promptly seized. Eyes flashing, Agricola ordered the pair put under restraint.

Furiously Cerrix fought the hold of his guard. "It is Mouric!" he shouted, trying to make himself heard above the clatter of nearly five hundred men preparing for battle. "Give me my weapons and free my warriors. This is our fight! Let us battle our own traitors!"

A hundred feet away Galen heard his cry. As surely as he had known something was wrong, he knew Cerrix was not a part of it and moved toward Agricola to vindicate his friend.

Another call of the war horn sounded, and a band of renegade warriors swept out of the forest like a sea wave rolling over a beach. The solemn ceremony of gilt and purple was about to erupt into a scarlet battle. As was their wont, the Ordovicians stood in a defiant line, working themselves into a frenzy for killing by beating their shields and screaming battle cries.

Even as he worked his way through the battle-ready formations to reach Agricola, Galen mentally assessed the enemy as at least three hundred strong. Pale hair flowing, they taunted their enemies—Roman and tribesmen alike—to take their heads if they could.

At the sight of their mutinous clansmen Cerrix's retainers were maddened by the challenge flaunted by the rebels. Soon the Romans attempting to do so would no longer be able to restrain them from breaking through and joining the battle about to occur.

Observing their rage and apparently recognizing the real target of their ardor, Agricola called out an order to the legionaries to stand down. As soon as the soldiers complied, the Ordovices rushed forward to prepare to engage their brothers. The same beating of shields and screaming of taunts ensued. Agricola then signaled for Cerrix's release. The leader of the Britons immediately retrieved his sword and ran, swinging the blade above his head to rally his warriors to his command.

Galen ceased then in his drive to reach Agricola. Across the remaining distance that separated them he heard the man shout to the centurions commanding the forward line to draw back their men and regroup, thereby allowing the Ordovices now under Cerrix's command to bear the brunt of the initial wave.

There was no panic. In the faces of the Romans Galen saw only a look of grim determination. At his side he heard a familiar voice raised in the guttural war cry of the Thracian race. The huge man—again in his element—fairly grinned at Galen as he swung his shield into place and hefted his *pilum*.

And then it came—the baying of the rebels' war horn answered by the high notes of the Advance.

From inside her hut Rhyca heard the baleful cacophony—the deep bray of the tribal horn followed almost instantly by the penetrating cry of the Romans' trumpets.

Once before she had heard those awful tones. . . .

Suddenly remembrance that had lain dormant, lulled by time and soothed by love, awakened like some truculent beast.

"No!" Her scream filled the small space, but there was no one save she in the room—no one to hear or heed her cries. "No, please, not again."

She slumped forward. "Not Galen. Please, not him," she sobbed. She squeezed her eyes shut and covered her ears with her hands. But she could not block the horrifying images she saw in her mind.

Gripped by terror, she ran from her hut. A force neither of her making nor of her control drew her. She raced down the path toward the edge of the forest and the scene of the trumpeter's call—one she knew was a call to battle.

Within moments of its outbreak the battle had narrowed to the space of a few feet between combatants. Their shouts and the clangs of their blows, mixed with the sounds of the horns and trumpets, drowned out the groans of those who fell and the cries of those

426

that lay dying. The Romans' burnished armor was now defaced with dust, sweat and blood. The smell of blood was everywhere.

Over three quarters of Mouric's force had broken through Cerrix's line. Another half of those had breached the Romans' defensive wall of shields. Perhaps a hundred remaining rebels carried on the desperate fight against three-to-one odds.

It did not matter that they were already defeated and would die. They had no fear of death. Indeed, they welcomed it. For a Celtic warrior there could be no better end than to die gloriously in battle. And for every enemy head he was able to take before being struck down himself, so much greater would be his honor and the higher his place in the Otherworld where the ghosts of those he slew would be brought into servitude.

Galen knew the greatest prize to be won was the head of either of the two men who had drunk a blood covenant to peace. Mouric's followers would never reach Agricola. Their numbers were already decimated, while the defensive circle around the pavilion remained intact. When one man fell, another came forward from the rear ranks to take his place. That same tactic was also being used to replace the tired men on the front line with fresh soldiers from the rear. Yes, Agricola was safe. But what of Cerrix?

The cloak of blue and green would have been discarded as a hindrance, so Galen looked instead for the black and gold tunic. Refusing to consider the possibility, he did not allow his eye to search for the man among the dead.

Forty yards to his left he found Cerrix paired in

combat with a Satyr-like figure Galen knew at once. He started to move rapidly toward them. Suddenly, three meters ahead, his path was blocked. Into his startled sight loomed a face permanently distorted by disfigurement.

Balor swung his sword, slashing at the air between them with a deadly intent. Beyond the man's back Galen saw Cerrix stumble and falter on rocky ground as he lifted his shield to block a slicing blow from Mouric's blade.

"Go! I'll take care of this one."

Sita's growl sounded to Galen's ear as the sweetest of music. Like a great lumbering bear the Thracian stepped in front of him, facing Balor, and Galen left him to his task.

As Rufus faced his foe, he rolled his massive, sloping shoulders forward in anticipation. Since the day of Mauricius's flogging he had waited for this moment of revenge. Though he had not expected to be the one to deliver it, he now gloried in the opportunity. He beckoned the warrior to him with a snarling taunt. "Come ahead, you ugly bastard. When I'm done with you that scar upon your face shall seem an insignificant scratch."

With a roar of fury the Briton lunged at him.

Of a height with his pale-haired opponent, Sita balanced out the disadvantage of his greater years with the width and bulk of his body and the power behind them. He blocked the long sword with his shield. Then, with a single step inside the warrior's guard, he thrust his short sword up under the ribs at an angle, until the blade's point reached the man's heart.

It had been almost too easy. As he thrust the lifeless

body from him, Rufus noted that the Briton died with the most surprised of expressions upon his twisted features.

At first it was impossible for Rhyca to see anything but masses of men and dust. Only the flashes of sunlight upon armor allowed her to distinguish Roman from tunic-clad Ordovician. Even as she drew nearer, she still was too far away to see faces.

She stumbled forward to the edge of the woods. As her body trembled in horror and fear, she leaned against the rough trunk of an oak, disbelieving what lay before her in the clearing. The ground was strewn with the bodies of dead and dying men. She shut her eyes. If only she could shut her ears as well.

The din was ear-shattering. Steel clashed against steel and mingled with screams of agony and shouts of triumph that were beyond words—or any sound made by men. They were the roars and bellows of savage beasts.

Somehow hearing the clamor and not seeing its cause was more terrifying, and the not knowing was worse than anything she could imagine. She opened her eyes and fixed her gaze upon the scene, held spellbound. Her very being seemed slowly to separate. Part of her stood to the side of her own body, watching the horror. Like the rape, she watched, but she did not feel. . . .

And yet a portion of her mind attended to the scene at hand. She could still think and reason—enough to realize that the battle she watched was not drawn upon any lines she could understand. There were tribesmen fighting against Romans; but also Romans fighting *alongside* tribesmen, and Ordovicians even battling their own warriors.

She searched for Galen across the field of battle, looking for the distinctive red crest. She needed to find him, to locate him among the hundreds of men wielding swords and fighting for their lives. She needed to know if he lived. And if he was destined to die—then she must know that as well.

Suddenly she felt hot and cold waves of fear wash over her. She had found him, drawn off in a fight with a tall warrior. Despite the distance she knew. It was Mouric.

At Galen's approach Mouric stayed his attack upon Cerrix. With his rival for the kingship struck unconscious by a bloody blow to his temple, there was no expediency in taking his head just yet. Instead, the wild-eyed warrior turned to confront a far more hated foe.

"Come to me, Roman," he taunted, a crazed look glazing his eyes. He swung his blade in a series of arcs as he closed the distance between them. "Come to me, and I shall finish in a few moments what was begun between us months ago."

With Mouric's first lunge Galen noted the marked difference in the warrior's style from when they had last crossed blades. A lack of rashness and an increase in caution were unmistakable.

Again and again Mouric circled his opponent, probing the strengths and weaknesses of his guard, wholly disinclined to take on the role of aggressor. Galen parried every thrust, also looking for any weakness. A sardonic smile touched his lips. Perhaps his hot-blooded foe might be goaded into a reckless move. "Obviously you have seen fit to learn from your previous errors, Briton. I am pleased that I was able to teach you something of the warrior's art."

Mouric's eyes narrowed into slits. "There is nothing that you could teach *me*, Roman. It is I who shall teach *you!*" With a growl he slammed his shield against that of his enemy and swung his long sword up over the top of it and then downward in a diagonal slash.

The blow was intended to slice bone-deep, but Galen raised his blade to block the stroke. Instantly, from the shoulder down his right arm went numb. Reflexively his fingers cramped, allowing him to maintain his grip upon his sword hilt. Yet he had no feeling; the arm dropped lifelessly to his side.

As if touched by fire, Mouric recoiled and stepped backward. "Not this time," he spat, his voice like the venomous hiss of a viper. "Not again will I fall prey to your demon's trick. You will pay for your cunning cowardice that day, as well as all your other offenses against me." An evil leer appeared. "And know this, Roman: When I am finished giving you your lesson, I shall begin with your woman's. Before I send the whore to join you in the Otherworld, I shall finish what was interrupted and left undone."

The mere thought of the bastard touching her caused Galen's body to shake in a white rage. But he forced back the hatred from his mind and the pain burning in his shoulder, struggling to regain control. This precious moment of delay had allowed some tingling sensation to return to his arm.

Galen chose a desperate tactic. Dropping his sword and transferring his shield to the weakened right hand, he plucked his dagger from its sheath with the left and lunged forward. Feinting a thrust with his shield, he then crouched, noting that the move seemed to have taken Mouric completely off guard. He found an opening.

He felt a familiar quickening of his pulse. The red haze that seemed to descend then across his field of vision he knew and recognized: It was blood lust. But this time he would not kill for Rome; this time he killed for himself. He drove the dagger into Mouric's gut. Angling the point up, he jerked his left hand downward, slicing the bastard's stomach open from chest to groin. He stepped back and allowed Mouric to sink to his knees. The man looked down and watched as his entrails spilled out in a quivering mass on the ground.

Galen tossed down his shield, sheathing his dagger. He picked up his sword and grabbed a fistful of the lime-stiffened locks. Cleanly he severed the head from the body—not for mercy's sake, but in fulfillment of a vow he had made for the death of a recruit whose name he could not recall, but whose face he had not been able to forget. Perhaps now, with the youth's murder avenged, the spirit might rest in peace.

The sound of Sita's voice, breaking through the blood mist filling Galen's mind, brought his head around and his sensibilities back to the present. He saw that the Thracian was kneeling beside Cerrix, inspecting his head wound. Galen retrieved his shield, preparing to fight his way to Sita's side to lend aid to the Ordovices' injured king. Then realization came:

The din of battle had subsided. What fighting continued was upon the perimeter of the field where those surviving rebels, each pursued by several Roman soldiers, now sought to save their lives by reaching the forest. But there would be no survivors, no prisoners taken or quarter given. Agricola would not let a single rebel escape to spawn a second generation of rebellion. Galen knew here and now it would end.

Suddenly his limbs trembled, not merely from physical exhaustion, but from emotional release. He felt drained. He waved for Sita to take the Ordovician king to the pavilion where the surgeon had set up his field hospital.

He sheathed his sword. Wearily he pulled the helmet from his head. Sweat dripped into his eyes, stinging them and causing them to water. He wiped the tears from his eyes with the back of his left hand, then the sweat from his brow with his forearm. Breathing deeply, he looked out over the field of dead and dying.

It was over. The wounded were being attended to. Everywhere there was the litter of weaponry, mixed with corpses and mutilated limbs. Blood reddened the soil and ran in rivulets in the cracks of sun-baked mud. And yet this day the gods had been generous. Agricola had lost only a small fraction of his men, less than one in eight. Galen had been in battles where one in eight survived.

He turned from the sight. Half of his life he had known this carnage. And yet always he had unquestioningly accepted his lot. But this day the sense of fulfillment that invariably sustained him was lacking. He felt no satisfaction or pride in the killing that had gone on, because he saw in it no end. Was he truly fated to know nothing else but war and its aftermath of death?

A woman's cry reached out to him from across the field. He turned and saw her struggling toward him. Like a gossamer cloak her unbound hair streamed behind her as she ran for him, straight to him.

Rhyca did not stop until she was safe in his arms. Then all of the emotion burst forth. She wept with the terror that had racked her at the thought that he might be killed, and with the joy that abounded in the realization that he had survived. She wept, too, at the agony of her heart. How could she survive another farewell—and then live, never to see him again?

Galen could do no more than hold her. He had resolved himself to living without her. But now, standing in the midst of this field of death, he realized she was his life. Without her he would be a shell, no more alive inside than the bodies upon the ground.

How long they stood there he did not know. He simply held her, his chin nestled in her hair, his eyes staring out unseeingly over the battlefield. Only when he heard footsteps behind him did he ease her away from him.

"Centurion."

Galen turned and faced his commander. This day Agricola had won his peace for Britain, and it had been hard fought for—by Roman spear and Celtic sword alike. There would be none again to rally under a banner of war. But it was impossible to read anything of the man's thoughts.

Agricola's gaze darted briefly to Rhyca. "This is no place for a woman, Centurion," he stated quietly in Latin.

434

"Yes, sir."

The same twitching half smile Galen had observed the previous day flickered across his commander's face. "But I don't suppose you would send her away unless ordered to."

Galen returned his stare. "No, sir."

"Very well. I suspected it would come to this, and now is as good a time as any to settle the matter." Agricola slowly untied the bindings of his helmet and removed it. His tone and stare had become almost fatherly. "During the council meeting I watched you. You hid it well, and yet it was still clear. Though your loyalty to the Empire remains staunch, Centurion, the heart of a soldier has ceased to beat in your chest. In its stead there now beats the heart of a man who has learned to feel compassion and love."

Defensively Galen stiffened. Though he recognized the truth of Agricola's words, pride demanded a response, a denial at least of sorts. Before he could offer either, Britain's governor raised his hand to command his silence.

"Make no mistake. These are traits to be treasured—for they are rare in men. But for a soldier they are encumbrances."

He paused then and looked upon Galen with the sharp, appraising eye of a man gifted in the judging of others. When he spoke again it was with the clear voice of command.

"With the first thaw in the spring I will take the legions northward. Once you would have been invaluable at my side. Now, however, I believe that your greatest effectiveness lies elsewhere than in the capacity of a field officer. You have sixteen years of service, do you not?"

Galen nodded, wondering what direction the man was taking with the question. At his side Rhyca shifted uneasily. He knew she could not understand what was being said. Reassuringly he laid his hand upon the small of her back.

Agricola discreetly ignored the gesture and continued to speak. "A permanent garrison shall be located here. Because of what I witnessed this day, I am prepared to offer you the command of it. In selfless disregard for your own life, you defended that of these people's king. This act will indebt Cerrix to you for the rest of his days. No other shall ever have the influence over him which you will now have. I would be a fool did I not attempt to exploit that to Rome's benefit. And too, by giving the position to you, I am also able to grant the petition of a small boy—" his eyes turned to Rhyca—"as well as the unspoken prayers of a woman."

He smiled and looked back to Galen. "Well, Centurion Mauricius, what say you? Are you interested enough to hear my terms?"

Galen looked at her. Her luminous eyes were still filled with tears. But no more, he vowed silently. He looked back to his commander. Unsure of his voice, he nonetheless managed to rasp, "You know my answer, Governor. But I ask that you speak Celtice, that the woman who shall be my wife may understand."

Smiling, Agricola inclined his head in polite respect to her as he complied. "It is not often that I am able to grant the impossible. Your posting here does, however, come at a price to you, Centurion. You would

436

serve out your remaining years of active service as military overseer of this area. At the end of those four years, instead of the five years of reserve duty you would normally owe, I would ask for ten. I caution you, you might find a domestic life rather boring . . . civil affairs as opposed to combat . . . peace instead of warfare . . . but I have always believed it is not for man to decide his destiny, rather for the gods. And only by listening to his heart can he hear their will. So . . . Galen Mauricius, are you content with my terms and do you accept your fate?"

This time Galen was truly unable to speak, for the woman at his side was suddenly in his arms, clinging so tightly with her arms about his neck as to render him mute.

Seated beneath the purple canopy Cerrix stoically endured the ministrations of Agricola's healer. He would have preferred Myrddin's attentions, but did not wish to appear ungrateful. Besides, the Druid was busy tending to the Ordovician wounded who lay alongside the Roman. Ignoring as best he could the dark little man who clucked in some strange tongue as he wrapped his head with a length of cloth, Cerrix watched the couple afield. Whatever Agricola had said to them a moment earlier had sent Rhyca flying into the centurion's arms with a look of joy upon her face the likes of which could shame the sun for brilliance.

Cerrix nodded in satisfaction and turned his gaze to the man who now approached. "It is said, Governor, that one who does a kindness to lovers shall in turn find good fortune. May the gods reward you."

Agricola grinned. "You honor me with your faith, King Cerrix. However, my motives are far from self-less." He inclined his head toward the now embracing couple. "I have seen such happen all over the Empire . . . unions from which babes sired by Roman soldiers are born to women of our provinces. There is nothing better to weld two peoples into one. In two generations there will be an end to hatred."

He squatted down next to Cerrix and placed his helmet on the ground between his feet. "Indeed, the time to raise up warriors is past, my friend. Now is the time for diplomats. In fact—" he looked at him in sudden thoughtfulness—"you happen to have now among your tribe a boy . . . With the proper rear-ing . . . yes, yes, indeed . . . With the proper foster-ing, say from an officer of Rome's Eagles, he would make a very fine diplomat . . ."

His voice drifted on the wind heavenward, his words to become a crippled boy's destiny.

Glossary

II Adiutrix One of four Roman legions garrisoned in Britain

Aegyptus Egypt

Agricola, Gnaeus Julius Military Governor of Britain, A.D. 78-84

ala Unit of auxiliary Roman cavalry containing five hundred men

amphorae Large two-handled vessels used to transport and store wine and oil

baine Celtic stick and ball game

ban-sidhe Celtic supernatural being whose wailing foretells death, pronounced "ban-she"

Batavia The Netherlands

Belenus Celtic god of reason

Belgica Belgium

bracae Type of close-fitting trouser worn by men of the Celtic tribes

bucina Roman army trumpet

castris Term for bastard-born sons of soldiers; children born in army camps

Celtae Celts; native tribes of the British Isles

centurion Roman army officer commanding a century

century Roman infantry unit of the Roman army containing eighty men

Cerberus Minor Roman deity portrayed as a three-headed watchdog of Hades

Charon Boatman who ferried dead across the River Styx to Hades in Roman mythology

cohort Infantry unit comprised of six centuries; ten cohorts made up a legion

colonia Settlements built for retired Roman veterans in the Provinces

Coritani Celtic tribe in central Britain

Cornovi Celtic tribe in southern Britain

Dalmatia Roman province bordering the Adriatic Sea

decimatio Severest form of Roman army punishment whereby one man in ten was killed for the offenses committed by one or more members of a military group

Deva   Legionary fortress in present day Chester, England

Erebus   Darkness through which the Romans believed the souls of the dead traveled to Hades

Frontinus, Sextus Julius   Military Governor of Britain, A.D. 74-78

Gallia   Gaul; parts of present day France and Germany

XIV Gemina   Roman legion garrisoned in the Rhineland

Germania   Germany

gladius   Roman short sword

Hispania   Spain

Iceni   Celtic tribe in eastern Britain

Italia   Italy

Judaea   Roman province in the Middle East

legio   Legion; body of infantry in the Roman army numbering approximately five thousand men

lorica   Roman body armor made of segmented iron plates

Lusitania   Portugal

Mauretania   Roman province in North Africa

Mithras   Persian god of light and truth; his worship was popular in the Roman army

Moesia   Roman province in the Balkans

Mona   Island of Anglesey, located off the northwestern coast of Wales

Ordovices   Celtic tribe of western Britain in what is present day Wales

Pax Romana   Roman peace; a system of administration for conquered lands and peoples through cooperative government

phalerae   Military decorations in the form of medallions worn on a leather harness across the chest of a Roman soldier

Picts   Tribe in northern Britain

pilum   Roman throwing spear

Rhoxolani   Tribe in the Balkans

Silures   Tribe which inhabited the area south of the Ordovices

Thracia   Thrace, kingdom in eastern Roman Empire, north of Greece

torc   Collar or necklace worn by the Celts as a symbol of a freeborn male

turma   Troop of Roman cavalry consisting of thirty-two officers and men

Typhon   Fire-breathing monster and according to Roman myth creator of hurricanes

XX Valeria Victrix   Roman legion garrisoned in Britain

Vespasian, Titus Flavius   Emperor of Rome, A.D. 69-79

Virconium   Legionary headquarters in present day Wroxeter, England

Author's Note

After subjugating the last of the rebellious mountain tribes of western Britain, Julius Agricola turned his attentions northward to what is now Scotland. In A.D. 85 he was recalled to Rome by the Emperor Domitian, son of Vespasian. For over thirty years following Agricola's departure Britain has no written history. But if history is like news, and "no news is good news," perhaps those thirty-five plus years do not appear in the history books because they were good years. If this is true, and if there had been a real Galen and his Rhyca, then they would most certainly have lived in a time of peace and prosperity.

I would like to think that it was so—and they did.

J.H.

Also by Judith Hill
Published by Zebra Books:

FIRES IN THE NIGHT
A KNIGHT'S DESIRE

WHAT'S LOVE GOT TO DO WITH IT?

Everything . . . Just ask Kathleen Drymon . . . and Zebra Books

CASTAWAY ANGEL	(3569-1, $4.50/$5.50)
GENTLE SAVAGE	(3888-7, $4.50/$5.50)
MIDNIGHT BRIDE	(3265-X, $4.50/$5.50)
VELVET SAVAGE	(3886-0, $4.50/$5.50)
TEXAS BLOSSOM	(3887-9, $4.50/$5.50)
WARRIOR OF THE SUN	(3924-7, $4.99/$5.99)

PENELOPE NERI'S STORIES WILL WARM YOU THROUGH THE LONGEST, COLDEST NIGHT!

BELOVED SCOUNDREL	(1799, $3.95/$4.95)
CHERISH THE NIGHT	(3654, $5.99/$6.99)
CRIMSON ANGEL	(3359, $4.50/$5.50)
DESERT CAPTIVE	(2447, $3.95/$4.95)
FOREVER AND BEYOND	(3115, $4.95/$5.95)
FOREVER IN HIS ARMS	(3385, $4.95/$5.95)
JASMINE PARADISE	(3062, $4.50/$5.50)
MIDNIGHT CAPTIVE	(2593, $3.95/$4.95)
NO SWEETER PARADISE	(4024, $5.99/$6.99)
PASSION'S BETRAYAL	(3291, $4.50/$5.50)
SEA JEWEL	(3013, $4.50/$5.50)